Shifted

SHIFTED

Roxanna Mason

ROXANNA MASON

Shifted

Roxanna Mason

The characters and events portrayed in this book are fictitious. Any similarity to real persons, living or dead, is coincidental and not intended by the author.

ISBN-13: 979-8-218-12243

ASIN: B0BNCBQT61

Cover design by: Benjamin Richard

Cover photo by: Joe Taylor

Typography by: Kristy Lynae Moore

Interior Art by: Simple-Line

Printed in the United States of America.

This book is dedicated to my tiny tribe of women:

To my mother, Gail, and the stories she dreamed she'd one day write. Thank you for the nest you chose to build instead so I might fly. To be called your daughter is the best title I have ever been given.

To my sister, Constance, and the stories she taught me to love. Thank you for your incredible mind, the fierce way you have loved me, and for never letting me doubt I was capable. You are and always will be my very best friend in all the world; the other half of my heart.

To my sister, Kayla, and the stories she taught me to tell. Thank you for the joy you bring to every person who knows you, for being my proof that family is a choice, and for walking with me through every step of my insane little life. I am so proud of everything you are and so very lucky we chose each other.

One

The silence inside my apartment was deafening.

My face fell. I had rushed back from Paris early to surprise my fiancé; I even made reservations at the restaurant where we went on our first date and picked up a bottle of champagne on the way home from JFK. Things were rocky between us before I left. It seemed like the closer we got to walking down the aisle the more distant he became. What used to feel like a perfect love story now felt like waking up to a stranger each morning. I didn't understand why he refused to come with me to Fashion Week or why he seemed to be pulling away, but I wanted so badly to get us back on track.

Naively, I believed I could.

I closed the door behind me and started to turn on the lights when I heard a soft sound from our bedroom. It almost sounded like a moan. I blinked a few times,

afraid I might have been so jet-lagged that I was imagining things. Then I heard it again. I hesitated a little. *Maybe he's watching TV?*

There I was, making excuses again. For months I had been coming up with so many explanations for Brian's behavior. It was exhausting.

I swallowed the growing lump in my throat and started down the hallway toward the bedroom. With every step I took, the sounds became louder and my feet felt heavier. I wanted there to be a logical explanation, but once I brought myself to open the door, the answer was right there in front of me, screaming my fiancé's name.

"Shit!"

I watched, horrified, as Brian pushed a tall blonde off him. She tumbled to the ground, landing on her side with a loud thud, and then immediately began scrambling. Brian pointlessly tried to cover himself with our sheets as she frantically searched for her clothes on my bedroom floor. The whole thing felt like it was in slow motion. I just stood there, my eyes wide, my feet glued to the floor.

"Babe! Babe! This isn't—"

I knew what he was about to say. It was that old cliché that every man said when they got caught. I lifted my hand to silence him. I didn't want to hear it. I couldn't bring myself to speak, but that didn't mean I had to listen to him try to gaslight me into thinking I wasn't seeing what was right in front of me — both of them naked, sweaty, and moments away from ruining 700 thread count Egyptian cotton. I turned my attention to the blonde who was desperately trying to get her clothes on, and that's when a terrible realization hit me.

I knew her. "Lexi?"

She froze and then slowly turned to look at me. The color drained from her face as her eyes met mine. "I'm so sorry. I swear this just—"

"Please, don't." I cut her off; I didn't want to hear the excuses. What could she possibly say? We worked together for years. She was the best assistant I'd ever had. More than that, we were friends. She was supposed to be in our wedding! I could feel the tears stinging my eyes, but I refused to let them fall. "I need to pack. Please don't be here when I'm done." My voice was shaky but direct.

I almost couldn't believe how calm I was, but I knew it was only temporary. As soon as the shock wore off, I would likely fall apart. I just had to make sure I was as far away as possible when that happened.

I started to gather whatever items I could from around the apartment until I heard Lexi leave. Then I mustered up the courage to get my clothes out of the bedroom. Brian sat on our bed, his eyes cast down at the floor in silence. At least by now he had managed to put his pants back on. I texted my best friend, Leon, who let me know he was on his way over. I just had to get my clothes and get out.

"Please don't go," Brian said. For a moment, he almost sounded like that sweet, nerdy video game programmer I fell in love with and not whatever it was he'd become.

I took in a sharp breath and shook my head. "You chose this, Brian. Not me."

My hands trembled as I slid my engagement ring off my left finger. I set it down on the bedside table quietly and continued to gather my things. There was no way I could get it all, but I had to keep myself busy long enough for Leon to get there.

"Please, talk to me. We can figure this out," Brian pleaded.

I whipped my head around and held out my hand. He just stared back at me as if I had lost my mind.

"What?"

"The watch!" I demanded.

I became even more horrified by it all when I looked down and saw he was wearing it. He was wearing MY grandfather's watch in our bed *while he had sex with my assistant.* I felt my stomach churn but I willed my face not to betray me.

"It's not yours, Jacey," he shot back at me.

"The fuck it's not!" I hissed. I could feel the bile rising in my throat.

"He gave it to me!"

Before he passed, my grandfather and Brian were extremely close. Brian didn't have grandparents of his own. In fact, he barely had any family at all, so I knew why he wanted to keep it. However, the watch belonged to my family. A family Brian was no longer a part of. How much could the watch mean to him when he was so willing to toss the family it came from aside?

"He's dead! He thought you were going to marry me. I'm sure the last thing he would want is—"

I paused at the sound of urgent pounding at the front door, so loud I was surprised it didn't fly off the hinges. Leon had been saving me since I was nineteen years old, and here he was, rescuing me again.

I opened the front door and Leon barreled in with a look on his face so feral, it made me take a step back. I couldn't remember ever seeing him this furious.

"*Where the fuck is he?*"

"Let's just go," I said, grabbing his arm.

"No," Leon growled before yelling towards the back of the apartment. "Fishman, get out here before I drag you out!"

I slowly turned as Brian emerged from the bedroom, but Leon's arm prevented me from getting a good look at him. I had no idea why he was stupid enough to approach when Leon had at least forty pounds of muscle on him.

"I'm going to fucking kill you!" Leon snarled.

"Right, like you weren't hoping this would happen!" Brain fired back.

"What the fuck is *that* supposed to mean?!"

I didn't know what that meant either, but Leon's hands were clenched so tightly that when he took a step forward I physically had to put myself between the two of them before Leon ended up charging him.

"Please, just take me home," I pleaded.

Leon's face softened when he met my gaze. "Do you have what you need?"

Brian watched as we grabbed my bags. I couldn't look at him. As far as I was concerned, if I never saw his face again, it would be too soon.

Leon tried to stop me when we got into the hallway. I could tell he was worried, but I marched right past him, down the stairs, and into the cab waiting outside. There was only so long I could hold the tears back, and I needed to be somewhere safe before I let them fall. I was silent as we drove. I just stared out the window at the wet city streets and the soft drizzle of rain hitting the glass in front of me.

"Are you okay?" Leon asked even though we both knew the answer.

"No."

I was trying to avoid speaking, afraid that if I said anything at all, the thread I was hanging onto might snap.

"What the hell was he thinking? He's an idiot. He literally just lost the best thing that—"

"Please..." I said, reaching for Leon's hand and interrupting the rant he was about to go on.

He didn't say another word. Instead, he gave me what I desperately needed. He turned his hand over, laced his fingers in mine, and held space for me.

It wasn't until I was home, back inside the loft I had shared with Leon for so many years, that it finally hit me. I only made it about four steps through the front door. I couldn't breathe. I couldn't think. All I could do was try to keep myself upright as helpless, gut-wrenching sobs ripped through my chest.

My best friend wrapped me in his protective arms, holding me tightly. "I've got you," he whispered.

I cried until I went numb again. Leon never once let go of me. We sat on the floor in front of our front door for what felt like hours. Once I'd been silent long enough, he helped me to my bedroom. All I could do was lay wide awake in my old bed, staring at the wall, trying to figure out how I ended up here.

We were weeks away from the wedding. *Weeks.*

Heartbreak wasn't exactly new to me. My heart was its own wrecking ball. Before Brian, I was in this vicious cycle of falling fast, rushing into bed, and giving too much of myself. I would throw myself head-first into men who would give me just enough to keep me hanging on, but never enough to actually make me feel safe and secure. It happened so many times I started to believe I might be cursed. When it came to building anything stable, I didn't have a clue. No matter what I did, I always ended up alone.

Like now.

Compared to my long-running streak of bad romances, my relationship with Brian Fishman seemed like a fairy tale. He might not be Prince Charming, but that was what I loved about him. He wasn't perfect. He was sweet and nerdy, and slightly awkward. Things moved slowly when I was with him, the way they were supposed to. The last thing I ever could have imagined was *this.*

If I was being honest with myself, the problems started long before finding him in bed with Lexi. Before we'd met, Brian and his best friend started designing a video game. It was their passion project, and for years, the two of them worked tirelessly to finish it. When they finally did, the game ended up becoming a huge success. The minute that money hit his account, Brain proposed.

Until I saw it first hand, I didn't realize how true that saying about "money changing people" is—and Brian made more money in those first few months than he'd seen in his entire life. The changes were small at first. He wasn't as kind to strangers, he seemed more impatient, and he had this thinly-veiled arrogance about him that I never noticed before. As the months went on, he would stay out a little too late getting drinks after work or suddenly need to go to unexpected dinner meetings. He was detached—vacant, even. The closer we got to the wedding, the more alone I felt.

Now I knew why, at arguably the most important moment of my career as a designer, my fiancé refused to show up. At the time he told me he was too busy with work, so I took Leon with me to France. Apparently, what he was too busy with was banging my twenty-two-year-old assistant.

Two

Everything inside me hurt. Each week I expected it to pass, but it didn't. It was only four months ago I had everything I'd ever wanted. The fashion line I had poured my heart and soul into was finally taking off. I was about to get married to the love of my life. Well, I thought he was the love of my life. After I found my assistant on top of him in our bed, I wasn't sure that Brian had ever really known how to love anyone.

The whole thing was devastating. Not only did I have to deal with the emotional wreckage of being cheated on, but I had to make hundreds of humiliating phone calls to the guests and the vendors to cancel the wedding. I hadn't been myself since then. I was walking through my life in a fog that everyone could see. I was more than heartbroken. I was shattered. No matter what I did, I couldn't seem to put myself back together.

One early Saturday evening, I sat on the large, dark

blue sectional in my loft. I used to spend Saturday nights lounging like this with Brian or out with friends. Now all I could bring myself to do was the weekly "wine and chat" that my twin sister set up, probably as an excuse to make sure I didn't have a mental breakdown.

I was shaken from my thoughts by the grating sound of the downstairs buzzer. Less than a minute after letting my sister into the building I heard a perky little knock at the door. I took a deep breath and forced a smile before letting her in.

"I'm so glad you live here with Leon. I swear every time I come over, there's some weirdo outside your building," my sister complained as she set her salmon-colored Birkin and a bottle of Chardonnay down on the end table near the door.

"You know what's weird...they're only here on Saturday nights. They must just show up to see you."

"Very funny," Elise said, rolling her eyes.

"Leon is useless," I added. "If someone broke in, I'm sure I'd be the one fighting them off."

That was entirely untrue. I knew if I needed it, Leon would do everything he could to protect me. He always did. I just made the joke to deflect my sister's need to insult our building. She thought any part of New York that wasn't Central Park South or Tribeca was dangerous. Elise was sweet, or she tried to be, but she was spoiled. Her fiancé was extremely wealthy, which was made evident by the giant, canary-yellow engagement ring she wore on her left hand. Elise's fiancé was from old money, and the more time she spent with them, the more entitled she became.

"How's the planning going?" I asked absently as I made my way into the kitchen to grab two wine glasses.

Nathan only proposed two weeks ago but Elise was already completely wedding-obsessed. Participating in wedding planning wasn't easy given what I recently went through, but she was my sister, and Elise had been waiting eight years for that ring. She deserved to feel like I was happy for her, which I was, even if the reminders stung a little.

"I still can't decide on a date. I was thinking of June, but maybe April is better? Do you think June will be too hot?" she asked me.

I grabbed the bottle of wine and headed for the couch. I poured Elise a glass and handed it to her before doing the same for myself.

"Everyone gets married in June. You're going to be competing with a ton of other weddings."

I stared down into my glass of French Chardonnay, the memories of my failed engagement twisted in the pit of my stomach. I knew I was better off without Brian, but I couldn't help but picture his face and imagine things that could have been.

"That's why I didn't choose May. I thought there would be too many other weddings. You think June is going to be the same way?" Elise asked me.

"Yeah..."

I had no idea what my sister had just said to me. Her words went in one ear and right out the other. My head was clouded with too many memories. I thought of the Alexander McQueen wedding gown that was gathering dust. What was once the dress of my dreams, was now a monster hiding in the back of my closet waiting to send me into hysterics any time I saw it.

"Are you okay?"

I had always considered Elise and I close, but I knew

I couldn't tell her how I felt. My perfect sister, with her fairy tale romance, couldn't possibly understand life-altering heartbreak. She met Nate when she was eighteen. She had never experienced any other relationship, and she certainly had never been cheated on.

It was almost comical how different Brian and Nate were. While money had turned Brian into an arrogant prick who couldn't manage to keep it in his pants, Nate had all the advantages in the world and he was easily one of the kindest people I had ever met. He was loyal to a fault. I had no doubt in my mind that he would be just as in love with my sister in his eighties as he was now.

"Yeah... I'm fine..." I lied as I fiddled with the rim of my glass.

"We don't have to talk about this if it's upsetting you."

I knew that Elise meant well, but she had this tone that made me feel like I was being lectured even when I wasn't. It was almost like I wasn't allowed to be upset. Apparently, my grieving period could only last until my sister added "soon-to-be Mrs. Montgomery" to her Instagram profile.

I shook my head and tried to get the negative thoughts out. I needed to focus on my sister. I was her maid of honor, after all.

"It's okay. I'm happy for you, Ellie. It's just..."

"I know," Elise nodded and softened her tone. "You know the offer still stands. I could totally murder him..."

I laughed at the notion. Elise, like me, was all of five foot five inches tall and about one hundred and ten pounds. Brian was no bodybuilder, but he was just shy of six feet tall and had always made me feel comparably tiny. There was no way that Elise would be a threat to him. I could only picture my petite twin sister screaming, limbs flailing everywhere as she tried to attack Brian in some adorable attempt to defend my honor.

"You're not exactly the fighting type, Ellie."

Elise thought for a moment as she took another swig of her wine.

"Fine, but I could find someone!" she said.

"Who? The mafia?" I asked sarcastically.

I could see it now, Elise in some stereotypical mobster costume complete with a fedora, trying to get some guy named Big Fishy Bob to take out my ex.

"No, but I *am* about to be a Montgomery..."

I rolled my eyes. In certain circles, that might have meant something, but to me, all it meant was that my sister was about to become even more pretentious than she already was. On some level, I understood. Nate's money was really the only weapon that Elise had to wield. I loved that she wanted to protect me, but the truth was, no matter how much I hated Brian for what he did, there was still a part of me that loved him. There was no future for us, but that didn't mean I wanted to see him harmed.

"Seriously though, are you okay?" Elise asked.

"It still hurts, but I think it's just one of those situations where the only way out is through."

"Maybe you should get back out there," Elise suddenly said.

Oh, here we go! It only took about a week before Elise started insisting that I sign up for dating sites. She even tried to set me up with her banker. I wanted to find love again...eventually, but I was nowhere near ready, and quite frankly I had never been very good at it to begin with. The last thing I wanted was to dive back into the chaos that was my dating life before Brian. I felt like the part of me that used to imagine "happily ever after" was now broken beyond repair. "Getting back out there" was not going to fix it.

"I think I need more time," I said as quickly as I could, hoping she would drop it.

"Really? It's been four months!"

I opened my mouth to snap back with something witty, but before I could, I heard the sound of keys outside the apartment. The door swung open, and there stood my best friend, his arms struggling to balance several overstuffed bags of groceries. I watched as Leon shuffled into the kitchen, dropping the bags onto the counter so loudly he now had all the attention in the room.

"What are we discussing tonight?" he asked as he made his way into the living room. His voice was even but I could already tell by the look in his eye that he was up to something.

"Nothing, we're just chatting about Ellie's wedding," I replied.

"Actually, we were just talking about how Jacey needs to get back out there and start dating again."

I winced, clamping my eyes shut and pinching the bridge of my nose. Sadly, this was a topic that Leon loved almost as much as Elise did. I knew there was no getting out of it.

"I want in on this one," he said. *Of course, he did.*

Leon walked back into the kitchen to grab himself a wine glass before he plopped down on the couch next to me, sandwiching me between him and Elise.

"Guys, I'm just not ready, I don't think -"

"Jace, you work with tons of guys. There's no reason you shouldn't be dating!" Elise said.

I knew that trying to reason with them was pointless.

Both Leon and Elise were relentless when they wanted something. I glanced over to Leon, pleading with my eyes for a subject change. I'd known Leon so long that when he looked back at me it was like I could hear him teasing me just by the look on his face. There was no getting out of this. He found it far too entertaining.

"I work with male models. There's a difference..."

I was a designer, so between photo shoots, runway shows, and fittings there were almost always male models around me. However, I had made it a priority from the start not to get involved with them.

"So models aren't your type?" Leon asked me although he already knew my thoughts on the subject.

I rolled my eyes. "I mean, they're nice to look at, but most of them don't have two brain cells to rub together."

Elise got up and looked around the apartment until she found a pen and something to write on.

"Okay, what qualities are we looking for here?" she asked me.

"I don't know!"

I wasn't looking to date, so it wasn't like I had some list of qualities I was hunting for readily available.

"Yes, you do! Now spill!"

Elise was impossible. I sighed heavily and looked over at Leon. He was looking at me with this deep concentration that I couldn't for the life of me understand. It reminded me of the way he watched ESPN. He didn't blink or look away, afraid to miss a single moment. *What is up with him?* Elise cleared her throat loudly, clearly unamused by my lack of response. I knew she wouldn't let this go, so I tried to focus on the question at hand.

"Okay, well...creative would be good."

I had a creative job, so it might be nice to be with

someone who understood that.

Elise nodded and started scribbling down notes.

"But smart... maybe successful; I'm not looking to date a starving artist."

That was true, too. I had known too many aspiring musicians and out-of-work actors before I met Brian.

"Got it!" Elise kept writing down everything I was saying. It felt like I was dictating some kind of shopping list to an assistant.

"Obviously, he has to be attractive."

Male models weren't my type, but that didn't mean looks didn't matter.

"Obviously!"

I was starting to find this kind of fun. I knew Elise wasn't all-of-a-sudden going to come up with my "dream man", but it had been a long time since I thought about what I wanted.

"Athletic is good too."

I spent a lot of time at the gym, so why not date someone with similar interests?

"Anything else?"

"Kind... and loyal..."

Those were, by far, the most important things on that list. No matter who came next in my life, there was no way that I was going to go through being cheated on again. I wanted someone so loyal that even the thought of them cheating on me would be laughable.

"Okay, so now we have the recipe for Mr. Perfect. We just need to find him. Leon, you must know someone from work, right?"

Leon worked for a high-profile men's magazine. Half the reason my line did so well was that he made sure I got in the right rooms. It made sense that Elise was asking.

His whole office was full of attractive, eligible men.

"I... um..." Leon ran a hand nervously through his perfectly-styled dark hair and cleared his throat. "Most of the guys I work with are married."

I snapped my head to the left and stared at him like he was crazy. I knew that wasn't true. I had been to that office a thousand times and almost never saw a single wedding ring. In fact, guys had come up to me at least a dozen times while I was there. I thought about calling him out, but maybe he just didn't want me dating his co-workers. I certainly wouldn't want him dating mine.

Elise threw her hands up in the air dramatically. I could only hope that was a sign she was about to give up.

"I have an idea!"

Now both of us turned our attention toward Leon.

"This whole finding Mr. Perfect thing isn't going to work." *Well, at least someone was making sense here.*

"What you need to do is just get back on the horse," he continued. *Okay... maybe not.*

"I'll make you a deal...you're going to say 'yes' to the next five guys who ask you out, no matter who they are or where you meet them," he explained.

"Okay... what do I get out of this?"

"If you go out with all five and you still don't like any of them, then Elise and I will never bring it up again." Leon looked so pleased with himself. There was a look of mischief in his eyes, like a kid who'd just figured out where his parents hid all the Christmas presents.

"What!?" Elise exclaimed, but Leon gave her a look, and she quickly gave in.

"Okay, fine." She rolled her eyes for good measure, her own silent way of having the last word.

"You're going to have to do better than that," I retorted.

He seemed to contemplate this for a few moments before a light bulb went off.

"I'll also give you the master bedroom back."

I went quiet for a moment. On the one hand, Elise and Leon were right. I did need to get back out there eventually. My real motivation, however, would be how badly I wanted my old room back.

When I moved out of this apartment to live with Brian, Leon took the larger room. When I moved back in, Leon welcomed me home with open arms, but he flat-out refused to give me back my bedroom. Still, the idea that I had to go out with any guy who asked me was a little unnerving.

"And what if I get asked out by some creeper on the street?"

Leon rolled his amber eyes at me. "You don't have to go out with anyone who doesn't seem safe." His tone made it clear he thought this was obvious. Perhaps it should have been, but I had to know what I was agreeing to.

"Alright, I'll do it, but I never want to hear another word about this if it doesn't work out."

He lifted his glass to mine.

"Deal."

Three

By Monday morning, I nearly forgot about the bet I'd made with Leon and Elise. I woke to the sound of the alarm on my phone and lazily hit the stop button as I squinted at the time: 5 a.m., an unbearably early hour for most, but I was accustomed to early morning workouts. I groaned a little as I pulled myself out of bed and found a sports bra and a matching pair of leggings from one of my dresser drawers. I twisted my shoulder-length brown hair into a messy bun on top of my head and shuffled my way to the kitchen downstairs.

I was still in a fog, fighting the urge to turn back around and crawl back into bed. The only thing I could manage to focus on was what flavor of protein powder I wanted - and even then I was struggling. When I turned the corner into the kitchen, I froze. Hanging over the stainless steel coffee maker, looking dead on his feet, was Leon. He was barely awake, with his eyes only

partially open as he fumbled with the buttons on the machine. I was surprised, to say the least. In all the years I'd lived with him, not once did I see him up at 5 a.m..

"You're up early..." I said hesitantly, worried that something might be wrong.

Under normal circumstances, Leon would wait until the last possible minute to get out of bed. Snooze was arguably his favorite word. I knew that he didn't have to be at the office until ten, and so the fact that he was desperately trying to make himself coffee five hours before he needed to be at work was strange, very strange. What was stranger was the look on Leon's face as soon as he'd registered what I was saying to him.

"I.... have an early meeting..." he muttered.

I didn't buy that for a second. *Why on earth would he have a meeting so early?*

"Are you okay?" I asked.

"Yeah, I'm fine. Why?" He shifted uncomfortably under my gaze.

There was something up with him. That was obvious. However, he seemed to be determined to hide it from me. Not only were early mornings unlike Leon, but so was being this secretive. We always told each other everything.

"You're acting like a weirdo," I teased, borrowing Elise's words.

I came close to him, reaching around him to grab the tub of chocolate protein sitting next to the coffee maker. Leon took in a sharp breath before abruptly shifting his attention back to the coffee pot as it finished brewing. He filled a mug with the dark, steaming liquid before looking back in my direction.

"What is rule number one of platonic mixed-gender

friendships?"

"I'm not naked! I'm going to the gym. What else am I supposed to wear?"

Leon and I had a long-standing list of rules that had been in place since we moved in together during our sophomore year of college. At the very top of that list was that we always had to be fully dressed around each other. Leon was never up this early, so I never felt the need to worry about what I wore before heading to the gym, nor did I feel like I had to apologize for it now.

"More than *that*! Oh, and don't forget our deal."

"Believe me. I didn't forget." I grumbled. I wasn't exactly thrilled about being reminded.

Something was definitely "up". Leon and I had been inseparable for years, and I just knew when something didn't feel right. It was more than just his half-assed excuse about a meeting or even the strange way he looked at me last night. I could tell he was hiding something.

I tilted my head to the side as I looked him over. Suddenly, the realization hit me that while I may have been lacking in clothing, Leon wasn't. Fully dressed at *this* hour? He wasn't wearing one of the tailored suits he regularly wore to work. Instead, his clothes were casual. He was in a familiar dark gray t-shirt and a pair of dark-washed jeans. He *definitely* wasn't going to a meeting.

"Did you just get home?" I asked.

It was the only other conclusion that made sense.

"Who are you? My mother?"

"No, but I could call her."

"You don't speak Portuguese."

"Isso é o que tu pensas!" I responded in what I was sure was the worst accent in the history of the language. *That's what you think.*

"Google translate?"

"Duolingo"

Leon cracked a huge smile. "You're learning Portuguese?"

"More like dabbling," I said with a shrug.

"What brought this on?"

"It's silly..." I said.

I glanced at the clock on the microwave and decided that maybe I could be a little late to the gym. Even though I saw Leon every day, he felt distant lately, so I wanted to take advantage of the opportunity.

"Sit. I'll make you breakfast."

I didn't need to tell Leon twice. He went around to the bar stools that sat on the opposite side of the kitchen counter. As he took a seat, I started to grab ingredients out of the fridge.

"So why the sudden interest in Portuguese?"

I shook my head. That man never let anything go.

"Promise you won't make fun of me?" I said as I started to chop red bell pepper.

"Promise."

"I've been thinking, and I realize that I don't know what I would do if something ever happened to you. I can't even communicate with your family."

"Wow," he breathed, and for a long moment, he was quiet.

"I mean, the only time I ever hear you talking to them you're arguing but —" I stopped myself, realizing that Leon was just staring at me like I'd said something he didn't understand. "What?"

"I just don't think anyone's ever cared that much before."

"You're my best friend. Of course, I care."

I started to whisk a bowl full of eggs and heat the

Four

Despite arriving at the gym later than usual, it was still pretty empty. Typically, anyone who came in before 8 a.m. was either getting in a pre-office workout or truly fitness-obsessed. Luckily for me, this meant that the treadmills were still largely unoccupied. I preferred the gym this way. I could focus on my workout and didn't have to worry about waiting for machines or being leered at by strange men. I climbed onto my usual machine in the front row of the cardio area, popped my AirPods into my ears, and cranked up my workout soundtrack: Metallica's *Fade to Black.*

After a few minutes of slowly increasing my speed, I was in the zone. I managed to push the thoughts of Leon's odd behavior, the bet I'd made with him and my sister, and even my cheating ex-fiancé out of my head and focus on my run. That was part of why I went

to the gym so often — it only took a few minutes for everything in my head to melt away. Plus, given that Nia, my business partner, was at work, and Leon at home, the gym was the only place I had any time to myself.

Out of the corner of my eye, I saw someone — a rather tall someone — take the treadmill next to me. I was too focused on my cardio to bother looking over fully, but I found it strange. Why did this person have to use the machine right next to mine? It was hardly proper gym etiquette, but I couldn't exactly tell someone where they should work out. I kept up my pace and tried as hard as I could to ignore the figure beside me.

It only took a few moments before I noticed that the person was just standing there, motionless, watching me run. *Great! Just what I need!* As I turned to tell whoever it was to take a hike, I was struck by how impossibly tall and painfully attractive he was.

He was stunning in all the wrong ways. I found it hard to keep my feet moving as my gaze moved from his long, dark hair over his ruggedly handsome features. I almost wanted to laugh. He was so unreasonably good looking that it seemed like some kind of cosmic joke. It didn't help that he was also built like he fell right out of a men's fitness magazine. I spotted tattoos along his muscular arms but refused to stop running long enough to get a good look at them. All I knew is that they were black and tribal looking. At least they seemed to be well done. There was nothing worse than bad tattoos. They were impossible to ignore. He pointed to my headphones and gestured for me to take them out. I obliged, though I stubbornly kept up my pace.

"What's up?" I asked, sounding disinterested. I didn't want to be rude, but I also didn't want to be interrupted, no matter how attractive this man was. I figured that he probably worked at the gym and was about to try and sell me on personal training or spin classes or something.

"Have you been coming here long?"

I looked around, a little confused, but I was determined to keep running.

"This gym?" I asked.

"Yeah... I just joined. I can't figure out where the weight room is."

The gym isn't that big, dude. There was no way he'd come over for directions, especially with the front desk only twenty feet away. The save was good enough however, that I decided to play along.

"Go down past all the cardio machines, hang left, past the locker rooms, and it's on the right." I somehow managed to tell him all of this while running, albeit breathlessly.

"Thanks."

"Don't mention it."

I expected him to head off in the direction of the weight room, but instead, he continued to stand there.

"I'm Owen."

"Jacey."

I turned back to face the wall in front of me, but I could still see him standing there. Instead of following the directions I'd given him, he started up the treadmill.

"So, you don't need the weight room?" I asked.

He smirked. It was sexy and a little wicked, definitely enough to make any girl weak in the knees. *Don't stare, Jacey.* The last thing I wanted to do was faceplant on a moving treadmill just because some obscenely attractive man said a few words to me.

"Need to warm up, first," he responded.

I continued running in silence. A few minutes passed, and I couldn't help but notice that my new cardio partner was now matching my speed. It was as if he was purposefully trying to keep up with me.

"How long have you lived in New York?"

"Are you always this chatty?"

I didn't mean to sound abrasive, but it wasn't even 7 a.m. yet. It reminded me of the rare occasions I'd work out with Leon. He always wanted to talk and talk. Cardio was hard enough on its own. I didn't need to try to keep up a conversation at the same time.

"Only when beautiful women are running next to me."

I audibly laughed. I couldn't help it. Sure, guys would hit on me once in a while — it wasn't a foreign concept, but they usually did not look like him and I usually wasn't drenched in sweat with no makeup on when they did it.

"Is this your thing? Picking girls up in the gym?"

"First attempt. How am I doing?"

I had a hard time believing that. I spent enough time watching my best friend pick up women to know a line when I heard one.

"Well, at least you're keeping up with me." Now he was the one laughing. It was a deep, throaty laugh that instantly brought a smile to my face. "I'm sure this isn't the only way I can keep up."

I glanced over at him with a raised eyebrow. *He definitely knows what he's doing.* His voice sounded so dark and smoldering. It was hard not to get pulled in by it. I started to decrease my speed and slowed to a walk.

"Look, I just moved here, and I don't know anyone yet, so... what are you doing after this?"

The look on my face was probably more skeptical

than anything else. How was it possible that less than twenty-four hours after Elise and Leon made me promise to say "yes" to any date that came my way, the most attractive man I'd ever seen appeared out of nowhere? I knew I needed to get back to my studio, but the rules were that I had to agree. I reasoned I could text Nia and let her know I was coming in later than usual. I shrugged a shoulder. "Hanging out with you, apparently."

"Really?" He sounded a bit surprised.

"Do you normally get turned down?" I really couldn't imagine any woman with a pulse saying no to him.

"You've got me there. I'm gonna hit the weight room, but I'll meet you back here in like...an hour?"

"Okay...sounds good," I said, though I wasn't altogether sure what I had just agreed to.

He got off the treadmill and started walking in the opposite direction of the weight room.

"Hey, Owen!"

He turned to look at me.

"It's that way."

I caught a quick look of embarrassment on his face before he turned and started walking in the right direction. It was kind of adorable. Once he was out of view, I grabbed my phone and sent two text messages.

The first was to Nia. I knew I didn't need to keep her posted on my schedule. She was my business partner, not my mother, but we were close. I knew if I didn't show up when I usually did, she would worry.

Hey, I got tied up with a few things. I'll be there in a couple of hours.

The second was a group text. I figured I'd keep Leon and Elise posted on the progress of their ridiculous bet at the same time.

Me: One down, four to go!
Elise: *Pics, or it didn't happen.*

I rolled my eyes before going back to my workout.

An hour or so later, I finished, took a quick shower, and put on a pair of high-waisted plaid pants, black Converse, and a black crop top. I looked more like I was about to jump on a skateboard than head into the office, but that was one of the many benefits of being your own boss: no dress code. Owen was standing outside the locker rooms waiting for me when I finally emerged.

"So, what exactly were you planning?" I asked.

"I have to get to work in an hour, but I figured I'd buy you coffee?"

I nodded, and the two of us stepped outside of the gym and onto the busy street. Thankfully, there was a coffee shop directly across from the gym, making deciding where to go easy.

I found myself looking over at Owen as we crossed west 56th. He was so attractive that he didn't quite seem real. I didn't necessarily have a "type". My romantic experiences were all pretty varied. Still, the list I made with Elise the night before popped into my mind. "Attractive" and "athletic" were both on that list, and even though I didn't know anything else about Owen, it was clear that he checked those two boxes.

Once inside, I ordered a cold brew while he ordered the house coffee, black. Another thing he seemed to have in common with Leon — black coffee. I didn't know why Leon kept popping into my head. Perhaps it was because this whole thing was his idea.

Owen's questions began the moment we sat down.

"How long have you been in New York?"

"Since college. My sister and I grew up in Connecticut, and then we both moved here when we graduated high school."

"You must be close."

"We're twins, we kind of have to be," I said with a shrug.

"Wait, you're telling me there's two of you?"

"Yes, but if you're about to tell me how hot twins are...."

Since high school guys made bizarre and downright disgusting comments about Elise and me. I had zero interest in hearing it again.

"I'm just shocked the universe made something so beautiful twice."

He was laying it on thick. That was for sure. I wondered why he felt the need to be so blatant about his advances, but that wasn't exactly the kind of thing you could flat out ask someone. Changing the subject seemed like the best policy. "So you said you just moved here. Where from?"

"Seattle, but before that, Hawaii."

I nodded slowly. Both Seattle and Hawaii seemed fitting for him. New York, however, didn't. "What brought you here?"

"I'm an athletic recruiter. I was working for Washington State, and then NYU made me a better offer."

"How are you liking it so far?" I asked before taking a sip of my coffee.

"I'm still getting used to it."

"The trick is just to figure out what makes a place feel like home to you and then try to recreate it here."

Owen nodded and seemed to contemplate that for a moment as he looked down at the table below us. .

"So, what makes a place feel like home?" I jumped back in.

"I'm big on being outdoors," he said as he glanced up at me.

Another laugh escaped me. "That one's a little tricky unless you count Central Park."

"I think if I went camping there, I'd probably get myself arrested."

"Probably," I said with a smirk. I kept contemplating how he could have the outdoors while living in New York when it hit me. "You could always go upstate. I mean, you'd need a car to get up there, but...."

"I have my bike," he said as he shrugged his broad shoulders.

"By bike, you mean...?"

"Motorcycle."

Of course he has a motorcycle. I was just starting to think he couldn't be any more appealing, and then he threw that particular fact in the mix. "Then there you have it. You have a place to camp."

"You should come with me," he said.

I blinked a few times, running the words back in my head to make sure I heard him correctly. He didn't even know me, and now he wanted to go camping with me. Either he was crazy, or he was one very hot serial killer.

"You don't know anything about me..." I said, thinking out loud. I looked Owen over, hunting for clues he might be more than just a gym bro with a few too many pick up lines. He seemed normal... or at least as normal as someone could when they were built like a house and made every woman in the coffee shop do a double-take. If he was a serial killer it was a poor choice of a hobby. It wouldn't exactly be hard to pick him out of a line-up.

"No, but I'm not going to learn anything about you unless I make a move, right?"

I shook my head, fighting the urge to roll my eyes. He knew exactly what to say. I reached across the table and grabbed Owen's phone. He didn't react at all. It almost took me by surprise given that Brian was always so secretive with his. The phone was the same version of iPhone that Leon had so it took me no time at all to figure out how to enter my number or call myself so I had his.

"I need a contact photo," I said before quickly snapping a photo of him. In reality, I didn't need one, but I wanted Elise and Leon to know I wasn't making up dates to win. "Let's start with this before I run off into the woods with a strange man I just met."

"It's a good start," Owen said with an amused smile on his lips. It was hard to ignore that everything that came out of his mouth sounded like an attempt at seduction.

We finished our coffee and then went our respective ways. I still didn't know how I'd managed to go on the first of my five dates so quickly, but all things considered, Owen wasn't a bad first option.

Six

Forty-eight hours ago, I swore to Leon and Elise that I wasn't ready to date. I might have agreed to their ridiculous wager, but I didn't honestly believe that anything would come of it. Yet I spent hours at the Brooklyn Heights Promenade with this completely random, obscenely attractive man I'd met at the gym. It was almost hard to believe. Not only did he look like someone sculpted him, but he seemed to know just what to say at every turn. Hell, he even had the same taste in music I did.

Owen wasn't perfect. No one was. He tended to come on too strong, and I got the sense that he didn't have significant ties to anything. I couldn't picture him settling down or wanting the things I ultimately wanted in my future. Instead, I imagined that, despite how much I liked him, he would likely roll right through my life and onto something new. I didn't love that idea, but

I was enjoying the ride.

I woke up completely exhausted the following morning. My lips felt swollen in a way that reminded me of the backseat makeout sessions of my adolescence. I didn't bring Owen home, though the thought had crossed my mind. Instead, he dropped me off at two in the morning, and I crawled into my bed, happier than I'd been in a long time.

Now it was nine, which for me was late. I groaned as I dragged myself out of my room and straight for the kitchen. I was happy to see that, unlike the morning before, Leon wasn't lurking around. I wasn't ready to hear him gloat about my love life and how right he was, especially when I'd just woken up.

I poured as much coffee as I possibly could into a large mug and then went back upstairs. I took my time getting ready for work. I didn't care about being late; I just didn't want to look like I'd been out all night. A hot shower, mascara, and a great deal of concealer later, I was climbing into a cab headed for my office.

Other than the fact that I did what I loved for a living, my favorite part about my job had to be my studio. It was an industrial-style loft space. I was only fourteen years old when I decided I wanted to be a designer. There was no way I could have imagined then that I would have made it out of Connecticut, let alone be successful. The studio was, in many ways, a reminder of how far I had come. It didn't matter what else was going on in my life. The studio made me feel like I did something right.

I was the first one there. Until recently, an assistant would open everything up before Nia and I arrived for the morning. However, since the incident with Lexi,

I was avoiding hiring someone new. I still couldn't understand why, of all the women in Manhattan, my ex-fiancé decided to sleep with the girl I had been mentoring since she was in fashion school. There were times I thought that maybe he just wanted to add insult to injury, but Lexi was a leggy blonde who made most men stop dead in their tracks. It likely had more to do with that than it did with me.

Just as I was disarming the alarm system and turning on the lights, I heard the distant sound of high heels clicking against the concrete floor of the building. In a matter of seconds, Nia breezed through the door in a stunning cream-colored Badgley Mischka dress suit.

"You need an assistant," she reminded me as she headed straight for her perfectly organized desk.

"I don't want to have to sort through resumes again," I groaned.

As if she knew what I was going to say, Nia pulled a folder out of the middle drawer of her desk and waved it at me. "Lucky for you, I already did the sorting for you."

I watched her walk over to my design desk and drop the folder onto it dramatically.

"Alright, I'll take a look...."

I felt no interest in doing that, and I could tell by the unimpressed look on Nia's face that she knew I had every intention of putting it off. "I have a five-year-old, do you really think I can't tell when someone is telling me what I want to hear?"

I held my hands up as I walked over to the desk, surrendering to her demands. I opened the folder and started flipping through the resumes. I didn't even read them. Instead, I eliminated them based on entirely trivial matters. Whether it was a ridiculous first name, fashion trade school instead of a university, or a weird font, I found any excuse I could to put them in the "no" pile. After a moment or two, I sighed heavily and looked up at Nia. "Can you just pick one?"

"That is not my job," she huffed.

"Yes, but—"

Nia held her hand up. "I don't want to hear it. I already told you, I picked your last assistant, and she was a nightmare, so I am staying out of it. However, that does not mean that you can avoid having one. I can't run a fashion line if you're so busy taking your own calls and answering your own emails that you aren't designing anything."

She had a point. The fact that Nia was never afraid to tell me exactly what was on her mind was one of the things I loved most about her. I did, however, wish she would stop holding onto so much guilt about Lexi. It certainly wasn't her fault.

"She wasn't a nightmare, she just—"

"I would call sleeping with your fiancé a nightmare."

Ouch. I couldn't exactly argue with that. Arguing with Nia at all was pointless. She always got her way.

"Fine, then; who's your favorite?"

"Look at Danillo Reyes."

I flipped through the stack of papers until I saw his name appear near the middle and pulled the resume out. It was impressive; he went to a good school, previously worked at another men's line, and possessed all the necessary skills for the job. Plus, it might not hurt to hire a man at a company that designed men's clothes. "I'll call him."

"Thank you," Nia said smugly before turning her attention to the giant iMac on her desk.

I grabbed a sketchbook and a handful of other items and took a seat on the small couch, intentionally placed against the only window we had in the office. I sat down and started to get myself sorted, but I felt this gnawing urge to tell someone about last night.

"I met someone," I said rather suddenly.

Nia's eyebrows shot up as she looked over at me from across the room.

"You what?"

"I met someone," I repeated. "We met at the gym, and we kind of went out last night...."

"What exactly is 'kind of' going out?"

"We both couldn't sleep, so he picked me up, and we went on a walk."

"Picked you up?" Nia questioned. I had to admit that I had expected her to be a bit more enthusiastic.

"...on his motorcycle...."

"You are not telling me that you got on the back of some man's motorcycle last night!"

I forgot just how much Nia liked to mother everyone around her. Before I could respond, I saw a familiar figure in the doorway.

The door was open, so Leon knocked on the door frame. His hair was slicked back, and the suit he was wearing told me that he had stopped by on his way to work. "Good morning, ladies," he said with a smile.

"Get in here! I feel like I haven't seen you in ages." Nia motioned him into the office. She hurried over and hugged him tightly before they both turned to me.

"Forget something?" Leon said, holding up my laptop case.

I had so much on my mind when I woke up this morning, I entirely forgot my laptop when I walked out the door. I had no idea how I'd managed to get to the studio without noticing it, but I was more than grateful that Leon brought it to me.

"You're amazing!" I said, leaping out of my seat to take it from him.

"Did you know she was out all night with some strange man?" Nia said to Leon.

I rolled my eyes. I intended to keep that particular fact from Leon. Apparently, that wasn't an option.

"Oh, did you?" Leon said, looking over at me with a triumphant smile on his face.

"I couldn't sleep."

"Next time you can't sleep, take an Ambien! Don't go riding off into the night on the back of some strange man's motorcycle!" Nia scolded me.

"Motorcycle, huh?" Leon said. I could see on his face that he was stifling laughter.

"It was a good night," I shrugged.

Leon looked at me for a little too long. I was trying to get a read on what he was thinking when he suddenly shook his head. "I should get going. I'll see you at home. It was so good to see you, Nia."

"Don't be a stranger," Nia said to him.

"Thank you," I called after Leon as he started towards the door.

Nia watched him leave before turning to me again.

"Tell me again why you aren't just dating Leon," she said, raising her brows at me.

"I'm not his type."

I headed back for the couch, but Nia continued to stand in the middle of the room with her hands planted firmly on her hips. "You know you're crazy, right?"

My eyes shifted back and forth as I tried to work

out whether this was about my middle-of-the-night motorcycle ride or the fact that I'd just said I wasn't my best friend's type. "Generally speaking, yes, but why specifically?" I asked.

Nia dramatically gestured toward the door that Leon just left through. She didn't have to say anything. I knew what she meant. Most women took one look at Leon and assumed I had to be insane for not falling all over myself for him.

"He's my best friend," I said to her dismissively.

"You do know most women would kill to have a best friend who looked like that?"

I shook my head, but in reality, I was used to this conversation. People had been implying that Leon and I were meant to be together since we became friends in college. It wasn't that I didn't find him attractive. Objectively, he was a ten. He was tall, athletic, tan, and classically handsome. He was well-dressed and successful. I couldn't think of any reason why someone wouldn't be interested. The first time I met him, the first words out of my mouth were, "you're so pretty". Granted, I was intoxicated at a college frat party, but regardless, his looks weren't lost on me.

"His last girlfriend was a runway model," I added, trying to further drive the point home that Leon had no interest in me.

"You don't give yourself enough credit."

"What do you think of royal blue for the winter line?" I asked, completely changing the subject.

"When it finally happens, just remember I told you so," Nia said before walking back to her desk.

I got busy sketching, but despite Nia's insisting that something was going to happen between Leon and me, there was only one man on my mind. Images of last night and the feeling of Owen's lips on mine kept flooding back to me. I didn't want to get too attached to him or fall back into familiar patterns. We just met, after all, but I decided to be a little bold.

I grabbed my phone and quickly typed out a text.

When do I get to see you again?

My heart raced a little, which I took to be a good sign, and before I could talk myself out of it, I hit the send button.

Seven

Owen and I decided to meet at a bar in Chelsea called The Jaded Anchor. I'd never been there before but, judging by the name, I had a pretty good idea of the kind of place it would be. When my cab pulled up to the aging brick building covered with mismatched pieces of street art and unwanted graffiti, I wasn't at all surprised. I couldn't say that I had Owen figured out just yet, but if I had to guess where he would take someone on a date, this would be it. I spotted him standing out front with a cigarette in hand.

When the cab stopped on the curb, I found myself staring at him, entranced. He made it impossible *not* to stare. He had this quality about him that felt like he'd just stepped out of some other place and time.

"That'll be $28.75," my driver said flatly.

I snapped my head forward, unsure of just how long I'd been sitting there watching Owen smoke. He was

like something straight out of fantasy with his strong jaw and his long, weathered hair. Owen noticed me getting out of the cab and came over to hold the door open as I stepped onto the sidewalk. I watched his eyes move up and down my body. Thankfully, it appeared that the outfit I'd spent hours agonizing over definitely worked.

"You look like a bad idea," he said with a smirk on his face.

I took a step closer to him, looking up at him through my lashes. "Who says I'm not one?"

He put out what remained of his cigarette and took my hand, guiding me inside. The bar was everything I expected it to be. The lighting was dim, and even though you could no longer smoke in bars in New York, the scent of tobacco had permeated the walls. It was the kind of place that seemed hazy even before the first dirt-cheap cocktail. There were pool tables at one end of the room and a stage that was little more than a foot-tall platform at the other.

A group of what looked like freshly twenty-one-year-old boys with far too much hair attempted to play something that vaguely sounded like rock. It was too loud and barely music, but the perfect soundtrack to a place like this. We slowly edged our way through the crowd and took seats at the bar. I looked around at the patrons. It was a strange combination of college kids who were there to see this tragedy of a band, and hardened middle-aged barflies who had been drinking since noon.

I could only imagine what my sister might think if she knew I was on a date in what could arguably be the biggest dive in the city. No doubt she would have a laundry list of complaints, but there was something

I found charming about it. I liked that Owen wasn't trying to impress me. He was simply taking me to the kind of place he would go. The last time I saw Owen, he talked about how I was intense, but not pretentious. I could easily say the same about him. Perhaps that was why I felt so comfortable around him.

"What can I get you?" an exhausted-looking bartender asked.

"What am I drinking?" Owen asked me.

His question felt like a test. We never discussed what his poison of choice was, and so I was left to make the best guess I could.

"He'll have a Guinness and a shot of Jack," I shouted over the band.

"And what about you?" the bartender shouted back at me.

"What am I drinking?" I asked Owen. I figured if he was going to make me work for it, it was only fair that I make him do the same.

He tilted his head to the side. "She'll have a vodka-cran."

As the bartender turned to start working on our drinks Owen looked over at me, raking a hand through his dark hair. "How did I do?" he asked me.

"I haven't had vodka since college," I laughed. "I'm more of a whiskey girl."

Owen looked a little surprised but the smirk that slowly formed on his face told me he approved. Turning back around, the bartender set our drinks in front of us before moving on to the next customers.

"How about me?" I asked as I picked up the cocktail in front of me. I tried not to look completely repulsed as I examined it, but vodka and I definitely didn't get along.

Noticing my lack of enthusiasm, Owen slid me the

shot of whiskey I'd ordered him.

"I'm more of a tequila kind of girl," he said sarcastically.

I threw back his shot of whiskey before looking over Owen's shoulder at the band. Anyone with ears could tell you that they were terrible, but I enjoyed his company so much that I didn't care. For months I hadn't felt like myself, but in that dive bar with Owen, I felt a little more like the person I used to be.

My eyes made their way back to him, and we held each other's gaze for a long moment until he reached forward and pulled the empty shot glass out of my hand.

"Come on..." he said as he stood up and reached for me.

I didn't know what Owen had in mind, but it was already obvious to me that I would go anywhere this man was leading. He kept his hand in mine as he guided me through the crowded bar and toward the pool tables. Thankfully, because the band was still playing, the back of the bar was far less populated.

"Is playing pool normally part of a first date with you, or are you just trying to get me alone?" I teased.

Owen took a step towards me, pinning me between him and the pool table.

"Both," he said with a smile on his face that I could only describe as wicked.

I tilted my head to the side as I looked up at him. "Let's make it interesting, then."

"Interesting?"

I took a step to the side, sliding out from between him and the ancient wooden table. I grabbed a pool cue off of the rack and tossed it to him before grabbing a decidedly smaller one for myself. "We're going to need more shots," I said to him.

A smile crept over his dark features. "My kind of girl..."

he murmured as he lowered his head towards mine.

"Nope, if you want to kiss me, you better plan on winning."

Owen shook his head and left me at the table while I started to rack the balls. A few minutes later, he returned with four shots; two of whiskey, two of tequila. I took one of the shot glasses filled with dark brown liquor straight out of his hand and threw it back. I winced as the alcohol made my throat close in on itself. The truth was, I might have been putting on a show. I enjoyed the way I felt around Owen, but I didn't know if I was as wild as I wanted him to believe.

"So what are the stakes here?" he asked me as he set the remaining shots on a nearby high-top.

"If you win, you get to take me home..." I said in a voice I barely recognized as my own. It was breathy and seductive. Those two shots apparently went to my head faster than I thought.

"And if you win?" Owen asked with a raised brow.

"If I win, I get a second date."

"Who said we can't do both?" he said with a chuckle.

I rolled my eyes. I didn't have this whole impulsive, whiskey-drinking, short skirt-wearing Jacey completely figured out yet.

Owen took a step towards me. He reached for my hips and pulled me toward him. "What do you really want?"

I could feel my pulse banging in my ears, and the loud, crowded bar faded into the background. He reached around my head, threading his fingers into my hair and tugging me towards him. I leaned forward, expecting him to kiss me, but his mouth hovered over mine.

"What do you want?" he asked again.

"You," I said, my voice caught in my throat.

"What was that?" he asked teasingly. His deep voice, vibrating through me.

"I want you."

Finally, he brought his lips to mine and kissed me deeply. Kissing Owen wasn't new to me; we couldn't stop kissing the night he drove me over the Brooklyn Bridge. But this was something else. I wasn't sure I even knew my own name anymore.

"*When* I take you home, it's going to be because you're begging me to...not because I won at pool."

I stood there with my mouth open, completely shocked and more than a little turned on by his statement. I started trying to regain my composure and, hopefully, the upper hand.

"That just sounds like you know you're going to lose," I purred.

He laughed a little and then stepped back from me. "Ladies first...."

I leaned over the table a little, aligning my cue with the cue ball and trying to concentrate. However, before I could pull the stick back to make my first shot, I felt Owen come up behind me.

"I know how to shoot, thank you very much," I said, glancing over my shoulder at him.

Owen backed up, and as soon as he was a fair distance from me, I took my shot. Only one ball managed to get into any of the holes, but it wasn't bad for a first shot.

"I guess you do..." he said before walking over to the other side of the table and lining up his cue.

I decided that two could play at his attempts at distraction, so while he was trying to place his shot, I slowly took off the leather jacket I was wearing, exposing the black bustier I had on underneath. I watched Owen's gaze quickly make its way from the table to me.

"That is not fair!"

"It's just hot in here," I said with feigned innocence.

"Right," he grunted as he raked his eyes over me once more.

We kept taking turns back and forth and kept making trips to the bar for shots. We were down to a couple of balls on the table when my turn came up again, but I was nowhere near sober enough to shoot pool with any level of skill. Owen grabbed another shot of tequila, but before he could throw it back, I took it out of his hand.

"Hey!"

"I think this belongs here," I said, taking the tiny glass and sliding it into the top of my bustier.

"Oh, we're taking body shots now?"

"Is that a complaint?"

Owen grinned, pulling the shot from my top and swallowing it before kissing me hard.

"Not at all," he said. "But we should probably get you home."

I was drunk and I was happy. I had no desire to go anywhere unless Owen was going with me, but as I teetered on the Jeffrey Campbell heels I had the bright idea to wear, I realized that he might be right. "Fine, but since you forfeit, I win!"

"Alright, you win," he said and placed his hand on my back, ushering me outside.

Out front, the two of us waited for a cab. Owen was doing a much better job of holding his liquor than I was. Everything was a complete haze for me while he seemed almost stoic. I started to wonder if maybe I did something to cause his silence when a bright yellow car made a turn onto our street. Owen waved for it, and when it pulled up, we both slid in the backseat.

"250 West 50th," I told the driver.

He pulled out onto the street and started towards my apartment. We both sat in silence for what felt like a little too long.

"You're quiet."

"I'm drunk," he said in response.

"Are you normally quiet when you're drunk?"

"It's probably the only time I'm quiet."

"That's okay. I can think of better things you can do with your mouth," I blurted out before kissing Owen again.

Before either of us realized it, the cab was pulling up to my building.

"Technically, since I'm the one taking you home, do I have to beg?" I wasn't sure that sleeping with Owen was the best idea, but there was no doubt in my mind that I wanted to.

He didn't answer right away. Instead, he kissed my forehead sweetly. "When you're sober," he said.

I crossed my arms over my chest and made a face like a small child pouting. "I know what I'm doing."

"When you're sober, Jacey," he repeated.

I rolled my eyes dramatically and then kissed him on the cheek. I doubted I was going to change his mind. Even in the short time I'd known Owen, I could tell he was rather immovable. Plus, I got the impression that this was a question of consent, and the fact that he cared enough to insist on it was endearing.

"Goodnight," I said and climbed out of the cab, resigning myself to go to bed alone.

Eight

I already lost the bet. There was no doubt about that. It had been two weeks since I agreed to say "yes" to the next five guys that asked me out. If I didn't like any of them, I would get both my old bedroom back and the luxury of having Elise and Leon refrain from any further meddling in my love life. When I agreed, I assumed it would be a cakewalk. I didn't have the slightest interest in dating. Yet less than twenty-four hours after I'd agreed to their ridiculous challenge, Owen Kahale appeared in my life.

I liked Owen. I couldn't deny that even if I wanted to. I still intended to go through with the bet, but it was with the knowledge that technically, I had already lost. I wasn't upset about losing. In fact, for the first time in months, I was excited. Owen brought out a side of me that I wasn't sure still existed. When I was with him, I felt reckless and sexy and brave. Still, there was some-

thing about him that kept me from calling the bet off.

Something felt like it was missing.

I woke up Saturday morning with a headache and the taste of cheap whiskey still in the back of my throat. I looked around the room and realized I hadn't made it to my bed, but instead fell asleep fully clothed on the couch downstairs. I hadn't even managed to change my outfit or take off my makeup.

"Good morning," I heard Leon call out from the kitchen as I struggled to get myself upright.

"Nope, not a good morning," I said in a pained voice.

"But was it a good night? That's the question."

On the one hand, I didn't want to tell Leon he'd won. I did like Owen, I just wasn't sure there was any future there. On the other hand, he was my best friend, and I wanted to tell him everything. "It was a very good night."

"So are you ready to admit defeat?" Leon asked with a grin.

My head started pounding as soon as I stood up and, as if he could read my mind, Leon placed a cup of coffee on the counter for me.

"God, I love you," I said before taking a large sip.

Leon just stared at me. I could only assume it was because I hadn't answered his question.

"He's hot and we have fun together, but I'm not giving up just yet..."

"Why?"

"He's kind of..." I wasn't sure why I was struggling so much to find the words.

"Kind of what?"

"Have you ever been with someone who's visually stimulating but not mentally stimulating?"

"You mean he's not smart enough?"

"I don't know. He just doesn't have a lot of depth," I said with a shrug before turning to head upstairs.

I could hear the muffled sounds of Leon starting an interrogation as I left, but I had no intention of giving him a play-by-play. It wasn't that I didn't want to talk to him, it was just that I didn't have the time to really dissect how I felt about Owen. I was wildly attracted to him, but the idea of him being something permanent in my life seemed completely unrealistic.

Weekends were a bit of a new concept to me. I still wasn't used to free time. From the day I graduated from college, my entire life was about making sure that my line was successful. Now that my dream had become a reality, I wasn't sure what to do with myself. Nia ran the business end of things, so I didn't have to do anything but design. I wasn't managing my books or sewing my samples. Hell, I didn't even have to manage my social media.

I thought briefly about calling Owen, but I didn't want to seem overly eager. We were only apart a few hours. I thought about hanging out with Leon, but by the time I'd managed to get myself functioning, he was gone, no doubt with that girl who kept him out all night.

I now had an entire day to myself and no idea what to do with it. I considered working; I had nothing else to do after all, but I was trying to teach myself moderation. I was a bit of a workaholic, and if left to my own devices, I'd never do anything for myself. My head was still pounding, and I was desperate for caffeine, so I decided I'd start with my favorite coffee shop.

Common Ground wasn't just a coffee shop; it was also a used bookstore. The whole place was filled with the incredible smell of old books, and I always found myself spending hours pouring over their selection of haphazardly organized titles. When I arrived, I headed straight for the back and ordered a cold brew before I began wandering up and down the aisles.

I was off in a corner thumbing through a copy of *The Great Gatsby* that was older than I was when I noticed someone join me in the aisle. He didn't seem to notice me. I looked him up and down briefly. I could tell he was attractive in a studious, vaguely unconventional way. His hair was curly and dark. He had glasses that I wasn't sure were for function or aesthetic, perfectly groomed facial hair, and an outfit made up entirely of muted earth tones. He didn't seem aware of my presence at all, so I went back to my book hunt, continuing to hold on to *Gatsby* as I did.

I was so busy with endless shelves that I didn't notice that Mr. Dark Academia had wandered closer to me.

"Please tell me you've read it," I heard him say.

I looked up with confusion and a bit of surprise written all over my face. He gestured to the book in my hand.

"Oh, Gatsby, yeah... a couple of times. I just don't own a copy."

"Do you need to?"

I raised an eyebrow. *Was this a new pastime I didn't know about? Criticizing strangers' book choices?* "I'm using it for reference material," I explained.

"Writer?"

"Fashion Designer."

He looked impressed or, at the very least, appeased. I found that his face, though handsome, wasn't easy to read.

"What are you designing that you need Fitzgerald?

Please don't tell me they're making some intolerable Gatsby musical!"

"That would make me a costume maker, not a fashion designer."

The look of disinterest on his face told me he didn't know, nor did he care, about the difference.

"Anyway, I'm thinking about using the 1920s as design inspiration for my winter line."

"Thank God you're not telling me it's your favorite book."

"Why, would that be a problem?"

I didn't even know why I was still standing there talking to this judgmental man who'd shown up out of nowhere. Perhaps it was because he seemed to become more attractive the longer I looked at him. I wouldn't call him my type, and I got the impression that his personality was severely lacking. Still, there was something about him I found fascinating.

"Where do I start?" he said dramatically.

I crossed my arms over my chest. It was clear this was going to take a while.

"The characters lack dimension. They're all just tropes, and the relationships lack any depth at all."

"You don't think Daisy and Gatsby have depth?"

"The relationship isn't rooted in anything. It's not rooted in sex or friendship. It's certainly not rooted in love!"

"I think there are a lot of people who would beg to differ," I said. I wasn't sure if he believed what he was saying or if he was trying to get some kind of rise out of me. The Great Gatsby was a classic and therefore was the sort of book that people got up in arms about.

"Okay, enlighten me."

"You're right. I don't think it's rooted in sex. The

book never mentions that. I don't think it's rooted in friendship, either. However, the only way you can argue that it isn't rooted in love is if you think love is some black and white construct where you can only love someone if your intentions are noble."

I half-expected this man, whose name I still didn't know, to start a debate with me, but to my surprise, he seemed to be listening with genuine interest.

"Go on...."

"The way Gatsby loved Daisy was messy and entirely self-serving, but most love is. We like to pretend it's a fairytale and that 'true love' has to be for the 'right reasons', but it's far more nuanced than that. Therein lies the depth you claim is lacking. I'll admit that he had no idea who she was, and what he was really in love with was the idea of her, but do you have to know someone to love them?"

"I would say so."

"What about mothers who love their babies before they're even born? Or love at first sight? What about first love? Would you say you knew everything about the first person you thought you loved? Probably not. You were probably fourteen, but you felt it, and I think if you feel it, it's real."

"Are you sure you're not a writer?"

I laughed a little. Why did I feel like I'd just passed a test? "Not a writer," I said.

"I'm August, by the way. August Henry."

His name was almost too fitting. It sounded like something out of an 18th-century novel, and as I stood there, I imagined him in a frock coat and cravat asking me to a ball.

"Jacey Lange."

"That's quite a name."

"So is August Henry," I shot back at him.

I couldn't decide if I was enjoying this conversation or if I was merely tolerating it. I certainly didn't mind looking at the man, but he seemed full of himself, to say the least. I got the impression that he thought he was the smartest man in any room. Maybe he was. I just had no intention of acknowledging it.

"Well, Jacey, I'm impressed," he said. "I don't often hear a perspective on Fitzgerald that's new to me."

"How often are you asking people's opinion on *The Great Gatsby*?"

"I'm an American Literature Professor."

"Got it." That made so much sense. August's whole demeanor and aesthetic screamed "college professor". Hot college professor, but college professor nonetheless.

"Well, it was nice meeting you."

"Yeah, nice to meet you too...."

It sounded almost as if he had more to say and I had just cut him off, but he turned to walk away. I went back to browsing books, glancing up briefly to see him turn down the next aisle. That certainly wasn't what I was expecting out of my Saturday morning, but at least I wasn't bored.

I picked up another book set in the twenties; this time, it was *Mrs. Dalloway* by Virginia Woolf. I had never read it before, and I began scanning the back cover when August abruptly returned.

"Forget something?" I asked.

"Yes, actually...."

I was tempted to hide the book in my hands behind my back, lest he starts criticizing that, too.

"Would you have dinner with me?" he suddenly

asked me.

I tried to keep from laughing. We just finished bickering over Fitzgerald. *Was this what he considered flirting? Could literary debates be considered a fetish?* My mind went to Owen. Things were new, and we were nowhere near discussing commitment, but something felt strange about agreeing to go out with someone else less than 24 hours after my date with him.

However, I could hear Leon's voice in the back of my head. *"Five guys, Jace."*

I'd agreed to say yes to five different men, and Owen was only the first, so I didn't have a choice. The only out I had was if I didn't feel safe. August might have been pompous, perhaps even annoying, but he wasn't threatening.

"Sure..." I agreed hesitantly. "Do you always argue with women before you ask them out?"

He seemed entertained by my question. "How else am I supposed to find out if they can keep up?"

I shook my head. This was certainly going to be an interesting dinner.

We exchanged numbers, and I made my way up to the front of the store with my book as I texted Elise.

Me: Just Agreed to Date #2.

Nine

Monday morning was a relief. Most people dreaded returning to work after the weekend, but I was looking forward to some semblance of normalcy. I couldn't exactly say I minded garnering the interest of not only one, but two shockingly attractive men. However, I wasn't used to it. I had gone from being in a long-term relationship for years to swearing off dating entirely. The attention felt good, but it made me feel a bit uneasy. Going into my studio put me back in my element. I walked in knowing, however, that today would be different.

I'd been without an assistant for months, and my productivity suffered because of it. Now that I was starting to work on the winter line, I couldn't exactly afford to keep putting off hiring someone. Nia had gone to the effort of collecting resumes and making her suggestions, which meant I needed to start interviewing.

I didn't want to spend weeks listening to hopeful fashion graduates tell me how much they loved my work or why they thought they'd be a good fit, so I called in the best candidate first.

Danillo Reyes arrived at the studio wearing a burnt orange blazer over his broad frame. He wore a pair of tan trousers cut high but perfectly suited to his ensemble. His hair was dark, and he had a young, albeit handsome face with a pair of rich brown eyes round with excitement. I knew I probably shouldn't have judged the outfits of my potential employees, but my first indication of someone's knowledge of fashion was what they wore. In this case, I approved. He knocked on the door frame, as everyone that came into the building seemed to do. A sense of recognition danced over his face when he saw me.

"Miss Lange, it's such a pleasure to meet you!" he blurted out excitedly.

"Jacey is fine," I said, motioning for him to come in.

The studio had an open floor plan. I always found I worked better that way than in the confines of a traditional office. Even so, Nia and I did have a small conference room we used from time to time. I led Danillo to it, attempting not to bother my business partner with the interview. I gestured for him to have a seat in one of the black leather rolling chairs.

"Did you have any trouble finding the place?" I asked casually. I wasn't the kind of boss who required a bunch of formalities, so I tried not to sound too uptight. I worked hard to create an environment where people felt like equals, and if Danillo was going to be a part of the team, I wanted him to feel that way from the beginning.

"No, my husband and I only live about two blocks

away, actually," he said brightly.

When he mentioned a husband, it made me smile. It didn't particularly matter to me whether my employees had spouses or not, but I found that people who openly mentioned their significant others were usually happy. Somewhere deep down, I was still a romantic.

I looked over his résumé. His qualifications were extensive. "I see your last employer was Yates-Richland?" I asked.

Yates-Richland was another menswear line that started much like mine. That was, until a huge department store chain bought them out. From what I'd heard, the quality suffered for it.

"Yes, I loved working there," Danillo responded a little too quickly.

My eyebrows shot up. The tone Danillo used made it sound like perhaps he'd been fired. I hoped that wasn't the case, because the last thing I wanted to do was keep searching. "Why did you part ways?"

I watched Danillo's youthful, happy-looking face drop a little, and he looked down at the dark wooden conference table in front of him.

"I was happy there in the beginning. I felt like I was part of a team, and they encouraged this creative, collaborative environment. When the company was bought out, everything changed. I started feeling like I was just there to get coffee. I wanted more than that, so I left."

His answer both surprised and resonated with me. I was lucky enough to have started my line right out of fashion school. It took a long time for me to build any success, but I had family to help me. However, there were a lot of creative people who took jobs as assistants or sample makers and I could understand how difficult it would be to feel like his only contribution was going to Starbucks.

"So, what do you want?"

"I want to work in a place where I feel like I'm contributing. I have experience, and I want to put that to good use."

He had perfect answers, and though I wasn't always great at reading people, the way he looked at me seemed earnest. For a brief moment, my mind went back to Lexi. She, too, seemed like a perfect candidate, and over the years I worked with her, she was not only a great assistant but became my friend. Perhaps that was why her betrayal cut me so deeply, and perhaps that was why it took me so long to find someone new. It was silly, but I put off hiring a new assistant the same way I put off dating. I knew that on both fronts, it was time to move on.

"Look, I've never been one for formalities, so let me be completely honest with you," I started. "I fired the person who had this position before you, and it was one of the hardest things I've had to do professionally."

"Why is that?"

I tilted my head to the side. *Wasn't I the one that was supposed to be asking questions here?* "Because, as you can see, I don't have a huge staff. The people that I work with are people that I consider friends, not employees. I don't want an assistant who's just going to run around and do my errands. I want someone who believes in this line and who wants to be a part of it."

"That's what I was hoping for," Danillo sighed, a look of relief on his face.

"Also, I would die before I sold my line to a department store," I said with a scoff, although there was some truth to it.

I wasn't sure if I was making the right choice, but I knew that I had to make one. "Can you start now?"

The biggest smile appeared on Danillo's face. "Y-yes! I can."

"Okay, let's get started then." I got up and motioned for him to follow me. He nearly tripped over himself trying to get out of his chair.

"This is Nia Carter, she runs the business side of the line," I said as Nia turned her attention towards us.

"Welcome to the team," Nia greeted with a smile as she got up to shake Danillo's hand.

"Could you get his paperwork started?" I asked her.

"Only if you tell me what happened with Mr. Motorcycle," she teased.

I wasn't sure that this was the best time to discuss Owen, but this was also what "normal" looked like at the studio. We spent almost as much time talking to each other as we did working. Sooner or later, Danillo was going to figure that out.

"We went out again this weekend..." I began as I walked over to Lexi's old desk. I sat down and logged into the laptop that had been gathering dust for months. As Danillo filled out paperwork, I started writing down passwords and other bits of information he would need.

"What is 'out'? Did you go on an actual date or did he just drive you around on that Harley of his in the middle of the night again?" Nia asked me.

I rolled my eyes. "We went to a dive bar in Chelsea."

"That's a date?"

"It was fun!" I responded, sounding a little more defensive than I intended to.

Nia seemed to spot the ring on Danillo's finger, so

she turned her attention to him. "You're married. Where did you go on your first date?" she asked him.

"He took me to a fashion exhibit at MoMa," Danillo responded with a smile though he sounded a little surprised that the conversation suddenly turned to him.

"See! Michael took me to Tavern on the Green."

"What's your point?" I asked impatiently.

"The kind of man you should be taking seriously doesn't take you to dive bars."

"Who says I want to take him seriously?"

I was protesting a bit too much. I didn't know if I wanted to take Owen seriously or not. I wasn't even sure that taking him seriously was an option. The jury was still out. I just knew that the idea that there was something wrong with him simply because he didn't take me on some expensive date was ridiculous.

"Why are you seeing him, then?" Nia asked.

I raised an eyebrow and then pulled out my phone. I airdropped the photo I'd taken of Owen to Nia's computer.

"Oh...*now* I get it!"

That seemed to end the conversation, and just as I was about to start training Danillo, the phone began ringing loudly from Lexi's old desk. Without missing a beat, Danillo crossed the room and picked up the phone. "J. Lange, how may I direct your call?" I was surprised that he'd taken the initiative to answer the phone without so much as a set of directions. "Please hold."

"Leon Acosta?" he asked, holding out the phone.

I made a confused face and then took the receiver from him.

My brows lowered in confusion. "Why are you calling my work phone?"

"Because it's work-related," Leon responded.

"Okay, hit me."

"What are you doing this afternoon?"

"I thought you said this was work-related."

"It is. The stylist we hired for this month's cover didn't show."

"I'm in the middle of—"

"Please! I'll make sure they mention the line in the feature," Leon begged.

He sounded desperate. I looked over at Danillo. It probably wasn't a great idea to drag someone I'd hired less than an hour ago to a shoot of this caliber, but at the same time, the fashion world could be fast-paced, and it would give me a good sense of how he performed under pressure.

"Okay, have them send a car in an hour," I said before hanging up the phone. I turned to Danillo. "Have you ever worked a photoshoot before?"

"When I worked at Yates-Richland, I did, but they did all their photography in-house," he responded.

"We do, too, but a friend of mine had a stylist drop out, so I'm doing him a favor."

"Okay, what do we need?" Danillo asked without skipping a beat.

I smiled. I was quickly starting to realize just how much I'd missed having an assistant. It was nice to have someone so willing to help, especially without having to hold their hand. "Two racks and all the jackets from this season. I'll pull the rest, and we're going to have to stop at Saks on the way."

Danillo nodded, looking rather determined, and started towards the opposite end of the studio. I got to work as well, loading up pieces into the plastic suitcases we used for fashion shows. I just hoped that whoever the magazine was shooting was a sample size.

About an hour later, Danillo and I loaded a huge, black SUV. It was strange, but in some way, we already felt like a team. I always assumed that my working relationship with Lexi was unique, and part of my hesitation to hire someone new was concern that I wouldn't find that again, but Nia seemed to have been right about Danillo. He jumped right in without a moment's hesitation, and on a day like today, I was grateful for it.

Ten

After a pit stop at Saks and an insufferable amount of traffic, the SUV arrived at *Cavalier* headquarters. Most magazines took a hit once people started reading their content online, but *Cavalier* was in a world of its own. It had been around since the 1960s. It took constant rebranding, a touch of elitism, and some excellent PR, but they somehow managed to maintain their status as the authority on the modern, sophisticated man. Leon had been working at *Cavalier* for years, so the place felt familiar to me. But when I looked over at Danillo, he was staring up at the high-rise building in complete awe.

"You didn't say we were going to *Cavalier*," he said, his gaze fixated out the window.

"We're going to *Cavalier*," I teased.

He was still staring as the driver came around to let us out and started unloading everything we'd brought

with us.

"I'll be right back," I told Danillo before heading into the lobby through the large glass doors. Seated behind a long chrome reception desk were Cavalier's four receptionists. Though they were distinctly unique, they were all stylishly dressed, effortlessly beautiful, and almost uniform in the way they answered the endless barrage of phone calls that came in. It took a long minute before Ana, my favorite of the four, looked up at me from under her mane of thick, dark curls.

"Hey, beautiful, I'll let Leon know you're here."

"I'm styling the cover shoot, so I could also use a bunch of interns to get this stuff up to 18."

"On it," Ana said before hopping back on the phone.

I went back outside to join Danillo, who I caught taking a photo of the building. When he saw me, he quickly shoved his cell phone back in his pocket.

"Sorry, I just..."

"Don't be. My best friend works here, so I forget that it's a big deal." I smiled, trying to sound reassuring.

He nodded, and before I could say much else, Leon hurried outside. He wrapped an arm around my shoulder.

"You are a lifesaver, Jace," he said, squeezing me tightly.

"Oh, don't think for a second you're not going to owe me," I said to him.

I quickly realized that Danillo and Leon hadn't met. "Danillo, this is my best friend, Leon. Leon, this is my new assistant, Danillo."

"Danny is fine," he said as he held out his hand for Leon to shake.

A small group of interns started to file out of the building, and Leon turned to give them instructions.

"Please tell me that's Mr. Motorcycle!" Danny said

under his breath.

I immediately laughed. It was clear we were going to get along just fine. "No, Leon and I are just friends," I explained.

I said that sentence to so many people over the years. I doubted that any of them believed me. I was never sure if it was strictly based on what Leon looked like or if it was that pesky misconception that men and women couldn't be platonic friends.

"Come on, let's head upstairs."

Danny followed me through the marble-floored lobby and up the glass elevators to the eighteenth floor. The doors opened onto a large photography studio and a crew of people shuffling back and forth trying to get set up. Before I could make my way towards the dressing rooms in the back, I heard a familiar booming Australian accent.

"Jacey Lange, look at you!" Oliver Berry, *Cavalier*'s photographer, called out.

"Oli!" I exclaimed as the muscular, forty-something man with salt and pepper hair kissed both of my cheeks.

"I was so happy when Leon told me you were coming in."

"I heard you had a no-show."

"I swear the stylists in this city..." he groaned, rolling his bright blue eyes.

"Who are we shooting?"

"Some actor. He's in some big-budget something coming out next month," Oliver said, waving his hand dismissively.

"Alright, let's get this going."

Just as Danny and I entered one of the dressing rooms, the interns dragged themselves through the door with arms full of racks and clothing. Leon trailed behind them.

"What can I do?" he asked me.

I was surprised. I styled shoots at *Cavalier* before, but Leon didn't usually hang around or attempt to help. "Don't you have a job to get back to?"

"You saved my ass. The least I can do is help."

"Alright, give me that," I said, pulling on the lapel of his suit jacket, or rather, my suit jacket. The piece was one of mine, and even though I had gifted it to Leon, there was no way I was going to see it get ruined. "And start putting racks together."

I left Leon to build racks and Danny to hang up and steam pieces while I went in search of Mr. Big-Budget Something. Luckily for me, he was indeed a sample size. Once everything was set up, getting him into something cover-worthy was easy. Oli's assistant eventually came to get him, and they started shooting. After that, all I had to do was sit there for the rest of the afternoon and occasionally pick out a new jacket or accessory. Getting there might have been the most difficult part.

I watched the shoot for a few minutes before joining my best friend and my new assistant back in the dressing room. I found Danny sitting in a white director's chair on one side of the room. Leon was glued to his phone on a small couch in the opposite corner.

"Now comes the boring part..." I muttered to Danny as I flopped down on the couch next to Leon and draped my legs over his lap.

"Are you kidding? I'm at a photoshoot at *Cavalier*. How could this be boring?" he scoffed.

"Well, we're not going to be doing much other than waiting around," I said, sounding a little apologetic.

"At Yates-Richland, I would be making coffee runs and answering emails right now. I have nothing to complain about."

I noticed that Danny kept looking at the door like he was quietly wishing he could see through walls. "You can go watch if you want."

Instantly, his eyes lit up. "Are you sure? I don't want to be in the way."

"Just stay off to the side, and you should be fine."

Danny clambered to get out of the room and watch the shoot. As soon as the door shut behind him, I turned to Leon. "I heard you on the phone this morning. Is everything okay?" I asked.

It wasn't exactly uncommon for me to hear Leon arguing with his family in Portugal over the phone. In fact, most of the phone calls he had with them sounded like that. I was never really sure if it was just a cultural thing or just really bad blood, but Leon never really cared to explain it to me.

"Yeah....it's fine..." he said absently, never once looking up from his phone.

Like the annoying little sister I often felt I'd grown to be, I snatched his cell phone out of his hands without warning. "Let's see who you can't stop texting..." I said playfully.

"Jace!" Leon warned as he tried to grab the phone back from me.

I jumped up out of his grasp and hurried to the other side of the room. However, when I looked down at the screen, I saw a name I'd hoped I'd never see again: Natalia Kasandrova, the model Leon dated last year. It was the only time in all the years I'd known Leon that I'd seen him get hurt. Needless to say, I wasn't her biggest fan. She was the coldest woman I had ever met, and since then, even the sound of her name made me angry. However, I couldn't make sense of the emotional reaction I was having. I just knew that for whatever reason, her name on his screen made my stomach drop.

"Sorry, I was just...joking. I — here." I hurried back over and handed him the phone.

Leon slowly took the phone out of my hands and looked down at it. I hadn't even bothered to read their text exchange. They could have been talking about the price of Bartlett pears at Whole Foods for all I knew. I was just so immediately uncomfortable that I wanted the phone as far away from me as possible. *What is wrong with me?* I didn't like Nat. That was obvious, but why was I having this bizarre reaction?

"We were just— " Leon started, but I jumped in before he could finish.

"You don't have to explain!"

Leon looked up at me through his dark lashes. I couldn't tell if the look on his face was concern or confusion. "Are you okay?" he asked me.

"Yeah, why?"

"You're acting like a weirdo..." he said, borrowing my words from not so long ago.

I opened my mouth to speak, but nothing came out. What could I possibly say to that? I couldn't be upset with him for interacting with someone I didn't like, especially when I'd found out by snatching his phone away from him. "I just didn't realize you and Nat were still talking, but it's none of my business."

I felt like I couldn't just stand there with him staring at me like that so, nervously, I started adjusting clothing items on their hangers, buttoning buttons, straightening sleeves, literally anything to avoid eye contact. I knew it was ridiculous, and yet I couldn't stop myself.

Leon got up from the couch and stood next to me so I couldn't continue to avoid looking at him. "Does it matter if we are?"

"No. Yes? I don't know." I stopped my fidgeting and turned to face him. "She hurt you," I finally managed to say.

"I wouldn't go that far."

I placed my hands on my hips and gave Leon a look that told him I wasn't buying that for a minute. "You were heartbroken."

Leon rolled his eyes, but he and I both knew the truth. "We're just catching up," he assured me.

I nodded my head curtly, stepping away from him yet again, this time looking around the room for my purse. "That's great," I said, but my voice was tight, and Leon always seemed to know when I was lying.

"Why is this bothering you so much?" he asked.

"I don't know."

I was telling the truth. I didn't know why I felt strange and panicked and uncomfortable. I just did. All that happened was that I saw my best friend texting his ex-girlfriend. The whole situation had absolutely nothing to do with me, and yet here I was, bent out of shape over it.

Again, Leon stood in front of me and stopped me from moving around the room. The confrontation was starting to feel like some weird dance between us. I wanted him to stop. I didn't want to answer any more questions. I wanted to forget I'd even seen his phone. Yet, in true Leondro Acosta fashion, he seemed determined to push the issue until he got the answer he wanted. The only problem was I didn't know what he was looking for.

"I think you do," Leon said this time with an unexpected smile on his face.

"I just don't want you to get hurt again," I said to him.

"Are you—" Leon started to continue to press me when the door to the dressing room opened unexpectedly.

"Hey Jacey, could we pull a second look? He looks amazing, but we want to try something a little darker." Oli's assistant asked.

"Yeah, of course," I responded.

I was saved by the photographer's assistant. I poked my head out the door and waved Danny back into the dressing room. Thankfully, with the room now filled with people, Leon didn't ask me any more questions. I focused on the job at hand and tried to pretend that the last few minutes never happened. It was easier that way.

Eleven

My life had felt like a metronome. Get up, work out, go to work, go home, eat dinner, stare at the ceiling, try not to think about Brian, eventually fall asleep, and then start all over again.

Then all of a sudden, everything around me started changing.

It was as if this bet Leon made was a catalyst. Not only were Owen and now August completely unexpected, but my very mundane routine was suddenly peppered with motorcycle rides, drunken nights, and flirty texts.

> **Owen:** *Have I known you long enough to take you camping yet?*
> **Me:** Sounds like you're just trying to get me alone in the woods.
> **Owen:** *I'm always trying to get you alone.*

I said yes, despite having briefly considered that Owen might have been a serial killer when he first asked me. I had to admit it might have been a bit early to disappear with him for several days, but with Owen, I was slowly starting to learn there was no timeline. He was one of those people who just did what he wanted regardless of the consequences. It was almost impossible not to get swept up in his spontaneity and wild energy. One look into those piercing brown eyes, and I was a goner.

Friday night, Owen rented a truck and picked me up from the studio. Both Nia and Danny watched from the window as we drove out of sight. My budding love life had become a constant source of office conversation, and so the two of them weren't about to miss an opportunity to see "Mr. Motorcycle" in the flesh.

The trip upstate wasn't exactly a short one. For four hours, we listened to heavy metal from the 80s, talked about our opposite upbringings, and even made out at a few red lights along the way. I learned a lot about Owen as we drove. He told me about being raised by a single mother. He had no family to speak of other than her. I liked the sound of his voice when he talked about her and the way he described her dark sense of humor. I watched his face light up as he started to tell me about growing up on O'ahu and how large bodies of water were the only thing that kept him from feeling homesick. He started playing football as soon as he could hold a ball. The sport had taken him all the way through high school and eventually landed him a scholarship to University of Washington. Something changed in his voice when he started talking about his college years. When he explained how he'd gotten injured before going to the

NFL, I quickly understood why: football was the only thing Owen ever saw himself doing for a living.

I let him do most of the talking. I wanted to soak up every piece of information he would give me. I couldn't remember the last time I was so content. Watching him while he drove and listening as he told me stories of his life filled me with a rare warmth. Slowly, the doubts I had about him started to fade. We had been in the truck for hours, but I didn't care if we ever got there. Camping wasn't important to me. I couldn't even say I liked camping. I did, however, like Owen.

The truck finally stopped and I glanced over at the clock on the dashboard. It was late and much too dark to make heads or tails of where we were. Owen however, didn't hesitate as he barreled out of the driver's seat, so I didn't question him. I stepped out of the truck and immediately heard the trickling of a nearby stream and a symphony of crickets chirping into the night.

"I'm guessing you're not the campground type?" I mused, still struggling to see in the darkness.

"I wouldn't call that camping."

I couldn't exactly argue with him. I knew next to nothing about camping. The closest I had come was an expensive summer camp that my parents sent Elise and me to as kids. What I did know, however, was that no campground meant no plumbing or showers or outlets. This was going to be quite the weekend. I thought for a moment about saying something, but when I first met him, Owen told me how much he loved camping, and the last thing I wanted to do was ruin it for him by complaining about the lack of amenities.

Owen flipped the headlights on so he could see while he grabbed the gear out of the back. I now had some idea where we were — at the bottom of a hill with a small stream a few feet away. I couldn't make out much else, but I could see the appeal. I watched as Owen made trips back and forth from the bed of the truck to the area he was setting up camp.

"Is there something I can help with?" I asked.

I might not have known much about camping, but it hardly seemed fair to stand there and watch him do all the work. I certainly enjoyed the view, but I wanted to make myself useful.

"Do you know how to start a fire?"

"The hard way or the easy way?" I asked.

He raised an eyebrow at me as a devilish smirk played at the corner of his lips. He grabbed a packet of Firestarter, his dark eyes never leaving me. He held it out to me for a brief moment but when I reached for it, he teasingly pulled it away.

"Are you sure you don't want to do it the hard way?" he asked, his voice lowering as he spoke.

I snatched the packet away from him. "I have plenty of time to make things hard," I purred.

I busied myself with building a fire. Despite having all the supplies, it was a bit of a struggle. It became embarrassingly clear that I didn't remember as much from summer camp as I thought I had. Owen moved around me while I worked, setting up a tent with expert precision. Once we finished, I sat down on one of the camping chairs and took a deep breath, enjoying how quiet it was compared to the city. It felt like I was in a whole other world.

Owen took my hand, pulling me up to my feet, and then proceeded to take my seat. He then tugged at the belt loops on my pants, nudging me to sit down on his lap.

"What are you thinking, Beautiful?" he asked me.

"I'm just glad we decided to do this."

He nodded, and for a while, we were both silent. We stared at the fire in front of us and listened to the sounds of the nearby water. It was peaceful, but there was one thing that had been bothering me since our first date. While I liked the feeling of being close to Owen, I couldn't completely relax with questions still bouncing around in my head.

"I need to ask you something."

Owen leaned to the right a little so he could look at me. "What's that?"

I froze. I realized as I thought of a hundred different ways to word my question in the span of a few seconds that I had no idea how to ask Owen what he was looking for without sounding like some weird, love-sick puppy. I was interested in Owen, and I was desperately attracted to him. I just wanted to know if what he wanted and what I wanted were aligned.

"Jacey?" he said. I had been in my head a little too long.

"I... um..." I decided to dive right in. "What are you looking for? I mean, if there was an ideal partner or an ideal situation...romantically...what would it be?"

His eyes shifted back and forth as he seemed to think about the answer. "I don't know."

"You don't know what you're looking for?"

"I think I'll just know when I find it."

That had to be the vaguest answer in the history of answers. I tried as hard as I could not to let it frustrate me. "Okay, but you have to have pictured the rest of your life, right?"

"Sure."

"Well, then, who's in it? Do you want to get married?

Any kids? Do you want monogamy at all? Polyamorous throuple? Dog? Hermithood?"

He laughed, and as usual, the deep rumbling sound of his laughter put me at ease.

"Maybe, yes, maybe, no, yes, and I don't think I'd hate being a hermit. Why all the questions?" he asked me.

"Because I like you. But we're really different, so I just wanted to know if we're looking for the same things. We've never really discussed it."

Owen reached up and tucked my hair behind my ear, and something in me melted a little. At that moment, he could have said that he wanted to spend the rest of his life on an alien spaceship, and I would have readily gone along with him. "You like me," he teased, sounding like a child who was just told a secret on the playground.

"A lot," I shrugged.

He kissed me hard, pulling my body closer to his. We may not have been the perfect match on paper and there was still something missing, but there was no denying the chemistry between us.

"Okay, now I have a question."

I wasn't expecting that, but I welcomed the fact that he wanted to get to know me better. "Okay, go ahead."

"This guy you're living with..."

"Leon? What about him?"

"There's not something going on there?"

"No, there's not," I laughed. Even though I hated that question, I realized that Owen wouldn't have been asking if he wasn't interested in pursuing things further. "I've known Leon since I was in college. He's my best friend, but it's never been more than that."

"Could it be?"

I shrugged. I had never really given that question any

thought. It had never been an option, so I never thought to consider what I might do if it were.

"I doubt it."

"Why is that?"

This line of questioning was starting to go from endearing to uncomfortable. I made a face at Owen, trying to break the tension between us. When he cracked a smile I decided it was safe to answer. "I think that if something were going to happen, it would have already. I have nothing negative to say about Leon. He's one of the most amazing people I've ever known, but after ten years, I think it's safe to say that it's unlikely."

"Okay, last question...Why is he the most amazing person you've ever known?"

"Why are you asking so many questions about Leon?"

"I just want to know about the things, and people, that are important to you."

I sighed. I wasn't sure I knew how to sum up how I felt about Leon, nor did I feel entirely comfortable doing it with someone I was dating. However, I figured if Owen was genuinely trying to learn about me, it was only fair that I gave him an honest answer. "Leon and I met because he literally rescued me from a bad situation when I was in college. He didn't know me or have any reason to care about what happened to me, but he stepped in. He didn't leave until he knew that I was okay. That's the core of who Leon is. He is so selfless. He would give the shirt off his back for complete strangers. I can't say that about very many people in my life."

Owen looked up at me for a long moment. I wondered what was going on in his head but he said nothing. Instead, he just pulled me closer to him and held onto me like he might not let me go.

We continued talking well into the night. In the truck, I had asked question after question about him and his life. In front of the campfire, he asked me question after question about me and mine. I may have liked Owen before, but the more we talked, the more I started to genuinely feel connected to him. Eventually, exhaustion got the better of us, and we put out the fire.

I was tired from the drive and from setting up camp but laying next to Owen in that tent had my mind running a mile a minute. I wondered if this was the point that we were finally going to act on all the sexual tension and loaded words we'd been exchanging since we met. I wanted to make a move, but it had been a long time since I'd had a first experience with someone. I talked myself up, telling myself that if there was ever a moment, this was it, but when I turned to my side to say something, I could see his breathing had grown heavier, and his eyes were closed tightly. It looked like taking things to the next level was going to wait.

Twelve

When I opened the front door of my apartment, I found Leon missing yet again. The thought that he might be off with Natalia crossed my mind, but I swallowed it down. Leon was a grown man. It wasn't my business who he spent his time with. I just hoped it wasn't a five-foot-ten blonde who smoked like a chimney and had an accent that sounded like a cheese grater on concrete. Before heading upstairs, I grabbed a sticky note from the kitchen and scribbled out a note, leaving it on top of Leon's laptop.

In the shower.
Don't leave!
Need to talk.

Once upstairs, I got in the shower. I let the water get as hot as humanly possible and tried to scrub away not

only the days of layered dirt on my body, but the terrible aftertaste the weekend had left in my mouth. I knew that I might have been overreacting. Objectively, the weekend had been fine. Owen and I didn't fight, and the place we set up camp was beautiful. It was just that after waking up next to him without anything "happening", I was frustrated. I proceeded to put myself out there on more than one occasion that weekend, and yet nothing. I couldn't figure out if I did something wrong or if it was just bad timing, but I left feeling like Owen was a dead end. Or worse yet, he didn't want me at all.

I hated that I cared. It was too early to care. I had almost forgotten what it was like to have feelings for someone and how such tiny things could tie me into knots. I didn't understand why Owen flirted with me so intensely and then backed off the moment I wanted intimacy. There was some part of me, however small, that thought something might work out between us despite my misgivings. Yet when I looked at the situation, we just weren't compatible. The more time I spent with him, the more abundantly clear that became.

After what seemed like an eternity in the shower, most of which I spent staring at the tiles on the wall as I tried to make sense of my thoughts, I got out and dried myself off. I put on a pair of sweatpants and a tank top and then padded downstairs, still barefoot with soaking wet hair. From the bottom of the steps, I could see Leon tapping away at his laptop wearing a pair of thick-rimmed reading glasses. Something about seeing him there was so comforting. It was a reminder that I was home and that I was with the one person I knew I could always trust. Leon didn't notice me, so for a while I just stood there watching him, letting the unexpected sense of relief wash over me.

"Are you going to keep standing there, or are you going to come talk to me?" Leon asked, never looking up from his screen.

I jumped a little. I hadn't realized that Leon even knew I was there. I didn't say anything, just headed straight for the seat next to him. He typed quietly for a second or two longer before shutting the laptop and setting it to the side.

"Are you okay?" he asked.

"Y-yeah, it was just a weird weekend."

"Weird how?"

"I guess...it just didn't go the way I expected it to."

I didn't know how to explain myself or explain how I felt. I just knew that I was relieved to be home, and that wasn't how I was supposed to feel after a weekend alone in the woods with someone that looked like Owen. I should have been on cloud nine. Instead, I felt defeated.

"Seriously? I thought you'd be calling off the bet by now."

"I'm not calling off the bet."

"You seemed really into this guy. What happened? Still too dumb?"

"He's not dumb, and I *was* really into him. That's the problem."

"Jace, you're talking in circles," Leon sighed. "What happened?"

Leon was right. I couldn't help but talk in circles. The downside to having a straight male best friend was that talking about sex could be rather uncomfortable. Be that as it may, I needed to confide in someone, and I knew that sharing this with Elise would only be met with judgment.

"Nothing happened," I muttered.

"I can't talk to you if you're going to make me pull —"

"*Nothing* happened," I said again, hoping that he would catch what I was implying.

"O-oh!" It finally dawned on him. "He turned you down?"

"Not exactly. I mean, he didn't outright say no. The first night he was already asleep by the time I worked up the nerve, and then I just felt like everything went downhill from there." I continued to spin the events of the last few days around in my head. "He even physically got out of the tent when I was changing. Who does that? By the end, he was basically avoiding touching me all together." I shook my head, realizing I was thinking out loud.

"Are you sure he knew you wanted it to happen?"

"Yeah! I'm sure! I couldn't have made it more obvious if I tried."

"What women think is obvious and what men think is obvious are usually two very different things."

I turned to Leon sharply and locked eyes with him. "Ask me if I'm sure I don't want to do it the hard way."

"What?"

"Just ask me!"

"Fine... are you sure you don't want to do it the hard way?"

I softened my gaze, lowered my chin, and looked up at him. "I have plenty of time to make things hard."

Leon looked at me with such intensity that he seemed to forget to respond. Suddenly, he realized what he was doing and shook his head quickly.

"Uh...yeah...that would do it," he chuckled nervously.

"It's probably for the best. I don't feel like it's going

anywhere."

"What makes you say that?"

"He's hot, like really hot, and we have fun together, but..."

"But?"

"He's too fun?"

Leon laughed. "What's too fun?"

"He's all drunken nights and random adventures, but no substance. He doesn't know what he wants."

"Do you know what you want?" Leon fired back, strangely defensive.

I didn't realize it until now, but Leon and Owen had more in common than just their taste in music and their love of black coffee. They were both major flirts with no sense of serious romantic direction. If I asked Leon the same questions I asked Owen, I was sure that I would get similar answers. Leon never once mentioned wanting to get married or settling down in the ten years I'd known him. His primary concern for the future was who was going to be in his bed that night.

"I know I don't want to date someone I can't see a future with. That's just setting myself up to get hurt again," I said honestly.

"So there's no convincing you to let go and date for fun?"

"I am dating for fun, but I want to know that if I fell for someone, taking things further would be an option," I explained as I pulled my legs up into my chest wrapping my arms around them.

Leon nodded, seeming to understand that. I didn't expect it to make sense to him, but it was nice to have a sounding board. "So are we going to talk about this whole Natalia thing?" he suddenly asked, switching gears on me.

"Do we have to?" The last thing I wanted to do was revisit that strange experience at the photo shoot. I still didn't know why the idea of my best friend talking to his ex-girlfriend again upset me so much, but I was trying to avoid dissecting it. The whole situation made me so uncomfortable that I would have been more than happy to pretend it didn't happen at all.

"You kind of freaked out on me, Jace."

"I know...I'm sorry."

Leon shook his head. "You don't have to apologize. I just want to know what happened."

That was the problem. I didn't know what happened. The best I could do was give Leon what little I did know. "Look, I know you're never going to admit to this, but I was there, Leon. You were a mess when it ended. I've never seen you like that before."

It probably didn't help that Brian had proposed right around the same time that Leon and Natalia stopped seeing each other. He was such a wreck. All he did was drink and mope for weeks.

"Okay... but you just seemed..."

"What?"

"Jealous?"

I thought about that for a second. For years, I had always been the only woman in Leon's life. His family lived in another country, and he didn't have committed relationships, so I was used to being a priority. Last year, when Natalia came into the picture, she threatened that. It wasn't fair, I was with Brian at the time, and it shouldn't have mattered that my best friend was seeing someone, but perhaps I was jealous in some way.

"Maybe you're right," I said with a shrug.

"Am I?" He seemed genuinely shocked by my answer.

"It's always been you and me against the world, and even though it is completely selfish and I hate admitting it, I think I hated the idea of someone coming in and changing that. It broke my heart to see you hurt, but in a way, I was relieved because it meant that we'd still be us."

"How do you think I felt about Brian?" Leon retorted. "When you moved in with him, I thought it was the end of an era."

I couldn't help but smile. It was one of the many things I loved about Leon. Here I was, saying something that made me sound selfish and possessive. Yet, instead of judging me for it, he was admitting I wasn't alone in the way I felt.

"Nat isn't going to change us," he added, nudging me gently.

"Promise?"

"Jacey, no one, not even Natalia, will ever mean more to me than you do."

I could feel my eyes welling up a little. Leon and I weren't usually so mushy. Our relationship was mostly built on sarcasm and bad jokes. However, he somehow knew I needed to hear that. "No one will ever mean more to me than you do either," I said, leaning my head against his shoulder.

Leon and I were both quiet for a little while before I chimed in again. "But like, maybe don't start dating her again..."

Leon laughed but didn't say anything. I didn't want to read anything into his lack of words, but I had a sinking feeling that he might already be doing just that. Despite spilling my guts to him, the thought of the two of them together still made me feel like something was crawling under my skin. I assumed after talking about the situation that I would feel better, but I didn't.

Did I just hate the possibility of growing distant from my best friend? Maybe I just hated Natalia that much? Perhaps I was just worried about him getting hurt again? I knew, deep down, there was one other possible answer to explain how I felt...but I refused to entertain the idea. Our friendship was too important to me to even consider it.

Thirteen

In the time since I'd met him, I learned one thing about August Henry: he was persistent. When I encountered him at my favorite used bookstore, he came off as wildly arrogant. He was well-dressed and handsome, but in my experience, arrogant men usually were. Never in my life had anyone challenged my views on a book before deciding to ask me on a date. Yet since we'd met, he texted me every single day without fail.

The first text was simple. August just wanted to ask me to dinner. I told him my schedule was crazy, which translated to going camping with Owen. Then the daily texts began, always in the morning. This alone was impressive enough, but August wasn't the type to settle for a mere "hi" or "good morning". He asked me profound and unusual questions.

August: *Do you think morality is*

learned, or innate?
Me: 100% learned. Morality is just the effect of culture and upbringing on your decision-making.
August: *Have I mentioned I can't wait to take you to dinner?*

At first, I found it a little peculiar. How often do you get asked things like the root of morality or the difference between honesty and truth? Yet as the week went on, I started to look forward to what question he would ask me next. Sometimes the questions sparked a discussion, and sometimes he just sent a quick but sweet response, and I didn't hear from him again until the following morning. That was, until Friday rolled around. I decided to take matters into my own hands. I texted August before he could text me.

Me: What is the biggest obstacle you're trying to overcome?
August: *Recently, I've been trying to overcome your lack of availability.*
Me: Luckily for you, I think you've accomplished that.
August: *Should I take that to mean you're free tonight?*

Hours later, I was in a cab headed for SoHo and a hip rooftop restaurant called Republic. It was strange how I'd gone from disinterest to excitement in a matter of a few days, but August intrigued me. He seemed to love to challenge me, and so I was curious how this date would turn out. Would he be the entitled, arrogant professor I ran into at the coffee shop? Or the persistent and charming suitor I'd been texting back and forth with all week?

When I arrived at the restaurant, a hostess directed me upstairs. Republic was one of those tragically trendy restaurants that were impossible to get into, at least until some other place became a hot spot and it disappeared into obscurity. On the roof, I found yet another hostess who informed me our table wasn't ready yet and that Mr. Henry was at the bar. I followed her directions, finding a gaggle of miscellaneous people drinking and chatting in front of a frantic-looking bartender. I scanned the crowd, only to spot a familiar silhouette facing away from me and gazing out over the city.

I could see the cream-colored suit he was wearing, his dark, shoulder-length hair, and the brown liquor that I could only guess was brandy in his hand. Though I hadn't noticed it when we first met, there was a way he stood that screamed of breeding, maybe even military school. He had perfect posture that was just a hair away from looking uncomfortable.

I also wasn't used to going on a date with a man who dressed for dinner. When I started dating Brian, I couldn't even get him to put on a shirt with a collar. But there was this quality about August that made him seem almost fictional. He was like a character from the classic novels he knew so well.

I made my way over and stood next to him, following his gaze over the skyline. He didn't seem to notice me at first and so I took a moment to really look at the city I loved so much. There was something miraculous about New York City. No matter how long I'd lived here, I was still amazed by the idea that something so vast and beautiful was created by other human beings. That somehow they created starlight out of rebar and steel. I opened my mouth to share what I was thinking with August but I found myself unsure of how he would react. I knew he had some depth, but I had my doubts about his creativity and the last thing I wanted was another one of his little lectures.

"Come here often?" I teased.

August's eyebrows lifted as he turned to face me. *God, he is so much more handsome than I remember.*

"I was starting to think I might get stood up," he said to me.

"A man doesn't dress like that expecting to get stood up," I responded, matching the crisp, impersonal tone of his voice.

"Does that mean you approve?"

I tilted my head to the side and gave him a once over. I definitely approved, but I also didn't want to put all my cards on the table. "I mean, it's not mine, but it'll do," I said, doing my best Anna Wintour.

He opened his mouth to respond, but before he could, the hostess came to show us to our table.

August pulled my chair out for me. The furniture at Republic was unique in that the tables were these strange interactive art pieces with lights that reacted every time you touched them. My natural inclination was to keep tapping on the table to get it to respond, like a kid with elevator buttons. I had to steel myself so I wouldn't do anything embarrassing.

"I took a look at your work, actually," August said.

I wasn't sure whether to be flattered or worried, given how critical he was when I first met him. "You did?"

"It's a little edgier than I expected, but impressive."

"Is edgy a bad thing?"

"I suppose that depends on who you ask."

I was getting the impression he was trying very hard not to say something judgmental. Instead of pressing the issue, I decided to pick up my menu and look at my options. Unfortunately, it was full of strange, trendy nonsense that I didn't recognize, like Atlantic halibut with *matbucha coulis* and deconstructed lasagna with a Brandywine and basil reduction. I felt like I was going cross-eyed just trying to make sense of it. "Have you been here before?" I asked.

"Only once."

"Any idea what I should order?"

August stood and dragged his chair closer to mine so he could look over the menu with me. I knew that he could have easily looked at his own, but the gesture made me smile a little. He was close enough that I could feel his arm brush mine, which, despite still being a little unsure of him, caused butterflies in my stomach.

"Avoid anything deconstructed, and you should be fine," he said after a moment.

"Really? I figured deconstructed food would be right up your alley," I said with a laugh.

"Why is that?"

I gave him a look, at which he immediately rolled his eyes.

"Just because I know my Fitzgerald doesn't mean I enjoy eating meals out of upcycled baby food jars."

"That's true. Now if you had argued with me on Hemmingway, that would be another story."

August just looked at me. Those almond-shaped espresso eyes of his were even more disarming up close. Any doubts I had about this date started to melt away.

He might not have made the best first impression, but he was quickly changing my mind.

"What?" I asked as he continued to hold my gaze.

"I have a confession...."

I looked back and forth, trying to figure out what he could have to confess. We barely knew each other after all.

"I have a Hemingway tattoo," he muttered with a guilty look on his face.

I didn't mean to, but a laugh escaped me. "You're kidding!"

"I wish I were."

"Why?"

"I was nineteen. I'd just moved to New York to be a writer. I don't know what I was thinking."

"Where?" I asked. I was now completely fascinated by the fact that he had such a stereotypical and arguably awful tattoo.

August pointed to the right side of his chest to the space between his collarbone and bicep.

"You have to show me!" I exclaimed, sounding far more excited than I should. I loved bad tattoos.

"Here?"

"Why not?"

"How's this? I promise I'll show it to you at the end of the night," he said, a hint of mischief in his voice.

I didn't exactly know how to take that statement. I couldn't tell if August was implying that he'd be taking his clothes off at the end of the night or simply trying to avoid having to show me his tattoo at the dinner table.

I shrugged. "I guess I'll take it."

After the waiter took our orders I expected August to move back across the table but he remained next to me.

I was surprised to find that in the moments we didn't speak, nerves started to bubble up inside me. I wasn't expecting August to make me nervous. I wasn't even sure that I was expecting to enjoy myself, but there I was. I tried to distract myself with my surroundings but when I turned back toward my date I found that his eyes had never left me. Thankfully, the food came out quickly, despite how crowded the restaurant was, but I was too distracted by the man sitting next to me to pay much attention to the pistachio-crusted chicken breast I'd ordered.

"So, how did you go from a nineteen-year-old writer with bad tattoos to a college professor?" I jumped back in.

"I only had one good book in me," he said, though I could hear a hint of sadness behind his straightforward tone.

"That can't be true," I blurted.

August looked at me like I had just jumped on the table and thrown our entrées off the rooftop.

"Painters don't have one painting in them, and musicians don't just have one song, so I refuse to believe that you only had one book," I explained.

He genuinely looked like he had no idea what to say to that, and I quickly realized that I'd overstepped. I wasn't trying to be rude. I just hated the idea of creative people giving up.

After a painful silence, he cleared his throat. "Unfortunately, my literary agent disagreed with you," he said somberly.

Great job, Jacey. I had only been on this date for forty-five minutes, and I already managed to put my foot in my mouth. The uncomfortable silence returned, and so in an attempt to salvage the evening, I said the first thing that came to mind. "Oblina."

"I'm sorry, what?"

"I have a tattoo of Oblina," I shrugged, sounding like it was the most normal thing in the world.

"What's an Oblina?"

"I'm guessing you didn't watch *Aaahh!!! Real Monsters* as a kid?"

August shook his head.

I grabbed my clutch and pulled out my phone. After a quick Google search, I handed him my phone, showing him a picture of an ugly, black-and-white striped cartoon monster. It resembled the bottom half of an umbrella with eyes.

"You're joking," August said, trying hard not to laugh.

"Not at all."

"Why would you put this on your body?"

"My best friend and I got drunk in college," I said with a shrug.

"Does she have a bad tattoo, too?"

"She's a he, but yes, he has an Ickis."

"Do I want to know what an Ickis is?"

I took the phone back and pulled up another photo of a similar monster, but this one was small and red with gigantic ears that resembled a rabbit.

"You know you're going to have to show me," he said.

Without a moment's hesitation, I pushed my chair back and crossed my left leg over my right, exposing the inside of my left ankle. There, as promised, was a tattoo of Oblina about two and half inches long.

"That is..."

"Fantastic?" I asked sarcastically.

"I was going to say strange, but the canvas is pretty breathtaking," he said with a wink.

That seemed to turn the conversation around. We spent the rest of our meal laughing and talking about books and music and the endless list of things that August seemed to be passionate about. It started to hit me that I had been wrong about him. He wasn't stuck up. He was just passionate about nearly everything he encountered. By the time the waiter brought him the check, I was sure I didn't want the night to end.

He insisted on seeing me home, which again seemed straight out of some other era. He rode with me in a cab back to Midtown. To my surprise, the conversation continued the whole way there without so much as a pause. When we pulled up to my building, I turned to him.

"This is me," I said, expecting an awkward goodbye.

"Can I walk you to your door?" he asked me.

"Um...sure."

I wasn't expecting that. Maybe August wanted me to invite him upstairs? I liked him well enough, but I wasn't intending on sleeping with him on our first date. He got out of the cab and held the door for me. As we walked up to the building, he grabbed my hand. I liked the feeling of my hand in his, even if it was brief.

"I believe I made you a promise," he finally said.

I watched as he took his suit jacket off and unbuttoned several buttons before pulling the shirt to the side just enough for me to see the singular line in a scribbled sort of script; *'write the truest sentence you know.'* It was a terrible tattoo, and yet it couldn't be more fitting.

"I think I win," I teased. My tattoo was definitely worse.

"Yes, I think you do. What's your prize?"

In a move that I certainly hadn't expected myself to pull, I wrapped my arms around August's neck, and I kissed him. If I was being honest with myself I had wanted to kiss him for hours. I had obviously taken him by surprise, but after a brief second, he wrapped his arms around my waist and kissed me back.

It was one hell of a kiss.

When we pulled back, I was breathless, and he was smiling.

"I should get upstairs," I said.

"Okay, I'll talk to you in the morning."

"The morning?" I asked.

"You didn't think I was going to stop asking questions after one date, did you?"

I smiled so hard it made my face hurt a little and turned to let myself inside. By the time I got to the elevator, there was a familiar *ding* from the inside of my bag. It was a text from August and another Hemingway quote.

I didn't want to kiss you goodbye, that was the trouble. I wanted to kiss you goodnight. And there's a lot of difference.

Fourteen

Since the beginning of my wager with Elise and Leon, I hadn't been able to keep my weekly wine date with my sister. She was understanding, of course. Not only was my active dating life partially her idea, she had a wedding to plan. Yet, I always found that if too much time passed without seeing Elise, it started to weigh heavily on me. Being a twin was strange in that way. Elise and I had very different lives and almost nothing in common, and yet we were connected in a way that seemed so much deeper than ordinary siblings. Plus, aside from Leon, Elise was my best friend. It had been three weeks too long. When I texted Elise to let her know that my Saturday night was free, she insisted that I come over to the apartment she shared with Nathan.

Elise lived in Lincoln Square in a high-rise apartment with a view of the Hudson. The Montgomerys, my sister's soon-to-be in-laws, owned a vast number of

buildings in Manhattan, including the one where Elise and Nathan lived. Somehow my sister ended up living in an apartment that retailed for almost ten thousand dollars a month without having to pay a dime. Anyone that knew Elise could tell you that this wasn't surprising. She was always the kind of girl who simply lucked into everything. In this case, her luck led her into the arms of one of the richest available men in New York City.

I was greeted by Elise's doorman, Charlie. "Now which Lange are you?" he asked, squinting his eyes at me.

"The pretty one," I said with a laugh.

"Don't let your sister hear you say that," he scolded me.

After Elise moved into the building, Charlie would let me upstairs without so much as a second glance because he thought I was my sister. He almost had a heart attack when he finally saw the two of us together. Since then, he would regularly make jokes about not being able to tell us apart despite eventually learning the subtle differences between us.

When I reached the top floor, my sister answered the door dressed as she always did, in some ultra-feminine, 1950s-inspired dress. This time the dress was mint green, and she vaguely resembled Natalie Wood with her perfectly placed dark curls.

"I feel like I haven't seen you in months," she sighed, hugging me briefly.

It had only been a few weeks, but I felt the same way.

"I know. I have so much to tell you..." I said as she stepped aside and let me into her lavishly decorated apartment.

I followed Elise into her living room where she already had white wine and a charcuterie board, that I was sure had taken her an hour to put together, laid out on her Restoration Hardware coffee table. I sat down carefully on her stark white sofa. I always felt like I was in a model home when I came to see her. Nothing was lived in or homey; it was all aesthetics and opulence.

"Boys or the wedding?" Elise asked me, though I knew she wanted to talk about her wedding desperately.

"Wedding first," I said as I grabbed a cracker and shoved it into my mouth.

"Okay, don't hate me...."

I knew any time my sister started apologizing before getting to the point that what she was about to say wasn't good.

"What's wrong?"

Elise scrunched her face up before finally blurting out what she wanted to say. "We've been thinking about a destination wedding."

"Where?" I asked slowly, trying to keep from reacting.

"Bordeaux," she responded just as carefully.

"France?"

Elise nodded.

I took a large gulp of my wine. "Why, exactly?"

"It was the first place Nate and I went on vacation together, and it's so beautiful, Jace. Katherine said we could get married anywhere we wanted, so I figured...."

"You figured you'd make everyone you know fly to France?"

In reality, it didn't surprise me that Elise wanted to get married in Bordeaux. She loved wine and French cooking. Plus, I had already expected with my sister's lavish tastes and the Montgomerys' limitless checkbook that this wedding was going to be over the top.

"You said you wouldn't get mad!" Elise exclaimed.

"I said no such thing," I reminded her.

"Do you really think it's a bad idea?"

I noticed the look on my sister's face, and I could tell she genuinely wanted me to approve. Going to southwestern France next spring was hardly convenient, but truthfully, if Elise said she wanted to get married on the moon, I would find a way to make it happen.

I placed my hand over hers. "I think you deserve the wedding of your dreams, Ellie. If that happens to be in Bordeaux...then we're going to Bordeaux!"

Relief washed over her face, and I knew I did the right thing. Attempting to make Elise think logically rarely ever worked, and ultimately I knew if this is what she wanted, it was going to happen whether I liked it or not.

"Okay, now that's out of the way. I need to know everything about these guys you're seeing!"

I sighed. I knew when I'd decided to visit that this was coming. I just didn't expect the focus to swing to me so quickly.

"I'm not seeing either of them. Owen and I didn't really work out, he basically ghosted me after we went camping, and August and I have only been on one date," I explained.

"I could have told you Owen wasn't the one. He took you to a dive bar and then dragged you out to the middle of the woods!"

"Why does everyone keep saying things like that?"

"Like what?"

"Nia said the kind of man I should take seriously doesn't take me to dive bars."

"That's because Nia is a genius," Elise replied as she picked up a bundle of grapes.

"This is true, but there's nothing wrong with dive bars."

Elise rolled her eyes with her signature dramatic flair.

"Tell me about August. He's a professor, right? What's the last name again?"

"Henry."

"Nate!" Elise called towards the back of the apartment.

Dutifully, my future brother-in-law wandered into the room. Nathan Montgomery was nothing like his family's money or name would lead one to believe. He was attractive but not stunningly so, shaggy-haired, good-natured, with a wide, infectious smile. He was, without a doubt, one of the most genuine people I had ever met. I found it sort of baffling that someone who grew up with all of his advantages could be so likable. I found it even more baffling that my sister had somehow managed to accidentally snag the wealthiest bachelor in New York. Granted, they were only 18 years old when they met, and Nathan was hardly sought after then, but I was well aware of the fact that there were now more than a few women who were envious of my sister.

"I didn't even know you were here!" I exclaimed as I stood up to hug Nate.

"How have you been, Jace? Elise says you're dating again?"

"Something like that."

"Do we know any Henrys?" Elise asked.

I looked at Elise, confused. Henry wasn't exactly an uncommon last name. I didn't even know if August grew up in New York. We never discussed it.

"I went to Grandview with a Henry. He teaches at Columbia now."

"August Henry?" Elise clarified.

"We all called him Gus so...could be...?" Nate mused, again shrugging his shoulders.

Nate had this non-committal way of speaking. It was

probably why he and Elise balanced each other out so well. She was headstrong and full of opinions while he was laid back and seemed perfectly content to follow where Elise led.

"Oh my god, marry him!" She exclaimed.

Nate took that as his cue to leave the room. "I'll catch you later, Jace."

"We don't even know if it's the same guy," I said to her.

"Oh, come on! How many Gus Henrys are there, let alone ones that are professors?"

When I thought about it, the idea that August came from money wasn't unreasonable. Grandview was a strict boarding school, which accounted for the way he held himself. If his family was anywhere near as wealthy as Nathan's, then it was no surprise that he came off so arrogant when we first met.

"Okay, that's fair, but that doesn't mean I should marry him."

"Come on, Jacey! He's rich, he has a good job, and you're attracted to him, so find out when he's free and go out with him again!"

I had no idea how to explain to Elise that his family's hypothetical money meant nothing to me. That concept just wasn't in her wheelhouse. My business was successful. I was doing well for myself. I didn't need anyone else's money. I didn't judge Elise because I knew she honestly loved Nathan. To her, everything that came along with being the future Mrs. Elise Montgomery was just a bonus. However, I'd always gotten the impression that my sister wanted me to live a life that was more like hers, and it appeared that she now saw August as a way to make that happen.

"What's wrong? You like him, right?" Elise asked.

"I think so...."

"Then go for it!"

"I'm not sure who he is yet."

"What does that mean?"

"When I met him, he was an entitled jerk, and then last night he was amazing. I don't know which guy I'm dealing with here," I explained.

"The only way you're going to find that out is by going out with him again," she said as if her opinion was fact.

If I was honest, I wanted to go out with August again. All I had been thinking about was him. While I might have moved on rather quickly from Owen, there was just something about August that got under my skin in both the best and worst possible ways. I wanted to dive into that mind of his. I wanted to understand what made him go from arrogant to charming and back again so quickly. I wanted to convince him to start writing again. Yet in the back of my mind, I knew this was all too much for one date. My unexpected attachment to him worried me. I didn't want to be the kind of girl who developed feelings for every guy she met, and I certainly didn't want to get hurt again.

"Okay, I'll text him," I hesitantly agreed.

I reached for my purse and dug around for my phone. To my surprise, when I unlocked the screen, there was already a message from August waiting for me. It was as if he'd somehow read my mind. I quickly typed back a response and then handed the phone to Elise.

> ***August:*** *I'm going to be bold here and say I can't stop thinking about you.*
> **Me:** Your ears must be burning. I've been thinking about you too.

August: *When can I see you again?*

"I'm telling you, this is The One!"

God, she never stops. All of these opinions about my love life were starting to make me want to stop dating anyone so Elise would get off my back. I knew that my sister meant well. I also knew that after what happened with Brian, she was genuinely worried about me. I tried to put myself in her shoes. If I'd seen Ellie go through the kind of heartbreak I experienced, wouldn't I want her to find someone who was far better for her?

"I love you El," I said with a sigh.

Elise looked at me, a little perplexed. "I love you, too. Where is this coming from?"

"Thank you for wanting me to be happy." I simply added.

I would probably never enjoy my sister's preoccupation with my love life, but I did love her, and at the end of the day, she was only doing this because she wanted to know that I was with someone who could, and would, take care of me.

Fifteen

Real dates weren't something I was used to. It was unfortunate, but hookup culture had spoiled most men my age. Their idea of a date was Netflix and Door-Dash, followed by a short and meaningless liaison with someone they'd "swiped right" on. August, however, seemed to be the last 29-year-old man on the island of Manhattan who made plans in advance, put on a suit, and showed up when he said he would. It was refreshing, but at the same time, there was something kind of unreal about it. I didn't know how I'd found the one man in the city that treated dating like a courtship and not a means to get laid.

In the middle of the Garment District was a small theater called The Howl. Even though I had lived in the city for the last eleven years and grown up just a stone's throw away, I was never particularly interested in the New York theater scene. I had nothing against it.

I just never took an interest in plays. However, I wasn't surprised that August's plan for the evening was some experimental show I'd never heard of. It sounded just like the kind of artsy, avant-garde, off-the-beaten-path thing that August would do. The reviews for the show were good, and the playwright was up-and-coming, but I was more concerned with which version of August was taking me out that night.

The theater was only a block away from my office, so instead of picking me up at the apartment, August showed up at the studio. I planned to meet him downstairs, but after getting a last-minute call from one of my fabric suppliers, I missed his text completely. The next thing I knew, Danillo stood in the doorway of the conference room where I was taking my call.

"There's someone here," he mouthed, pointing over his shoulder.

I muted myself quickly. "Who?"

"I forgot to ask his name...super hot, though...."

"Shit!"

I glanced over at the clock on the wall and realized that while August might have been right on time, I was not.

"Can you just offer him some water or something? I'll be right there."

Danny nodded, and I tried to finish my phone call as quickly as possible.

When I emerged from the conference room, August stood leaning against the door frame. I could feel my breath get caught in my chest. He looked incredible.

"This late thing is starting to become your calling card," he teased with a slight smirk on his face.

"I am not late!" I protested. "You are just alarmingly

on time."

"I see." His smirk slowly turned into a full smile.

I was about to suggest we head out when I heard Nia clear her throat from behind me. When I turned, both she and Danillo were looking on expectantly.

"I'm sorry.... August Henry, this is Nia Carter, my business partner, and Danny Reyes, my assistant."

I watched as August went over to them and shook their hands. "Pleasure to meet you both," he said before turning back to me. "Should we get going?"

I nodded and stepped over to my desk to grab my things. When I turned back, I could see the look of stunned approval on Nia's face. I smiled at her as August held out his arm for me to take.

We only got a few feet into the hallway before August stopped me.

"Wait..." he said, turning me to face him.

"What?"

Instead of responding, he took a step toward me and kissed me hard, my back hitting the wall behind me.

"Well, hello to you, too," I breathed, smiling against his lips.

"I have wanted to do that since the last time I saw you," he murmured.

"The feeling is mutual."

We both straightened ourselves out and continued out of the building. The walk from the studio to the theater only took a few minutes, and we were both quiet most of the way there. I started to realize that, for me, dating wasn't as easy as it had once been. I had a hard time staying out of my head. The idea of going with the flow was completely lost on me. Instead, my mind ran in circles.

With August, it was worse than it had been with Owen because I didn't know what to expect. Owen possessed this fixed personality; he was impulsive but predictable. I only had two encounters with August so far, but the person I'd experienced was completely different each time. I told myself it was two out of three and that tonight would decide which version of August was the one I should learn to expect.

When we arrived at the theater, I noticed how sparse the audience seemed. I had never been to a show at The Howl, but the threadbare curtains and worn-down seats of the tiny theater gave me the impression that sold-out shows weren't exactly common. August and I sat down in the middle of the center row, waiting for the show to start.

"Two truths and a lie." I was trying to kill time and perhaps stop thinking so much.

"Okay, let me think..." August turned his gaze from me to the empty stage in front of us. "Cats freak me out, the first book I wrote was a romance novel, and I love horror movies."

I thought for a moment that if he loved horror films, he and Leon would get along just fine. That also seemed like the most obvious truth of the bunch. Cats or romance novels, that was the question. Try though I might, I couldn't picture August writing a romance novel. In the time that I knew him, he had a few romantic moments, but overall he seemed a bit too smart and much too cynical to write a story that ended with happily ever after.

"I'm going to say the romance novel is a lie," I said.

"Wrong."

"What? You wrote a romance novel?" I asked, completely shocked.

"It was never published or anything, but yes, the first novel I ever finished was a romance novel," he said.

"So, what was the lie?"

"I actually love cats," he said with a laugh.

"I could see that." I imagined August chasing some little orange tabby around what I assumed was an apartment full of books.

"Your turn," he said to me.

I also took my time, trying to think of the hardest possible facts to decipher about myself. "I once ate a Costco-size bag of chocolate macadamia nuts in one sitting, I have a birthmark in the shape of a heart, and my middle name is Isabelle."

"No, it's not. Your middle name is Morgan," August said without batting an eye.

I froze. "How did you know that?"

August looked a little shocked himself. "I...saw it on your ID when you ordered wine at the restaurant the other night."

"You remembered that?" Most guys couldn't even remember to text a girl back, let alone such an insignificant detail.

"Believe it or not, when I like someone, I tend to notice things about them, Jacey Morgan Lange."

I smiled at that. "Well, it's only fair that I get to know yours then."

"Oliver."

"August Oliver Henry?" I asked with a laugh.

"I didn't name myself!"

"I never said I didn't like it." Truthfully, now that I heard it out loud, "Oliver" seemed to be the only name that could follow "August".

More people began to enter the theater, and the lights dimmed around us. The date was nowhere near over, but I felt like I had my answer already. I was willing to let go of the bad first impression I'd gotten of August in favor of this version of him. As we watched the performance, I laid my head on his shoulder. *I could get used to this.* It was nice to feel something again without having to second guess myself.

The play wasn't exactly my thing. The words were beautiful, and the actors were talented, but there was something uncomfortable about it. It was almost as if they were trying too hard to create reality out of a very unrealistic subject. However, it didn't really matter to me that experimental theater wasn't my thing. I was more concerned with the brilliant, gorgeous man sitting next to me and the feelings I was starting to develop for him.

When the play was over, we left the theater, and August started to hail a cab. I grabbed his arm to stop him.

"My apartment is only a few blocks away. Let's walk." I wanted to prolong the night for as long as I could.

August smiled at me and slid his hand into mine as we started walking.

"I wanted to ask you something..." I began. It was the first time, possibly in years, that I was the one asking someone out, but the night so far made me feel confident about where things were headed.

"Alright."

"I know that it might not exactly be your thing, but..."

"What might not be my thing?" he said, smiling at the uncomfortable look on my face.

"I have a show for my line coming up, and —"

"A fashion show?" He cut me off, but the tone of his

voice was far from gentle.

"Um...yeah..." I said, completely unsure how to react. I felt like things took a sudden hard left somewhere, and the way he looked at me was alarmingly judgmental.

"I'll pass."

I quickly pulled my hand from his and folded my arms over my chest. The warm budding of feelings I had only moments ago was now gone. It was like he was someone else entirely.

"Should I even bother to ask you why?"

August had a baffling look on his face as if he was struggling with the answer to my question. I couldn't understand what was going on. All I'd done was ask him to come to something important to me because I thought there might be something between us. I knew that if he'd asked me to go to something important to him, I would have happily said yes.

"I get that you somehow manage to make a living drawing pictures of overpriced suits, but you can't expect me to take that seriously, Jacey," he finally said.

I stopped dead in my tracks. All I could do was stare at him in disbelief. *Where the hell was this coming from?* I understood that fashion design might not have been up his alley, but he could have just said so. Why was he suddenly insulting me? I couldn't understand what was going through his head, but I refused to stick around to find out.

"You know what, August? I think I can get myself home." I started to walk away.

"I'm not letting you walk by yourself," he argued as he followed behind me.

I turned sharply to face him. "That's the thing. You don't get to *let* me do anything. It's not up to you."

"Alright, I'm sorry, just—"

"We are done here," I snapped.

Unfortunately, he continued to follow me.

"Please leave me alone."

"We don't have to talk, but I'm not leaving you out here by yourself."

I just wanted to get far away from August as fast as I could, but it appeared that the only way I was going to do that was by getting back to my apartment. As promised, he followed behind me in silence for the nearly fifteen minutes it took to walk back to my apartment. When we arrived, I didn't so much as even turn to look at him. I buzzed myself into the building and let the heavy iron security door slam behind me.

I was done.

Sixteen

Fashion was the proverbial love of my life. I could remember sewing clothes for Elise's and my Barbies and the countless notebooks I filled with sketches. Design had been a part of my life long before I'd decided to make a career out of it, and when it was all said and done, fashion stood by me longer than any relationship I'd ever had. I loved my job, and I believed in my art. I didn't have much of an ego, but one thing I knew for sure was that I was good at what I did. These were the reasons I was angry with August Henry, but the reason I was angry with myself was that I had somehow managed to let my guard down just long enough for him to hurt me.

I shoved my way up the stairs of my building with my gaze fixed straight ahead. I knew that August wasn't following me any longer, but I couldn't shake the feeling of him staring holes into the back of my head while he

followed me home. I unlocked the door and threw it open, calling out for the only person I knew could calm me down at a time like this.

"Leon!" I nearly yelled into the abyss of our empty loft.

There was no response. I suspected that Leon probably wouldn't be home, but I hoped I would have somewhere to vent my frustrations.

Unfortunately, there was no such luck. Instead, I opted for throwing my body down on the deep blue couch cushions and screaming into the crushed velvet fabric. Emotionally exhausted, I just lay there, face-down for what could have been minutes or hours. I didn't know. The only thing that distracted me from my child-like fit was the sound of keys in the front door. Leon was home. That meant everything would be okay again.

A laugh escaped my best friend as he noticed my impression of a dead fish on our sofa.

"What are you doing?"

"Trying to muffle my screams," I sighed dramatically.

"It was that bad?"

I hadn't yet looked up at him, but I could hear Leon shuffling around the room.

"Worst date of my life!" I moaned.

I heard Leon's footsteps come closer and then felt the sofa cushions shift as he sat down next to me.

"What the hell happened?"

I lifted my head just enough to see the dark gray dress pants he was wearing. He must have been at work.

"They kept you late?"

"Yeah, dinner meeting," he explained.

I dropped my head down again, smashing my face back against the cushions.

"Why are men the literal worst?"

"Fire escape?"

"Please," I responded as I pushed myself up off the couch.

Off our living room window was a fire escape that Leon and I had effectively been using as a balcony since we'd first moved into our apartment. Occasionally, when one of us needed to talk, we would both sit out there and watch the city move. We could sit out there for hours. I had no doubt that was exactly what I needed.

We crawled out the window, first me and then Leon. We adjusted ourselves, so we were both sitting with our legs crossed like we had so many times before. Neither of us said much of anything for a while. We watched the city lights and the strangers walking up and down the sidewalk across the street. New York was always moving, yet there was something peaceful about being above it instead of a part of it. I was still angry and frustrated, but as soon as I felt the cold night air, I started to feel a little better.

"August is not the one," I finally spoke up.

"Did you think he was?" Leon asked. He sounded like he genuinely wanted to know, but I was painfully aware of how ridiculous it was that I even imagined my interest in August going anywhere.

"No...maybe...I don't know..."

"I'll take that as a yes," Leon said, laughing at me.

"Look, I'm not crazy! I just really liked how intelligent he was, and I thought maybe there was something there."

"No one is calling you crazy, Jace. You liked him. I'm pretty sure that's what's supposed to happen when you're dating someone."

"Well, I don't anymore," I said, looking over at Leon as he continued to stare out at the city.

"Why?"

I sighed as I rested my head against the brick wall behind me. "I asked him to come to that Collective show I have coming up," I explained. "He told me that there was no way he could take my job seriously."

"He what?" Leon blurted.

"He said that even though I somehow managed to make a living drawing overpriced suits, I shouldn't expect him to take that seriously."

"What the hell?"

I threw my hands up in defeat. "I know! I don't know what the hell is wrong with him." Leon was quiet for a moment. "Maybe he's just intimidated."

I laughed at the ridiculous notion.

"He's a professor at Columbia. I don't think I intimidated him," I said, shaking my head.

"You have a highly successful creative career. How is that not intimidating to someone whose whole world is academic?"

I paused. I never considered that. August didn't exactly seem like the type to be easily intimidated, but Leon did have a point. I also never considered that August once tried to have a creative career, and it didn't work out for him, so perhaps that also factored into his strange behavior.

"That makes sense, but...I'm not seeing him again."

"I don't blame you," he nodded.

"Maybe I just need to find someone in fashion," I sighed with a shrug.

"Are we tossing out the no-models rule?"

"At this point, as long as they actually respect what I do — I'll date a model, a designer, a photographer, hell, I'll go out with someone who works in the shoe department at Saks!"

Leon laughed, and then there was silence again, but it was comfortable. The sounds of the city filled the spaces where we would normally have to speak. I turned my head to look at Leon. I watched headlights dance over his strong features, and I couldn't help but wonder what he was thinking. "What's on your mind?"

"A lot."

"Like what?"

Leon turned to face me and smirked. "First, I'm trying to decide whether I should murder August," he said.

"No murder necessary."

"Second, I'm trying to figure out what you're actually looking for."

"We made a list, remember?" I teased.

"I remember Elise writing down five random qualities, but there's more to finding someone right for you than just checking off some boxes on a list."

I nodded. Leon was right. I just hadn't taken the time to dissect what would make someone the right person for me. Even though I agreed to the bet and started on this journey, the truth was I didn't have a destination in mind. I just dove headfirst into dating with no idea what I wanted in a new partner or a new relationship.

"Okay, then you tell me," I said to Leon.

"Tell you what?"

"If you could pick the ideal guy for me, what would he be like?"

"Seriously?"

"Yeah," I said with a laugh. "I'm clearly not very good at picking for myself. Plus, who knows me better than you do?"

Leon seemed to ponder my question for a while.

"If I could pick the right guy for you..." he mumbled under his breath. "I'll leave the list-making to Elise. I just know that you deserve someone that sees you for what you are."

"And what is that?"

I hadn't been thinking much of myself recently. I was still only one foot out the door of the dark place my failed engagement sent me to. I was doing better, but after hearing August reduce my art to "drawing overpriced suits," I wasn't exactly feeling great about myself.

"I'm only saying this because you need a pep talk. Tomorrow I'm going to go back to complaining about the fact you never take your clothes out of the dryer," Leon said.

"Okay, deal."

"You are easily the most talented person I know, so let's just get that out of the way. But what I want for you is someone who looks at you and feels like they can't breathe. You deserve someone who gets your weird quirks and doesn't mind that you set alarms for ungodly hours of the morning. They need to think horror movies are funny and that the best metal comes from at least the early 90s, if not earlier. I don't think you've ever really been with someone that recognizes all the tiny things about you that make you so amazing, and that's a shame because you deserve that."

I couldn't help but smile. When it came to women, Leon was rarely ever romantic. Yet, here he was, saying what could arguably be one of the most romantic things I'd ever heard. It amazed me that the same man who could say something like that could also talk a girl he barely knew into bed in five minutes flat and not remember her name in the morning.

"I'm not sure that guy exists..." I admitted.

Leon opened his mouth, and I could tell that he wanted to say something, but he seemed to think better of it. I briefly wondered what it might be, but I assumed he was just going to tell me that I needed to keep looking, that the perfect guy was out there somewhere.

"If he doesn't, we'll just be spinsters together," he said, nudging my side.

"Is it called a spinster when you're a guy?"

"I have no idea what a male spinster is called."

"It doesn't matter. You're too pretty to end up a spinster." I looked over before rolling my eyes. If it was possible to be so attractive it was annoying, Leon had it down to an art. "Even if you don't settle down, we both know you're not going to be alone," I added.

"Actually, I've been giving the settling down thing some thought lately."

My mouth dropped open and I sat there motionless as I stared at my best friend in complete shock. I couldn't imagine what on earth would suddenly make the great Leon Acosta want to settle down. Then it hit me. It was the girl, the one he was seeing. Whoever she was, she had to be the reason he was reconsidering his firmly established bachelorhood.

"You like this girl that much?" I asked.

"What girl?" Leon shot back at me a little too quickly.

"The one who's keeping you out all night."

"I just think there could be something there. I don't know where she's at, but...."

"I'm sure she feels the same way," I reassured him.

"What makes you say that?"

"I've yet to meet a girl who didn't do a double-take

when you walk into a room."

"You're ridiculous..."

"No. I'm honest," I responded.

"She's different. The things I usually do, don't exactly work," Leon explained.

I tried not to laugh. I had never seen him sweat over anyone before. "Maybe that's a good thing."

"It's a frustrating thing."

"If what you usually do doesn't work, then maybe you'll just have to be yourself, which you're going to have to do anyway if you're thinking about anything serious with her."

Leon shook his head. "When did you become a relationship expert?"

"They always say that those who can't do, teach."

Seventeen

I did my best to push August out of my head. That was made easy by the fact that he'd essentially disappeared. One minute he was texting me daily, and the next, he was just gone. The night after our date, he'd sent an apology text, but when he received no response, he didn't attempt to contact me again. Weeks passed and I didn't have any more unexpected suitors. The only explanation I could give myself for the sudden boom in my romantic life was some weird coincidence. Things slowly started to feel normal again, and the bet began to fade to the back of my mind.

Thursday afternoon, I was at the studio, busy working on a sketch while Danny sat across the room tapping away on his laptop. Nia, however, had rather secretively snuck off to the conference room nearly an hour earlier to take a phone call. She had yet to return. Just as I started to wonder why she was taking such a long phone meeting, the door to the conference room

was thrown open, and Nia stood triumphantly in the doorway.

"I got him!" she exclaimed.

Danny and I both just stared at her. Neither of us had any idea what she was talking about.

"Got who?" I asked, taking the bait.

"Alexander Duran," Nia said, a smile slowly spreading across her face.

"Oh my god, you're kidding!" Danny exclaimed.

I sat there looking perplexed. I had no idea who or what Nia was referring to. "Who is Alexander Duran? And what exactly did you get him for?"

Both Nia and Danny turned to me, shocked.

"You know, for a designer, you know absolutely nothing about models," Nia said.

"Okay, so he's a model...." I still didn't know why that was a cause for so much drama.

Danillo looked at Nia and then back at me. He took out his cell phone, and after scrolling for a few moments, he handed it to me. On the screen was an Instagram account with several million followers. "He's huge right now," he said.

I scrolled, looking through a few of the photos. It was clear why this man was so popular. He had a head of dirty blond hair, a strong jaw, and two of the most piercing blue eyes I had ever seen. Everything about him screamed "Americana". It was no wonder my entire office seemed so excited about him. I handed Danny back his phone. "How much is this costing us?" I could only assume that she hired him for the print campaign that we were doing for the winter line, and, given that this man seemed to have quite the career, that would mean he was probably expensive.

"Let me worry about that," Nia responded.

I gave her a stern look, making it clear that I wanted to know the answer. Under most circumstances, I trusted her business instincts, but we had a whole network of models we could use. We didn't need to hire someone who was going to cost an arm and a leg.

"It's less than you think," she quickly added. "Alex is a big fan of the line and wanted to be a part of the shoot."

I had to admit that was flattering. I just wasn't entirely sure why this was necessary. I could have kept prying, but all of the fanfare over this man was distracting me from my work. "Okay, I trust you," I said simply with a slight shrug of my shoulders and went back to my sketch.

"He's coming in this afternoon to sign a contract."

Danny abruptly turned to look at Nia. "Alexander Duran is coming here? Today?"

I was starting to become accustomed to the bright-eyed way that Danny saw the world and how he seemed to find every little thing about this job so exciting. Even though he had been in fashion for some time, I got the sense that his previous employer didn't give him much hands-on experience.

The afternoon passed uneventfully, though I could sense both Nia and Danny's excitement. I didn't see why it was such a big deal. Sure, he was objectively stunning, and, from a business perspective, a following like that meant more exposure for the line, but they were both acting like Jesus Christ himself was about to walk through the door.

"He's here," Nia suddenly announced as she got up from her desk.

"He can't walk upstairs by himself?"

"I'm just being polite," she explained. "This building

can be confusing."

That wasn't true. We were the only ones on this floor. I watched her hurry out of the room and return several minutes later with a tall, blond man following behind her. I was sure that I was going to be as disaffected by him as I had been by the dozens of other models who walked through that door, but instead, as soon I glanced up into those icy blue eyes of his, I completely froze.

"As you know, this is Jacey Lange," I heard Nia say, but I couldn't bring myself to react. I just stood there, stunned.

I had been around attractive men before; it was essentially part of my job description. This man was otherworldly. The photos Danny had shown me didn't do him any justice.

"We've met, actually..." he said.

That immediately snapped me back to reality.

"I'm sorry?" I questioned. "I don't think we've—"

"Paris Fashion Week. I walked the show before yours. I almost mowed you down backstage," he said with an amused smile on his face.

I blinked several times. I couldn't recall that happening. Anyone who'd been backstage at a fashion show could tell you that things could get frantic, but there was no way I would forget someone who looked the way Alexander did.

"Are you sure? I'm pretty sure I would remember you..." I said.

"I'm sure. There's no way I would forget you," he responded with a wink.

Yet again, I had no words. I just continued to stare up at Alexander Duran like some mystical creature had just waltzed through the door. Thankfully, I was saved from my impression of a deer in headlights by Nia clearing her throat.

"Should we go over the contract?"

Alexander nodded, and we both followed her into the conference room. Nia and I took seats on one side of the table while Alexander sat opposite us. She handed out several sheets of paper, first to him and then to me. The three of us sat silently, looking at the documents. I didn't need to read them. I trusted Nia. Plus, it wasn't like I had any background in law or contracts. I couldn't make heads or tails of the words in front of me. I was just there because it was my line and therefore, my money. I glanced up from the small stack of papers to Alexander's face and his long eyelashes as he scanned the page in front of him. I got a little lost looking at him until, out of nowhere, he looked up at me, and a slow, painfully sexy smirk crossed his face.

"There isn't an agent or someone you want to look over this?" Nia asked.

"I went to law school before I started modeling. I can read a contract," Alexander responded. His tone was cool and even; the confidence in his voice was almost intimidating.

Nia raised a brow but didn't question him. I couldn't tell what she was thinking, but knowing her, I would find out as soon as he left the office.

"As you can see, it's pretty standard. It outlines the pay rate which we've already discussed with your agent, the usage of any photographs or videos taken during the session..."

I couldn't take my eyes off Alexander. I knew Nia was talking, but I couldn't tear my eyes away.

"This all looks—" Alexander started, but he was interrupted by a knock at the door.

Danny poked his head in with a hesitant look on his face. He resembled a puppy that was about to get in trouble. "I'm so sorry, but Nia, there's a call for you," he said.

"Can you—"

"It's your daughter's school. It sounds urgent."

"Excuse me for a moment." Nia followed Danny out of the room, leaving me alone with the ethereal-looking man in front of me.

We just stared at each other in uncomfortable silence for what felt like forever.

"I don't know anything about contracts," I said awkwardly.

He reached forward and grabbed a pen from the center of the table before scribbling his name across the bottom of the page. "It's okay. It looks fine," he said.

"I'm sorry you had to come down here—"

"I'm glad I did."

"Why is that?"

"I got to see you again," he responded.

There it was again. Just enough time had passed that I thought I might have forgotten what butterflies in my stomach felt like, but there it was. "You're sure we've met?" I asked. I kept trying to replay that show in my mind, but I couldn't recall the memory of running into someone backstage.

"You have a tattoo of flowers wrapping around your left wrist," he pointed out.

He was right. I did. I might have considered the idea that he'd seen the tattoo when he walked into the office, but I was wearing a sweater that covered both my wrists completely.

"I guess we have," I mused. "I don't know why I can't

seem to remember..."

"I guess I wasn't very memorable," he said with a hint of sarcasm in his voice.

I laughed at the notion. I had only been sitting across a table from this man for twenty minutes, and yet, I already felt like that face was seared into my brain. "You're definitely memorable! That's why I thought you were mistaking me for someone else. I couldn't imagine forgetting you," I explained.

"Maybe you'll let me make a better first impression?"

My mouth dropped open. *Is he asking what I think he's asking?*

"How do you plan on doing that?" I asked hesitantly.

"Do you have dinner plans?"

That was exactly what I thought he was asking. Mr. Two Million Instagram Followers just asked me on a date. I stalled for a moment. Under normal circumstances, I would have jumped at the chance to go out with this man. Anyone on planet earth would have jumped at that opportunity. Yet, there was a conflict of interest here and a big one. I'd just hired him. Plus, I had a long-standing rule about not dating models.

The fact remained there was a bet. I had to say yes to any man who asked me out. If I said no to this one, I was just looking a gift horse in the mouth.

"I - um - no, I'm free... I think..."

I had been resting both elbows on the table, and Alexander reached forward and pulled my copy of the contract out from under me. He started to write on the top of the page before turning the sheet around to face me.

"Call me when you're done for the day?"

I nodded. For at least the fourth time in less than an hour, this man left me speechless.

He stood up from the table and turned to leave the conference room when Nia hurried back in. "I'm so sorry about that, shall we—"

"That's okay, the contract looks great. I look forward to working together," he said.

"Are you sure you don't have any questions about anything?" she asked him.

"If I do, I'll just ask Jacey later tonight..." he responded with a smug smile on his face.

With that, he turned and left the room, leaving me with Nia, who just stared at me in disbelief. Uncomfortable under the scrutiny of her gaze, I tiptoed out of the room and back towards my desk.

"What's happening later tonight, Jacey?" She called after me.

"Um... dinner?" I said.

"What!" Danillo yelled.

"He asked me out."

"Wait, you mean to tell me that you have been going on and on about how you won't date models since the day I met you, and now you're going to dinner with the biggest male model in the country?"

"Yes?" I said, bracing myself for a lecture.

"Right after we hired him?" Nia clarified again.

"Yes?" I repeated uncomfortably.

"You think that's a good idea?"

"Not exactly, but...."

"Come on, Nia! If you were single, would you say no?" Danny responded.

That seemed to resonate with her, and she took a deep breath before speaking again. "Just please don't do anything that might risk him quitting. I worked too hard to get him on board."

Eighteen

I told Alexander that I would let him know as soon as I got off work. However, there was no way that I was going to dinner dressed in torn black jeans and an oversized sweater with a man that looked like him. I spent most of my time at work hovering over sketches and drawing programs, so I rarely dressed for anything but comfort. I had no idea where Alexander planned to take me, but I knew that what I was wearing was hardly ideal.

Instead of shooting him a text, I decided to hurry home and change. Despite the short distance between my studio and the apartment, it was no easy task to get home during rush hour. I crashed through my front door, tossing my purse and everything else I'd brought with me to work on the floor as I began the dash toward my bedroom.

"Where's the fire?" I heard Leon call out.

I was surprised to hear his voice. He typically got home later than I did, but I didn't have time to think about my best friend's unexpected change in schedule. I needed to look incredible.

"I have a date!" I yelled down from the top of the stairs.

I didn't wait for Leon to respond. I wanted to look devastating, and I needed to do it fast. I started ripping through my closet like a cartoon character, throwing outfit after outfit onto the floor. I wasn't even sure if I was taking the time to breathe. I finally pulled a short, black, off-the-shoulder dress out of my closet before indecision got the better of me. There was no time to second-guess my instincts, so I put it on as quickly as possible.

I fished a pair of strappy heels off the floor and then hurried into my bathroom to put just enough makeup on my face to make it look like I'd freshened up, but not enough to betray the full-blown panic attack I was having about this date. Determined to get back to the studio as quickly as possible, I took off down the stairs. I made it to the last few steps before teetering on my four-inch heels and completely losing my balance. I stumbled forward, catching myself only seconds before I wound up with a black eye before my date. I straightened myself out before entering the kitchen to find Leon in front of an open refrigerator contemplating his dinner options.

"What do you think?" I asked.

Leon looked up at me, silent and motionless. He stared for so long, I started to worry that I'd miscalculated my outfit. "Do you hate it?"

Leon cleared his throat and shook his head. "No... you...uh..."

"What?"

"You look amazing, Jace."

I smiled. That was the reaction I was hoping for, though I couldn't help but notice a trace of something sad in Leon's eyes. I wanted to ask about it, but I knew him, and I knew that he wasn't exactly forthcoming when he was upset. I mentally put a pin in it, reminding myself to check on him when I got back from my date.

"Who is this guy?" Leon asked.

"His name is Alexander Duran...."

"The model?"

"Why does everyone know who he is but me?"

"He shot for us about a year ago...wait! He's a model."

"Right..."

"I guess you weren't kidding about dating anyone as long as they're in fashion."

"I thought you said I had to say yes to anyone who asked."

"Fair enough."

Noticing the time on the kitchen clock, I realized that I needed to get back to the studio. "I have to get going, but I'll tell you all about it later!" I said as I hurried out the door.

I shot Alexander a text before jumping into a cab. The ride back to work was quick but not quick enough to keep me from overthinking. I felt ridiculous. I'd spent years swearing off models and here I was rushing around trying to get ready for a date with one. Technically, I didn't have a choice. The rules of the bet were clear, but there was no denying that I was going on this date because I wanted to, not because I had to. When I arrived at the studio both Nia and Danny were gone for the day so I sat mindlessly flipping through my phone as I waited. All Alexander told me was that he was on his way but I had no idea how long that might be.

I got wrapped up reading an article on environmental sustainability in the fashion industry when I heard someone clear their throat. There was almost no light in the studio. I didn't bother turning on a bunch of lights only to have to turn them off again, and so there, haloed by the light from the hallway, was the first and only male model I'd ever agreed to go on a date with. He was still breathtaking, and I was still clumsily unable to speak. I didn't know why I expected that to change in a matter of hours.

"You ready?" he asked me.

I nodded and stood up from my seat, straightening myself out briefly before making my way toward him.

"You didn't have to change on my account," he said as his arctic gaze made its way over my body.

There was just something about the way this man looked at me. I had no idea how someone whose features were so angelic could look at me in a way that was so seductive and dark. Forget speaking. I couldn't even remember how to breathe.

"I..." *Get it together, Jacey.* "I had to drop something off for my roommate, so I figured I'd just throw something on..." I said, trying my best to sound casual.

He smirked, almost as if he was trying not to laugh at me. "I guess I'll have to thank your roommate,"

Alexander nodded for me to follow him. I closed up the studio, and when I turned, he offered his arm. I took it carefully, and he led me downstairs to a waiting town car.

I wasn't surprised, though I couldn't say that I was impressed either. It was flashier than Owen's Harley or taking a cab to meet August, but the type of money a man made didn't make me any more or less attracted to him. The driver got out and opened the door for the two of us. We both slid into the car quietly before the driver started to pull out.

"Where are we going?" I asked.

"It's a surprise," he said.

"What makes you think I'm the kind of girl who likes surprises?"

"I guess I'm just hoping...."

The drive wasn't long, and we didn't talk much, although I kept catching my date staring at me out of the corner of my eye. Mentally, I told myself to start wearing this dress more often.

The car stopped rather abruptly, and when I glanced out the window, I noticed that we were outside what appeared to be a restaurant. The only problem? It didn't seem to be open. There was no way that a restaurant, even a Red Lobster, in New York City would have absolutely no one going in or out on a Thursday night. Yet this building remained dark and motionless.

The driver opened Alexander's door and then came around to let me out. He offered me his arm again, and I took it as he led me into the building. What was it with guys taking me on dates to places that felt like they were straight out of a 90s slasher film?

We stepped through the dark heavy door, and standing behind a hostess station was a tall redhead in all black. She almost did a double-take when she got a look at Alexander. I knew exactly how this girl felt.

"We've been expecting you, Mr. Duran. Right this way..." she said before he could even open his mouth.

As I suspected, the restaurant didn't seem to be open, or at least not to the public. I could hear the kitchen staff in the back, but the dining room was completely empty.

The hostess led us to a secluded table off in a corner and then left us to our menus.

"Empty restaurant?" I asked as soon as she'd stepped away.

"I'm friends with the owner. Their grand opening isn't until Saturday, but I called in a favor," he said.

I looked around again. I had to admit that I never had a man go to quite this much effort on a first date before. I was impressed and perhaps a little intimidated. I just tried as hard as I could to avoid letting that show.

Because there were no other diners to attend to, a waiter came to take our order within a matter of minutes. I didn't have a chance to look at the menu, so I let him make a recommendation and then focused back on my date.

"So tell me about how we met..." I teased.

Alexander gave me a confused look.

"I can't remember it, so tell me what happened...."

"You were wearing a blazer and this little cropped shirt with your hair in this half-up, half-down thing..."

I was almost shocked. How did Alexander remember exactly what I was wearing? It was months ago, and I couldn't remember him at all.

"Do you have a photographic memory or something?"

Alexander shook his head slowly. "I told you I couldn't forget you," he answered.

I smiled, but I still couldn't understand how this was real.

"Okay, so what happened?" I asked.

"I was walking in two shows that day, and as soon as I got off stage, I started booking it to make it to the second. I took off and wasn't paying any attention to where I was going until I ran into this tiny person..."

"Hey, I'm not that small!" I protested.

I suspected that, like Leon, he probably spent plenty of time around female models. Even if he didn't date them, he must have had to work with them often. Comparatively, I probably did seem minuscule.

"I stand by 'tiny,'" he chuckled. "You fell back, and I caught myself right before I completely crushed you."

Alexander had to be telling the truth. He knew about the tattoo on my arm and the outfit I was wearing. Unless he was a crazed stalker, he had to have been there that day. Yet, no matter how hard I tried, I couldn't remember a single thing about his story.

"This is cheesy, but I thought you were beautiful, and I wanted to ask for your number, but I didn't have the time to get the words out, so I just apologized and bailed," he continued.

"Okay, so how did you end up in my office?"

"I asked around trying to figure out who you were and even went to the after-parties hoping to find you, but when I couldn't, I just figured it wasn't supposed to happen. I just happened to be in my agent's office when Nia called, and I thought...here's my chance..."

I sat back in my chair and just looked at him. I felt like I was on some hidden camera show. I didn't know how it was possible that someone as good-looking as Alexander Duran was even interested in me. Now, I was supposed to believe that this whole thing was happening like the script to a poorly written rom-com?

"This doesn't seem real," I blurted out.

"What doesn't?"

"You don't. Don't get me wrong. I believe you, it's just..."

"Okay, well then let's start over. Hi, I'm Alex."

I laughed a little. It seemed a little late for introductions — the waiter already brought out our entrées.

"I'm Jacey," I said.

"What do you do, Jacey?" he asked me.

"I'm a men's fashion designer. And you?"

"I'm an accountant," he said flatly.

I started laughing again. "Oh really, an accountant?"

"What can I say? I love math." He grinned.

"Have you ever thought about taking up modeling?"

"Modeling? I've heard the guys that do that are meatheads," he gasped, feigning shock.

We continued playing this little game of Alex the Accountant much longer than we probably should have. We couldn't stop laughing, and I enjoyed the fact that Alex could poke fun at himself. For my first date with a model, I was having a perfect time. In fact, it was one of the best first dates I'd ever been on. It was like I'd known him for years.

Nineteen

"The Collective" was as ominous as it sounded. It was a group of fashion professionals who decided what was "in" at any given moment. I had seen them make designers' entire careers. I had also seen them destroy them without so much as a second glance. If New York had a fashion mafia, The Collective was it. For years, I remained blissfully under their radar. I always assumed it was better if they never noticed me. That way I couldn't possibly get on their bad side.

That was, until last year.

Other than my designs, there were two reasons why J. Lange was a success. The first was that Leon used his connections from Cavalier to get me into the right rooms. The second was that The Collective decided they liked my work. Twice a year, once before spring collections and again before winter, The Collective held a series of fashion shows. Last year was my first, and as

luck would have it, I was invited back for a second.

I felt like I had been planning the show for months. No matter what I did, it weighed heavily in the back of my mind. Though I successfully pulled off one Collective show in my career, I was worried about how I was supposed to manage a second. Thankfully, my team was incredible, and the first pieces from the winter line were some of my best work. Yet, I couldn't help but feel my nerves piling up as the show got closer.

The morning of the show, I woke up to the sound of my alarm screaming. I had no time for the gym, but as I headed downstairs to get some caffeine in my bloodstream, I found Leon already in our kitchen again.

"This is for you," he said to me as he pushed a mug full of coffee and a plate full of avocado toast and scrambled eggs across the kitchen counter towards me.

I was baffled. I couldn't remember the last time anyone made me breakfast for any reason other than a birthday or a holiday.

"You didn't have to do all this," I said as I picked up both the plate and mug and sat down on one of the barstools opposite him.

"I know I didn't, but I know how important today is, so I wanted there to be one less thing for you to worry about."

If Leon wasn't my best friend, I could have kissed him. One of the downsides to being your own boss was that no one seemed to worry about taking things off your plate. Instead, they falsely assumed that if you could manage a company, you could handle anything. It meant a lot that someone was trying to make things easier for me.

"I knew I married you for a reason," I said playfully.

Leon smiled at me and then wandered out of the

kitchen, leaving me to my breakfast. I sat picking at my food and going through a mental checklist in my head. What time did I need to pick the pieces up from the studio? What time were the models showing up? What was I going to wear?

I was suddenly shaken from my thoughts by the sound of my downstairs buzzer.

"Are you expecting someone?" I called out to Leon, wondering if this unexpected visitor was his.

The buzzer rang again, and when Leon didn't respond, I just assumed it was a neighbor or a delivery person trying to get into the building and buzzed them in without even using the intercom to find out who it was.

No sooner had I sat back down did I hear a knock on my door. I paused for a long second before walking over to peer out of the peephole as quietly as I could. I don't know why I thought an intruder would be knocking, but the time of morning paired with the fact that we weren't expecting anyone felt insidious. No one had even texted to say they were coming by. However, when I looked out the peephole, I found the familiar sight of my sunny, bright-eyed assistant standing there expectantly.

"Good morning!" Danny said brightly as I opened the door.

"Good morning?" I squinted at him before taking a long sip of my coffee.

"I know it's early, but when I asked Nia what time I should get here, she said as early as I could."

"Nia sent you?"

"She said you're going to need me all day, so here I am!" he said.

I shook my head, mostly out of relief that I wasn't about to be robbed by a very polite burglar. "Come on in," I said and stepped out of the way to let him enter our apartment.

Danny followed me inside, and before I could sit back down to my breakfast, he already had an iPad out with an itinerary on it. He placed it down next to me as I shoved a fork full of eggs into my mouth. "Does this all look correct?" he asked, sounding a bit nervous.

I could tell that he'd put a lot of work into it, and it was a far more organized schedule than the one I had been making in my head. "This is amazing, Danny. Thank you!"

The smile on his face was so genuine. I was happy to see that he was proud of his work. He deserved to be.

"So, what can I do to help you?" he asked.

I laughed a little in response. "You've done plenty... but, if you want to help me pick out what to wear..."

"Of course I do!"

I loved the enthusiasm in his voice. I finished the last couple of bites of my food and motioned for Danny to follow me upstairs.

"The layout of this apartment is so weird," he mumbled, more to himself than to me.

He was right. The kitchen, living room, and master bedroom were all on one floor, and the second bedroom was all alone on the floor above it. We chose it because, at the time, Leon and I were both single. It only made sense that if we wanted to bring someone home that our rooms be as far apart as possible. Now that I was the one living upstairs, I liked to make *Flowers in the Attic* jokes. I really couldn't wait until this bet was over so that I could go back to the master bedroom and Leon could be the one living in the random upstairs room.

Despite not being the room I wanted, it was uniquely

mine — exposed brick walls, a giant canopy bed, and a bunch of eclectic and vaguely whimsical decor. As I looked over at Danny I realized that this was the first time I'd brought anyone up here since moving back in with Leon. He was only here to give me fashion advice but it felt a little strange, nonetheless.

The best part about my room was that one wall was composed entirely of closet space. Instead of a walk-in, this room had one very long closet with multiple french doors that opened into different sections.

"I take it back. This apartment is great!" Danny exclaimed when I started opening the multiple closet doors to reveal the space in all its glory. "So what are we going for?" he asked me as he examined my options.

I thought back to August briefly. I didn't know why, after I had such a great date with Alex, I was thinking of some snobby professor who ridiculed my work. I read once in some terrible self-help book that people are always attracted to what rejects them, and there was no question that August rejected me.

"Well, since the guy I invited isn't showing up, we don't have to impress anyone."

"Alex?"

I shook my head and laughed a little. "August."

"The hot librarian?"

I laughed even harder. "He was a professor," I explained.

"Your dating life is insane," Danny said as he started pulling a few things out of my closet and tossing them on my bed.

"Tell me about it," I sighed, rolling my eyes.

Danny was quiet for a minute before he pulled a hideous pink lace cocktail-length dress out of my closet.

"What the actual hell is this?"

"It was a bridesmaid's dress, but believe me, it gets worse..." I said before finding the pair of white, bedazzled cowboy boots I had to wear with it and holding them up.

"Oh please, tell me there are pictures!" Danny said through his laughter.

I grabbed my phone and started to dig through the bowels of my social media to find photos of my cousin's wedding.

It was then I realized that I was having fun. It was like we were old friends. I had been trying to keep myself from getting too close to Danny because of what happened with Lexi, but the truth was, Danny did nothing but prove himself to me since I hired him. He deserved a little credit for that.

We eventually decided on thigh-high boots, a sheer maxi skirt, and a studded leather jacket. It was edgier and probably light-years more flashy than most designers wore to their shows, but I liked how confident I felt in it. The Collective caused me more stress than I cared to admit, but dressed like that, I could take on the world.

Danny and I got in a cab headed toward Industria in the West Village. On the way there, we went over the rest of the schedule for the day. I was surprised at how relaxed I felt and how easy everything seemed to be going. This time last year I was terrified. Today, I felt on top of my game.

As the afternoon leading up to the show wore on, everything seemed to fall into place. The models showed up on time. The rehearsal went perfectly. Before I knew it, people began filling the audience. The mad dash of being backstage during a fashion show began, and everywhere I turned, there were models frantically putting on outfits, makeup artists trying to finish their looks, and various other people trying to pull this show together. I loved getting lost in it all, and as I turned the corner to make sure the first model was ready to get on stage, an unfamiliar face greeted me.

"Are you Jacey Lange?" an eighteen-year-old kid in an oversized hoodie asked me.

"Um...yeah..."

"These are for you," he said, shoving a large bouquet of dark red roses into my arms. He turned to leave before I could ask who the sender was. Luckily, there was a card, or rather a Polaroid, with a few words scribbled at the bottom.

Good luck tonight, Gorgeous.

I smiled. I didn't know how it was possible, but even in a poorly lit Polaroid, Alex was still breathtaking.

The show began, and I found somewhere to quickly stash my flowers as I stood at the front of a line of male models, checking their outfits before they went on stage. Each of them had two looks, so as soon as they finished walking the runway, they would run backstage and change before going back out again. There was so much going on all at once, and yet, the show felt like it was over in a matter of minutes.

At the end, all the models took to the runway one last time, and I followed behind them. As soon as I hit the stage, the crowd of people stood up, clapping enthusiastically. It was arguably one of my favorite feelings. There were a ton of faces in that crowd, but my eyes only found one person. The one person I could always count on to be there. At the end of the runway, in the very front row, was Leon. The smile on his face was so big, and he looked so proud of me that it almost brought tears to my eyes.

After the show was over, Leon was the only person I wanted to see. I made my way through the crowd as fast as I could, but people kept stopping to congratulate me. The sentiment was appreciated, but I was starting to get frustrated. I wanted to see my best friend. I wanted to thank him for being there, for being my cheerleader. In that entire room, Leon was the only person who showed up for me. He wasn't there for my art or the press. Leon couldn't care less about The Collective. He was there because it was my show. Finally, I spotted him talking to someone toward the back of the room. I started to make my way toward him when a pair of bony fingers caught my arm.

"Oh my god, Jacey! I haven't seen you in ages!"

The sound of her voice violently turned my stomach. I whipped my head around, hoping that perhaps it was my imagination, but there, with her perfectly manicured hand around my arm, was Alexis Atkins.

Twenty

I wanted to slap her clear across the face. But as I pulled my arm sharply out of Lexi's grasp, I made a horrifying discovery: I couldn't hit her. It wasn't because we were in public or because of The Collective. I certainly didn't feel any fondness toward her. I couldn't hit her because as I looked over the blonde in front of me, I noticed the unmistakable shape her stomach made in the form-fitting dress she was wearing.

Lexi was pregnant.

She was *very* pregnant.

She towered over me at five foot nine, and as if she knew exactly what I was thinking, I watched her left hand protectively move to her stomach. On it was an engagement ring so large, it almost rivaled my sister's. It was cushion cut and haloed in smaller diamonds. It looked just like my old ring, only hers was larger.

"You're....um..." I just pointed at her stomach, unable

to get the words out. "C-congratulations," I finally managed.

I didn't mean it. The last thing on earth that woman needed to do was procreate. I just didn't know what to say. I wanted to speak, but the words just wouldn't come out. The only thing worse than Lexi trying to mother anyone was the idea of Brian as a father. They were the two most selfish people I had ever met. I had no way of knowing it was his. I just assumed.

"Oh! Thank you!" she beamed. Her voice was thick and sweet and completely false. Just being around her made me nauseous. "I can't believe I'm almost twenty-four weeks!" she added.

I started doing the math immediately. *Twenty-four weeks? Twenty-four divided by four was six. Six months? She was six months pregnant?* That couldn't be right. It had only been five months since I caught them together.

Another terrible realization hit me. I always assumed that the night I caught my assistant in bed with my fiancé was the first and only time they'd ever been together. However, if Lexi was six months pregnant and this child was, as I suspected, a baby Fishman, that meant...

My stomach clenched tighter around itself and the room started to tilt on its axis. I thought for a second I might throw up. I leaned forward a little as Lexi stared down at me with a self-righteous, smug little look on her face.

"Are you okay?" she asked in a way that sounded more disgusted than concerned.

However, before I emptied the contents of my stomach all over the nude Dior sling-backs she was wearing, I felt a protective arm wrap around my shoulder and pull me upright.

"I have been looking everywhere for you, Beautiful," I heard Leon say before he kissed the top of my head.

I blinked a few times before my brain caught up to what my best friend was doing.

"I was coming to find you when I ran into Lexi," I said through the gritted teeth of a forced smile.

As if he were just now noticing that Lexi was standing there, Leon shot her a vaguely repulsed glance. "Lexi, you're looking...healthy...." he said, staring directly at her stomach.

"Thank you! Brian and I are so excited!" she exclaimed.

There it was: confirmation of what I feared. Brian didn't just make one mistake one time. He had been cheating on me for months, and I never knew. He might have even been cheating on me since I'd hired Lexi. At that moment, I felt like a complete idiot. *How could I be so blind*?

"It's a good thing you're so big-boned, you'd never know you were pregnant." Leon smiled.

I looked up at Lexi's face which was growing red with anger or perhaps embarrassment. I had no idea how he'd done it, but Leon took me from feeling like the room was closing in on me to suppressing my laughter.

He reached for my face and tilted my chin to face him. "You were amazing," he murmured.

I felt my heart bang in my chest unexpectedly. I knew that Leon was playing at being my boyfriend for two very distinct reasons: first, like most women who came into contact with him, Lexi spent years obsessed with Leon, and the attention he was giving me would likely make her jealous. Second, he knew that if she thought the two of us were dating that it would most likely get back to Brian, who felt threatened by Leon from Day

One. I couldn't count the number of times Brian told me that Leon was secretly in love with me. Yet even though both Leon and I knew it was an act, there was still some part of me that couldn't help but feel something under his amber-colored gaze. The way he looked at me was a little too...*real.*

"I'm sorry, are you two...?" Lexi asked, interrupting Leon's unexpected display of affection.

Before I could respond, Leon jumped in. "Together?"

We looked at each other, and again, my heart threw itself violently against my rib cage. I still didn't know why. It wasn't the first time Leon had pretended to be my boyfriend in an attempt to protect me. Maybe it was the emotions of seeing Lexi again and pregnant, no less, that had me feeling jumpy.

Leon gently tucked a stray hair behind my ear as he gazed down at me. If this was just a show for Lexi, it was quite a show.

"It was inevitable," Leon said, never looking away from me.

Okay, maybe this isn't just for Lexi. I didn't exactly know what was going on here, but I did know that Leon never looked at me like that before.

"Brian always said something was going on between you two," Lexi scoffed, rolling her blue eyes.

"Oh, you're still with Brian? Is that...?" I glanced down at her ring. "Good for you!" I mimicked her falsely sweet tone. I was doing a decent job of pretending, but the truth was I could still feel bile rising in my throat when I thought of how long Lexi and Brian might have been sleeping together.

Frankly, the two of them deserved each other. If I knew anything for certain, it was that men like Brian didn't change. Lexi may have been pregnant with his child, and she may have his ring on her finger, but I knew that if he was willing to cheat on one fiancée, there was no doubt he would do it to the next. If her betrayal didn't make me so angry, I would have felt bad for her. I tried so hard to hold back the poisonous words racing through my mind that my body started to rebel against me, and I could feel myself shaking. Thankfully, so could Leon.

"Jace, my boss is here and wants to talk with you about the winter line and maybe have one of our reporters do a write-up on it, so we should catch him before he heads out," he said.

I nodded, and without another word, Leon ushered me away from Lexi as quickly as he could. She had come there for one reason, to get a rise out of me, and the only reason she didn't was Leon.

His boss wasn't there. Instead, he led me straight through the crowd of people and out a side door into the alley. As soon as the heavy metal door shut behind us, I lost it. I completely lost it. I gasped for air — unaware that I had been barely breathing the whole time she was in front of me. My back hit the brick wall behind me, and I slid down until I was sitting on the ground with my knees bent in front of me. I knew my outfit was too nice to be sitting on the asphalt in an alley, but I couldn't hold myself up anymore. All I could do was panic.

Leon got down on his knees in front of me. My brain was spinning in circles, and my vision blurred at the corners.

"Hey, Jace. Jacey, look at me. I need you to look at me," he said calmly, turning my face toward him.

Tears stung my eyes. I didn't know why I was crying.

I didn't want to cry, but I couldn't stop myself. "He...he... he...six months..." I choked out, though I knew I wasn't making any sense.

"Six months? Jace, you gotta breathe, okay?"

"They were...she is...six months...it wasn't...."

"Okay, okay. I've got you. It's okay." His tone was gentle and calming. He adjusted and sat down on the ground next to me before wrapping his arms around me and pulling me close to him. "You were such a badass in there," he said, running his hand up and down my arm.

I didn't feel like a badass. I felt like a child who was freaking out over a playground bully. It was exactly what Lexi wanted. She didn't care about my designs, and she certainly didn't care about me. She had dragged herself clear across town for one reason: to gloat. The only thing I could be thankful for was the fact that, yet again, Leon came to my rescue.

My breathing started to slowly return to normal, though my heart was still racing. "She's six months pregnant," I finally managed to get out.

"You're kidding?" Leon said as a familiar flash of anger crossed his face.

"That means he was with her for at least a month before I caught them and who knows if it was longer. They could have been sleeping together since I hired her!"

Leon held me closer. "Just breathe," he whispered into my hair.

It took several minutes before I could pull myself together. I was sure that the two of us looked ridiculous huddled together in a dirty alleyway, but Leon never let go of me. Not until my breathing was even, and the panic had subsided.

"Are you okay?"

I nodded as I sat up straight. "I'm okay," I said softly. "Thanks for the rescue."

"Anytime," he said before getting up off the pavement and extending a hand to help me up.

I took his hand and stood up, dusting myself off.

"Now, as your boyfriend, first I'm going to take you to Di Fara, then I'm going to buy you a stupidly expensive bottle of wine, and then I'm going to take you home."

I laughed a little. "Why didn't I start dating you sooner?"

"I ask myself that all the time," he mused sarcastically. He slid his hand into mine and led me back inside to get my things.

The following morning, I was shocked at how okay I was. Leon and I spent the whole night getting wine drunk, eating far more pizza than two human beings should have been able to handle, and making fun of Lexi.

I laughed until my face hurt, and somehow I forgot all about everything that happened. Somewhere in the back of my mind, I was still aware that Lexi was now engaged to Brian and pregnant with his child. I was also aware of the fact that what I thought was just a one-night stand for Brian was a months-long affair. Yet once the initial shock wore off, it didn't hurt the way I thought it would. I hoped that meant I was healing.

I rolled out of my bed, late yet again. However, this time it wasn't because I'd been out all night with some new man; it was because I was up until 3 a.m., cackling about the fact that Leon called Lexi "big-boned".

When I got downstairs, I found the familiar sight of my best friend pacing around our living room with a phone pressed to his ear.

"Não me interessa quantas vezes é que explicas. Eu não sou como ele!"

"O que é que não percebes? Não!"

As soon as he spotted me crossing the distance from the stairs into the kitchen, Leon lowered his voice.

"*Para de me ligar*," he said in a hushed tone before hanging up. *Stop calling*. It was the only sentence I could completely understand.

"If you hate talking to them so much, why don't you just change your number again?" I asked as I poked around the freezer, hoping we still had toaster waffles.

"They always get it somehow," Leon responded.

Yet again, information about Leon's family always left me with more questions than answers. I wondered if he'd ever tell me what that was all about, but after ten years, I knew it was pointless to push him. He always found a way to dodge my questions or change the subject.

"You want coffee?"

That was Leon for, *are you going to make coffee so I don't have to*? I closed the freezer door and turned toward the coffee pot when I noticed a box with a sticky note on it.

Open me.

"What is this?" I asked as I picked it up.

"Just open it."

"Are you finally proposing?" I teased.

I pulled the lid off the rather unremarkable black box and immediately my heart stopped. Inside was a worn, silver Rolex Oysterquartz with a blue face. I just stared at it for a moment before pulling the watch out of the box and turning it over. Just as I'd suspected, there it was.

To Christopher,
My best friend.
My love.
I am forever yours.
- Marie.

I was speechless. It was the watch Brian refused to return to me after we broke up. I couldn't believe I was holding it in my hand. I honestly believed I would never see it again. I pressed the hard piece of metal against my chest before turning to Leon.

" How did you–? Where did you–?"

"I found it."

"You found it?"

"Well, it kind of found me," he explained, though I still wasn't following. "Everyone at work has been looking for a rotary phone from the 30s for the shoot we're doing for next month's cover. When I was passing that pawn shop on 47th, I stopped to see if they might have something. They didn't, but I saw the watch. It looked familiar, and when I saw the inscription, I realized it was yours."

I couldn't believe it. The story made sense, but I didn't understand how it ended up at a pawn shop. If Brian wasn't willing to give it to me, why was he willing to sell it? It wasn't like he needed the money. Maybe he lost it? It didn't really matter, and I wasn't about to call Brian up and ask. All that mattered was that I had it back.

"Leon, this is a vintage Rolex. This thing had to cost

you a fortune."

"Don't worry about it."

"I'm paying you back."

"Don't you fucking dare," Leon warned with a smile on his face.

I hurried around the counter and wrapped my arms tightly around Leon's neck. It wasn't something either of us did often, but I was so caught up in my emotions I didn't care. "You are amazing,"

"I didn't do anything. I was just in the right place at the right time," Leon said.

"Jesus! Why am I crying?" I exclaimed as I pulled back and quickly tried to wipe the tears out of my eyes. I hadn't expected seeing that watch again would affect me so much, but it wasn't just a family heirloom that Brian had taken from me, it was my entire sense of self-worth. In some tiny way, it was like Leon was giving that back to me. "Thank you," I said, still struggling not to turn into a mess.

"Don't mention it."

I turned the watch over again, running my finger over the words. I still couldn't wrap my brain around how it ended up here.

"So what's the story with that?" Leon asked.

"The inscription?"

"Yeah..."

"My grandparents grew up next door to each other. They were practically raised together. My Grandpa Chris said that he decided he was going to marry her when he was five years old and that he was too stubborn to change his mind."

Leon laughed at that. "So they spent their whole lives in love with each other?"

"Not exactly. My grandma actually never thought of him romantically and wound up engaged to another guy."

"So what happened?"

"The guy got drafted before they got married and while he was gone, my grandma spent all her time with her best friend to try to keep herself distracted. She ended up realizing that she was in love with my Grandpa Chris and the two of them got married before she'd even called off her engagement. She gave him this on their wedding day."

"Sucks to be the other guy," Leon said.

"I think it's the true love rule."

"The true love rule?"

"You can do something completely morally screwed up, but only if it's in the name of true love. No one can really judge you for what you had to do to end up with the love of your life."

Twenty-One

Alex had to fly to Milan for a shoot. He would be gone for a week, and given that we'd only been on one date, I suspected I wouldn't hear from him. I took our great first date and the roses he sent me as an indication that I would see him again after he got back, but I assumed the shoot would keep him too busy to call.

Alex, however, had other plans.

At midnight the day after he arrived in Milan, I woke up to the sound of my phone. It wasn't a ring, but rather the distinct sound of a FaceTime call. I was asleep for only an hour, so I hadn't yet gotten my bearings. As if on auto-pilot, I picked up. My end of the screen was pitch black, but on his was the view of a gorgeous Italian sunrise from what I could only assume was his hotel balcony.

"I know it's late, but I just wanted you to see this," I could hear his voice say.

I didn't yet know much about Alex, but he certainly knew how to charm a girl.

Without fail, every morning around that time, Alex would call. It was doing nothing for my sleep schedule and everything for the feelings I was developing for this man. How could I not? He wasn't just beautiful, he was attentive, charming, and even funny. Plus, I couldn't deny that I found his interest flattering.

By the time Alex got back, I was dying to see him. He was all I could think about. Luckily, he seemed to feel the same way. As soon as he arrived in New York, I got a text:

> ***Alex***: *I'm going to need you to start packing*
> **Me:** For the night or forever?
> ***Alex:*** *Don't tempt me. Renting a car. Be there in an hour.*

True to his word, Alex was parked downstairs in exactly fifty-five minutes. I realized that yet again, I was running off with a man I didn't know very well. One of the things I was starting to realize about myself was that I got caught up in the moment a little too easily, and Alex was quite a moment. When I got downstairs, I took a quick peek out my living room window.

He was like something out of a black-and-white film. The clothes he wore clung to his body in a way that made my mouth dry, and he leaned against the side of the rather flashy rental in a way that would put James Dean to shame. Seeing Alex standing there was enough to make me question why I'd ever sworn off male models. This man was a masterpiece.

I didn't want to wait for a second longer. I hurried downstairs, nearly tripping over myself to get out the front door of the building. The moment it swung open, Alex looked at me from behind his aviators. I bound up to him and immediately wrapped my arms around his neck.

"Hello there," he said, smiling.

"Hi, I missed you," I greeted with a grin.

"Oh really?"

"No." I shrugged as I stepped away from him. "I just figured if I start seducing you now, I won't have to go to H&R Block when tax season rolls around."

Alex laughed and then reached for my face. For a moment, I thought he might kiss me, but instead, he tilted his head to the side and his lips met my cheek. "I missed you, too."

He stepped to one side and held the car door open for me. Despite being a rental, it still smelled of new leather. I sank slowly into the expensive seats and let out a sigh. As soon as Alex joined me, I turned my gaze to him.

"So, where are you taking me?"

"The Hamptons."

"Seriously?" I asked.

It wasn't that I had something against the Hamptons; on the contrary, it was beautiful. There were just two issues. First, it was hardly the time of year most people went to the Hamptons. Second of all, *was this real*? Not only was I going on a date with Alexander Duran, but he was whisking me away to one of the most beautiful places in the state.

"As long as that's okay with you," he said.

I wanted to laugh, not because what Alex said was

funny, but because I couldn't imagine any reason I would object to his plan.

"Let's go," I said with a smile.

The drive from Manhattan to the Hamptons took two hours. It required passing through Queens, Long Island, and several other suburbs. I could tell I was there when the grass turned an unreal shade of green and the houses started to look like something out of an architectural magazine. There was such a stark difference between the Hamptons and the city that it was almost like being transported to some other world. The streets were spotless, the beaches all looked like they came out of paintings, and the buildings were all a blinding shade of white. If there was any place that could be described as too perfect, the Hamptons was it. As we drove, I couldn't help but look over at the man next to me and realize I could describe him the same way.

Alex held my hand the entire way there and we never once stopped talking. Whether it was about his trip, the fashion industry, or random stories about our lives, I found that talking with Alex was just as easy as it had been on our first date. While Owen was great once I got him to open up, it took me a while to find out anything about him. August was a good conversationalist, but only when he found the subject to be intellectually stimulating. Otherwise, he was just judgmental.

Alex, however, had an ease about him that not only made me feel like I could tell him anything, but gave me the impression that anyone who met him would feel the same way.

I didn't press Alex for details. All I knew was the area we were going to, but I didn't know where we were staying or why he chose the Hamptons in the first place.

Eventually, the car slowed as we turned down a residential street. The houses were breathtaking and perfectly manicured. I stopped talking to Alex entirely in favor of staring out the windows. It wasn't the first time I had been to the Hamptons, but the change in scenery was always so dramatic that it left me a little speechless.

We pulled into a long driveway that ended at a large steel gate. I watched as Alex punched in a code without any hesitation, and the gate slowly creaked open in front of us. I wondered who the owner of this house could be and why Alex already seemed so comfortable here, but I didn't ask. Instead, I just sat in silence as we parked, and Alex opened my door for me.

The house was a gigantic, white, three-story home. While I knew that Alex was successful, there was no way that he was *this* successful. The house likely cost tens of millions of dollars. So the question remained, where were we?

Before I could ask, Alex took me by the hand. Again, without any hesitation or difficulty with the keys in his hand, he was able to get the door open. I had to admit that it was strange how comfortable he was with this place. I looked around, but I couldn't yet find a hint of who the house belonged to. Maybe it was just a rental? It certainly didn't look very lived in.

"Should I give you the tour?"

I looked at Alex skeptically. "Of the rental?"

He looked back at me just as confused. "I grew up here."

"This is your—"

"My parents' house."

I froze. *Are you kidding me?* Alex wasn't just rich, he was *loaded.* Suddenly, his comfort with the house made so much more sense, but the shock didn't leave my face. I let him lead me through the giant mansion. There was a pool and a tennis court, and even a deck on the roof. I couldn't imagine growing up in a place like this. My parents were more than comfortable, but there was a difference between a six-figure salary and owning a forty-million-dollar estate.

When we got to the bedrooms, I felt the tension between us shift a little. We entered what appeared to be one of many guest bedrooms, and Alex turned to me.

"So if you want, you can sleep in here tonight," he said carefully.

I tilted my head to one side, pretending not to know what he was implying. "What if I don't want to sleep in here?"

A dangerous smirk crossed his face, and he nodded for me to follow him. We entered yet another bedroom directly across the hall.

"Then I guess you'll have to sleep in here."

The room I was now standing in was much larger than the one we'd just come from, and based on the stylish yet masculine decor, I had to guess the room was his.

"What happens in here?"

Alex didn't respond at first; he just moved closer to me, causing my knees to hit the back of the enormous four-post bed.

"What would you like to happen here, Jacey?"

He was provoking me. That was obvious. His body pressed flush against mine, and I could feel the heat rising in me with every second those blue eyes of his danced over my face. I couldn't deny myself or him any longer, and so instead of answering his question, I slid my hands onto his defined shoulders and pulled him against me as I kissed him hard.

If I could rate every first kiss I'd ever had, this one might take the cake. It felt hungry and intense and wild. Alex pushed me back onto the bed as he continued to kiss me. I didn't care if I'd known this man for two weeks or twenty seconds.

I wanted him.

My hands roamed over his body as his hands moved slowly over mine as if he was trying to memorize me with his fingertips. We couldn't stop kissing each other. It was intoxicating. Still, I sensed a certain level of restraint coming from him, and as if he could read my mind, Alex pulled back from me. He didn't go far. He just moved from hovering over me to laying next to me, propping himself up on one elbow.

"Nope, get back here!" I said as I grabbed the collar of his shirt and collided my lips with his again.

He smiled against my mouth before pulling away a second time.

"As much as I just want to roll around in bed with you all day...I had a plan."

"Oh, you did?" I asked, though I wasn't particularly interested. I started to trail my lips down his neck in an attempt to get things back on track. I'm sure that whatever Alex planned was lovely, but I had other things in mind.

I heard a quiet gasp escape him, and for a minute, I thought he might cave. But instead, he got up out of bed.

"Just trust me."

I sighed heavily and got up. As I straightened my now disheveled outfit, I turned to face Alex. "Okay, so what's the plan?"

"Follow me."

I didn't like it, but I did as I was told. I followed Alex through the house until we reached the kitchen.

"Your plan is in the kitchen?"

"My plan is to make you dinner," he chuckled.

I could hardly think about food after what just happened, but I had to admit that the gesture was sweet, so I decided to let him have his way. A male model just brought me to a mansion in South Hampton, kissed the hell out of me, and now wanted to cook me dinner.

Did I really have room to complain?

Twenty-Two

In the forty-five minutes it took Alex to cook lemon rosemary chicken and scalloped potatoes with gruyère, I admitted to myself that I was starting to fall. While he cooked, I sat at the island with a glass of white wine and watched every move he made. He was stunning. I couldn't tear my eyes away. It was more than what he looked like, it was the lines across his forehead that only appeared when he was concentrating and the way the warmth in his voice made me hold my breath. Once in a while, he would glance up at me, and I was sure I would melt right into the floor. I tried hard not to imagine what life would be like if this were a regular occurrence and not just an over-the-top second date.

Somewhere, deep in the back of my mind was a small voice urging me to be careful. I may have been enjoying this multi-million dollar home and this mind-numbing-

ly beautiful man, but I didn't know enough about Alex to be coming so unraveled. Plus, if my last two romantic encounters were any indication, things could, and likely would, go south quickly. It was just hard to keep my guard up when everything seemed to be going so well.

"What are you thinking about?" Alex asked me as he started plating our food.

"It's just — it's nothing..."

He raised an eyebrow and I could immediately tell he didn't believe me. "You looked pretty deep in thought."

I sighed. "I was wondering when this is going to go wrong."

"Does it have to?" Alex casually leaned over the island, resting on his elbows so he was eye to eye with me.

I wanted to tell him "no" and that I hoped it wouldn't, but instead, I opted for the truth. "These things normally do for me."

"These things?"

I had to choose my words carefully. I didn't want to give Alex the impression that I thought there was more to this than there was. We were only on our second date, after all. "Dating...I guess..."

"These things normally go wrong for me too," he said.

I had a hard time believing that. I doubted there was anyone on earth that wouldn't give their right arm to be where I was sitting right now. He was wealthy, so good-looking that he got paid for it, and as if those two things weren't enough, he was also funny and sweet and could cook. Alexander Duran was basically Prince Charming and the closest thing to perfection I had ever experienced.

Alex grabbed our plates, and I grabbed the wine as I followed him outside. He led the way down a long, narrow wooden path that eventually led to a seating area overlooking the beach. It was beautiful. The sun had just started to set, and the sky was striped with orange and pink. We sat on two chairs facing the water with a table between us.

"I have an idea," Alex said.

I raised an eyebrow and turned to look at him. "What might that be?"

He poured wine into our glasses and then turned his attention back to me. "If things normally go wrong for both of us, then maybe we should do something different."

"Like what?"

"I'll do the opposite of everything I would normally do, and you do the opposite of what you would do, and we'll see where it takes us."

I mulled over that thought for a moment. What was the opposite of what I would normally do? Normally, I let myself get caught up too quickly and rush into bed too soon. Every romantic encounter I'd ever had was like a race to the finish line, except maybe with Brian. I met someone I liked, and in a matter of seconds, I had tunnel vision. I didn't know how to handle things casually. If I was going to do the opposite, that meant not allowing myself to fall for Alex, at least not yet. The problem with that, however, was he'd already gotten under my skin. I'd been in the house with him all of two hours, and already I didn't want to leave. I couldn't exactly stop feeling the way I did about Alex, so doing the opposite would have to mean pretending this was all casual to me. *Could I do that?*

"I guess it's worth a try," I said, trying to sound as detached as possible. "So, what is it that you normally do?" I asked as I took a sip of my wine.

"Sleep with someone right away and then base all my feelings on sex," Alex bluntly answered.

I choked on my wine. I tried hard to clear my throat and pretend it wasn't a reaction to what he'd just said. What I *usually did* wasn't all that different, but it still caught me off guard.

"What about you?"

"I...um...jump in too fast. I meet someone, and I like them, and then it's like I have blinders on," I admitted.

"I'm sure that would be awful," he said, rolling his eyes at me.

"I'm sure jumping into bed with you would be terrible, too."

That was a lie if I'd ever told one. I was pretty much dying to get into bed with Alex. It was all I'd been thinking about since we left his bedroom. I could still feel his lips on mine long after we'd stopped kissing. The only reason I wasn't in bed with him right now was that he insisted on dinner.

"You didn't seem so against the idea an hour ago."

"Well, let's just say it's a good thing you cook better than you kiss," I lied as I took a bite of my chicken.

Alex made a shocked face, though I could tell that he knew I was teasing him.

The two of us ate our dinner and drank nearly the entire bottle of wine. We talked for what felt like hours without even a pause between us. Eventually, I found myself sufficiently buzzed and blissfully happy.

"What am I supposed to do if I'm not supposed to like you?" I asked, though I wasn't sure I was making sense.

"Who said that you weren't supposed to like me?"

"You said that I was supposed to do the opposite of

what I usually do."

"Take a cold shower?" Alex teased.

I wasn't sure if it was the alcohol or the mood I was in, but I stood up from my seat and started walking toward the ocean. "Okay," I said with a shrug.

"Jacey, what are you doing?" Alex called after me.

"You said take a cold shower...but I don't see a shower, so....the ocean is cold!" I yelled over my shoulder.

"Get back here! You're going to freeze!"

"If you want me, you'll have to come get me!"

I kicked my shoes off and started walking into the water. Alex was right, it was freezing, but I didn't intend on backing out now.

I was up to my knees in the Atlantic when I heard him jogging to catch up with me. Bravely, he marched right into the freezing ocean.

"I want you," he responded, grabbing me by the waist and kissing me hard.

Just as I began to kiss him back, a giant wave kicked up and covered the front of us in water. I pulled out of Alex's grasp, gasping in shock.

"I told you it was cold!" He laughed. "Let's get you inside."

Alex took my hand, and I walked closely beside him back up the wooden path that led to the house. When we got inside, he took me straight upstairs to his bedroom. "I have to clean up from dinner, but you should get in the shower," he said.

"And you...should come with me." I tugged at his shirt, making him take a step closer to me.

A smirk played on his lips, but he just kissed my forehead and left me to my own devices.

I took my time in the shower, trying to get the salt

and sand out of my hair. This whole day made me feel like my head was spinning, so it was nice to have a second to myself, though I kept hoping that I'd hear Alex open the bathroom door. After spending way too long hoping he'd change his mind, I finally decided to get out.

I wrapped myself in a towel and stepped out of the bathroom only to find Alex quietly sitting on the bed, flipping through his phone. He looked up at me and, again, I thought I might fall apart looking into those icy blue eyes. I didn't say a word. I couldn't even think of words. I just walked over to him, still wrapped in a towel. His eyes moved from my face down to my chest. I took that as my cue and reached up to unwrap the towel from around my body. However, before I could, Alex reached up quickly and grabbed my hand. The look he gave me was painful, as if he had to fight himself to stop me.

"What's wrong?" I asked.

"Nothing. I just..." His eyes trailed over me again. His gaze was low, and longing, and I knew he didn't want to say the words that came next. "I like you."

"Ditto," I responded as I leaned down to kiss him, but he stopped me again.

"Which is why I can't sleep with you," he added.

I took a deep breath. I had a feeling that was what he was going to say. Alex said he wanted to do things differently than he usually did, and he usually rushed into bed with women. I nodded my head and took a step back.

"Should I..." I started, looking towards the door. I didn't know if this meant that I should sleep in the guest room.

Alex shook his head. "That's up to you...but I don't

want you to."

I smiled. "Okay, I'll get some clothes on."

I grabbed my bag and headed back into the bathroom before emerging yet again, this time in a lacy pair of shorts and camisole.

"I'm guessing you don't have a floor-length nightgown in that bag?"

"I wasn't exactly planning on wearing much," I said with a laugh.

Alex groaned dramatically. "Why am I doing this to myself!" he said while tossing himself back onto the bed.

I crawled into bed next to him and turned on my side so I could face him. I looked him over and it suddenly hit me that whether I was pretending this was casual or not, I was falling right back into my old habits. I wanted to hit the brakes, but that seemed impossible when I couldn't find a single flaw.

"What is wrong with you?" I asked abruptly.

"What?"

"There's no way you're this perfect."

"I'm not perfect."

I stared at Alex as if he'd lost his mind. "You're a model who was smart enough to get into law school, you apparently have an obscene amount of money, you can cook, you can dress, you can kiss...so what is wrong with you?"

"I...don't know..."

"What do you mean, you don't know?"

"Where is this coming from?"

I sighed. I knew I wasn't making any sense, but I also didn't know how to explain it. "I'm sorry. I think I'm just overthinking things."

"Well, maybe I can help with that..." Alex said before

his lips found mine yet again.

Eventually, Alex and I fell asleep. It was the perfect ending to a perfect date with a perfect man. The problem was, it was too perfect to make me feel safe. I had no idea where this was going, or if I wanted to follow. If the last two guys I'd dated were any indication, it might not be going anywhere at all, but I did know that there was something about Alex that made me hope that I was wrong.

Twenty-Three

Alex got booked again. This time, he would be gone for weeks. He promised he'd call and that we would resume things when he got back, but I tried not to get my hopes up. I liked him, more than I should, but I wasn't sure that being in a relationship with someone who had to pack up and go halfway across the world every few weeks was reasonable.

I couldn't seem to find Alex's flaw and yet there it was, staring me right in the face. I'd only known him a short time and he had already left the country twice. How was I supposed to build a relationship with someone who was jet-setting across the world at a moment's notice? I wasn't exactly sad. I wasn't sure what I felt. There was just this cloud of melancholy that followed me around since he first told me he was leaving and I hadn't been able to shake it.

Being away from Alex felt like being distanced from the sun. Everything just seemed dull and gray.

The best thing I could do was to focus on my work, so that's what I did. I dove headfirst into my daily grind. The problem was that I couldn't keep my mind from wandering. When I got into the office on Wednesday, no matter how hard I tried to focus on the work in front of me, my mind kept finding its way back to Alex. I kept thinking about how good it felt falling asleep next to him. Then it would switch to August and why he'd pulled a Jekyll and Hyde on me. Then Owen and why he seemed to be so in the dark about what he wanted. I was thinking so hard I began to give myself a headache.

"I'm gonna go drop off the mail," I announced to both Nia and Danny, who were quietly typing away at their desks.

"Isn't that my job?" Danny asked, glancing up at me from behind his laptop.

"I just need some air."

To avoid explaining myself, I hurried over to the packages waiting by the door and gathered them quickly into the oversized tote we used for mail runs.

I thought getting out of the studio would help, but as I walked towards the post office, I still couldn't shake the thoughts about my unexpectedly booming love life. Anyone would have killed to be in my shoes right now. First, there was Owen, who looked like a god. Then August, who was classically handsome and impossibly brilliant, despite his faults. Now, Alex, who could arguably be one of the most attractive men on the planet. The problem wasn't them, however. The problem was that I wasn't ready from the start, and now three men into this dating spree, I still felt lost. I liked all of them.

I liked them too much for how briefly I'd known them and yet not enough to look past any of their red flags.

I made it through the endless line at the post office, but I still didn't feel any better. Instead of heading back to the studio, I decided to take a detour through Central Park.

It was beautiful this time of year, and the change of scenery from the busy Mid-Town streets to the serene greenery was desperately needed. I walked for a while, just trying to clear my head and think of something other than the men popping up like daisies in my life. Eventually, I found myself in a secluded area and took a seat on a bench under a large maple tree. I knew eventually I was going to have to go back to work, but for the time being, I just enjoyed the momentary solace of being alone.

I wasn't sure how much time had passed, but out of the corner of my eye, I noticed an elderly woman wandering rather aimlessly. She was well-dressed and clean, so it was unlikely she was homeless, yet she seemed very lost. Central Park was huge, and it would be easy for anyone to lose their bearings. The longer I watched her, the more I felt like she needed help, so I got up and approached her.

"Ma'am, are you lost?" I asked.

The woman looked at me and then at her surroundings. I could tell she wasn't altogether sure what was going on.

"Y-yes dear, I think I might be," she answered.

"Well, would you like to come sit with me, and maybe I can help you find your way home?"

She nodded her head and unexpectedly took my arm. I walked with her slowly back towards the bench, and the two of us had a seat.

"What's your name?" I asked gently.

"I'm Gail, dear. What is your name?"

"I'm Jacey. It's nice to meet you."

"Jacey, that's a funny name."

"My parents were funny people."

That wasn't true. My parents were exceedingly normal people. The story of my name was just a mouthful. When my mom was pregnant, my parents knew they were having twins. They just thought they were having one girl and one boy. They decided to name my sister Elise Marie after my parents' mothers, and I was supposed to be Jacob Christopher after my parents' fathers. When, much to their surprise, a girl came out, they scrambled to find a name. Jacob Christopher was J.C., which became Jacey.

"What part of town do you live in, Gail?"

"Oh, I live on the Upper East Side."

I nodded slowly. We were in the southwest corner of the park. If she wandered from the Upper East Side, she had been on quite a walk.

"Do you know your address?" I asked, hoping that maybe I could put her in a cab, but she shook her head no.

"Could you call Gabriel for me, dear?"

"Who's Gabriel?"

"He's the nice young man my son hired to help me around the house."

I was relieved to hear that she had a caretaker, though I was concerned that they'd let her wander so far from home. "Do you know Gabriel's number?"

Gail reached a shaky hand into the small beaded clutch she'd been carrying with her. She then pulled out a cell phone and handed it to me. "My son gave me that, but I can never figure out how it works," she said.

I looked down at the newer model iPhone in my hand. This woman had to be in her 80s. I had no idea why her son thought she'd understand how to use technology this new, but it wasn't my place to judge. Instead, I scrolled through the contacts until I found the name "Gabriel Warren" and dialed.

"Gail? Where are you?" I heard an exasperated voice on the other end say.

"Um... hi... I found Gail wandering in the park, and..."

"Central Park?"

"Yes."

"I thought that's where she might have gone. Where are you? I'll be right there."

"Southwest corner... I can drop you a pin."

"Great, thank you so much!"

He hung up; now all we could do was wait. Gail started to tell me about her family. Her son's name was Julian, and he was some high-powered divorce attorney. She told me that she was proud of how successful he'd become, but she wished he practiced some other type of law. According to Gail, marriage was sacred, and people these days were too quick to throw in the towel.

"What about you, dear? Are you married?"

I was surprised by her question, but I answered honestly. "No... no, I'm not."

She smiled a mischievous kind of smile. "You know Gabriel is very handsome."

Great! Just what I need! Yet another person trying to meddle in my love life. Gail looked at me expectantly, but I didn't know what to say. "I'm sure he is," is all I could settle on.

Before I could say anything else, a man's voice

interrupted our conversation.

"Gail?"

I turned my head to find a sandy-haired man approaching us. He was wearing a pair of burgundy scrubs, and as I glanced over at Gail, there was a look of recognition on her face. *This must be Gabriel.*

Gail was right. He was handsome. Gabriel had a mess of wavy, light brown hair and a large pair of olive-green eyes. He reminded me of something out of a Jane Austen novel. He wasn't terribly tall or muscular, but he was captivating. I found myself unable to look away.

"Gail, how did you—" he started. "You can't just—"

He seemed to be struggling not to get upset. I watched him pause and take a deep breath. This likely wasn't the first time Gail had done something like this. Instead of trying to figure out why Gail had run off, Gabriel turned his attention to me.

"Thank you so much for calling," he said, his eyes finally meeting mine.

"Of course," I said with a smile. "Gail was telling me all about you."

"She's single!" she said in a sing-song way.

I didn't know why this old woman was playing matchmaker for me, but now that I'd seen Gabriel for myself, I didn't mind so much.

"Can you stay here for a minute Gail, I'm going to talk to your new friend," he said to her.

"Take all the time you need," she responded.

I stood up, and Gabriel and I walked a few feet away.

"I'm so sorry about this. I'm sure this isn't how you wanted to spend your afternoon," he said to me.

I shook my head. "I don't mind. I'm just glad I was able to reach you. She got really turned around."

"Yeah, she can be..."

"A handful?"

"Something like that." He held his hand out to me. "I'm Gabe, by the way."

"Jacey...Lange... it's nice to meet you."

"You too. I really appreciate your help."

"It was nothing," I said with a shrug.

I had sort of hoped that Gabe might show some interest. It seemed like every time I turned around, someone was asking me out. Unfortunately, without another word, Gabe started walking back over to Gail.

"Let's get you home," I could hear him say to her.

"Not until you get that girl's number," she said to him rather assertively.

I tried not to laugh. I didn't imagine that my new elderly friend was suddenly going to become my wing woman.

"Gail, that isn't appropriate. Let's get going..."

"I'm not going anywhere," she said, crossing her arms over her chest.

I watched him open his mouth to argue with her, but before he could, I decided to do something rather unlike myself. I took a pen out of my purse, walked over to a man I knew nothing about, grabbed his hand, and scribbled my number on it.

"I... um...." he started.

"I hope you use it," I said with a smile, then turned my attention to Gail. "It was so nice to meet you."

"I'm sure I'll be seeing you again soon, dear," she responded.

I gave Gabe one last meaningful look. "I hope so," I agreed.

With that, I started back toward the studio. I didn't

necessarily expect I would see or hear from either of them again, but I was happy knowing that Gail was now safe, and I was proud of myself for being so bold.

Twenty-Four

Timing is everything. A few days passed, and I didn't hear from Gabe. Maybe he just thought I was just trying to be nice and help him get Gail home, or maybe he wasn't interested at all. Perhaps it was for the best. I had too much on my plate already, but I had to admit I was ever so slightly disappointed. Thankfully, Alex was a great distraction. Just as we had while he was in Milan, he called me every night. It was starting to feel like there might be something real happening between us.

That was, until he stopped calling.

The first night that Alex didn't reach out, I assumed he was busy or still sleeping. When he didn't call again on Saturday night, I started to get concerned. I texted him, simply saying I'd hoped he had a good day. A read receipt showed up immediately, but there was no response. I had no idea what I'd done or why he had suddenly gone cold. I couldn't understand why he was

ignoring me, but it felt awful. Leon was on a business trip, so there was no one to vent to. It was right about the time I was considering a large glass of red and a rom-com to drown my sorrows that I got a text.

> ***Unknown Number:*** *Hi, Jacey?*
> **Me:** Yes? Who is this?
> ***Unknown Number:*** *Gabe. Gail's Caretaker. We met on Wednesday.*
> **Me:** Oh, hi! I didn't expect to hear from you. How are you?
> ***Gabe:*** *Honestly, I was working up the nerve to text you.*
> **Me:** Well, I'm glad you did.
> ***Gabe:*** *Do you have plans tomorrow night?*

I didn't exactly believe in fate, but I couldn't help but notice how perfectly timed Gabe's text was. Instead of focusing on Alex and his sudden decision to ghost me, I decided to focus on this date instead. Plus, Gabe would be the fourth guy, which meant I was one step closer to getting my old room back. All I knew was that he wanted to take me to a gallery opening, and that I was supposed to meet him there at eight the following night. So I spent my Saturday night picking out the perfect outfit, painting my nails, and blocking out any thoughts of Alexander Duran.

When Sunday night rolled around, I was more than ready. I practically watched the clock. Most of the dates I went on made me nervous, but this time I was excited. I might have been looking forward to the distraction from Alex more than I was about seeing Gabe himself, but regardless, I was dressed to kill and in a cab at seven-thirty exactly.

When I arrived at the gallery, there was a long line outside, and I spotted Gabe near the front. I wasn't sure what it was about him. As soon as I caught a glimpse of him, I genuinely felt butterflies. He looked a little different without the scrubs. I was surprised that he had a sense of style. Anyone I knew who wore uniforms for a living didn't put much effort into what they wore off duty. My dad was a perfect example of that. He was a surgeon, and he always wore one of two things: scrubs or sweatpants. Gabe, however, had this effortlessly cool, lived-in vibe that I could appreciate.

As I approached him, his eyes locked onto mine. The most heart-stopping smile formed on his face. He was still a stranger, but when he smiled at me like that, the pull inside me felt like a longing for something I'd been missing.

"Hi there," I said, a little unsure of how to greet him.

"Hi...um...you look...great. I mean...beautiful? You look beautiful."

I had to smile at the way he fumbled his way through the sentence. The fact that I seemed to make him nervous was rather adorable. "You look pretty good, yourself," I said honestly. I watched him rub the back of his neck and look away from me for a minute. I could tell he didn't know what to say, and so I jumped right back in. "So, what are we doing?" I asked.

When he asked me out, Gabe gave me an address to meet him but didn't tell me why. I knew nothing about the artist or if there was a reason he chose this particular event.

"Well—" Gabe started, but before he could finish

his sentence, the doors opened up, and the line started to file into the vast, dimly lit gallery. It was a beautiful space, and larger than most galleries I'd been to in the city. Everything was minimalist and white. I already found the place beautiful and oddly romantic, even though I hadn't yet looked at a single thing hanging on the walls.

"Where should we start?" I asked.

"How about here?" Gabe pointed to a painting off to our right. The gallery was in the shape of a U, so it made sense to pick a place to start and work our way around. We walked over to the large canvas, and I tilted my head as I looked it over. It appeared the artist chose fabric instead of paint, covering the canvas in vibrant hues of pink and orange tulle in a way that reminded me of a sunset. It was absolutely beautiful.

"What do you think?" Gabe asked after a long moment of silence as we both looked at the piece.

"It's amazing."

I started to wander towards the next painting a few feet away, and I realized that not only had the artist chosen to use fabric for the first painting, but every piece was done in a different type of fabric. I was amazed and a little surprised. Given that fabric was my own artistic medium, I wasn't sure how Gabe came up with such a thoughtful date, especially when he didn't know what I did for a living.

"How did you...?" I started to ask. I wasn't sure how to word my question. "Why did you pick this opening?"

"I might have Googled you," he said sheepishly.

I opened my mouth to speak, but it took a moment for actual words to come out. "That's... really sweet..."

"I just figured since you also make art with clothes..."

"I love it. Thank you."

Gabe's smile was wide and so genuine it almost made my heart ache a little. I knew that to him, the gesture was probably small. However, this was the first time I'd been on a date with someone who'd taken the time to learn something about me so he could take me somewhere he was sure I would like. Our date had just started, but he was already winning me over.

We continued walking through the gallery, looking over pieces, and chatting with each other as we did.

"So, what made you decide to become a caretaker?" I asked.

"I got a nursing degree because I wanted to help people, and I tried working in a hospital for a while, but high-stress environments aren't really for me. I also tend to get invested in people. It was hard not knowing what happened to patients after they left. Instead, I decided to do something where I could still help people, but I could be a more active part of their lives." I didn't know if it was possible, but the more Gabe spoke, the more I liked him. "What made you decide to go into fashion?"

"I've wanted to be a designer since I knew what fashion was. I used to make clothes for mine and my sister's dolls, and I was always sketching. I didn't decide that I wanted to design men's fashion until I was in college, though."

"From what I've seen, your work is...something else."

I had no idea whether he meant that as a compliment or if he was trying not to say something impolite. "Is that a good thing or a bad thing?"

"It's a 'you're so talented it's intimidating' thing."

Anyone who knew me could tell you that the fastest way to my heart, other than pizza, was taking an interest in my work.

"There's no reason to be intimidated," I said.

Gabe stopped out of nowhere as we were making our way from one painting to the next. "Are you serious? You are the single most intimidating woman I've ever met," he said.

Immediately and without warning, I laughed. I was plenty of things, but I hardly considered myself intimidating.

"I'm serious," Gabe protested at my laughter. "I've never really..." he started, but trailed off before he could finish his sentence.

"Never really what?"

"Dated anyone who's made so much of themselves before."

"You must not date much," I teased.

"I don't... exactly..."

How was that possible? Gabe might not have been stereotypically hot, but he was certainly attractive enough to have plenty of options. Those dark green eyes, that giant smile; he was beautiful. Plus, he took care of old ladies and had been doing nothing but paying me compliments since I got here. I didn't understand why there weren't women lining up around the block to go out with him.

"Why is that?" I asked.

"Uh...." Gabe started to shift uncomfortably.

I got the impression right away that whatever the reason was, it was something he wasn't sure he wanted to tell me. He had been so sweet that my instinct was to reassure him that I wasn't going to judge him. Before this bet, I hadn't been dating much either, so I understood, but I didn't say anything. Instead, I just waited for the other shoe to drop. Usually it took a little longer for me to find the red flags, but the pessimist in me was sure that Gabe was about to drop a bomb.

"I'm demi..."

I paused. *What was "demi"?* I'd never even heard the term before. Was it short for something? At least he wasn't telling me he was married, but I was at a loss at what he was saying. "Demi...what...?"

"Demisexual."

I considered myself progressive in most things, but this was new to me. I tried to clear the confusion from my face; the last thing I wanted was for Gabe to mistake it for judgment. I just didn't know what he meant. "I'm not sure I know what that means..." I admitted.

Gabe bit down on his bottom lip. He still looked uncomfortable, but he bravely decided to explain. "Okay, do you know what asexual is?"

"Yes."

"Well, if asexuality is white and sexuality is black, it's like a gray area."

"I'm still not sure I understand," I admitted.

"I guess the easy way to explain it is that for me to be sexually attracted to someone, I have to form an emotional bond with them. I don't date much because that's sometimes a hard thing for women to understand."

It was starting to click now. I didn't necessarily know how that translated to dating someone or being in a relationship, but I was at least putting the pieces together. "So, does that mean you aren't attracted to me?" I said, trying to make sure my tone was playful enough that he knew I was teasing him.

"No! No... I am— you are—"

I couldn't help but smile. I leaned forward a little as he struggled to find the right words.

"Gorgeous."

I didn't think I'd ever gone out with anyone who seemed to mean the words they said as much as Gabe did. The way he complimented me was so earnest. There were no pick up lines or over the top flattery. The way he looked at me really felt he was actually seeing me.

"I was kidding," I said honestly.

I watched a sense of relief wash over his handsome face.

"I'll be honest with you, I don't know if I completely get it, but I'd like to."

That same irresistible, wide smile formed on his face. Gently, Gabe slid his hand into mine, and while we continued to wander around the gallery, he opened up. I learned more about him in the few hours I spent on that date than I knew about Brian after dating him for years. I felt so close to Gabe. He was so easy to get close to, and when the night ended, I felt like something had changed in me. I didn't know what it was, but I knew that Gabe had left a mark.

Twenty-Five

I had a long list of things about the fashion industry that I loved. However, there was also a list of things I hated. At the top of that list were two words: industry parties.

There was nothing worse than networking, schmoozing, and feigning interest in someone in the hopes of one day getting ahead. However, the publicist I hired for the line was adamant that they were a necessary evil, so there I was, wasting a Saturday night in a painfully pretentious nightclub in Chelsea.

I was sure no one actually networked at these kinds of parties. They pretended to, but for the most part, they just got wasted on free liquor and forgot the names of the people they met. It also didn't help that, like any nightclub, the lighting was dark, the music was loud, and it was almost impossible to imagine having a serious business conversation of any kind. It was all

for show, and I had little interest in performing for anyone. As far as I was concerned, my work should speak for itself.

Case in point, since arriving, the only conversation I'd had was with a girl with incredibly bloodshot eyes who called herself "Flower" and designed hemp jewelry. I decided that if I was required to be here, the only way to make it bearable was to head to the bar. I ordered a Jack and Diet Coke. I watched the bartender pour me a glass that was about 85% whiskey and 15% soda. Just looking at the concoction made my stomach turn. Getting drunk was clearly going to be a lot easier than I thought.

"You don't want to drink that," a voice said as a tattooed, masculine hand grabbed my drink and placed it back on the bar.

I turned to my right and looked up into the face of possibly the most interesting-looking man I had ever seen. He was tall and lithe with hair that was so blonde it was almost white. His eyes were deep-set and a striking color of cerulean blue. He hailed the bartender back over and ordered two beers with hip-sounding names. When the bartender returned, he handed me a bottle.

"I'm Cash," he said as he tilted the neck of his beer towards mine as if to toast to this rather peculiar introduction.

Of course his name was Cash, with those tattoos, his punk-rock sense of style, and the staggering amount of confidence he had; it was almost too fitting. I wanted to ask if that was the name his mother gave him or if, like many people in New York, he invented that particular moniker. But I thought better of it.

"Jacey," I said.

"Jacey... Jacey... Jacey, what?"

"Lange."

"Why do I know that name? Are you an artist?"

"Designer."

His blue eyes went wide with realization. "J. Lange!"

I opened my mouth to speak, but before I could, he jumped back in.

"This is yours!" he said, pulling on the jacket he was wearing.

I didn't know how I'd missed it, but sure enough, he wore a leather jacket that I'd designed a year and a half ago.

"I don't know..." I said playfully. "It could be a knock-off. I should probably take a look."

I held out my hand, expecting Cash to take off the jacket. He scoffed a little, but then an ever-so-slightly-crooked smile crossed his face, and he shrugged it off his narrow shoulders. Underneath, he was wearing a black v-neck shirt, which made it easy to see just how many tattoos he had. He was covered in them, his arms, his chest, his hands, and though I couldn't see much else, I could only imagine where else he might have them. He handed me the garment, and I pretended to examine it, although I already knew it was mine. My brand might have been gaining popularity, but I wasn't at the point people were making knock-offs of my work.

"I just met her, and she's already got me taking my clothes off," he said sarcastically.

I looked up from the jacket and raised an eyebrow. I had to admit, as soon as that jacket came off, I started wondering what he looked like under those clothes, but I wasn't about to give him the upper hand by admitting it.

"I guess I just have more game than you do," I playfully retorted.

Cash looked away, trying not to smile. "I guess so..."

"So what do you do, Cash?"

The way he looked at me when I asked that question was like I'd just slapped him. However, it quickly changed to a look of intrigue. Apparently, he liked being slapped. "You don't know?"

"Am I supposed to?"

There were plenty of people in New York who were renowned for what they did. It was a creative mecca. That, however, didn't mean that I knew every one of them or cared to keep track. The idea that I should know who he was bordered on obnoxious. Still, the fact remained that he was attractive, and I needed something to keep this party interesting.

"I'm an artist," he finally said.

"That's vague," I replied.

"You're not fucking with me? You really don't know who I am?"

I rolled my eyes. His ego was starting to get old, fast. "Are you going to tell me or not?"

"I'm a painter."

"Is there a reason you're so aloof about this?"

The only way I could describe how Cash looked at me was a cross between maddening insult and utter fascination. He started to say something, but instead of words, he hesitated, still staring at me in disbelief.

"If you make art, then tell me about it. Don't just give me three-word sentences," I said.

"It's uh... this cross between baroque-style paintings and street art."

I had to admit, that sounded more than a little impressive. At least, I admitted that to myself. I was rather enjoying knocking Cash down a peg or two.

"I'd tell you about my art, but you're wearing it," I said with a smile.

Cash shook his head and just stared at me for a minute as if he was contemplating something. "Do you wanna get out of here?" he asked me.

I looked around the club at people I didn't want to talk to and took stock of the horrible music that was growing increasingly louder, and then I looked back at Cash. He seemed like a much better option.

"Yeah, let's go."

Cash led me out of the crowded nightclub with his hand on the small of my back. I was aware that I didn't know him and that I once again found myself running off with a strange man just because I found him attractive, but that didn't stop me.

The two of us ducked into an Uber before I'd even bothered to wonder where we were going. Cash, however, seemed to know exactly where he wanted to take me because the driver had already entered our destination into the GPS on his phone.

"Where are we going?"

"If I'm going to tell you about my art, I might as well show it to you," he said.

I knew that showing me his art was likely a poorly disguised way of telling me he was taking me back to his place. I wasn't surprised. I'd assumed that's what I was in for as soon as he asked me if I wanted to leave the club. This wasn't exactly typical of me, but there was something about this night and this particular man that made me feel like someone else.

We pulled up to a brick building that looked more like a warehouse than an apartment building, but like many buildings in New York, it had been converted, and the inside resembled any other complex. I followed him up a set of stairs and into his loft. Though I was feeling a little reckless, I did take a second to text Leon the address and the apartment number. He didn't respond, but it made me feel better knowing that he knew where I was.

"Can I get you a drink?"

I nodded in response as I looked around his apartment. The decor was this strange and eclectic collection of items that didn't quite seem to go together. As soon as Cash went into the kitchen, I turned my attention back toward him. I wasn't about to let him make me a drink I didn't pay attention to. He poured me a rather unremarkable vodka-soda and slid it over to me.

I sipped on the bitter-tasting liquid, leaning against his kitchen counter as I watched Cash down not one but two shots before making his way over to me. He stopped in front of me, placing his hands on either side of the counter.

"I've wanted to do this all night..."

Cash leaned in and kissed me. He tasted like my poorly made cocktail with a hint of smoke behind it. Regardless, it was definitely a good kiss. I wrapped my arms around his neck and deepened it.

I didn't know what the hell I was doing. I wasn't the one-night-stand type. I was a hopeless monogamist, but the truth was, that didn't get me anywhere. I had been chasing true love my whole life, and it only got me hurt, so tonight, I chased something else. Tonight, I just wanted to get lost.

"God, you're fucking beautiful..." I heard him whisper as his lips left mine.

I assumed the next place we would go was his bedroom, but I was mistaken. Cash took yet another shot. I didn't understand the rapid-fire drinking, especially when he had company, but Cash didn't exactly strike me as logical.

"I'm gonna go smoke," he said, sounding a little more inebriated than he had before.

I decided that I needed to catch up. Maybe a few more drinks in me, and I wouldn't be thinking quite so hard. I downed the rest of my cocktail, and while Cash disappeared out the sliding glass door onto his balcony, I poured myself another drink.

He was outside longer than I expected. I had completely finished my second drink by the time he came back in. It was clear it wasn't cigarettes he'd been smoking. It didn't bother me, but I couldn't help but notice that he seemed pretty intent on getting himself wasted in any way he possibly could. *Is this what he usually does when he takes a girl home?*

"I think you have paintings to show me," I said.

"Right."

Moving slower than he had before, Cash took my hand. He led me into one of two bedrooms. As soon as I walked in, I could see that he didn't sleep in this one. It was a mess of canvases and art supplies. Leaning up against the walls were several huge paintings. They were just as he'd described: beautiful, classical pieces that had modern street-art additions to them. I wasn't just impressed by his work. I was blown away.

"These are incredible," I said softly.

"You're incredible," Cash responded as he kissed my neck gently. "There's more in the other room," he said suddenly as he led me across the hall.

True to his word, there were two other pieces in

Cash's bedroom, but before I could say anything about them, he was kissing me again. His lips and mine danced desperately against each other as he backed me toward the bed. Both his hands and his mouth were frantic, but it wasn't a moment I cared to savor. I wanted him just as badly as he wanted me, and I wanted him then and there.

He laid me down on the bed, and his fingertips slowly started to move up my leg and underneath the dress I was wearing. I could feel my pulse pick up when suddenly he just...stopped.

"Nope. No. I probably should..."

With only those few words, he rolled off of me and onto his back. He was out of it, and as much as I wanted him, I was well aware of the fact that nothing was going to happen.

I looked over at Cash. His eyes were heavy, drifting open and closed gently. I took a deep breath and started to get out of bed when I felt him grab my arm and pull me back in.

"Where are you going?" he asked, almost sounding like he was whining.

"I should get going," I said, trying not to sound as disappointed as I was.

"Just stay with me."

I considered following through with my plan and leaving, but I'd had quite a few drinks, too. The idea of trying to get a cab home sounded more than a little daunting. I knew that Cash wasn't going to do anything I didn't want him to when he could barely keep his eyes open, so there was no harm in sleeping off my buzz and getting a cab home in the morning.

"Okay," I said to him.

I had no idea why he wanted me to stay, but I got out of bed just long enough to take off the dress I was wearing.

When I climbed back into bed with Cash, he immediately pulled me close with a kind of familiarity that made my heart hurt. I lay there for a while, just listening to the sound of his breathing. Eventually, despite how strange it seemed, I started to drift off to sleep with my head on the chest of a man I didn't know at all.

Twenty-Six

I awoke in an unfamiliar bed.

I was on a giant king-size mattress wrapped around a heavily tattooed man I'd only just met the night before. I wished this was the only time in my life I'd woken up somewhere I didn't belong, but it wasn't. When I opened my eyes, my mind raced to figure out where I was. The memories of last night didn't immediately catch up with me. I propped myself up onto one arm and looked over Cash's sleeping face.

He was more handsome than I'd remembered. I took in his long dark lashes followed by his long, perfectly straight nose. He also seemed less chaotic than I remembered, but that, of course, was because he hadn't yet woken up. In his sleep, Cash looked oddly angelic. I felt the urge to stay there in that bed and watch him for a while, but I remembered I had texted my best friend an address with no explanation, and I was sure that Leon

would be panicking.

I got out of bed as carefully as I could, trying not to disturb Cash. As soon as my feet hit the cold concrete floor of his loft, I dashed into the living room to find my phone. It was sitting with my bag on the kitchen counter. To my surprise, my missed texts weren't from Leon. They were from Gabe.

I wasn't sure how to feel. I was a little disappointed that Leon hadn't thought to check on me. He didn't respond at all, and it had been hours. Yet, I couldn't help but smile at the prospect of seeing Gabe again. Despite how it might have looked at that moment, I felt a fondness for Gabe, and I was excited he'd reached out. It dawned on me, however, that I couldn't exactly go to breakfast with him. The skin-tight white dress I wore to the club last night was the only outfit I had with me, and I was still wearing day-old makeup. Anyone with half a brain would take one look at me and know I was doing the walk of shame. I stared down at the screen, trying to decide what to do, when I felt a pair of arms wrap around my waist and pull me close.

"Good morning," Cash whispered in my ear. His voice was husky and still full of sleep.

"Morning," I said as I quickly closed out of my messages, hoping he hadn't been reading over my shoulder.

"You were great last night."

"At sleeping?" I said, trying my best to hold back my laughter.

"We didn't...?"

"Oh, come on, you were not that wasted!"

Cash drank a little and smoked a lot, but he hardly seemed impaired enough to forget we hadn't slept together. We didn't even get past first base.

"I was feeling pretty good before I got to the club," he admitted.

I could only take that to mean that he'd been drinking long before we met and was just fantastic at hiding his buzz.

"Right..." I said. I wasn't sure how to respond to that. Maybe, if I could get out of here fast enough, I could get home, shower, and make my breakfast with Gabe a brunch. "Well, thanks for letting me crash," I said with a shrug and started to grab my purse.

I had to admit, this was completely uncharted territory for me. I didn't know much about the man I'd spent the night with, but there was no doubt that this was not the first time he'd woken up next to a stranger.

"Hold up, what's the rush?" he asked as he put his long-limbed body right in my path.

"I'm... um..." I had to think of something, but my mouth started moving before I'd thought of a good excuse. "I'm meeting a friend for breakfast," I said.

If I could avoid it, I tried not to lie. I told myself this was more like a necessary stretch of the truth. Gabe and I weren't exactly friends. I didn't know what we were or if his sexuality would allow us to be anything more, but I did know that I was interested and that, comparatively, I would rather be spending my time with him. The longer I stood in that loft with the walking, talking, red flag that was Cash Mason, the more I wanted to see Gabe. This whole thing felt like a terrible idea.

"Or you could blow them off, and we can finish what we started..." he said, his voice low and seductive.

"What's my name?" I asked, skeptical. The man couldn't even remember what we did last night. I had my doubts he could remember my name.

I expected Cash to back down, but instead, he reached out for my hips and pulled me towards him forcefully. My body collided with his, and I immediately felt a familiar heat inside me.

"Jacey," he whispered into my ear.

Everything in my body wanted to drag Cash back to his bedroom. Instead, I mustered up all the willpower I could and stepped away from him. "I really have to go," I said, grabbing my things before he could convince me otherwise.

"Wait!" Cash called out before I could close the distance between myself and his front door.

I turned and looked at him over my shoulder. He came up to me, took my cell phone out of my hand, and started entering what I could only assume was his number. It was unexpected, but I doubted that I was going to use it.

"We should hang out again," he said.

To me, that meant he wanted to hook up sometime. Cash didn't seem like the type to be interested in anything more than that. I didn't have the time to turn him down, and so I just shrugged my shoulders. "Sure."

I hurried out his front door and waved down a cab as soon as my feet hit the curb. As I sat in the back of the yellow sedan, I fumbled with my phone, typing out a text to Gabe as quickly as I could.

Thankfully he agreed to brunch instead.

When I arrived home, I didn't see or hear Leon anywhere, but leading from the living room to his bedroom was a trail of clothing—most of which I didn't recognize. I picked a short black skirt up off the floor and looked at the brand and size. I felt my insides twist and immediately dropped the garment. There weren't very many women that were small enough to fit in that skirt. I only knew of one: Natalia. I pinched my eyes shut and tried to drive the thought out of my head. Leon may have been my best friend, but who he chose to spend the night with was none of my business. Plus, I didn't have the time to sit around and let it bother me.

I stripped out of the dress I'd worn on my walk of shame and jumped in the shower. By the time I got dressed and put my face on, I was a new person. Quietly, I crept downstairs with the hope that Leon would be there and his companion for the night wouldn't be. Yet the apartment was again silent, and the clothes remained on the floor. I sighed as I looked at his closed bedroom door. I didn't want to admit that the scene bothered me, but like it or not, it unsettled me all the same.

The diner where Gabe wanted to meet me was only a few blocks away. I decided to walk. I hoped that by the time I got to the restaurant, my head might be clear. Luckily for me, it didn't take that long. By the time I was standing in front of the ultra-modern diner and its bright pink sign, I could see Gabe sitting at a booth next to the window, and my confusing thoughts about Leon completely disappeared.

I had no idea how those large green eyes and puppy dog face could make me so happy, but the smile that tugged at the corners of my mouth the moment I saw him was impossible to deny. As if he could read my mind, Gabe glanced out the window at me. His eyes immediately lit up, and I watched as he motioned for me to come inside.

"Get over here," he said to me as he stood up and wrapped me tightly in his embrace.

Just as it had been on our first date, the moment I

got close to Gabe, it felt as if I'd always known him. I couldn't make it make sense. I didn't believe in fate or soulmates, but the feeling I had when I was around Gabe made a good argument for both of those things.

"How have you been?" I asked as I sat down in the booth.

"Good. I just..." he started, but couldn't seem to finish his sentence.

"Just...what?"

"This is weird."

"Brunch is weird?"

"No, I just mean... This is going to sound weird, but... are you feeling what I'm feeling?"

I didn't know if I liked the idea of showing all of my cards so early on in the game, but when I looked at the hopefulness in Gabe's eyes, I realized something. He wasn't playing a game at all.

"Yeah. I think I am," I said softly, as I placed my hand on top of his.

He turned his hand to brush the top of my fingers with his thumb, though his eyes never left me.

"I wasn't kidding. I don't think I've stopped thinking about you since Sunday," he blurted out.

I couldn't help but find his shameless honesty adorable and rather refreshing. "I know what you mean," I said.

"I swear this isn't normal for me."

"It's not exactly normal for me, either."

It felt an awful lot like being a teenager again. That was the last time I could remember developing feelings for someone so quickly without so much as kissing them. Still, I had my reservations, especially when it came to his demisexuality.

"Can I ask you something?" I said after a moment had

passed between us.

"Yeah, of course."

"I really like you—"

"Why do I feel like there's a but coming?"

"Not exactly. I guess I just need some help understanding what this might look like given your..."

"Sexuality?"

"Yeah."

"First, I'm demisexual, but I'm not demiromantic."

"Here's the thing, I want to understand the way you identify, and I'm sure I will, but for right now, could you explain it to me without the technical terms?"

"Okay. I don't experience primary sexual attraction. That comes secondary after I've formed some kind of bond with someone. I do, however, experience primary *romantic* attraction."

That made sense, or at least the most sense it could, given how new the concept was to me. "So, you're interested in me?"

"Very," he responded without a second thought.

"But we can't have sex?"

A blush grew in Gabe's cheeks as he looked down at his menu.

"It's not that we can't...or won't...it's just..."

"It takes time," I said, finishing his sentence. I didn't want to make him uncomfortable with my line of questioning, but if I were to consider Gabe with any level of seriousness, I needed to understand the whole picture.

"It's like the way you date when you're in school. You like someone, you start dating them, and the physical part of the relationship usually comes later."

Of all the things he said, that part was clearest to me. However, I found myself questioning it immediately.

Could I work with that? It wasn't a decision I had to make right away, we were only on our second date, and yet I found myself rushing to answer it. Rushing seemed to be the only thing I knew how to do once I liked someone. The truth was, there was nothing difficult about taking things slow. All I had to do was let things develop naturally, so why did it feel like this was such a big deal? I wanted to tell myself it was because Gabe wasn't like any of the men I'd known and because I was starting to develop an affection for him, but I knew it was more complicated than that.

"I have a question too," he said to me after we'd placed our orders. "What does the rest of your day look like?"

"I haven't figured that out yet."

"How about our third date?"

I was a little confused. "We're on our second..."

"Yes, and this afternoon will be the third, and maybe tonight I'll take you on a fourth," he responded.

"So you're asking to spend the day with me?"

Gabe nodded with a warm smile. How was I supposed to say no to a face like that?

"I'd like that."

Twenty-Seven

There was an ease with Gabriel Warren. The only other time I'd felt something like it so quickly was when I met Leon. I often said I knew within the first few hours of meeting Leon that he and I would always be close. It was like we belonged to each other. I had been right about that feeling, and so there was a part of me that hoped I was right about Gabe, too.

He was unlike anyone I had ever met and certainly unlike anyone I had ever dated. Gabe held open doors, held my gaze when he spoke, and he answered every question with a level of honesty that was almost baffling. I may not have known very much about his demisexuality, but what I did know was that it left no doubt that he was interested in more than sex. It was comforting, in a way. I didn't even have to consider the possibility of sex being all Gabe wanted because, for the time being, sex was off the table.

When we finished brunch, Gabe and I left the diner and headed back to the place we met: Central Park. We walked for a short while, but I couldn't help but notice that rather than aimlessly strolling, Gabe seemed to have a destination in mind. I followed alongside him, my arm linked with his, but eventually, curiosity got the better of me. "Where are we going?"

"We're almost there," he simply answered.

Moments later, we arrived at a rather unremarkable bench, and Gabe stopped unexpectedly.

"We're at a bench..." I said, a little confused.

"Read it," he said as he sat down.

I followed his instructions and twisted a little to read the aging metal plaque nailed to the wood.

"'This is a place to dream things that never were and ask why not.'" I read out loud.

"So, tell me something that you dreamed of that never happened and why it didn't."

I turned to face forward and thought to myself for a few moments. There was only one thing I could think of that I dreamed of but never managed to accomplish. I peered over at Gabe out of the corner of my eye. "How deep do you want me to go with this?"

"Mariana Trench."

"I was a hopeless romantic once, and I always thought by this point in my life I'd be married," I said, choosing my words carefully so that my admission wouldn't scare him.

"So what happened?"

"I was engaged, but... he wasn't who I thought he was."

"Is that your 'why not'?"

I considered this, perhaps for the first time. *Why didn't I marry Brian?* There was the obvious answer to that: he cheated on me. However, that wasn't the Mariana Trench. That was just the surface-level answer. The truth was, I still could have married him. There were plenty of couples who worked through infidelity, but I never even considered that as an option. My silence felt like it went on forever while I contemplated Gabe's question.

"I don't think I've ever told anyone this before, but some part of me always knew he wasn't right for me. I loved him. I loved him so much that I completely blocked out all the red flags, and then when he proposed, he gave me the one thing I'd always wanted, and so I thought marrying him would be the solution to all of those problems. I'm just glad I woke up before I went through with it."

Gabe listened intently. I never once got the sense that he was judging the words coming out of my mouth. When I finished, he stood up from the bench.

"Okay, let's go find the next one."

"Wait! What about you?"

Gabe sat back down, though the look on his face told me he didn't expect me to turn the question around on him. "There was a time I wanted to be a musician," he said.

"So why didn't you?"

"I just found something else I loved. I also realized that it's okay to love something and do it because you love it, not because it's going to make you money."

I nodded. I couldn't help but remember that August also had a dream that he never accomplished. Unlike August, however, I didn't get the sense that Gabe was living a life unfulfilled. He just found a new dream. I couldn't fault him for that.

We walked a little further until we came to yet another bench.

"'How perfect this is. How lucky we are.'" I read the plaque aloud again.

"So, what makes you feel like you're lucky?" Gabe asked.

"Overall, or at the moment?"

"Both."

"I'm lucky for a lot of reasons. My line is doing well. I have amazing people around me. Generally, my life is pretty good," I said. I turned in my seat, my eyes meeting his, before I spoke again. "At the moment...you make me feel pretty lucky," I admitted.

He ran a hand through his hair as he smiled. Self-conscious, he couldn't bring himself to look at me, and so instead, he looked down at my hands in my lap.

"You make me feel pretty lucky, too," he murmured.

I placed my hand on the side of his face, and Gabe looked up at me. I wanted to kiss him, but I wasn't sure it was a move I could make without making him uncomfortable, so I hesitated, and the moment passed by us. "What about you?"

"Similar things. I have great people in my life, and I love my job."

"And what about at this moment?" I asked.

"A few days ago, I was panicking because Gail had disappeared again, and then I got a call from this amazing woman," he said.

"Oh really? Then what happened?" I asked.

"When I showed up, she was the most beautiful thing I'd ever seen."

"That sounds pretty lucky. What happened next?"

"I was petrified, so it took me days to work up the

nerve just to ask her out."

"But she went out with you?"

"She did. Then we went on a second date, then a third..."

"So, how does the story end?"

Gabe reached out, his fingertips grazing my forearm. "Maybe it doesn't."

I was a little confused and searched his olive-colored eyes for understanding. "Doesn't what?"

"End."

There weren't many times I could remember someone taking my breath away with just the words they said, but this was one of them.

We continued walking around the park for most of the afternoon, reading plaques that ranged from inspirational to bizarre. By the time the sun started to set, Gabe turned to me and said exactly what I was hoping he would.

"Do you want to go back to my place?" he asked me.

I didn't even have to think about the answer. The two of us got in a cab and took the long ride from Central Park to Brooklyn. Eventually, the car pulled up to a brownstone, and I followed Gabe inside his building and up several flights of stairs to his tiny studio apartment. It wasn't much, but the exposed brick, the extensive vinyl collection, and the vast collection of houseplants all seemed to fit perfectly with the picture of Gabe I had in my head.

"Do you mind waiting here for a minute?"

I was surprised, but nodded my head. I watched as Gabe grabbed what looked like a gym bag and disappeared out of the apartment without another word.

I briefly considered poking around a little to see what I could find out about Gabe that I didn't already know, but I thought better of it. Instead, I took a seat on the unnecessarily firm Ikea couch. I wasn't sure how long he'd be gone. It felt like an eternity, and I found the idea of letting someone in your apartment only to disappear a little strange, but I decided to suspend my judgment until I knew what was happening.

Just as I was about to get concerned, the front door to Gabe's apartment opened, and he poked his head inside.

"Come with me, please?"

I got up and did as he asked, following him out into the hallway as he locked his apartment. He led me back down the stairs of the building and out a side door. What I found was more than a little surprising. Apparently, while I was sitting in his apartment Gabe was busy at work turning the community garden in his apartment into what was easily the most magical thing I had ever walked into. On the ground, he had laid soft, woven blankets and a handful of adorably mismatched pillows. He had created some cross between a picnic and a fort. The whole thing was made even more dreamy by the golden, industrial string lights that hung from the vine covered awning overhead.

"You just did all this?"

"It's our fourth date. I had to do something special," he teased.

"If this is what I get on the fourth date, I wonder what happens on Date Twenty."

"Stick around and find out."

Gabe and I both sat down, and he wrapped his arm around me, pulling me close to him.

"Thank you for this."

"Thank you for spending the day with me."

The two of us sat quietly in the tiny little oasis that

Gabe built. We decided to order dinner, and once the delivery was confirmed, he turned to me.

"I have to admit something."

"Again?" I asked playfully. I was, of course, referring to the first admission that he was demi.

"I had a goal in mind when I did all this."

"What might that be?"

"I wanted to make sure there was no way you'd forget our first kiss."

I opened my mouth to speak, but no words came out. I had decided not to initiate anything physical with Gabe because I didn't want to cross any lines, but I desperately wanted to kiss him. He was right. There was no way I was going to forget this. He gently touched my face and then pressed his lips to mine. It was the kind of kiss I felt tingling through every inch of my body. When he pulled away, I had to mentally restrain myself from jumping right back in.

"You're right. There's no way I'm going to forget that," I breathed.

We spent what was left of the perfect day eating Chinese food and continuing to talk like two old friends who hadn't seen each other in ages. No matter how much he wanted to know about my life, I never once hesitated to tell him. I didn't even consider how short the time had been that we'd known each other because there was one thing I was sure of: I felt safe with Gabe.

We talked so much we nearly ran out of words. When I finally looked down at my phone, it was nearly midnight.

"Well, unless you have a fifth date planned, I should probably get home," I said.

"Or you could stay..." Gabe said cautiously.

I didn't know what that meant. Part of the problem

with dating someone whose desire for sex was so different from my own was that I didn't know how to gauge where his head was. If anyone else I'd dated gave me that line, I would have immediately thought they wanted to get lucky, but with Gabe, it was difficult to tell.

"What does staying mean?" I asked.

"I don't know. I just know I don't want you to go," Gabe said.

That answer was good enough for me because the truth of the matter was I didn't want to go either. I was starting to think I might not want to be anywhere that Gabe wasn't.

Twenty-Eight

For the second night in a row, I woke up in a bed that wasn't my own. This time, I was alone. I wore a well-loved Sonic Youth t-shirt in an apartment that smelled like incense and looked like it had been decorated by the manager of an Urban Outfitters.

It reminded me of the first time I met Leon. I woke up in his dorm room wearing his high school math team t-shirt. Thankfully, this time I wasn't hungover or confused about where I was. I knew I'd spent the night with Gabe. I just didn't know where he'd run off to. I sat up in his bed and looked around the apartment for some sign of him, but I quickly realized I could hear the sound of a shower running from across the room.

I didn't want to leave without saying goodbye, so while I waited I decided to check my phone for the first time in nearly twelve hours. The screen was full of alerts — text messages, voicemails, missed calls, all of

them from Leon. It had been two nights since I'd been home, and I spent them with two men Leon had never even heard of. It wasn't that Leon was entitled to know who I spent the night with, but we'd been looking after each other for the better part of ten years. I couldn't exactly blame him for being worried.

> ***Leon:*** *Jace, please pick up your phone!*
> ***Leon:*** *You haven't been home in 2 days! This isn't like you.*
> ***Leon:*** *I called Elise. You aren't there. Where are you?*
> ***Leon:*** *Please, Jacey.*
> **Me:** I'm sorry. I didn't mean to worry you. I'm on my way.

A feeling of guilt washed over me as I read his messages. I wanted to spend more time with Gabe. However, I knew that Leon was most likely crawling out of his skin with worry. I certainly would be if I were in his shoes. I got up and started to put my clothes on, hoping that I wouldn't offend Gabe with my disappearance. He'd been so sweet. The last thing I wanted him to think was that he'd done something wrong. I found a pad of paper sitting on his kitchen counter and wrote him a note, left it on the bed, and then hurried out the door.

I wasn't sure what to expect when I got home, but before I'd even stepped through the threshold of my front door, Leon grabbed me and tightly held me against his chest.

"Jesus, Jacey!" he said, sounding exasperated.

Leon and I weren't huggers. It happened on occasion, but it was never really the way we showed affection. The fact that he now held me like I might disappear was sweet, but only made me feel more guilty.

"I'm sorry," I mumbled.

In my defense, I texted him where I would be when I spent the night with Cash. I also did come home. He was just so busy with the woman whose clothes were all over our living room floor he didn't notice.

"Where the hell were you?"

"I met someone at that industry party. I was too drunk to get home, so I just crashed."

"For forty-eight hours?"

"Um...not exactly..."

"Then where were you?"

"I had a date," I said sheepishly.

"A date with who?" Leon sounded strangely shocked. It was as if my date was somehow more shocking than the fact that I'd crashed at a stranger's apartment.

"Someone I met in Central Park."

"This is a joke! This has to be a joke!"

Leon stepped away from me entirely and turned his back as if he couldn't bear the sight of me.

I stood there silently for what felt like an hour. I knew that I worried Leon with my absence, but I felt like he was overreacting. I didn't understand why he was so upset, and I definitely couldn't figure out why he seemed to think the date I had with Gabe was a bigger problem than the night I spent with Cash.

"Who was this guy?" he demanded.

"I told you. He's someone I met in Central Park," I said with a shrug. Gently, I put my hand on Leon's shoulder, urging him to turn around and look at me. "Look, I'm so sorry. I should have called. I just really like this guy, and I got caught up," I tried to explain.

The turn Leon made toward me was sharp and abrupt. The anger in his face was something I'd seen maybe once or twice in all the years I'd known him, and never once was it ever directed at me. It was so intense that it made me step back. "You're sorry?"

"Yes, Leon. I'm sorry."

"For what, Jacey? For not calling or for gallivanting all night with complete strangers?"

"Where have you been the last few months? All I've been doing is gallivanting with strangers!"

"That's not—"

"It is the same thing. You weren't mad when I went camping with Owen or when I spent the night in the Hamptons with Alex, so why is it such a big deal now?"

I hated fighting with Leon, but this was completely unfair. I knew he was worried about me, and for that, I was genuinely sorry, but he was my best friend. He wasn't my mother.

"You're such a child," Leon said angrily as he started towards his room.

I, however, was not good at backing down once a fight had started. I quickly darted in front of him, blocking the path to his bedroom.

"You know what's funny? I did come home. I came home to shower and change my clothes, and you know what I found here? Natalia!" I nearly shouted at him.

Leon closed his eyes tightly. I couldn't tell if he was remorseful or just embarrassed, but the truth remained that he lied to me. Worse yet, he lied to me about *her.*

"I just—"

"Save it! You can't get mad at me for not coming home when you lied to my face!"

"Oh yes, I can! You could have been hurt, or worse!

I get that you don't like Nat, but that doesn't give you a free pass to scare the hell out of me," he spat.

"You lied to me! You *lied*! You told me that you weren't seeing her again, and then I find size 36 Gucci on our living room floor. I'm not stupid, Leon. Who else is that small?"

"This is ridiculous. I'm not going to apologize for who I sleep with."

"So, you *are* sleeping with her?"

"That's not the point!"

"Just admit it!"

"Why do you care?"

My voice got stuck in my throat. I didn't know why. I didn't even want to admit that I cared, but the idea of the two of them together felt like it was clawing at my insides. Every time I pictured the two of them together, I felt like I was going to throw up. "I don't! If you want to get hurt again, be my guest!"

"Why are we even talking about me?" Leon snapped.

"Because we're not doing this! You don't get to criticize my choices while you're running around doing something twice as stupid!"

"How is spending the night with my ex-girlfriend more idiotic than spending the night with a guy you just met? Twice! You could have been murdered!"

"I didn't do it twice. I only did it once. Last night I was with someone I've been seeing."

"Who?"

"Why do you keep asking me that?"

"You're going through them so fast I can barely keep track," he said.

His words crashed into me. If it was Leon's goal to get me to stop fighting with him, he'd certainly accomplished that.

"You're the one who told me I had to say yes to the next five guys that came along," I said quietly, averting my gaze.

The moment he heard the hurt in my voice Leon's volume dropped immediately. "Jace, I'm sorry... I just..."

"It's fine." I stepped out of Leon's way and started towards the stairs that lead to my bedroom. This time he dashed in front of me, putting both hands on my shoulders to stop me.

"I said it's fine, Leon. Let me go," I groaned, tossing my head back.

"I'm not letting you go!" he said as he gripped my shoulders, shaking me gently, though I was sure it was just out of exasperation. "We need to talk about this."

"No, we don't." Please, just let this go.

"Can we just—-"

"How about we just agree to stay out of each other's love lives?"

Leon dropped his head and took a deep breath before taking a step back.

"I don't like the idea that there's a part of your life that I can't know about."

"I'm not trying to keep any part of my life from you, but you can't judge me for it. That's not who we are. We don't judge each other. We've never judged each other."

"You're right," he said.

"But I don't want to know about Natalia."

"I still don't get it."

I looked deep into the warmth of Leon's eyes and sighed.

"I don't know if I get it either. All I know is how it makes me feel, and I don't like it," I admitted.

"Okay," Leon said.

I could tell that he wanted to say more, but I appreciated that he didn't keep pushing for answers I didn't have.

"I'm really glad you're okay," he added.

"Thanks."

As much as I wanted to reassure my best friend that the two of us were okay and that I wasn't angry, the truth was I hadn't even begun to process how I was feeling. I just needed space. It wasn't the first time we'd fought over Natalia, but it was the first time we fought over someone I was seeing.

I went upstairs to my room, shutting the door behind me. I collapsed onto my bed and looked up at the ceiling for a while. I knew I needed to figure this out, but I didn't even know where to start. I had known Leon my entire adult life, and never once in all that time had things felt so complicated.

Before I could start digging into my feelings, I heard the text alert on my phone go off several times in a row. I assumed that it was Gabe and grabbed my phone, ready to apologize for my disappearance from his apartment. However, to my surprise, the messages weren't from Gabe at all.

> *Hey, it's Cash.*
> *I want to see you again.*
> *Fuck that. I need to see you again.*
> *Come over?*

I now had two options. I could be responsible and take the time to figure out what was going on with my friendship, or I could go running back to Cash. I wasn't even sure that I liked Cash, but the idea of picking apart my relationship with Leon until I came to some profound epiphany sounded more than a little daunting.

Truthfully, I was afraid. I was scared that when I got to the bottom of the way I was feeling, it would change everything. I wasn't ready for that. I wanted things to go back to the way they were before Natalia and before this stupid bet. Avoiding the problem was the only way I knew how to ensure that nothing would change. Instead of taking the time for myself that I ultimately needed, I decided a chaotic, 6-foot-4 painter was a better option.

Twenty-Nine

I nervously descended the stairs into my living room. I didn't want to explain to Leon why I was leaving yet again. However, in what was becoming a regular occurrence, Leon was gone. I wasn't sure how it was possible to feel both relieved and sad, but I did. There was some part of me that wanted Leon to start another fight with me. I wanted him to demand I stay home and hash out whatever was going on between us. I hated arguing with him, but deep down, I knew it meant that he cared about me.

Having it out with my best friend made me feel emotional and raw, and the truth was I needed to feel those things. Right about now, I needed to feel anything. Unfortunately, my only option appeared to be Cash, and while he was devilishly handsome and painfully sexy, he hardly struck me as someone I should be hurling my emotions at.

As my cab pulled away from the building, I realized I didn't know what I was walking into. Was this a booty call? A date? A mindlessly nondescript hang? I wasn't sure how much it mattered. The whole reason I was heading across town was to distract myself. As long as I could avoid thinking about my fight with Leon and the subsequent feelings they pointed to, it didn't matter what I was doing.

Cash buzzed me into his building without so much as asking who it was. I followed the vaguely familiar path upstairs to his apartment. It wasn't until I knocked on the door and stood there waiting for what seemed like ages that I started to question why I felt the need to do this in the first place. I strongly considered just turning around and going home, but before I could, the door to the apartment creaked open, and I was face to face with Cash again.

"Took you long enough," he said through a crooked smile.

He wore a black open-knit sweater and a pair of jeans. They both hung loosely around his lanky body. His platinum hair was a shaggy sleep-induced mess to the point that he barely resembled the man who'd taken me home from the club the other night. Yet there was still something about him that drew me in and I had to admit there were butterflies. The weekend had been a complete whirlwind, so I'd somehow forgotten just how otherworldly Cash was. My attraction to him was more than just the simple observation that he was good-looking. It was the kind of thing that could stop someone dead in their tracks, and it did. All I could do was stand there.

"What? No comeback?" he asked, feigning shock.

"You're so much hotter when you're quiet," I said before pulling at his sweater, urging him to bring his lips to mine. His kiss oddly reminded me of Owen. It was the way someone kissed you when they wanted to devour you. We stood there passionately making out in his doorway for a little too long.

"I resent that," Cash said as he pulled his mouth from mine and shut the door behind me.

"Resent what?"

"That you think I'm hotter when I'm quiet."

"Did you invite me over here to talk?" I responded.

"What if I did?"

I searched Cash's face for any sense he might be joking, but he appeared to be serious.

"That...would be disappointing," I said honestly.

He laughed, but there was an edge to the sound of it. I didn't know how, but I somehow managed to insult him.

"Look, I'm sorry...I just...thought you wanted...something else, and I could use a distraction," I explained.

"Come with me," Cash commanded more than asked. He grabbed my hand and started to lead me toward the back of his apartment.

I hoped that we would turn right and end up in his bedroom, but instead, we made a left into the room he used as a studio. Inside was a painting that I hadn't seen the other night. It was similar in style to the others, although this was arguably my favorite. It seemed more emotional and frenzied than his other pieces.

"Did you just do this?" I asked.

Cash stepped behind me, wrapping his arms around my waist and pulling me flush against him. "I was inspired," he whispered into my ear in a way that sent shivers up my spine.

Slowly, I turned to face Cash, unsure if I understood what he was trying to imply.

"By what?"

"Dude, I've been stuck for weeks. I couldn't paint anything. Then I met you and..."

"And?"

I had a hard time believing that our brief encounter suddenly struck him with inspiration. Honestly, the whole thing sounded like some highly calculated strategy to get women into bed. Who wouldn't want to be a muse? Let alone to an artist who looked the way Cash did. It was somehow swoon-worthy and cringe-worthy at the same time.

"How many times have you used that line?" I asked.

"I'm serious," Cash insisted.

To my surprise, there wasn't a hint of deception in his voice, and the look on his face was completely earnest.

"This is why I wanted you to come over," he added.

"To show me your painting?"

"To thank you."

"And how are you planning to thank me?" I coyly asked.

Cash leaned in and gently traced his lips along my neck before whispering in my ear again.

"By taking you out."

I groaned, tossing my head back in annoyance.

"That's how you react to me asking you on a date?"

"How often do you actually go on dates?"

"You think you have me all figured out, don't you?"

"Don't I?"

I knew that wasn't fair. The only thing I knew about Cash was that he partied hard. Most of my assumptions came from the way he looked and the night we met. I wasn't giving him a chance. Plus, technically, I was supposed to say yes to five dates. Cash and I might have spent the night together, but that wasn't exactly a date. If I agreed now, I would have successfully reached Date Number Five.

"Okay, you're right. I don't do this," he admitted. "I don't even know what I'm doing. All I know is that this is the best work I've ever done, and I did it right after I met you."

"Okay..."

"Okay?"

"Yes, I will go out with you," I said, though my tone was less than enthusiastic.

"Yes!" Cash said, hopping up and down a little like an excited child.

The next several hours with Cash were both whirlwind and fairy tale. He dragged me all over Manhattan. His idea of a date was half pub-crawl, half gallery crawl, and a lot of making out. By the time we clamored back to his apartment, I was drunk, not just on the unreasonable amount of alcohol I had consumed, but on the aqua blue of Cash's eyes and the way his mouth tasted.

"Sit. I'll make you a drink," Cash said to me as we walked back in the door.

"I cannot have any more drinks. I am... too small," I slurred.

I attempted to sit down on some ultra-modern piece of furniture. I couldn't quite tell if it was a chair or a sculpture, but it didn't matter. I made one very poor attempt at leaning on it, missed the uniquely shaped hunk of plastic entirely, and crashed onto the floor.

"Shit!" Cash exclaimed as he rushed over to me. "Are

you okay?"

I nodded my head.

"Be careful baby," he said as he pushed away a stray strand of my hair.

"Be careful with that word," I warned him.

"You don't like it when I call you baby?" he asked me in a way that made it clear he already knew the answer.

"I like it too much."

In my drunken stupor, I decided that laying on the floor was a much better idea than continuing to sit upright, so without warning, I dramatically collapsed onto my back and stared up at the high ceilings of Cash's apartment.

"You are so drunk," Cash laughed, shaking his head.

"Then come be drunk with me," I responded, pulling at his sweater, urging him to join me on the floor.

He laid down next to me, head next to mine, but his body angled in the opposite direction. I slid my fingers into his platinum hair as we both lay there swimming in thick, euphoric intoxication.

"What's going on in there?" Cash asked me slowly.

"In where?"

Softly he tapped on my forehead, indicating that he wanted to know what I was thinking.

"I don't want to like you," I said honestly.

"Too late," he responded with a laugh.

I shook my head, but he was right. When I left his apartment forty-eight hours ago, I thought I had no interest in the man, and yet here I was, wanting to drown in him. If I were a bit more sober, I might have thought for a second about what I was doing. I would have considered that only hours ago I was in the middle of some huge emotional fight with Leon, and hours before that I was asleep in Gabe's arms. I kept throwing my feelings at every man that showed up in my life, hoping that something would stick. What started as some stupid wager with my best friend had now turned me into someone I didn't recognize.

I was suddenly grateful that I couldn't keep my head straight enough to sort anything out. Deep down, that was the whole reason I came here. I didn't care about Cash. I just wanted him to numb the aching in my chest that started when I saw Natalia's clothes all over my living room floor.

"Tell me something real," I said.

"Something real?" Cash repeated.

"Yes."

"Alright..." he said before looking away from me, turning his attention to the ceiling above us. He lay there for a long time, completely motionless.

"You showed up too soon."

I didn't respond right away. I wasn't sure if my lack of understanding was due to him being intentionally vague, or because the alcohol in my bloodstream was preventing me from grasping something.

"What does that mean?" I finally asked.

"I was not ready to be into someone the way I'm into you," he said.

Despite myself and my disbelief, I smiled. "So, what are you going to do about that?"

"I don't know. Inconveniently fall in love?"

I let out a loud, over-the-top laugh.

"Has anyone ever told you, you're hard to impress?" he playfully complained.

"I'm not," I said, trying to maintain my staring contest with the lighting fixture above me. Each time I looked over at Cash, I lost a little more of my resolve not to fall for him, and so I refused to meet his heavy-lidded gaze. "I've just done this before," I added.

"Done what before?"

"There are two types of men. There are conquerors, and there are poets."

"And which am I supposed to be?"

"You are a poet," I said.

"Okay, what does that mean?"

"Conquerors want women because they want to feel superior to them. They usually don't even like women. They just want to possess them. Now, poets, those are the dangerous ones. Poets fall madly in love for a night or a week or a month until their next muse comes along, and they fall right out of it."

I expected Cash to deny that was the case, but instead, he reached for my face, making me look at him. When I did, he kissed me. Unlike the dozens of other times he kissed me in the short time I'd known him, this kiss was tender. Every encounter my lips had with his was loaded with need and testosterone. This kiss was different, special even. He wasn't trying to seduce me or convince me of anything. He just wanted to connect with me.

That was when it occurred to me: I could dismiss him as many times as I wanted, but there was something about Cash. It was something, despite my better judgment, that made me want more.

I knew I was at a crossroads. It would be easy to spend the night with Cash. I could crash my mouth back into his and drunkenly drag him back to his bedroom. I would get the distraction I wanted, and Leon would be forced to sit at home wondering where I was, but I kept picturing his face the moment I walked through the door.

Leondro Acosta, my rock, my best friend, and perhaps the strongest person I knew, was legitimately terrified for me. As mad as I was at him, I couldn't do that to him again, so I made a choice.

"I should probably get home," I said, sitting up slowly.

"You're not staying?"

I shook my head and looked over at the clock on the wall. "I haven't been home in the last couple of nights, and my best friend worries," I honestly explained.

"But you're drunk," he said, grasping at strings to try to get me to stay.

"Yeah, but I'm just going to jump in a cab. I'll be fine."

"At least let me ride with you. I don't want anything to happen to you."

I was surprised at Cash's sudden sense of chivalry, but instead of questioning it, I just nodded.

He stood up and offered me his hand. When he pulled me to my feet, he wrapped his arms around me and lowered his lips to my ear. "Are you sure I can't get you to stay?" he asked.

This time I didn't hesitate at all. "I should go home."

Cash and I rode quietly in the cab from his apartment to mine. He had his arm wrapped around my body as I leaned into him. I wasn't sure if our silence was because we had nothing to say to each other, or if we'd simply run out of words after spending the entire day together.

When the cab stopped, I wordlessly kissed Cash on the cheek and got out. The walk to my front door seemed endless. When I got inside, the lights were off, and Leon's bedroom door was closed. Thankfully, there were no tiny designer garments slung across the floor. I didn't want to wake him up, or worse yet, get into another fight, so I just fished a piece of paper out of my purse and scribbled down a note.

I love you. I'm sorry.

Thirty

If there were rules to falling for someone, I didn't know what they were. I didn't know how long I was supposed to know someone or how many dates I was supposed to go on. I certainly didn't know if they were supposed to be the only person in my life or if it was possible to fall for someone while still wading through a sea of others. What I did know, however, was that Cash Mason now took up every inch of space in my mind. It had been two weeks since I went over to his apartment in an attempt to distract myself from Leon, and in those two weeks, I completely lost myself.

"Intense" was the only way I could describe it. According to Cash, he was addicted to me. If I was honest, I couldn't bring myself to stay away from him, either. I rarely went home, spending my days at work, my nights in his mess of a bedroom, and my weekends laying on the floor of his studio working on designs while he

painted. I never felt this way about anyone before. We fed off of each other creatively, and he understood me in a way that even the people closest to me couldn't.

Yet one fact remained: despite spending every day of the last fourteen together, Cash and I didn't have sex. I wasn't sure how it was possible, especially when everything about Cash screamed seduction, but something seemed to come up night after night. I was starting to wonder just how long he could come up with excuses. I didn't understand why Cash wouldn't sleep with me. I got the impression he slept with plenty of women, but he seemed to have no interest in doing so with me. I didn't feel comfortable enough to question him. One of the things I'd discovered about him was that he wasn't exactly open to explaining himself. Instead, I just went along with it, hoping for some logical explanation for his sudden chastity.

I enjoyed living in a bubble with Cash, but eventually, the real world came calling in the form of Elise's first bridal gown appointment.

There was probably nothing more exquisite or pretentious than the bridal salon at Bergdorf Goodman. Each gown was worth more than some people's entire yearly salary, and the chandelier that hung in the center of the room was enough to put the stage decorators from *Phantom of the Opera* to shame. Everything was a nauseating shade of cream except for the over-the-top red velvet sofa I sat on with Elise's two bridesmaids, Emma and Claire.

Emma Thorpe was Elise's roommate in college, and arguably her best friend. She sat a good six inches taller than me with a head of honey blonde hair and cat-like green eyes. She and Leon dated for a short time when we were about twenty. Though they both seemed more than happy to pretend it never happened. Claire Hastings was our childhood playmate. She grew up in the house next door, and we sometimes joked that she was "the third Lange daughter". Her petite frame, chestnut hair, and brown eyes all resembled ours, so it was easy to assume we were related.

Both women had been a part of our lives so long they felt like family, and yet I felt out of place. Perhaps it was because the last time I was in a bridal salon, I was trying on my wedding dress, and here I was, unmarried. I tried to push the negativity out of my mind and focus on my sister. It was her day, after all. I didn't want to ruin it with my less than sunny attitude.

While Elise and the bridal consultant went to work getting her into the first gown, the attention in the room suddenly turned to me.

"Okay, please catch me up on everything! What is going on with you, Jace?" Claire asked before taking a sip of complimentary champagne.

"Um...not much, just..."

"Elise says you're dating again?" Emma chimed in.

I wanted to respond with some sarcastic remark or roll my eyes, but instead, I just plastered a smile on my face.

"A little, yeah. It was time to get back out there," I answered.

"Totally! You're such a catch! Have you met anyone special?" Claire said in her typically cheery tone. She looked at me expectantly as she leaned forward in her seat.

"How's Leon?" Emma asked before I could answer Claire.

Emma was not the ball of sunshine that Claire was.

She was practical, maybe a little cynical, but most importantly, she broke up with Leon years ago because she was convinced something was going on between us. I figured, after all this time, she would have given up on that idea. Yet, I couldn't help but notice how perfectly timed her question was.

"Leon's good; he just got a promotion, and I think he's been seeing his ex again," I said with a shrug.

"You think?"

"Wait, I don't want to hear about Leon's love life. I want to know about yours!"

The two of them talking over each other was starting to make my head spin, so I decided to answer both questions at once.

"Leon and I don't talk about our love lives, and I'm seeing someone right now. It's new, but he's—"

"Since when do you and Leon not talk about your love lives?" Elise jumped in.

I'd been so busy being grilled by her friends that I hadn't noticed Elise emerge from the dressing room. She wore an ivory-colored architectural gown that hung off one shoulder and had cutaways on the sides. It was a beautiful dress from a high fashion perspective, but it certainly wasn't "her".

"I don't know about this one," Emma unknowingly agreed, tilting her head to the side in obvious confusion.

"It looked better on the runway," Elise said dismissively before turning her attention back to me. "You and Leon tell each other everything," she said, still waiting for my response.

"He started seeing Natalia again, and I'm not supportive of that, so we decided to keep our romantic relationships private," I explained.

Both Elise and Emma looked at me skeptically while Claire seemed to have no idea what was happening. Thankfully the bridal consultant came out with another dress in hand. "Why don't we try the Vera?" she asked.

Elise followed the consultant back to the dressing room while I was, once again, left with the bridesmaids.

"What's wrong with his ex?" Emma asked.

What she was doing was completely transparent. I generally liked Emma, but I didn't like the way she was digging. "She hurt him really badly the last time they dated, and I don't want that to happen again," I said. In an attempt to appear disinterested, I picked up a catalog of gowns off the mirrored coffee table in front of us and started to flip through the pages.

"So who's this guy? What does he do?" Claire asked me.

I wanted to shut down all the questions, but what else were we supposed to do while Elise was trying on dresses? Either I answered the invasive questions or told them to cut it out and sat there in uncomfortable silence. I sighed heavily. For the sake of my sister, I decided to play nice.

"His name is Cash. He's an artist," I said, looking up from the magazine in my lap.

"Do you think it's serious?"

I thought about the question for a second before I answered it on auto-pilot. It was far more complicated than a yes or no answer. On one hand, I was spending more time with Cash than I did with any of the other guys I had been seeing. On the other hand, I had a hard time imagining Cash wanting to settle down with anyone. He was too erratic. He was rarely sober, and while he liked to call me things like his muse or his drug, neither implied permanence.

"I don't know. It's new but I really like him." I responded carefully.

"You really like who?" Elise said, appearing again.

This time it was a strapless lace and organza ball gown. The dress was beautiful and much closer to the mark, but I couldn't help but notice how the huge skirt seemed to overshadow my tiny sister.

"That's a lot of dress," I said to her, hoping that she wasn't madly in love with it.

"Who are we talking about?" Elise said, paying no attention to my comments.

"Cash," I responded.

Repulsion pulled at the corner of Elise's upper lip, and I instantly regretted saying anything at all.

"The one with the tattoos?"

Elise only knew the guys I dated by the photos I sent her to prove I was taking the bet seriously. She didn't bother to remember their names or much of what I told her about them.

"Yeah," I responded before quickly turning to the consultant. "Do you maybe have a similar silhouette without the huge overskirt?" I asked.

"I'm sure we have some options. Let me go take a look," the consultant said.

As the woman went digging through the racks, my sister jumped right back in.

"What about August?"

"We've been over this, Elise. August was a dick."

"You barely gave him a chance," she whined.

As soon as Elise heard that August and her fiancé might have gone to the same private school, she was convinced this meant he had money and made it her mission to convince me that he was the one. I thought she'd let it go after I stopped seeing him. After all, I never even bothered to confirm that August went to school with Nate, but my sister insisted on bringing him up anytime she had the chance. Regardless of how Elise felt about it, I refused to date someone who could say the demeaning things August had about my work.

"I think I might really have something with Cash."

August Henry was a thing of the past, and while I couldn't say I knew for sure that Cash was in my future, I was starting to think I might want him to be.

The bridal consultant pulled a few more options, and my sister continued her fashion show.

"Do you have a picture?" Claire said, scooting closer to me on the sofa.

At least someone was excited for me. I unlocked my phone and scrolled a bit until I found a picture of Cash and me together and handed the phone to my childhood friend.

"Elise wasn't kidding. That's a lot of tattoos!"

This time I didn't hold back in rolling my eyes. Emma reached across me and pulled the phone out of Claire's hands.

"Damn..." she said, sounding almost surprised.

"I know," I said.

Tattoos or no tattoos, Cash was beautiful. I took the phone back from her and looked down at the picture for a long moment. I had no idea what it was about this mess of a man that brought me to my knees, but what I did know was that there was no escaping the way I felt. I had long accepted that Cash was going to be a mistake. Yet, I missed him. I wanted him.

I was falling in love with him.

Elise once again emerged from the dressing room.

This time the dress was a cap sleeve ball gown with a tulle skirt that reminded me of Audrey Hepburn in *Funny Face*. It was stunning. The polished, vintage look matched Elise's style perfectly and the pure white fabric was the perfect contrast to her dark hair and eyes. I'd never seen my sister look more beautiful.

"Oh my god!" Claire exclaimed, nearly jumping out of her seat.

"Wow!" Emma echoed.

I just sat there looking up at her. Elise looked incredible. The dress was everything I wanted for her. I'd always pictured my sister walking down the aisle in something that was uniquely Elise: timeless, elegant, strong. Anyone looking at her face could already tell this was it. It was her dress.

"I like it but... should I try on more gowns? Three doesn't seem like enough."

"Are you kidding me? It's perfect!" Claire said.

"I just don't know..." Elise turned around, craning her neck to see the v-shaped open back, her eyes narrowing as she tried to pick out any visible flaws.

There was no way I could let my sister walk out of this salon without that dress. It was perfect for her. I stood up and grabbed Elise by the shoulders, turning her back around to face the wall of mirrors behind her. "This is it, Ellie," I said to her.

I wrapped my arms around her from behind and rested my chin on her shoulder.

"Are you sure?"

I nodded my head, and as I looked at my sister in the mirrors in front of me, I could feel the tears welling up behind my ears.

"Don't cry! You're going to make me cry!"

"Shut up! I'm not crying," I sniffled with a laugh.

It was a perfect moment, but as I stepped away so the consultant could start taking Elise's measurements, a wave of sadness washed over me. I not only remembered the wedding gown gathering dust in the back of my closet, but I also realized, despite how badly I'd always wanted this, I might not ever have it again.

Thirty-One

In the twenty-nine years I had been alive, I never really found myself in the position to break someone's heart. One could argue that I broke Brian's heart when I left him, but leaving was merely a reaction to finding him underneath my assistant. It wasn't exactly a choice I made. Plus, I wasn't sure I believed that Brian ever had a heart to begin with.

Gabriel Warren, however? That was an entirely different situation.

It was impossible not to like Gabe. He was the kind of guy that would make any girl want to settle down. He was handsome, sweet, and patient. Hell, he took care of little old ladies for a living! There was nothing not to like. It could be argued that of all the guys I'd met during this bet, Gabe was the best of them. That was precisely what made the situation so hard.

During the two weeks I spent glued to Cash's side,

Gabe reached out to me more than a few times. I didn't know what I wanted. I just knew that I would rather be spending time with Cash than anyone else. I told Gabe that I was going through something and that I just needed some time. He was respectful of that, but it didn't stop him from sending me encouraging texts, checking on me when he had the chance, and even sending me flowers. Every time I looked down at my phone and saw Gabe's name, my heart ached a little. I felt terrible, not only for lying to him, but because deep down, I knew that Gabe was the better choice. I just couldn't let Cash go. He was this fixation I couldn't shake.

After helping my sister pick out her wedding dress, a realization hit me. I was falling in love with Cash. I didn't know how a man I gave no regard to when we met had somehow become the center of my universe, but he had. I wasn't sure I was ready to say it out loud, but I knew I couldn't leave Gabe thinking that I was having some crisis while in reality, I was falling for someone else, so I decided to be brave.

I could feel my heart fall into my stomach as I approached Gabe's aged, brick building. Logically, I knew that my flirtation with him had been brief and that I didn't owe him anything. Yet, I also knew that he was special. I'd known it from the day I met him. He wasn't the kind of person I was just going to ghost and forget about. What scared me was the likelihood that I would live to regret the choice I was about to make.

I pressed the button labeled "G. Warren" on the intercom before hearing a loud buzz and the click of the lock opening. I took the stairs slowly, each step making my legs feel heavier than the last. I couldn't seem to figure out if the reason I didn't want to do this was that

I didn't want to hurt Gabe, or because I didn't want to hurt myself. No matter how slowly I walked, I knew I would eventually reach the front door.

I stared at his door for a long time and then knocked, but before I had a chance to steady myself, the door opened and there he was. I opened my mouth to speak, but before a single sound escaped me, Gabe wrapped me tightly in his arms. I took in a deep breath and inhaled the familiar scent of his cologne. Hints of cinnamon reminded me of Christmas. I had to admit, it was hard to step away.

"God, I missed you..." he murmured into my hair before pulling back to look at me.

"I missed you too," I said awkwardly.

I didn't know if it was the tone of my voice or the uncomfortable look on my face, but it was as if Gabe immediately knew what was going on in my head. I could see the worry written all over him.

"Come in..." he said.

He took me by the hand and brought me to the tiny, taupe Ikea couch in the middle of the room. We sat in awkward silence for much too long. We were only a few feet apart, but to me, it felt like miles. I didn't want to do this. For a moment, I rationalized that I didn't have to. Cash hadn't asked me for a commitment. I wasn't even sure that he was interested in one, but the fact remained that Gabe deserved better than that. I couldn't keep seeing him with one foot out the door. We had only known each other for a short time, but I could already tell that Gabe was one of the best people I knew. He didn't just deserve better than the way I'd treated him. He deserved better than me.

"You said you needed to talk?" Gabe said, finally

ending the silence between us.

I nodded my head slowly. "Yeah, I just don't know how," I responded.

I watched Gabe shift nervously before he spoke again. "Why do I have a feeling I'm not going to like this?" he asked me.

"You're probably not."

Another uncomfortable silence fell over the room. I watched Gabe continue to fidget, unable to make eye contact with me.

"Can I say something first?" he interjected.

"Sure."

"I can guess what you're about to say, and I can guess why. This kind of thing happens to me a lot, but I want you to know that I think you're amazing, and even if you think being with someone like me is too difficult, I would still really like to be a part of your life."

"Someone like you?"

"This isn't about...?"

"No! No. God, no. Your sexuality isn't the issue," I quickly reassured him.

"Then I don't understand."

The truth was, I didn't understand either. I knew that people always said the heart wanted what it wanted, but now that I was sitting here, all I could think was that I wished my heart was smarter.

"Can I be honest?"

"Please."

"There's someone else."

I saw the shock of that statement hit Gabe, yet he didn't say anything for a long moment. It was almost as if he was coming up with the best possible reaction.

"Thank you for being honest about that," he said

carefully.

"Don't thank me." I didn't understand why he was so kind about this.

"I'm sure that's not easy to say to someone."

"None of this is easy."

"You know you don't owe me an explanation, right?"

"I know that. I'm not here because I think I owe you something."

"Then why are you here?"

Now I was the one fidgeting as I tried to come up with an answer to that question. Why was I here? Gabe and I had been on a handful of dates, kissed a few times, and slept in the same bed once. He wasn't my boyfriend, and I'd never promised him that he would be, and yet I was treating this like a breakup.

"You know how you said that you would still really like to be a part of my life?"

"Yeah..."

"Well, I would still really like to be a part of yours, but the only way I can do that is if I'm honest with you," I explained.

Gabe nodded, seeming to finally understand why I was making such a big deal out of something so seemingly small.

"Okay, then be honest with me," he said.

"His name is Cash. I met the two of you around the same time, and the last thing I was expecting was that I would develop feelings for him but...I did."

"I can't hold that against you."

"I feel terrible about it," I admitted.

"You shouldn't," he said. Gabe scooted a little closer to me on the couch and hesitantly took my hand in his. "I'm not saying I don't wish things were different, because I do, but you can't beat yourself up for the way you feel, or I guess in this case...don't feel."

"That's just it. I do have feelings for you. That's why this is hard. No part of me wants to do this, but I genuinely care about you, and so I don't want to mislead you."

"Thank you," he said.

"Stop thanking me," I gently protested with a laugh. "You're the only person I've ever met who thanks someone for breaking up with them."

"Are we breaking up?" he laughed.

His laughter was a pleasant distraction. It made me feel a little less terrible about the possibility of hurting him.

"Am I overthinking this?"

Gabe moved closer to me yet again. This time he was close enough that I could feel his knees brush mine. I knew it was wrong, and perhaps even selfish, but there was a part of me that wanted to keep him near. I knew I couldn't have my cake and eat it, too. I also knew that there was no way I could have something serious with either one of them. Not if I was seeing them both. The problem was, there was no denying the way I felt about Gabe.

"You're not overthinking it. I just don't want you to beat yourself up about it."

A thousand conflicting emotions churned in my head. The grace with which Gabe treated this was nothing short of incredible. I doubted that I would be as kind if someone I was interested in unexpectedly decided they would rather spend their time with someone else.

"Does that mean we're okay?"

"Jacey, I'm not going to pretend like this doesn't sting or like I might not need a little time, but I meant it when

I said I would like to be a part of your life."

"I meant it, too."

"Then let's do that. It doesn't have to be so difficult."

I sighed. Gabe made this whole thing so easy, and yet I didn't feel better.

"Okay," I relented.

He reached out and pulled me into him, hugging me yet again. I closed my eyes and tried to remember everything. I committed to memory the depth of his kindness, the feeling of his arms around me, and any other detail I could pull from such a fleeting moment.

While Gabe seemed optimistic that we could still be friends, I wasn't so sure. I wanted his friendship, but I'd never actually seen two people who were once romantically interested in each other successfully become platonic friends.

"I hope he knows how lucky he is," Gabe said to me as he pulled away.

I leaned in and kissed his cheek gently. "I hope you know how amazing you are."

We talked for a while longer. I got the sense that Gabe was trying to cheer me up. It baffled me how anyone could be so selfless. Here I was, telling him that I no longer wanted to see him and all that seemed to matter to him was that I was okay. I didn't know how a man like Gabe existed and stranger still, I didn't know how it was possible that I was giving him up.

Thirty-Two

I took a cab back to Cash's apartment. Inside the musty, yellow sedan, I stared out the windows while a ballad in a language I didn't understand played in the background. I felt sad, sadder than I thought I would be. I knew that I did the right thing by telling Gabe the truth. Yet, something didn't feel right. If I was honest with myself, nothing felt quite right. I couldn't name the actual feeling, but it was as if everything in my life was just slightly off. I'd always thought that the only two things I needed were art and romance. I figured that if I could create and I was in love, I would be happy.

Yet here I was, unhappy.

For some reason, the face that kept running through my mind as I stared at the traffic next to me was Leon's. Sure, I would miss Gabe's optimism and the beautiful lens through which he saw me, but I knew that ultimately, I could live without him. Leon, however, felt

further and further away with every passing day, and I felt helpless to fix it. Maybe this was just what happened to friends over time. They get into relationships, and the focus shifts until what used to be the center of your entire world turns into the occasional text message on holidays. The thought of not being close to Leon pained me. That, paired with knowing how badly I would miss Gabe, made me feel like I was suffocating.

When the cab dropped me off, I was in no condition to see anyone. However, I knew Cash expected me, and I feared what I might find if I went home. I knew the last thing I could handle was another trail of Natalia's clothes all over my living room. I decided to swallow down my feelings and hoped that seeing Cash would make me feel better somehow.

By now, I knew the code to get into Cash's building. I made my way to the front door and opened it without knocking. It was strange how comfortable I had become in this space in such a short time.

"Is that you, Babe?" Cash called out from his studio.

"Yeah!" I yelled back.

"I'll be right out."

I flopped down on a rigid white armchair. It certainly wasn't comfortable, but nothing in Cash's apartment was. Leather furniture, concrete floors, modern angular sculptures that didn't go together; even the fridge was devoid of anything but ketchup packets and vodka. Not unlike the man himself, the apartment was all aesthetics and very little substance.

A few minutes passed, and then I watched breathlessly as Cash emerged from the back of the apartment. He was shirtless, covered in paint, and his hair was a complete mess. It was the version of Cash that I was sure I was in love with: chaotic and beautiful. My eyes never left him as he took long strides toward me, stopping directly in front of the chair. I gazed up at him through my lashes, and he smiled at me before leaning down and kissing my forehead.

"You look sad," he observed.

"I'm fine," I said.

I had no interest in discussing the war zone in my head with Cash, or anyone for that matter. He wasn't exactly the most understanding person I'd ever met.

"Everyone knows that when a girl says she's fine, it's code for 'I'm about to lose it,'" he gently teased.

"I'm not about to lose it. I just had a hard day."

"Tell me about it." He nudged me over so he could fit sideways next to me in the chair. I moved over slightly, and the two of us adjusted. It wasn't exactly comfortable, but being close to him was nice.

I tilted my head to one side to look at him, gauging whether I should be honest about how I was feeling.

"Are you sure you want to hear about this?" I asked.

"Out with it."

"I kind of had to break up with someone today," I sighed.

As soon as the words came out of my mouth, I realized I phrased them completely wrong, but it was too late. Cash's face already started to contort with anger.

"What the fuck?"

"I mean...I was..."

"Seriously, what the fuck, Jacey?"

"It's not..."

I kept trying and trying to come up with the words, but my lack of explanation was only making him angrier. Abruptly, he stood up and took several steps away from me before crossing his long arms over his chest.

"Talk!"

I felt the absence of his warmth next to me like some kind of hole. I wanted to rewind the last several seconds and start over. I should have just kept my mouth shut.

"'Breakup' is the wrong word. There was someone interested in me who I went on a few dates with before I met you, and he has been trying to get a hold of me in the last couple of weeks, so I told him I couldn't see him anymore," I explained.

That wasn't exactly true. I knew very well that there was some overlap between Cash and Gabe, but I wasn't about to tell him that, especially when he was so angry.

"You can see whoever the fuck you want," he snapped before stomping his way to the kitchen and the bottle of vodka in his fridge.

I didn't know why, but instead of feeling like I'd done something wrong, my emotions immediately switched to anger.

"You're right! I can!" I fired back at him loudly. "It's not like you're even interested in being in a relationship with me!"

Cash opened the bottle and quickly hammered back a shot's worth of vodka before glaring daggers at me. "Is that seriously what you think?"

"What the hell am I supposed to think? We aren't dating unless you consider 'dating' getting drunk with your friends or hanging around this apartment, and we certainly aren't sleeping together."

"Great, so if I fucked you and never spoke to you again, you'd think I was an asshole, but when I care about you enough to hold back, you think I don't want you. I can't win!"

"Okay, Mr. Communication, how the fuck would I know that?"

It was the first fight Cash and I ever had. Much like my fight with Leon, I both hated and quietly loved it. On the one hand, he was being completely unreasonable, and I had no idea how this would end. On the other hand, I knew that if he was fighting with me it meant he cared about me.

"You cannot be serious right now. You tell me you've been seeing someone else this whole time, and suddenly I'm the bad guy."

"Great, now not only can he not communicate, but he can't listen, either! That is not even close to what I said."

Instead of responding, Cash took another shot, and while his drinking typically didn't bother me, this time, I was in no mood to put up with it. "You know what? I don't need this!" I marched over to my purse and slung the oversized bag over my shoulder before turning back to him. "This is ridiculous. You're not my boyfriend, you're not in love with me, you're just mad that someone else wanted something you thought was yours, and so you're throwing a fit."

I expected Cash to keep fighting with me or perhaps kick me out entirely, but instead, he crossed the distance between us in mere seconds. He towered over me, and while Cash might not have been all that intimidating under normal circumstances, when he was angry, he was downright scary.

"Say that again," he demanded.

I didn't think that Cash had any intention of hurting me. That didn't make the way he was standing over me any less aggressive. I, however, refused to back down from this. I was too angry. "What is this? Are you trying to scare me now?"

Cash grabbed the strap of my purse, pulling it off my arm. He roughly threw the bag toward the floor. It landed with a loud thud that vibrated through the room. "Say it again!"

"Say what again? What the hell do you want, Cash?"

He pulled me toward him forcefully and brought his mouth dangerously close to mine.

"Tell me again I don't fucking love you," he growled.

Before I could say a word or even process what he just implied, he kissed me hard. It was the last thing I expected. I froze before my thoughts were able to catch up with me. Once they did, I wrapped my arms around his neck, pulling him closer to me as I kissed him back. My head was screaming at me to leave. I was still so angry, but my heart banged loudly in my chest, and my body desperately wanted him.

When he pulled back, I gasped for air. "Please," I begged him, assuming that he knew what I wanted.

I was tired of nights spent cuddling, I was tired of excuses. I wanted Cash, and I wanted all of him. I could feel he wanted me, too, so I didn't understand what it was we were waiting for.

"I can't..." he said quietly.

"Why?" I asked, my voice pleading.

"Because the first time we do this isn't going to be when I'm pissed at you," he seethed.

I couldn't exactly argue with that, but the pent-up need inside me made me want to scream. I clamped my eyes shut. I had to get a hold of myself and I knew I couldn't do that when I was positively feral.

"Maybe I should go home," I said slowly as I willed myself to calm down.

"This weekend," he said.

"What about it?"

"I have a gallery showing."

"Yes, I know. What does that have to do with—"

"After."

My eyes searched his to make sure I understood what he was trying to say.

"Okay," I said to him. "I should still probably go."

"You don't have to—"

"I know. I just need to clear my head, okay?"

I didn't know that I needed to clear my head so much as I knew I couldn't spend another night in his bed without being "with" him. It was too hard, and I was dealing with far too many emotions to put forth the effort that holding myself back would take. In the back of my head I knew that this was yet another example of the pattern I repeated over and over again. Why was I always so convinced that if someone wasn't sleeping with me, they didn't want me? Even now. Even when I knew better.

"Okay." He picked my discarded purse up off the floor and handed it to me carefully. "I'm sorry," he said.

"Me too."

With that, I turned and headed for the door. I didn't kiss Cash or assure him that things would be okay because the truth was, I wasn't sure that they would be. I just knew that I couldn't figure that out if I stayed the night there.

I spent another long cab ride staring out the window in silence. I just kept replaying the last few minutes of our fight in my mind. Cash had all but said that he loved me, and I knew I was falling in love with him, so what was wrong with me? I should have been jumping out of my skin with excitement, but instead, I felt worse than I did when I left Gabe's apartment.

When I got home, I went straight to my room. I didn't even bother looking in the living room. If Natalia was there, I couldn't handle seeing it, and while it might have been nice to tell my best friend what I was going through, I was exhausted and simply out of words. I wanted normalcy, and at that moment, the most normal thing I could do was hide out in my bedroom and watch old *Project Runway* episodes until I fell asleep.

Thirty-Three

The week went by slowly and without incident. Instead of camping out in Cash's apartment, I decided to give the fight between us some air. I was well aware that Cash and I were burning too hot, too fast. If we didn't come up to breathe, something bad was bound to happen. We both apologized to each other, but my life still felt crooked. Without Cash to distract me, the sense that something was wrong only amplified.

Work kept my mind occupied. When Alex disappeared, it was not only from my life but from his contract. Nia wanted to get a lawyer involved, but I convinced her it was better to find another model. The last thing I needed was to start a war. Alex might not have been handling this professionally, but spending the weekend with him in the Hamptons was hardly professional, either. Luckily, we found another model, and for far less than what we'd agreed to pay Alex, which

was enough to make Nia happy. I did, however, have to bribe her with babysitting to keep her from giving me the world's longest lecture on not mixing business with pleasure, which was how I ended up with a five-year-old in my apartment before Cash's opening.

"There's my little monster!" I said as I opened the door for Nia and her daughter, Nichelle.

"Aunt Jacey!" Nichelle exclaimed before rushing towards me and wrapping her tiny arms around my legs.

"Who is this? You can't be my Shelly! You're too big to be my Shelly!" I playfully gasped, squatting down to her level.

Nichelle giggled. "Where's Leon?" she asked me.

It seemed that all women, even the tiny ones, were in love with my best friend.

"I don't know. Maybe he's hiding. Why don't you go find him?"

That was all Nichelle needed to hear. She immediately took off running into the apartment.

"What time are you leaving for that show?" Nia asked me absently.

"Around eight."

"Okay, I should be able to come to pick her up around 5."

"Sounds good," I said.

"Thank you for watching her."

"Thank you for not lecturing me," I responded with a cheeky smile.

"We both know you're gonna earn yourself another one sooner or later."

"Alex is long gone, don't worry."

"Yes, and now you're hung up on some artist with more tattoos than brain cells."

"Hey!"

"You know it's true, Jacey."

"It's serious. I think I might be falling for him," I explained.

"What?" Nia all but yelled in response. "You are not in love."

"How would you know?"

"You don't think I've known you long enough to know when you're in love?"

"Who's in love?" Leon said, entering the room with Nichelle in his arms.

"Apparently, your best friend is," Nia answered, rolling her eyes.

"I—"

"Guess you're not getting your room back," Leon teased.

"Don't you have plans?" I said to Nia. Both to change the subject and verbally nudge her towards the door.

"Alright, I'm gone. I'll see you in a few hours," she said before turning her attention to her daughter. "What are we today, Shell?"

"Brave!" the little girl said excitedly in response.

"That's right! Be good for your Aunt Jacey."

With that, Nia kissed her daughter on the cheek and disappeared down the hall.

"Aunt Jacey, I'm hungry," Nichelle complained as soon as I shut the door to the apartment.

"I guess we have to make some food then," I said, reaching out and taking Nichelle out of Leon's arms and adjusting her on my hip. "Sorry, I didn't mean to interrupt you," I muttered as I shuffled past Leon into the kitchen.

"Are you kidding me? I couldn't miss the chance to

hang out with my favorite princess."

"Mama says I'm not a princess. I'm the hero!"

I smiled. As soon as Nia found out she was having a girl, she was determined to take a progressive stance on parenting. Nichelle played with any toys that interested her, no matter the intended gender. She picked out her own clothes. She wasn't pushed to do anything traditionally feminine, and every day she and Nia would pick out an affirmation about what kind of person she would be that day. Today Nichelle was brave. Nia wanted to raise a strong little girl, and anyone who spent more than five minutes with her daughter could tell that was exactly what she was.

Leon dramatically hit himself in the forehead as if he should have known this.

"You're right! Look at how big and strong you are!"

Nichelle held her arms up like she was flexing her muscles, and Leon quickly did the same.

I had to admit that it was nice seeing Leon like this. It had been too long since I'd seen him laughing and acting like a kid. It reminded me just how much I had missed him.

"Do you mind if I hang out?" he asked me.

"I'd like that," I said with a smile before turning to look in the fridge to see if we had anything fit to feed a five-year-old. "So, what does the hero want to eat?" I asked Nichelle.

"Chicken fingers!"

Her answer wasn't exactly surprising, though I wasn't aware of any chicken fingers in our fridge.

"Do you need me to go to the store?" Leon asked me.

I spotted some uncooked chicken breasts and decided to get a little creative. "We're going to make chicken fingers," I announced.

"How?" Nichelle asked me.

"You'll see," I said as I pulled the chicken and a carton of eggs out of the fridge. I set Nichelle down on the counter and grabbed various other ingredients from the pantry. As I set things up and started to cut the chicken into strips, Leon kept Nichelle busy.

"Are you and Aunt Jacey married?" I heard her ask him.

Leon and I both looked at each other for a brief second before he responded. "No, your Aunt Jacey is my best friend, but sometimes we act like we're married," he said.

"Like you play pretend?"

"Something like that."

"I like to pretend I'm a pangolin!"

"What's a pangolin?" Leon asked.

I laughed. "It's like if an anteater and an armadillo had a baby."

Leon made a face as he tried to imagine what the creature might look like.

I finished laying everything out, grabbed a bar stool for Nichelle to stand on, and then plucked her off the counter. "Come on, little pangolin, let's make some lunch." I made sure Nichelle was securely standing on the stool and then pulled four bowls—one with chicken slices, one with egg, one with flour, and one with breadcrumbs close to her.

"What do we do?" she asked me.

"First, we have to grab the chicken," I said, handing her a slice.

"Ew! It's slimy!"

"That's why we have to put it in flour and bread crumbs," I explained. I showed her how to coat the chicken before putting it on a baking sheet.

"You know what's even more fun than putting flour on chicken?" Leon asked Nichelle.

We both turned to look at him. Leon came up behind me, reaching around to the bowl of flour and grabbing a pinch of it before sprinkling it on my head.

"Putting flour on Aunt Jacey," he said smugly.

"Yay!" Nichelle said, her voice full of excitement as she grabbed a tiny handful of flour and tossed it at me.

"Oh my god, you're going to get it!" I squealed as I tossed flour in Leon's direction.

"No, I'm not. I've got a pangolin on my team!" he said before grabbing Nichelle and more flour and hurling it at me.

"Oh no! Not a pangolin! They always win a flour fight!" I cried out.

The three of us laughed, tossing flour and eventually bread crumbs all over the kitchen and each other.

I reached for the bowl on the counter, hoping to grab the very last handful of flour, but before I could get to it, Leon had me by the waist. He picked me up and pulled me away from the counter.

"Oh no, you don't!" he said.

"Why do you have to be so strong!" I yelled out in frustration before we both collapsed into a fit of laughter.

I turned to face Leon, not realizing just how close he was to me. He gently reached up and dusted some flour off my cheek. There was something about his hand on my face and the intensity in his gaze that made me forget how to breathe. Without thinking about it, I closed my eyes and savored the feeling of his fingertips against my skin. It was the smallest of moments, and yet I felt it send shock waves through me. *Why does this keep happening to me? I need to get a grip.*

"Are you pretending to be married now?" Nichelle asked.

We both awkwardly stepped apart like kids who'd been caught under the bleachers.

"You know what? We still need lunch! How about we go clean up, and I'll take you to the Play Café?" I said to Nichelle.

"Yay, let's go!" she squealed, bouncing up and down.

I took Nichelle upstairs to try and get some of the flour off of her. By the time we returned, Leon had managed to clean up the tornado in our kitchen.

"You wanna go to Brooklyn?" I asked, unsure if he had plans that my babysitting duties were keeping him from.

"Are you kidding me? It's called the Play Café. Of course, I want to go!"

Leon, Nichelle, and I got in a cab headed for the children's themed restaurant across the bridge. By the time we arrived, Nichelle was bouncing off the walls in anticipation.

The Play Café was a brightly colored cross between a trendy café and a McDonald's Play Place. I only knew about it because Nia and her husband lived nearby, and the restaurant had quickly become Nichelle's favorite place on earth. I could only get her to sit still long enough for our waitress to take our order before she started begging to leave the table.

"Can I please go play now, Aunt Jacey?"

"Okay, but you have to come back when the food gets here," I said.

With that, she was off running full speed toward a giant ball pit in the middle of the room.

The moment she was gone, I realized I was alone

with Leon for the first time in weeks. I sat there silently for a moment, unsure of what to say. "Thanks for hanging out with us," I finally managed to get out.

"I'm glad I—"

"Excuse me?" A woman's voice called out, interrupting whatever Leon was about to say. We both turned to look at a blonde woman with short, textured hair and a terrifying pair of khaki capri pants standing next to our table. "I just wanted to say I think that it's so wonderful you two adopted. You're such a beautiful family," she said.

"Actually, we—" I started, but Leon reached out and grabbed my hand, effectively stopping not only my response but my entire train of thought.

"Thank you so much," he said.

With that, the woman waddled back to her table.

"She was just going to keep talking to us unless you took her weird compliment," he explained.

I wasn't paying attention. Instead, my gaze was fixed on Leon's hand, still wrapped around my own.

For ten years, Leon and I had been exceedingly platonic. There was nothing between us, not so much as a lingering glance or an inappropriate comment. Yet, recently, there was this unexplained jealousy of Natalia and these tiny little sparks that kept going off like fireworks inside of me. The more I tried to shut them out or explain them away, the more they bubbled up again.

I pulled my hand away and looked over my shoulder at Nichelle tossing around brightly colored plastic balls.

"You still don't think you'll ever want this?" I asked.

We'd discussed the topic many times, and Leon was always adamant he'd never have children. However, after watching him with Nichelle all day, it was hard to imagine that he'd never be a father. It was up to him, of course. I just got the sense he would make a really good one.

"Kids?" he clarified.

"Yeah, I just—you're so good with Nichelle, it's hard to imagine you never having children," I explained as I turned back to look at him.

"I have some genes I don't exactly want to pass on," he winced.

That wasn't news to me. I didn't know what Leon was afraid of passing on to a child, but I did know he always had the same answer anytime the subject of children came up.

"You could always adopt," I suggested with a shrug.

"Apparently, we already did," Leon said sarcastically.

"Oh, if we're adopting, it's going to be a boy."

"Why?"

"Do you know how much makeup and prom dresses and designer bags cost?" I sighed dramatically.

"Okay, okay...we'll have a boy, then."

"Great, what are we naming him?" I asked.

I didn't know why we were both playing along with this idea of having children together. I wasn't even sure where the sarcasm stopped and the truth started. I just knew that this was the best day I'd had in a long time.

"It's going to have to be Portuguese, or my mom is never going to let us hear the end of it," he scoffed.

I took out my phone and started googling Portuguese baby names. "Hm.... how about Teodoro? I'll call him 'Teo' for short."

An unexpected smile spread over Leon's face. "That was my grandfather's name."

"Teodoro it is, then," I announced.

We were both quiet for a while before I decided to

speak up again.

"I'm sorry we fought," I said honestly.

"I am, too."

"I missed you."

"God, I missed you, too," he whispered.

Those four simple words were all I needed to feel my world shift back into focus. I hadn't realized how much the distance from my best friend was eating away at me until it was gone. I felt lighter, like suddenly everything was okay again. I just hoped it would stay that way.

Thirty-Four

Leon and I brought Nichelle home. Nia came to pick her up an hour later. Exhausted, we sat sprawled across the opposite ends of our sectional in silence. I had to give it to anyone with kids—they're draining. Despite my lack of energy, I was still riding a wave of happiness. Leon and I were going to be okay. I had been so afraid that we would quietly fade from each other's lives that I almost forgot who we were. He was my best friend, my family. He had been and probably always would be my hero.

The night I met Leon was one of the most frightening nights of my life, yet I would always be grateful for it because it gave me him.

I was nineteen and in my sophomore year at NYU. I studied fashion, and though I would have much rather gone to Parsons, my parents somehow convinced me that NYU was the safer choice. I didn't care about safety.

I just wanted to be a designer.

I was laser-focused then. I didn't go out or party. Instead, I spent any free time I had studying or working on my designs. However, the one distraction I couldn't avoid was boys.

One afternoon in early spring, I sat at a picnic table in the courtyard, sketching between classes, when an attractive boy with ash-blonde hair approached me. He was on the short side, but broad and muscular. His eyes were dark brown, and he had this confidence about him that I couldn't quite put my finger on.

I would later learn that he was on the wrestling team. I would later get him kicked off that wrestling team.

"You're Casey, right?"

I raised an eyebrow as he got my name wrong. I didn't exactly have a common name, but it was a mistake I found annoying no matter how many times people made it.

"Jacey," I corrected him.

He looked a bit surprised but shook it off quickly. "I'm Bryce. We have Econ together."

Economics was a requirement for most majors, so the class took place in a huge lecture hall. There was no way I could remember who was in that class even if I tried. I decided to take his word for it. "Okay, what's up?" I asked.

I assumed he wanted notes or perhaps he had questions about something he missed in class. It was odd that he would ask someone he didn't know, but he was cute and seemed friendly, so I wasn't on guard.

"What are you doing tonight?"

"I...um..."

Before I could form a response, he sat down across

from me.

"Look, I know this is lame, but do you wanna grab dinner with me?"

It was the first time I'd been asked on a date since I started NYU, and I certainly didn't expect the invitation to come from someone I didn't know. "We just met..."

"I know, I know. This probably seems weird, it's just...I've wanted to get to know you since September. I just never got the chance to introduce myself," he explained.

He seemed so genuine, and it was impossible not to be charmed by his boyish good looks. I weighed my options. It wasn't like I had plans. My schedule for the night included eating Easy Mac and studying for my fashion merchandising exam.

"Okay...sure..." I said, shrugging my shoulders.

"Sweet!"

He pulled out his cell phone, and we exchanged numbers. Then, just as quickly as he'd appeared, Bryce ran off to his next class.

I didn't have the experience in my wheelhouse to know whether this was normal. It felt normal, and Bryce seemed nice. It was just dinner, so what did I have to lose?

During the day, Bryce and I texted back and forth. He was adorable, and at nineteen, I was a romantic. I thought maybe this could be the start of something. It was silly. I knew nothing about him, I didn't even know his last name, but I hadn't yet learned how to see male attention for what it was and not some epic romance in my head.

Hours later, I found myself across a table from Bryce at a cozy little Italian place on East 4th. It was early, so we managed to beat the dinner crowd. We sat in a corner towards the back and I listened as Bryce spent most of our meal talking about wrestling and his fraternity. Neither were of much interest to me. However, the dimples that appeared in his cheeks and the flecks of gold in his eyes were. By the time we finished our meal, I was completely enamored and totally oblivious to the fact I had barely gotten a word in edgewise.

When we finished, Bryce and I started walking back toward campus.

"I don't really want this to end," he said.

"Yeah, I had a great time," I responded, fidgeting uncomfortably as I glanced away from him.

"There's this party I'm going to tonight if you wanna..."

"Um..."

I once again had a choice to make. On the one hand, I typically avoided parties entirely, and going to a frat house was intimidating, to say the least. On the other hand, I liked Bryce, and I liked the idea of spending more time with him.

"I have to study, but I guess I can go with you for a bit," I said hesitantly.

That was all Bryce needed to hear. He took me by the hand and started leading the way.

Alpha Phi was precisely what I expected out of a frat house. It was a large, two-story brick building with all the classic charm of an old east coast home and all external damage that a bunch of drunken, rowdy boys in their early twenties could cause. Though it wasn't particularly late when we arrived, the party was clearly in full swing. On the front lawn were a handful of people throwing back the contents of red Solo cups and running around like children while music blasted from inside the building. Before we walked in the front door, Bryce wrapped an arm around my shoulder. I wasn't sure if the gesture was protective or possessive, but it made me feel special.

The whole place smelled of old beer, and all of the people piled into the house overwhelmed me. I had assumed that a frat party would be wild, but this was on another level entirely. The music was too loud, the people were too drunk, and things seemed to get more and more crazy with every passing moment.

"Let's get you a drink," Bryce said as he shuffled towards the kitchen.

I carefully trailed behind him trying to avoid spilt drinks and stumbling people. I pressed my back against the counter top as I watched him grab a bottle off the counter.

"Hold on," he said before he started to pour.

"What?"

Before I could blink, I felt his mouth hungrily crash into mine. The kiss was clumsy and a little short of what I hoped it would be, but I kissed him back. I was just excited that he seemed to like me.

When Bryce pulled away, I stood there a little stunned as he started to fumble around the kitchen. He returned to me with a tiny plastic shot glass. I didn't drink, but I wanted to impress him, so I took the clear liquid from his hand and threw it back like a champ. It stung going down, and I squeezed my eyes shut as I forced myself to swallow.

"Attagirl!" he said before kissing me on the cheek.

I felt victorious and on top of the world.

"I'm going to go say hi to some people. I'll be back," Bryce said.

With that, he wandered off while I remained in the

kitchen. I felt the slightest bit of buzz from the alcohol, but I knew I was nowhere near drunk.

I spotted a few girls I knew from the fashion program and started toward them. It was just a relief that I'd managed to find people I knew, and the four of us began chatting for a while. Eventually, Bryce found his way back to me with another drink in hand. This time it was in a red Solo cup. He wrapped his arm tightly around my shoulders again.

"You having fun, Jacey?" he asked me.

"Yeah, this is Ama—"

"I got you another drink," he said, interrupting me. He was far less sober than he had been when I last saw him.

He pressed the cup into my hand. The contents were a yellow-orange, like some kind of juice, but it smelled like lighter fluid.

"What's this?"

"Just some vodka and pineapple juice. I'll be back," Bryce slurred.

He left again, and immediately the three girls all looked at me with concern.

"Do you know that guy?" One of them asked me.

I looked back in Bryce's direction and smiled. Maybe it was the alcohol talking, but the next thing out of my mouth was, "Yeah, we're dating." I justified to myself that what I just said wasn't entirely untrue. We had just been on a date, after all.

The girls exchanged looks, but they didn't press the issue any further.

We continued talking for a while as I nursed my drink. It was strong, and I could feel my vision start to blur at the sides. I knew I was getting drunk, but I was surprised that it was coming on so suddenly. I'd only had one shot and about half the contents of the cup I was holding. My thoughts started to become disjointed, but I kept reasoning that I was at a party and this was what people did in college. By the time my cup was empty, I knew I wasn't making any sense, and the three girls I had been talking to decided to ditch the party altogether, leaving me alone to try and find Bryce.

Everything was spinning. I wasn't sure I was even making any progress from the place I started until I suddenly felt my shin hit something. I toppled onto a couch and directly into the lap of a complete stranger.

"Woah there!"

The voice was startled, but gentle. I focused my increasingly difficult vision on the face looking down at me.

"Are you okay?"

I nodded, though my head felt like it was full of lead. "You're so pretty," I managed to say to the man holding me. My eyelids grew heavy as honey-brown eyes and jet-black hair faded in and out of focus.

"Hey! Hey! Come on, stay awake for me."

I didn't know who this person was, and though I could feel him lightly shaking me, I couldn't make myself tell him I was okay.

"Yo, Leon, it's cool. I've got her," I heard Bryce's voice say.

"Do you know her?" Whoever this guy was sounded protective.

"I'm..." I started, but my mouth wasn't doing what my mind wanted.

"Yeah, man. This is my girl. She just had too much to drink."

"Your what?"

"We're dating, dude. It's fine."

I wanted to smile, although I didn't know if I was smiling. Apparently, we *were* dating.

"Come on, Babe. Let's get you home."

I felt Bryce's arms pull me up off the couch and brace me to start walking. My eyes kept fluttering open and shut. I couldn't focus no matter how hard I tried.

"Dude, she's really out of it. Let me help," I heard the unfamiliar voice say.

"I got it, man. She's a Kappa. I'm just taking her next door," Bryce rattled off.

What? I wasn't a Kappa. I wasn't even part of the Greek system. I shook my head, but again, I couldn't form any words. I just started dragging my feet along with the pace of Bryce's steps. I wasn't sure what was in front of me or behind me. We took a turn down a dark hallway and walked for a while longer before we stopped, and I heard a door open. I was ushered inside, and then the door slammed hard behind us.

Bryce started kissing me. The kiss was sloppy and hungry. I couldn't kiss him back. I didn't know what he was doing or why. Somewhere in my foggy mind, I knew this wasn't safe.

"No, I wanna go..." I muttered.

He somehow got me onto a bed. I could feel a scratchy comforter underneath me and Bryce clumsily trying to get my clothes off my body. I grabbed at the fabric, desperately trying to keep it on, but it was no use. It felt like a bad dream. I couldn't control my own body. His hands started to roam over me. I knew they were in places they shouldn't be, but I couldn't stop him.

I started to panic. *What is he doing? I said no, right?* I wondered if maybe this was just some terrible nightmare when I heard the door swing open again.

I felt Bryce spring off the bed. "What the fuck?" he yelled.

"Dude, that girl isn't even conscious."

The voice I heard was the same one that had been trying to make sure I was okay in the living room. I didn't know who this person was, but I knew he was rescuing me, and I took momentary comfort in the fact someone else was there.

"So what? Get out of my room!"

I heard a rustling sound. It sounded like two people shoving each other, but I couldn't lift my head to look.

"I'm not going anywhere without her, so either let me take her home, or I'm calling campus police. Take your pick!"

"This is bullshit," was the last thing I heard Bryce say.

My eyes fluttered open to see a tall silhouette over me. I didn't know the handsome face staring down at me, but something told me I would be alright. Whoever this guy was, he wasn't going to hurt me.

"Hey..." I could tell he didn't know what to say or do by the sound of his voice. "Are you okay? Where do you live?"

"Greenwich," I mumbled. I didn't know how I'd managed the name of my dorm, but I did.

"Shit!"

I didn't know what was wrong. I just closed my eyes again.

"Hey — no, don't go to sleep!" There was panic in his voice, and then silence for a little while. "I'm going to get you out of here, okay?"

I felt an arm slide behind my back and another behind my knees. I didn't know what items of clothing were left on my body. I told myself I would be okay; I had been saved. Then everything went black.

Thirty-Five

I woke up the morning after the party in the skirt I'd been wearing the night before and an oversized, dark green t-shirt that read, "Hillsborough High School Math Team". Startled, I sat up abruptly, and as my eyes adjusted, I realized I had no idea where I was. I scanned the room for some clue before both panic and a splitting headache settled in. I felt more nauseous than I had ever been in my life, and my stomach churned as I noticed the shirtless man sleeping on the floor below me. My eyes darted around, searching for someplace I could throw up. Thankfully whoever put me to bed was smart enough to put a trash can nearby. I grabbed the gray plastic container and emptied the contents of my stomach.

The horrible noise woke up the person sleeping on the floor below me. He jumped up as soon as he heard it, and without thinking twice, he grabbed my hair,

holding it back until I finished. I sat up slowly, both mortified and confused.

"Where am I?"

"There's a lot to unpack. Um..."

I watched as he carefully got up and sat down on the opposite side of the bed. He was clearly tired, and he rubbed his eyes before speaking again.

"You're at Alpha Phi. I'm Leondro, but everyone calls me Leon."

I pulled my legs into my chest. My head hurt so badly that I was having trouble processing anything he was saying. "I'm Jacey," I said slowly.

He smiled, and it was then that I realized just how gorgeous he was. His teeth were white and perfectly straight. He had dark hair, a strong jaw, and his uniquely colored eyes seemed incredibly kind. The longer I looked at him, the more self-conscious I became about the fact I'd just hurled my guts up in his dorm room. He, however, didn't seem at all upset or even phased. He just seemed concerned for my well-being.

"How did I end up in your bed? Did we...?"

"No! No. You don't remember anything?"

I shook my head. I watched his face change as I did. He seemed to be weighing something in his head.

"What happened?"

"Do you know Bryce McReynolds?"

I ran my hand over my face. I didn't know what happened, but something told me it wasn't good. "Yeah, we just met. He brought me to the party last night."

"I think he might have drugged you."

"What?" My heart started pounding in my chest. *What happened to me? How could I have let this happen? I was always so responsible.* "Did he...?" I couldn't even bring myself to finish the sentence.

"No," Leon said, taking my hand to reassure me.

I was so panicked that I pulled my hand away immediately.

"Hey, I'm sorry. You fell into my lap at the party, and I could tell you weren't okay."

I vaguely remembered tripping and looking up at someone I didn't know.

"Bryce said you were his girlfriend and that he was taking you home, but I've known him for two years, and I'd never seen you before, so I knew something was off."

I just started at Leon blankly as he continued.

"I heard Bryce's roommate complaining about him bringing a girl back to their room, and so...I don't know...I just felt like I had to do something."

I tried hard to remember, but most of the night came up blank. I remembered Bryce handing me a drink. I remember the girls I was talking to, but the rest was just empty.

"I found you before he did anything. I told him I was taking you home, or I was calling campus police, so he bailed."

"How did I end up here?"

"You managed to tell me what dorm you lived in, but I knew I couldn't carry you that far, so I just put you in my bed and crashed on the floor."

I looked around the room. I still had no idea how to process this. "Thank you," was the only thing I could bring myself to say, and the words came out barely above a whisper.

"I'm just glad you're okay."

I wasn't sure if I was okay. I was scared and confused, not to mention embarrassed. I looked down at the shirt

I was wearing, remembering that it wasn't my own.

"Is this yours?" I asked.

"Yeah...you...um...weren't wearing much, so..."

"Thank you," I said again.

"You don't have to keep thanking me."

"Yes, I do. If you weren't there, I would have..."

I still didn't want to say it. If I said it, it was real, and I wasn't ready for that. We were both silent. I doubted that either one of us knew what to say. It was hardly a normal way to meet someone.

"I should get going," I muttered, standing up slowly, unsure if my stomach or my head could handle it.

"Can I walk you home?" Leon asked me.

"You don't have to do that. You've already done so much..."

"I want to," he insisted.

The truth was, I didn't feel all that confident in my ability to make it home on my own, and Leon seemed to genuinely want to help me. Who was I to turn him down?

"Okay, sure," I said.

I looked at myself in the full-length mirror that was attached to the back of his door. I was a mess. I had mascara running down my face and remnants of my winged eyeliner was so smeared that I looked like a raccoon, not to mention my hair was all over the place. I knew walking out of a frat house wearing a men's t-shirt and a mini-skirt was going to make it look like I was doing the walk of shame. I was ashamed, but not for the reasons anyone who saw me might assume.

I tried not to stare as Leon tossed a shirt over his naked torso. The last thing I needed to be thinking about was how attractive this guy was. As far as I was concerned, I was swearing off men forever. Luckily, it was early enough in the morning that the hungover frat boys hadn't yet managed to drag themselves out of bed, so I didn't need to worry about unwelcome glances or childish comments.

I followed Leon down a hallway, through the tornado of a living room, and out the front door. There was an awkward silence between us for a while, but we had a long walk ahead of us, and the last thing I wanted was to spend it stuck in my head.

"Are you from New York?" I asked.

"Portugal, originally, but I grew up in New Jersey," he explained. "What about you?"

"I'm from Connecticut. What made your parents leave Portugal?"

"It was just my mom. She doesn't talk about it much. I think she just needed a change. She moved back to Tavira when I got into NYU."

"So you don't have any family here?"

"No, not really."

"That must be hard."

"I've just learned to make a family out of my friends."

"Is that why you joined a frat?"

"No, I'm just in it for the sorority girls," he teased.

Even though our initial meeting was rather unusual, I was quickly starting to find that I liked this handsome stranger.

"So, can I ask you a personal question?" he asked.

"Sure...I guess..."

"How did you end up at that party with Bryce in the first place?"

I sighed. I wished so much that I had just blown off Bryce when he asked me out or told him I had to study when he invited me to the party.

"He just showed up randomly and asked me out. I don't know why I said yes."

"Do you normally go out with guys you know nothing about?"

"I don't normally go out with guys at all."

"What does that mean?"

"I dated in high school a little, but I haven't gone out with anyone since I moved to New York."

"That seems...hard to believe..."

"Why?"

Leon looked over at me in a way that implied I should know what he meant.

"It's not hard to imagine someone wanting to take you out," he politely explained.

I glanced away from him and smiled. I could feel the blush creeping up in my cheeks, so I quickly changed the subject, and Leon and I talked about school and our classes until we reached my building.

"This is me," I said with a shrug as we reached the outside of my dorm.

"Okay, well, it was nice to meet you," he said a bit uncomfortably.

"Yeah...you too." I turned and started to walk up the front steps.

"Hey! Wait!" Leon called out before rushing up the steps I'd just taken to meet me. "Can I give you my number? I don't know if you're going to report Bryce or not, but if you decide to...or...if...you know...you want to return that Math Team shirt or...you just don't want to be alone after what happened...."

Not only was he handsome, but he was sweet and still worried about me despite the fact he barely knew me.

"Sure, I'd like that," I said as I handed him my phone.

I couldn't help but smile at the way his face lit up as he took it from me and entered his number. It was bad enough that he was gorgeous and kind but did he have to be so endearing?

Unsure of what else to say, I thanked him again and went upstairs.

My roommate had dropped out mid-semester, and the school didn't assign me another. My room was quiet and cold. It wasn't until I was alone without Leon to distract me that the terror of what I'd just endured started to hit me. I couldn't remember anything beyond that red Solo cup filled with toxic yellow liquid, but that made it all the more insidious. I sat down on the edge of my bed, and I could feel my breathing hitch in my throat. It was like I couldn't catch my breath, so I did the only thing I could think to do.

> **Me:** Wait. I don't want to be alone.
> ***Leon:*** Which room?
> **Me:** L102

By the time I heard a knock on the door, my eyes were clouded with tears. I couldn't think of anything but the panic rising inside me. I couldn't bring myself to respond.

"Hey Jacey, I'm going to open the door now," Leon said carefully before slowly stepping inside.

As soon as Leon saw me, he entered the room and shut the door. He knelt in front of me.

"Hey, breathe with me, okay?"

Leon breathed in and out in a slow, exaggerated way. I tried my best to follow along until eventually, my breathing returned to normal.

"Tell me what you need?"

"Just stay with me, please," I practically begged him.

"I'll stay with you as long as you need."

I suppose, in a way, Leon never left. We spent the rest of that afternoon watching horror movies on my laptop, and, despite assuring him repeatedly that I would be alright, he slept on my old roommate's empty bed that night. After that, we were inseparable. I was the family he didn't have, and he was the protector I didn't know I needed. I had never been so close to anyone, and even now, ten years later, he was still the most important thing in my life.

Thirty-Six

I laid around the living room with Leon for as long as I possibly could before I needed to get ready for Cash's opening. There was a small part of me that didn't want to go. I knew that tonight was supposed to change everything for Cash and me. Yet, I was hesitant. It was like I was under some spell when I was around him. He was all-consuming, and being around him was like being drunk. All I wanted to do was drown in the creative, chaotic energy he gave off. Yet, as soon as I was away from him, the hangover set in, and I found myself exhausted, unsure if I ever wanted another drink.

Despite my hesitations, I knew that if I wanted to find out where this relationship with Cash was going, I needed to show up. Maybe this was the beginning of our story. Maybe I could find love again. I would never

know unless I was willing to put on a dress and go to his opening.

As I sat in the cab on my way to some warehouse space in the Red Hook neighborhood of Brooklyn, I began to regret my choice of outfit. I shifted uncomfortably in the impossibly short satin dress I was wearing. It had virtually no back, and the only thing holding the dress against my body was a complicated weaving of black lace that resembled a corset. The heels I'd chosen were no more comfortable. I glanced down at the studded pointed-toe pumps, and while they may have looked incredible, they certainly didn't feel that way. However, I ignored my pinched toes and the fact that I was one wrong move away from a wardrobe malfunction. Tonight I'd give myself to Cash completely. Presents were a lot more fun when they were beautifully wrapped and so I had to look incredible.

I could hear the pounding of bass as I got out of the cab. Outside a dingy-looking warehouse were a bunch of attractive 20-30 somethings lined up like they were trying to get into a club. I hadn't even walked into the building yet, but this was somehow exactly what I expected. While most artist openings in New York were quiet rooms with white walls where the elite bought paintings they knew nothing about, this event was what most things in Cash's life were: a party.

I approached the bouncer and gave him my name, much to the dismay of the girls standing in the front of the line. Security ushered me into a dark room with a large poster warning me of the use of strobe lights. I stood in the dark while a handful more people followed into this makeshift holding area, then a blonde in the signature fishnets, tiny shorts, and bustier of a bottle service girl opened a door and let us inside.

The warehouse was outfitted with temporary walls. The whole place was dark and lit only by black lights. Cash's pieces hung on the walls, and above them were lamps that turned on and off to the beat of the deafening music. When the lights were on, you could see the entire painting for what it was, but when the lights went out, the graffiti in his paintings was the only thing you could see. It was genius. I'd never seen anything like it. However, I had already seen most of the paintings on the walls. What I came to see was Cash.

I wandered through the crowded halls past art patrons, influencers, and bottle service girls passing out shots of vodka. Cash hadn't told me where to find him and there was no use in texting him when the music was so loud. Thankfully, about halfway through the maze of artificial walls, I spotted a familiar mess of platinum hair. He stood a full head above the people he was talking with. As if he could read my mind, Cash's eyes met mine as soon as I noticed him, and for a brief moment, it was like the rest of the world disappeared.

I knew this was Cash's night, but selfishly, I wanted it to be over so I could be close to him. I watched as he completely ignored the two people in front of him and pushed himself through the crowd to get to me. When he reached me, Cash didn't say a word, he just pulled me in, and right there, in the middle of the crowd, he kissed me. The moment it happened, I felt the same familiar rush that showed up each time he was near. My head swam, my pulse quickened, and my whole body ached to be closer to him than I could ever possibly be.

"Follow me," he shouted over the music before taking my hand.

We made our way through the rest of the exhibit and toward a green room. There were still people scattered everywhere, but it was far less crowded, and the music dulled out just enough that I could hear myself think.

"So, what do you think?" Cash asked me.

I shook my head. It was amazing that someone as talented as he was would be the slightest bit concerned with what I thought.

"It's amazing," I said honestly.

"You look amazing," he said in response, pulling me closer to him.

"I figured I'd give you something to look forward to later."

I assumed that Cash's reaction to that would be a positive one, but instead, his attention was suddenly on a woman in the corner waving him over. She carried a clipboard and wore a dress suit, so I had to assume that she was his publicist or someone in charge of the event.

"I'll be back," he said before wandering off and leaving me on my own.

Now that I was alone in a room full of people I didn't know, I started to think of Leon and even wished I had thought to bring him with me. I stood off in a corner. I was sure that I probably looked awkward, and so to occupy myself, I took my cell phone out of my clutch and started scrolling through my Instagram feed.

"How do you know Cash?" I heard a voice say.

When I looked up, a tall, raven-haired girl with bronzed skin and a striking pair of green eyes stood over me.

"He's my boyfriend," I replied.

I was rather shocked at how directly I said that, considering we hadn't yet talked about being in a relationship. Something about this girl and her body language told me that she wasn't just asking out of curiosity. She was asking because she was interested.

The scoff that came out of her mouth made it clear that I was right. "If Cash had a girlfriend, I would know about it."

"Oh really? Why is that?"

"Let's just say Cash and I know each other really well," she said.

I rolled my eyes. I didn't know who this woman was or what she was to Cash, but I wasn't about to engage in the fight she was trying to start. "Apparently, you two haven't talked in a while."

"Let me just give you some advice, woman to woman..." she started.

No good advice starts with that sentence.

"You should be careful. Cash does this all the time. He falls for some pretty face he meets at the club or some bar and then swears up and down that you inspire him more than anyone ever has... until the next pretty face comes along, and then he forgets you ever even existed."

"What is this? Are we on the CW? I don't know what happened between the two of you, but you're not going to scare me off."

"Honey, I'm not trying to scare you. I'm just trying to be honest with you. Let me guess, you rarely go out, you just hang around his apartment, and on the rare occasion you're around his friends, they barely speak a word to you?"

She was right, but I refused to dignify what she was saying with an answer. I had to believe that what I had with Cash was special, even if the girl in front of me was trying to push me to think otherwise.

Before I could think of something to say, Cash returned.

"Jenna, I didn't know you were coming," he said, sounding polite but disinterested.

"I was just introducing myself to your girlfriend," she said.

I wanted to hide. I hadn't expected this Jenna girl to repeat what I just said to her. But I didn't know why it surprised me so much. She was angling for something, that much was clear. I was afraid to look up at Cash's face and see what his reaction might be, but to my surprise, he wrapped an arm around me.

"Yeah, I got lucky with this one," he said, kissing me on the top of the head.

I couldn't remember the last time I smiled so hard. I finally allowed myself to look up at Cash. I didn't know if this meant that he saw us as something serious or if this was just an attempt to upset the unpleasant girl in front of us, but I allowed myself to enjoy the way it made me feel. It was the validation I was hoping for. I wanted tonight to be the start of something, and I was beginning to realize that maybe Cash did, too.

Suddenly, Jenna's tone was all sugar. "It was so nice to meet you," she said. "Just remember what I said," she added before turning to leave.

"What did she say to you?" Cash asked me.

I waved my hand dismissively. I didn't want to give this girl any more attention than I already had. Instead, I turned to the tray of shots passing by me and reached over to grab one. I threw it back and coughed a little as it went down.

"It doesn't matter," I finally responded.

I couldn't tell whether Cash was impressed or

concerned.

"We can go somewhere and talk if you–"

"I'm good," I interrupted.

I knew I probably should have taken Cash up on his offer. My head was a war zone of questions. I wanted to know if he and Jenna had ever been together. I wanted to know if there was any justifiable reason for her warning. I wanted to know if he was just letting this woman believe I was his girlfriend to get her to go away or if that's what he actually wanted me to be. However, I refused to ask, opting instead to play the cool girl. It seemed easier to appear unbothered by her comments. In reality, I was just afraid to ask or just afraid I already knew the answers.

For the next several hours, Cash dragged me around, introducing me to dozens of people. I couldn't hear their names over the loud music, let alone remember anything about them except that each one seemed more self-involved than the last. I wanted to feel like I belonged in Cash's world but instead I found that the more time I spent in it the more it made my head spin.

By the end of the night, I was exhausted.

As the crowd thinned out and the loud music stopped playing, I found myself wandering around the exhibit alone while Cash tied up whatever loose ends he needed to. I stopped to look at a familiar piece. It was the same painting he'd said I inspired when we first started seeing each other. As I examined the piece, I felt a pair of arms slowly encircle my waist.

I looked down at the familiar tattoos on Cash's forearms.

"You see the title?" he asked me.

I honestly hadn't even noticed the plaques next to

each painting. I stepped away from Cash and moved toward the painting. It read one word: *Jacey*.

I knew then that Jenna had to be wrong. There was something real between Cash and me. It was arguably one of the sweetest things anyone had ever done for me. It was the sign I was looking for. I rushed back over to him and closed the distance between our lips.

"Let's get out of here," he whispered.

As we got in a cab and headed towards his apartment, I couldn't help but think I might be on the way to the rest of my life.

Thirty-Seven

On our way back to Cash's apartment, neither one of us spoke. It was like something went off inside us. We kissed like we'd never see each other again. There was nothing between us except for this frantic, unspoken need. It was the way teenagers kissed when they first learned how. If it weren't for the middle-aged man in the driver's seat, the first time I slept with Cash might have happened right there in that car.

When the vehicle finally came to a stop outside his building, Cash pulled his mouth away from mine just long enough to throw whatever money was in his back pocket at the cab driver. He pulled me out of the car with him. We continued kissing as he fumbled with the front door of his building, through the hallway, and only stopped long enough for him to shove his apartment door open.

I only had a brief second to catch my breath before

Cash was dragging me toward his bedroom. I followed willingly, but as soon as we were there, something stopped me. I wasn't sure what it was. Between implying I was his girlfriend, the painting, and the way he couldn't take his hands off me in the car, it almost felt too good to be true. This night was what I'd desperately wanted since we met, and yet I found myself needing reassurance of some kind.

Maybe it was because this was the first time I had been with anyone that wasn't Brian in years. When he moved in to kiss me again, I placed my hand against his chest, stopping him before that addictive mouth of his sent my head spinning again.

"What's wrong?" he said breathlessly.

"What is this?" I asked, though I instantly regretted the question.

A cocky smirk played on Cash's lips.

"I don't know. You tell me, Jacey. You're the one going around calling yourself my girlfriend," he said.

"Am I?"

The smile faded quickly. Cash didn't seem upset, but the question did affect him in some way. I just wasn't sure how to read him. "Are you asking to be my girlfriend?"

"I'm asking what we're doing," I corrected him.

"And I'm asking you what you want."

Everything about the conversation was confusing. To me, my question seemed simple, and yet Cash had to make everything so complicated.

"I want you."

"Do you?"

His questions were starting to migrate from confusing to insulting. It felt like he was playing a game that I was losing just by participating. I just wanted to know where this was going, but it was clear that he didn't want to answer the question.

"Just forget it," I said before moving back in to kiss him.

This time Cash stopped me and held me at arm's length by both of my shoulders.

"Do you really want this?"

"Yes! I love you," I said, sounding exasperated.

The words just flew out of my mouth. I believed at that moment I meant them, but it only took a minute for my head to catch up with my emotions. I immediately wished I hadn't said it. It wasn't because I was worried about how Cash would react, but because the tiny part of my brain that wasn't completely consumed with him clicked on. I looked around the mess of a bedroom I was standing in and then up into Cash's clouded blue eyes. I realized that I wasn't so sure.

"What if I told you to prove it?"

What the hell does that mean? I expected one of two reactions: he loved me or he didn't. Instead, he wanted me to prove it? "How am I supposed to do that?"

"You love me?"

"That's what I said."

"And you want me?"

"Yes! How many times do I have to say it?" I was starting to get annoyed at having to repeat myself. Was Cash so insecure that he needed to hear I loved him forty times before he could respond?

"Only me?"

"Only you, Cash. There's no one else."

I was so lost. Maybe Cash had more to drink than I thought. He possessed the unique ability to seem completely sober until he'd had one drink too many.

Then there was no turning back. I tried to count back the number of drinks I'd seen him finish that night, but I quickly realized I hadn't been watching him closely enough to be sure.

"That's bullshit," he said.

He had to be drunk. No other explanation I could come up with made any sense. Was he talking about Gabe? I'd stopped seeing him weeks ago. I also never bothered to tell Cash about any of the guys I had been dating before we met.

"You're seriously telling me you're not into that Leon guy you live with?"

I stepped away from Cash's grasp. I suddenly didn't want his hands on me. I had never seen this side of him before and frankly, I didn't like it. "Yes, that's exactly what I'm telling you. Where is this coming from? You've never even brought Leon up before!"

"You're the one who said you wanted to be with me!"

"Yeah, I'm not so sure about that anymore."

"So you *are* into him." There was a look of expectation on his face that I didn't understand. It was as if he genuinely believed I was going to admit he was right.

"No, Cash. I'm not, but maybe we should have this conversation when you're sober."

"Fuck that. We're having it now!"

I threw my hands up in the air. It occurred to me that this was yet another moment where Cash and I were about to get intimate, and he did something to avoid it.

"Are you just doing this to avoid having sex with me?"

I was far more direct than usual. I no longer cared what he thought of me. I wasn't even sure it mattered if we continued seeing each other. I just wanted answers.

"What if I told you, you had to choose?"

“Answer the question, Cash.” I insisted. I wasn’t going to let him play this manic little interrogation game without answering my questions, too.

“I’m not avoiding shit. I’m just making sure the girl I’m falling for isn’t fucking her roommate,” he said.

I don’t know what bothered me more, Cash insinuating that I was having sex with Leon or that he referred to him as my roommate. Leon was much more than that. Cash didn’t know everything about my life. I didn’t expect him to. But I did expect him to understand how important my best friend was to me.

“Now you answer the question...” Cash said, crossing his arms over his chest.

“What question?”

“What if I told you that you had to choose?”

“Between you and Leon?”

This whole conversation was absurd. I could understand jealousy. I could understand being suspicious of a mixed-gendered friendship. I couldn’t count the number of times someone had assumed that Leon and I were secretly in love with each other or destined to end up together. What I didn’t understand was Cash being jealous of someone he hadn’t even met yet. He didn’t know if Leon was gay or straight or attractive or even single. Leon’s gender was the only thing Cash saw as a threat. That was a red flag and a big one.

“Yes.”

“Are you telling me I have to choose, or are you asking how I would react to the question?”

Cash’s gaze hardened in a way that made me immediately want to get the hell out of there. I didn’t understand how this happened. Things with this man went from incredible to awful and back again at the drop of a hat. It was maddening. Did I want to be in a relationship like this?

"Choose, Jacey!"

I was so shocked I almost laughed. It was the only kind of reaction I could give. It was all so ridiculous that I couldn't even get myself to respond properly. "No problem," I said and sidestepped around Cash for the door. If he thought I would choose him over Leon, he had another thing coming.

"Wait," he said, following behind me as I stormed into his living room.

I didn't wait. I just kept moving through the apartment as quickly as I could.

"Wait, I'm sorry I—" he said as he grabbed my arm.

"Don't fucking touch me!" I spat out as I spun around to glare at him.

"So, I was right." I wanted to slap the smug look right off his face.

"This is fucking ridiculous!" I said as I turned for the front door.

"Just admit it!"

I turned again. This time I promised myself after I said my piece, I was gone. I wouldn't waste another moment on the jealous, overgrown teenage boy in front of me, no matter how much I thought I might have loved him.

"Admit what? That I would choose someone who's stood by me for the last ten years over you? I'm sorry that the fact that Leon is a man threatens your fragile little ego, but you are out of your fucking mind if you think I would ever walk away from him! I need him. I don't need you!"

"I'm so done with this!" Cash fired at me. Just when

I thought I couldn't be any more shocked by Cash's behavior, I caught the faintest of smiles as it crossed his face. It left me not only questioning whatever feelings he claimed to have for me, but his sanity as a whole. *Was he actually enjoying this?*

"What a coincidence! So am I!"

I reached for the door handle. This time, Cash didn't stop me. I stepped into the hallway and slammed the door behind me. I struggled to catch my breath. That wasn't how I'd pictured this night going at all. An hour ago, I thought Cash was The One, and now I never wanted to see him again.

I wiped away the tears brimming at the corners of my eyes and willed myself to start walking. I just kept telling myself to put one foot in front of the other. It wasn't the first time I had to hold myself together so a man couldn't see the way he'd just hurt me. I expected to hear the sound of the door opening behind me. I wanted to turn to see him following me down the hall. But there was nothing, just silence.

Outside his apartment building, I felt like I was suddenly on another planet. The cold air hit me almost as hard as the realization I was alone. Every feeling of warmth I'd had for Cash was gone, and so was he. The sobering reality sank in my stomach. I wanted to go home. I wanted to drink half a bottle of wine while Leon played cheerleader, but I needed to clear my head first. Otherwise, I knew I was going to be in hysterics. I didn't exactly feel safe walking home so late at night in such a short dress, so I just sat down, right there on the front steps of Cash's apartment. I let it out. I descended into a fit of sobs. Maybe I still had hope in me that he might come looking for me, but he never did.

Why was it that of all the men I had been seeing, I managed to fall for the very worst of them? I didn't know if I was crying because I felt stupid or because I knew how badly I would miss Cash, but I cried nonetheless. I bawled so hard that my makeup ran down my face, and my chest hurt from the heavy sobs coming out of me. Eventually, the tears just stopped. I sat numbly for several minutes before I pulled out my phone and requested an Uber.

It was too late to hail a cab in a residential area. Luckily for me, Marco in a silver Toyota Prius was only four minutes away. When he arrived, I slid into the back of the car and sat in silence as I waited for it to take me back to the only safe place I knew.

Thirty-Eight

Marco pulled onto my street and up to my apartment building. I thanked him absently before I made my way inside. My eyes were glossed with tears, I was disgusted with the dry, smeared makeup covering my face, and my chest felt like it weighed a ton. I just wanted to climb into my bed and forget all about Cash Mason.

My hands shook as I fished my keys out of my purse. I fumbled with them as I tried to get them into the door but instead they slipped out of my fingers. The metal loudly hit the concrete floor and I groaned before slowly bending down to get them. Just as I'd managed to grab them, the door opened for me. *Why is Leon home?*

"Jace, are you okay? Why are you home?" I could hear the concern in Leon's voice before I even stood up to look at him. When he finally got a look at the state I was in, I heard him take in a sharp breath.

I started to respond, but was immediately distracted by the fact my best friend stood there, shirtless. My eyes seemed to have a mind of their own. They slowly moved from his worried expression down the defined muscles of his chest. This situation was exactly why we had a rule about walking around the house half-naked. Fortunately for Leon, I was too upset to lecture him about it.

"No," I responded. It was the only thing I could get out. My voice sounded small and stuck in my throat.

Leon didn't say anything, he just grabbed me as fast as he could and pulled me in protectively. I held back tears as I felt his arms wrap around me. He felt like home, like the one place I always knew I would be safe. I took in a breath I didn't know I was holding. The familiar hints of amber and leather in his cologne surrounded me. It didn't matter to me that Leon and I rarely hugged; in that moment it was exactly what I needed. He was exactly what I needed. We stood in that doorway for what felt like ages and yet when he pulled back to look at me, it still wasn't long enough.

"What do you need?" he asked.

"Wine," I groaned.

Leon shut the door behind me and then ushered me over to the sofa. I slid my aching feet out of the heels I'd been wearing and pulled my knees into my chest. He went to the kitchen and returned with two glasses and the remainder of a bottle of Malbec in hand. He handed me my drink and then sat down next to me. "Do you want to talk?"

I didn't look over at him. Instead, I took a large swig of wine.

"Put a shirt on first."

"I'm doing laundry!"

In his defense, I could hear the distant rumbling of the washing machine in the hallway. However, I knew there was no way he was washing every single shirt he owned. "I don't care. Put on your tenth-grade math club t-shirt. You're distracting!"

Dramatically, Leon sighed heavily and stomped off to his bedroom. When he returned, he was wearing a wrinkled black t-shirt.

"Thank you."

He rolled his amber eyes at me before jumping back in. "Now talk."

"Cash and I are over," I explained. I could see the concern on his face as I spoke.

"What happened?"

I took a second and chugged the rest of my glass before pouring another. "I'm pretty sure he thinks I'm repulsive."

"What are you talking about?"

"We've been dating for weeks, and we never... every time I would try to... take things to the next level, he'd come up with some weird excuse. We were supposed to tonight, but he started this huge fight, and I stormed out." I peered over at Leon, whose eyes shifted back and forth. It was clear that he wasn't quite getting it.

"Okay. Why does that mean he's repulsed by you?"

"I did everything right. I went to the opening. I wore this stupid dress. I met all the horrible people he calls friends. He was acting like I was the best thing that ever happened to him, so I thought, 'this is it. I'm choosing Cash. I'm ready.'"

Leon nodded, but he didn't say anything.

"Then some impossibly hot girl comes over and starts

telling me that he does this with tons of girls and that he'd bail as soon as he finds a new muse."

"Seriously?"

"Yeah, I didn't ask if they'd ever been a thing. I guess I just wanted to believe she was crazy."

"That doesn't mean anything, Jace. She's probably just some jealous art groupie."

"Oh, I'm not done," I said. "We went back to Cash's apartment, and the whole way, we were all over each other..."

"Are you sure you want me to hear this?"

"Why not? I tell you everything. As soon as we got inside and things were about to start happening, I asked him what we were doing..."

"You didn't," Leon said, shaking his head.

"I just wanted to know if we were in the same place, but instead of answering me, he started this huge fight and accused me of sleeping with you."

"He what?"

"I guess I just read everything wrong..." I muttered, my voice getting small again.

"He's an idiot," Leon grumbled.

"I don't think it's him. I think it's me. I've dated five guys, Leon. Five! I couldn't get a single one of them to sleep with me."

"Maybe you just chose nice guys..."

"Or maybe I'm just some gross, pathetic thing they felt sorry for," I said.

"You are many things Jacey Lange but gross and pathetic are not on that list."

"Then why is no one sleeping with me?"

When I asked that question, something crossed Leon's face. It looked like guilt, but I couldn't understand why. I used to feel like I knew everything about the man next to me. In the last few months, however, I just couldn't seem to figure him out.

"Why do you do this?" he demanded, seemingly out of nowhere.

"Do what?"

"I've been try–" he started but stopped himself long enough to take a breath. "I've been trying to figure this out for years. You are unbelievably talented and beautiful and smart and funny, and that's just the surface level stuff. Yet you are sitting here basing your entire sense of worth on whether strangers want to have sex with you or not. It's insane. I love you, Jace, but it is seriously the most annoying thing about you."

I sat there wide-eyed and more than a little stunned by Leon's rant. I knew he was right, I just wasn't sure how to explain it to him. I wasn't even sure I knew how to explain it to myself. Somewhere in my warped perception desire felt like love, but as for why, I still wasn't sure.

"I need a pass," he suddenly said.

"What?"

"Rule number three. I need a pass."

Rule number three was no sexual comments. I shrugged my shoulders. It was the topic of conversation, after all. "Pass granted."

"Jace, why do you think we have the rules?" Leon asked, sounding frustrated as he raked a hand through his dark hair.

"I don't know. We made them up a million years ago. We didn't want to screw up our friendship," I shrugged.

"It's because if we didn't, it would be impossible not to want to sleep with you."

It was like someone sucked all the air out of the room. I struggled to comprehend what my best friend was saying to me.

"I'm sorry. What?"

"I'm just saying that resisting you is *not* easy."

We were both quiet for a minute. Leon seemed to be struggling with whether he should say more. "It might as well be an Olympic sport," he added.

"Wait..." I said. I was confused. I'd been friends with Leon since I was nineteen years old, and he never once said anything remotely like this. Maybe he was trying to make me feel better? I glanced over at him. His strong features were tangled as he waited for me to say something. He definitely wasn't just trying to boost my ego.

"Leon, what are you talking about? I'm not even your type," I said with an awkward laugh.

It was true. The girls Leon had been involved with over the years were so similar they could be sisters. They were all tall, leggy blondes that looked like they'd just walked off a catwalk. I was none of those things.

"I don't have a type."

"Oh yes, you do! Let's examine the evidence... Katie, Natalia, Leanna, Kris—"

"Okay, okay! My point was, I'd be lying if I said I wasn't attracted to you."

"W-why is this the first time you're saying this?" I stammered.

I glanced down at the bottle of wine. There wasn't enough of it missing to blame his admission on the alcohol. It wasn't that I didn't appreciate what he was saying or that I wasn't aware of my own thoughts and the way they could wander. I just couldn't seem to process why he was dropping a bomb like that out of nowhere.

"Look, we probably shouldn't unpack all of this right now. The point is, I don't want you sitting around thinking that anything that's going on is because you aren't desirable."

I turned and faced forward. I just stared at the wall across the room for several seconds. I knew Leon said he didn't want to unpack it, but my mind was reeling. The only thing I could think to do was change the subject. "Since we're having a heart-to-heart... what's been going on with you lately?"

"What do you mean?"

"I know I said I didn't want to hear about Natalia, but if you guys are back together, I swear to God Leon, I'll—"

When I turned back to look at him, he was grinning so wide he was almost laughing. "You'll what?"

I hadn't planned out the end of that sentence, but never one to back down, I just said the first thing that came to mind. "I'll tell her about nerdy high school Leon!"

"You wouldn't dare!" he mocked.

Once upon a time, my best friend had been a lanky mathlete with bad skin and braces. He didn't turn into the built, well-dressed man next to me until the summer before he went to college.

"We're not back together," he assured me.

"Then what is it?"

Leon looked at me for a long second and then moved in closer, too close. My heart started racing. *What the hell is he...? Is he...?* Before I could get any of my thoughts to make sense, Leon grabbed my glass of wine and downed the rest of it with a triumphant smile.

"Hey! That's mine!"

"Fine, I'll just drink this," he said, grabbing the bottle of wine by the neck and taking a huge gulp.

"Give me that!" I protested. I pulled the bottle from his hands and gave him a look of pretend shock. "You have your own glass!"

"Nope, no more glasses. If you want to know what's going on, then we're drinking from the bottle."

I rolled my eyes, but the truth was, Leon already turned my night around. He always had a way of doing that. My whole world could be falling apart, yet he always knew what to do or say to make it all okay again. "Okay, deal!" I said before taking a large sip from the bottle. The wine was starting to hit me now, and I could feel my face beginning to flush.

"There's... this girl," he said.

"I knew it!"

"It's not that simple."

"I have never met a girl you couldn't seduce."

"Yeah, you have..." His tone changed as if I was somehow supposed to know what he was implying.

"Wait! It's someone I know?"

The alcohol was starting to settle in, both from the drinks I had at the opening and the pity wine I'd been throwing back. I was louder and warmer than usual. "Let me guess... you're in love with Elise!" I teased sarcastically.

"You're drunk," Leon laughed.

"Not yet... but I'm getting there!" I beamed as I took yet another gulp.

"Normally, you're right. I don't have a problem in that department, but this one... she's..."

I took stock of the look on his face. I'd never seen Leon seem so completely enamored before. He didn't even have the words to tell me how he felt about this girl. He'd always been such a player — one girl to the next. Other than Natalia, he'd never been serious about any of them. This, however, was something else. The realization struck a chord inside me that I couldn't explain.

"Leon's in love! Leon's in love!" I started singing like a child on the playground.

I was both teasing him and trying desperately to shake the heavy feeling out of the pit of my stomach. I expected some sarcastic response, but instead, he just dropped his head, letting it hit the back of the couch. He looked up at me through his dark eyelashes, and suddenly it hit me.

"Holy shit!"

"What?" he asked cautiously, his dark brows knitting together.

"You don't have a comeback."

"What am I supposed to say?"

I grabbed both sides of his face in excitement. "You are in love!"

"Okay, it's officially time for you to go to bed," he said.

I crossed my arms over my chest and shook my head. "Not until you tell me who it is!"

"She doesn't feel the same way about me, so it doesn't matter."

"Leon!"

"Jacey!"

"I'm not getting off this couch. You can't make me!"

"Oh, really?" he said with a laugh.

Suddenly, Leon stood up, and without warning, he picked me up off the couch and practically tossed me over his shoulder.

"Put me down, you ridiculously muscular man!"

I playfully hit his arm, but he just laughed and started toward the staircase that led to my room.

"This isn't fair! Why are you so strong?" I continued

to protest.

The truth was, I probably did need to go to bed, but I was dying to know who this girl was that had suddenly brought the great Leondro Acosta to his knees. I wasn't even sure that I cared who she was. I was just happy that it wasn't Natalia.

It only took a moment for Leon to carry me into my room and toss me onto my bed like a rag doll.

"I'm going to find out!" I shouted as he headed for the door.

"Goodnight, Jace."

Thirty-Nine

An hour later, I still wasn't sleeping. I hadn't moved from the spot Leon left me. I just laid there, staring at the ceiling. There was this gnawing feeling that started when I saw the look on his face. When I realized that he genuinely had feelings for some mystery girl, I began to feel the same way I did when I thought of him with Natalia. It was like he turned into another man when he talked about her. Why did I care? He was my best friend, so of course, I cared about his well-being, but why couldn't I shake this? Each time I tried to put Leon out of my mind, I would spiral and start thinking about Cash. I felt awful no matter what I thought about, and the only thing that had been able to get my mind off it was Leon.

I looked over at the clock on my nightstand and realized how long I had been contemplating this. I was immediately annoyed with myself. Why couldn't I go to

sleep? It didn't help that I was still wearing the dress and makeup I'd worn to the party, so at the very least, I had to take those off. I dragged myself out of bed, yanked the skin-tight dress off my body, and tossed it to the floor. I grabbed a robe and slid it over my shoulders. I realized I didn't want to be in bed at all and decided to check if Leon was awake. I promised myself I wouldn't ask about his girl again, lest I get thrown back in bed, but I still felt this urge to be near him.

I left my bedroom, quietly creeping down the stairs to the kitchen. I reasoned with myself that from there, I would be able to look into the living room and see if Leon was still up. If he was, I could casually pretend to be getting a glass of water.

Who was I kidding? There was nothing casual about this.

I looked, but there was no Leon. I paced around for a moment before I spotted a bag of cookies sitting on the counter and shoved one into my mouth. I contemplated what to do. I still wanted Leon, or at the very least, I didn't want to be alone. I decided there was no harm in seeing if he was awake and made my way toward his bedroom.

Outside the door, I listened for a moment but didn't hear anything. Leon might've already fallen asleep, but I timidly tapped twice on the door anyway. When he opened it, he was shirtless, yet again, and more than a little surprised to see me. This time, I willed myself not to let my eyes wander. It was his room after all; I couldn't demand he put a shirt on. Even if I could, I wasn't entirely sure that I wanted to.

"Are you okay?" he asked me.

I shook my head. "I can't sleep. I just don't want to

be alone right now."

Leon opened the door further to allow me inside. I stood there, uncomfortable for a moment. I didn't know what to do with myself, so I just sat down on the edge of his bed. There wasn't so much as a wrinkle in his Egyptian cotton sheets, so I knew he also hadn't been sleeping.

"You couldn't sleep either?" I asked.

"I just have a lot on my mind."

I wanted to jump right in and ask him what was wrong. I wanted to know if it was this girl and his unrequited love for her that kept him awake, but I decided not to pry. "Yeah, I get that."

"Well, what's on your mind?" he asked me.

I hesitated. I couldn't tell Leon that he was the one keeping me up. I wasn't even sure if it was his fault. Some part of it was, but I had also just broken up with Cash. I just felt alone. I was a wreck, and honestly, I was having a hard time wrapping my mind around anything that happened that night. I didn't know what to say, so I decided to go with the obvious.

"I'm just upset about my fight with Cash."

"I'm still not sure I understand what happened," he said.

"I do," I admitted. "Cash wanted me to choose."

"Choose?"

"Between you and him."

"And you chose me?"

"I will always choose you," I admitted softly.

Leon paused, never breaking his eye contact with me. My eyes searched his, but I was unsure of what he was thinking. "I just want you to know that you're the most incredible woman I've ever met, Jace," he finally said.

Leon got up and knelt in front of me, those eyes still boring into me as he spoke.

"It baffles me that anyone would push you away, and anyone that is that stupid doesn't deserve to take up space in your head," he added.

My heart was banging out of my chest. It was beating so hard it made my ears ring. The men I'd been seeing gave plenty of compliments but there was something about hearing it from him, from someone who really knew me. We stared at each other for what felt like ages. I don't know what came over me, but I couldn't stop myself. I leaned in and captured his lips with mine.

Leon froze. It was like he was stunned but before I could start to hesitate, I felt his lips move with mine. There was only a breath between us before his hands reached up to both sides of my face and he deepened the kiss into something hard and desperate. I couldn't breathe. I couldn't even think to breathe. I didn't know what the hell we were doing, but it felt so right. The kiss could have lasted for seconds or hours; time just stopped. But just as abruptly as I kissed him, he pulled away. His handsome face was full of questions.

"Are you sure you—"

I didn't let him ask them. I just kissed him again. It was a bad idea, I knew that, but my body and my head were on two completely different planets.

Leon got up just enough to push me back onto the bed, his mouth never leaving mine. My whole body was screaming. It screamed so loud that I couldn't hear the tiny voice in my head trying to remind me that this was my best friend, and worse yet, he'd just told me he was in love with someone else.

My fingers slowly made their way down his chest. I

hooked them into the elastic waistband of his sweatpants, but just as I started to pull at them, he pulled away from me again.

"Stop! Stop! We have to stop."

I didn't think I could handle being rejected again, not twice in one night.

"Who am I?" he asked me.

I looked up at him, completely confused, but answered his question. "Leon."

"Where are we?"

I still didn't understand, but he wasn't giving me much choice. I had to go along with this strange line of questioning. "Our apartment? Midtown? New York? The United States? Earth?"

"Are you drunk?" he asked me.

A lightbulb went off, and I suddenly understood what he was doing. Leon was trying to figure out if I was so drunk that I'd just kissed him by mistake or if I was, drunkenly, thinking he was someone else. He was trying to get consent. It made perfect sense, especially given how we'd first met, but it still made my heart melt a little.

"Vaguely buzzed but no, not drunk."

I was telling the truth. I'd spent an hour in terrible, sobering self-reflection. There was still alcohol in my system, but I knew what I was doing. At least, I thought I did.

Before Leon could ask me any more questions, I slid my arms around his neck, pulled him down towards me, and kissed him again.

"I consent. I consent so fucking hard," I said against his lips.

He smiled. It was clear that was all he needed to hear. Leon hovered over me, leaning on one hand as the other untied my robe. The way his eyes moved over my body was painstakingly slow. It was like he was trying to memorize it. I should have felt self-conscious. No one had ever looked at me that way before, but instead, I just felt safe.

"You're so beautiful," he whispered to me.

I knew how irresponsible this was, and I knew that I was hardly in the right mindset to be sleeping with anyone, but I didn't care. It was like the moment I kissed Leon, something snapped inside me, and all of this pent-up need and desire came rushing to the surface. There would be a time to deal with the repercussions later. I wasn't naive enough to think I could sleep with my best friend and not have to face the consequences, but my overwhelming need for him was the only thing that mattered at that moment.

"I want you," I responded as my hands slowly made their way lower. Touching him in a way that I knew I couldn't come back from.

"Say it again," he all but growled in response.

"I want you, Leon. I need you. Please."

I was so afraid the same thing that happened each time I tried to get intimate with the other men I'd been dating would happen now. I was scared that he would come up with an excuse or pull away from me. I sounded like I was begging. In a way, perhaps I was.

He kissed me again before slowly trailing his mouth to my neck. My back arched into him, bringing my body closer to his as his hands started to explore me.

There was something familiar about all of this. It didn't make sense because I knew that Leon and I had never been together before. Usually, there was this awkward way people fumbled through their first encounter together, but with Leon, it was like we already knew exactly how to please each other. It was instinctive. We just knew.

"Tell me you're feeling this..." I gasped out.

"I'm here. I'm with you," he whispered.

The entire room felt heavy and electric. The space between our bodies was on fire. I never experienced anything like it. All I knew was that I didn't want it to end. If I could live in that exact moment with Leon forever, I would.

Everything he did was just right. I didn't know how that was possible. We never came anywhere near crossing this line before, and yet it was like our bodies just fit together, understood each other. Every time his fingertips moved from one part of my body to the next, I ached for more of him. That same ache continued building and building inside me to the point I no longer knew anything but the need for his touch. I wanted more of him than I thought could even be possible.

Until I had all of him.

We spent that night wrapped around each other. We barely spoke. Perhaps we were both afraid that if we said too much, if we questioned what we were doing, we would ruin it, and it was perfect. Each time I thought we might have exhausted each other, we started again. Neither one of us was able to get enough of the other. It wasn't until we were lying lifeless on his bed, watching the sun come up from his bedroom window, that we could no longer keep our eyes open.

Forty

I woke up the following morning utterly confused. Not only was I not in my bed, but I was in Leon's? I looked over at my best friend, who was wide awake and lying next to me. When he saw me open my brown eyes, I watched the biggest smile form on his face. Paired with the morning light peeking through his window, it was a breathtaking sight. I couldn't comprehend how anyone could be so beautiful. Unfortunately, my head had not yet caught up with me. What I did manage to figure out was that he was naked, and I was naked.

"Good morning," he beamed.

Leon was still smiling. He looked unspeakably happy, though I didn't understand why. He shouldn't be this cheery. I had just—the memory of the night before hit me like a truck. I shot straight up in bed, my hand covering my mouth.

"What's wrong?"

Was he crazy?

"We slept together!"

Leon's expression dropped as if I had slapped the smile right off his face. *Okay, he's catching up now.*

"I'm so sorry, Leon!"

I felt guilt creeping up in me with every passing second I sat naked in my best friend's bed.

"Wait. Why are you apologizing?" He looked both confused and hurt. I was sure that I looked shocked and somewhat insane. I certainly felt that way.

"The-the girl!" I said. I was scrambling and not quite awake enough to make sense. I took in a sharp breath. "You were telling me about this girl and how you had feelings for her, and my needy, pathetic ass decided to seduce you! God, I'm terrible! I'm so sorry."

The last response I was expecting was laughter, but that's what I heard. It was this deep, throaty laugh that only escaped Leon when he thought something was genuinely funny.

"What?" I demanded.

"Can I make you breakfast?" he asked me, shaking his head.

"You want to make me breakfast after what I did?" I gaped.

"Yes, I do," he said calmly.

I tried to avoid watching him get up and put clothes on. Instead, I stared down intently at the sheets covering my body.

"I'll be in the kitchen," he said before leaving me alone in his room.

I sat there for a while in complete shock. I wasn't just shocked at myself, but at Leon and how calm he seemed to be. I found my robe and slid it on before leaving his room. True to his word, I found him whisking eggs in a bowl while the coffee pot loudly brewed.

I sat down on one of the barstools and just watched him. I was puzzled by how unaffected he seemed to be. I wanted to say something, anything, but I couldn't. Was this just what post-sex Leon was like? Blissfully happy and making scrambled eggs? He glanced up at me every once in a while. Each time, he seemed to be holding back more laughter.

When he finished cooking, Leon put a plate down in front of me and then took the barstool next to mine. I worried about the state our friendship was in and the state of Leon's relationship with his mystery woman. I felt so guilty that even the thought of eating made me sick to my stomach. Instead, I just poked at my food, pushing it around the plate absently with my fork.

"Jace, stop it," he said.

"I just feel so awful," I responded.

"You don't get it?" he asked.

"Get what?"

Leon rolled his eyes and dropped the piece of toast he had just taken a bite of back onto his plate. "It's you."

"What's me?" I wasn't following at all.

"You're her," he said as he turned to face me.

I froze. If I *had* taken a bite, I would have choked.

"Are you saying that..." I started slowly. I didn't want to say the wrong thing, and I certainly didn't want to hurt him. I just didn't know how to react.

"Yeah, I am."

I looked down at my plate, and for a moment, my brain just shut off. I wasn't sure how long I'd been staring at my breakfast. Nothing about this seemed real. Was I dreaming? Yesterday, my best friend and I were just friends. Now it was morning, and he was telling me he wanted more than that. Not only that, we'd already crossed that line.

"Say something, please," he said.

I didn't know what to say, but I could hear the pleading in Leon's voice, and I knew I needed to try. I loved this man. I didn't know if I was in love with him or even if I could be, but I did love him, and I was sure that he was terrified right now.

"I'm sorry. I just..."

I finally made eye contact with him, but quickly looked away. The need in his eyes was too much for me. "I'm scared," I finally admitted.

Leon was amazing in every sense of the word. He was everything a girl could want. However, that didn't change the fact that we had ten years of history together. I was afraid to risk that.

"Why are you scared?"

I looked at him as if he'd just asked me why we don't have a pet hyena. The answer was obvious. And yet... "I-I don't know," I said.

"Then talk me through it. What's going on in your head, Jace?"

Leon was so gentle with me, even though I knew he was probably freaking out internally.

"You're my best friend," I said to him.

"Yes, and that's not going to change."

"How could it not?"

"We've been friends for a decade. That's not going to change because we slept together once," he said.

"But you..."

"Have feelings for you?"

I nodded my head.

"That's been going on for ten years, too, and I've managed to keep it from changing anything. The only difference is, now you know."

"You've had feelings for me this whole time?" I asked Leon in complete disbelief.

"Since the second I laid eyes on you," he said.

"Why didn't you tell me? We tell each other everything!"

"When we met, this terrible thing had just happened to you, Jace. You needed a friend, and I wanted to be that for you. By the time you were doing better, we were so close that I was afraid of screwing it up," he explained.

"I don't understand." I still tried desperately to wrap my mind around what was going on.

"What don't you understand?"

"This! Any of it! Leon, I've watched you date every blonde with a modeling contract in the tri-state area for years. Now you're telling me that you wanted to be with me that whole time? That doesn't make any sense."

"If you were trying to hide the fact you were in love with someone close to you, don't you think a good place to start would be dating people who were nothing like them?"

"What about Natalia?" I asked, completely bypassing the implication that Leon was in love with me.

"What about her?"

"You were such a mess when you two broke up," I said.

Leon shook his head. "What was happening in your life when Natalia and I broke up?" he asked me.

"Brian and I had just..." I started, but the realization of what he was implying hit me immediately.

"Gotten engaged," he finished for me. "I wasn't a mess over Natalia. I was a mess over you."

"I need some air," I said abruptly, getting up from the

counter and making my way over to the fire escape. I didn't care that I was still in a robe. I slid out the living room window. It was cold, but the blast of air that hit me and the sound of traffic below me helped snap me back to reality.

It wasn't that I didn't have feelings for Leon. After last night, I couldn't deny that I did, but just because I could admit I had feelings for him didn't mean that I was supposed to be with him. I crossed my arms over my chest and started trying to sort things out.

My mind wandered back to the hundreds of times I told people over the years that there was nothing going on between Leon and me. My parents, my friends, my co-workers, and even people we were involved with all constantly implied there had to be something going on. Apparently there was, I was just blissfully unaware of it. I glanced toward the window and then back out at the street below me. After last night, there was a part of me that knew I could fall into Leon and never look back. However, there was also a part of me that knew I wouldn't survive losing him if it all went wrong and the fear of that pain was paralyzing.

I wasn't sure how long I'd been standing out there before I heard the window open. Leon held out an oversized hoodie for me to take. My mind still raced, but I couldn't help but smile. I was probably wrecking him with nerves, and yet he still cared enough about me to try to keep me from getting cold. He didn't ask for answers. Leon just wanted to keep me warm.

"Should I give you some space?" he asked.

"No, it's okay," I said before he climbed out the window and stood next to me. "I have one last question," I sighed.

"I'll tell you anything you want to know."

"Why did you push so hard for me to start dating if you were—"

"Jacey, I've wanted you since we met, but I pretty much resigned myself to the fact it wasn't going to happen," he explained, taking a step closer to me. "You weren't interested, and I was okay with that. I wanted you to date because you'd just gotten your heart broken, and I wanted you to be happy again," he added. I looked up at him as he gently pushed a strand of hair out of my face, his fingers lingered against my cheek for a long moment . "I still want you to be happy whether that's with me or not," he said, his voice growing quieter as he didn't want to say the last two words.

"I was," I corrected him.

"You were what?"

"Interested."

Leon looked confused, and so I continued.

"The first thing I thought when I woke up in your bed in that frat house was, 'this is the most beautiful man I've ever seen. I can't believe I just threw up in his room.'"

Leon laughed and wrapped his arms around me. He pulled me close and kissed the top of my head.

"Do you want to know the first thing I thought when I woke up in your bed this morning?" I asked.

"What's that?"

"This is the most beautiful man I've ever seen. I can't believe he's in love with someone else."

"He's not. He's in love with you," Leon said softly.

I didn't know why I felt tears behind my eyes when he said those words. Perhaps it was because I didn't know what any of this meant. Was I about to jump into a relationship with my best friend after all these years of denying we were anything but platonic? Should I even be jumping into a relationship at all? It was less than twenty-four hours ago that I told another man I loved him.

I needed to think, and I couldn't do that with a six-foot-two Portuguese man professing his love to me. I knew that Leon needed me to tell him how I felt, and tell him if this had a future, but he meant too much to me to jump into this impulsively.

"Can I have today? I just need to clear my head and think, and then...we can have dinner or something? I'll try to figure out where I'm at with all of this by then," I said, trying hard not to sound discouraging.

"You don't have to rush, Jace."

I nodded. I knew that I didn't have to rush, but at the same time, I knew my best friend's heart was on the line, and it would be cruel to leave him waiting. "I just need until tonight," I reassured him.

I turned to go inside, intent on going up to my room and showering before I tried to get ahold of my sister, but before I could crouch down to slide back inside, Leon grabbed my arm. He turned me around to face him. Gently, his hand brushed my face as I looked up at him. He kissed me deeply, filling my body with the same need I'd felt last night.

"In case I don't get to do that again," he murmured.

Forty-One

When I returned to my bedroom, everything was still. I just stood there listening to the deafening quiet. It was peaceful compared to the war that raged inside my head. At the foot of my bed was a long, dark blue ottoman. I sat down, burying my head in my hands.

I *had* a plan. I was going to shower, text Elise, and then leave the apartment for the day, but now that I was alone, all I wanted to do was crawl into my bed. My mind was rapidly spinning. One minute, I tried to wrap my head around the fact that my best friend just confessed his love for me. The next minute, I'd start remembering the feeling of Leon's fingertips against my skin or the way his mouth felt against mine the first time we kissed. Then I'd flip to panicking about how I was possibly supposed to figure out something so life-changing in a matter of hours.

I needed someone's thoughts other than my own to

get me through this. I took out my phone and texted my sister and Nia, telling them it was an emergency. My sister was at the bakery she owned on the upper west side, but according to her, it was a slow morning, so the three of us decided to meet there. I jumped in the shower, dressed quickly, and rushed out the door in an attempt to avoid any further conversation with Leon. I wasn't upset with him. It was just that I didn't want my mind clouded with any more memories of that perfect body or all of the things I now knew it could do.

Frosted Rose was Elise's baby. When the two of us started at NYU, I knew what I wanted to do with my life, but Elise wasn't so sure. After she dabbled in some culinary classes, it became clear to her that she had a calling. As soon as Elise graduated, she went to full-time culinary school. Somehow she managed to convince both my parents and the Montgomerys to invest in a bakery. The result was a shockingly pink exterior right on the corner of 65th and West End. Everything inside was pastel, floral, and perfectly curated to be as Instagram-able as possible. The business was successful overall, but once in a while, there were slow moments.

Elise wasn't exaggerating when she said no one was around that morning. As I walked into the bakery, the only sounds were of Taylor Swift playing through the overhead speakers, and the only person there was Madison, Elise's cashier. She was idly scrolling through her phone until she heard the entrance chimes go off as I opened the door. I watched her stash her phone under the counter and sit up straight in the hopes that I didn't see what she had just been doing.

"You're fine Maddie, it's just me," I said. "Where's Elise?"

As if on cue, my sister emerged from the back

carrying a large tray of baby blue cookies. "Oh good, you're here," she said before setting the tray down on the counter. "Maddie, those are for the Galvan baby shower. Can you pack them up for me?"

The eighteen-year-old got to work while Elise came out from around the counter and wrapped her arms around my neck.

"What's going on? Are you okay?" she asked.

I had to admit that I was surprised at how much concern there was in my sister's voice. I knew she cared about me, but Elise always seemed to be the main character of any story. She could be more than a little self-involved, especially as her wedding drew closer.

Before I could respond, the entrance chime went off again.

"This better be good," Nia announced as she walked through the door.

As soon as I turned to look at Nia, she stopped in her tracks, and her tone changed completely. "Honey, what is wrong?" she said, crossing the distance between us and grabbing my hand.

The worry, doubt, and confusion I was feeling were all over my face. I wanted to hide it, but I just couldn't. "Can we sit?" I asked.

The three of us took seats at the closest table. They were the same signature pink as the outside of the building with tiny flowers embossed onto the glass tabletop.

"Are you pregnant?" Elise jumped in, grilling me immediately.

If I wasn't so twisted up inside, I might have laughed.

"Oh no, not with tattoos' baby! That is *not* happening!" Nia interrupted a little too loudly.

"I'm not pregnant," I assured them.

"Okay, then tell us what's wrong," Nia said.

I didn't know where to start or how to explain how I was feeling. I just knew if I didn't just get it out, I was going to go insane so, I blurted out the truth.

"I slept with Leon."

"What!" Elise almost screamed in response.

"I knew it!" Nia sounded far more excited than surprised.

"Knew what?"

"Oh, come on, Jacey! You don't have to pretend anymore," Nia said, shaking her head.

"Pretend?"

"Anyone who has ever seen you two together could have told you this was going to happen sooner or later."

I turned to look at my sister for confirmation of what Nia just said.

"He's been in love with you since we were in college, Jace," she shrugged.

"How did you know?"

"I didn't! I've just seen the way he—wait! Did Leon tell you he had feelings for you?"

I looked back down at the table, trying to avoid the prying eyes of the women in my life.

"He said he's in love with me," I said softly.

"Oh my god!" Elise squealed.

"Okay, hold on. What exactly happened?" Nia asked.

"Cash and I...broke up or whatever. When I came home, Leon and I hung out and drank wine. He tried to cheer me up, and he started telling me about this girl he had feelings for but that she didn't feel the same way. I had no idea who he was talking about, and eventually, we went to bed, but when I was up in my room, all I could think about was the fight with Cash, and I didn't want to be alone, so I went back downstairs to see if he was awake, and..."

"Were you sober?"

"Yes, I knew what I was doing." I rolled my eyes at her. It was a fair question, but it didn't make it any less annoying. "I wanted to do it. I didn't even do it because I was angry at Cash. I just...wanted...Leon," I explained with a blush.

"I don't see the problem here," Elise chimed in, tossing her hands up as she spoke.

"Okay, let's try 'Leon is my best friend', for starters!"

"Calm down! Some of the best relationships start as friendships," Nia assured me.

I covered my face with my hands. I knew that Nia and Elise were just trying to be supportive, but I started to regret opening up about this.

"Do you have feelings for him?" Elise asked carefully.

"I think so."

"You think?" Nia asked with a laugh.

"I don't know. I've never had to think about it until now!"

"Alright, I want you to be completely honest when you answer this..." She turned her chair to face me directly and leaned forward before she continued. "Was there ever a time that you had thoughts or feelings about Leon that you didn't want to admit to or ignored because you were friends?"

I paused before I responded, but I already knew the answer. I checked Leon out more times than I cared to admit. I was more than a little jealous of Natalia. If I was honest, I had been jealous of every woman he'd been with in one way or another. Plus, there were all these little moments when he would accidentally touch me or look at me a little too long, and I would fall apart. I kept telling myself that it was nothing, but some part of me always knew there was more to it than that. I was just too scared to admit it.

"Yes."

"How many times?" Nia prodded me.

"More than I can count."

"Then I think you have your answer," she said before turning her chair back toward the table.

"Oh my god, this is so exciting!" Elise said, bouncing a little in her seat.

"Why are you so excited? A couple of weeks ago, you were still trying to get me back together with August."

"I mean...if August is still an option..." Elise teased.

"That's the last thing I need," I said, rolling my eyes.

"The only reason I wanted you to date August was that I knew if he went to school with Nate, that meant he had money. If he had money, that meant he could take care of you. With Leon, I don't have to worry about that. I already know he'd move mountains to take care of you," she said.

Elise was right. Over the years, Leon had done everything he could to make sure I was safe and happy, and that was just as my friend. I was still really scared, but something clicked. Leon was the right choice. He had to be.

That was, until the one person who could make me question that choice came walking through the door.

My heart stopped as I watched his wavy hair and long limbs move across the floor of the lobby without even noticing I was there. "Hi, I'm picking up for Lily Galvan," he said to Elise's cashier.

I just stared for a long moment, unable to make

words come out of my mouth. I wasn't even sure that he was there or if it was my imagination.

"Gabe?" I finally said.

He turned in my direction with a startled look on his face, but his olive-green eyes softened as soon as he recognized me. "Jacey? Hi! How are you?" he asked me.

I didn't even turn to give my sister or Nia an explanation. I just got up out of my seat and hurried over to him. Gabe didn't hesitate at all. He wrapped his arms around me and hugged me tightly. He still smelled of cinnamon, and he still hugged me in a way that made me never want to let go.

"I'm okay, I guess. How have you been?"

"I'm good, really good."

I looked over at Madison, who was packing up the eight boxes of cookies.

"Are you having a baby?" I asked sarcastically.

"Not that I know of, but my sister is," he said with a laugh.

"That's great!" I said, sounding more cheery than I had in hours.

"What are you doing here?" he asked me.

"This is my sister's bakery," I explained, pointing over my shoulder at Elise.

The two awkwardly waved at each other before I realized how rude I was being. "I'm sorry. Gabe, this is my sister, Elise, and my business partner and dear friend, Nia."

The three of them exchanged pleasantries before he turned his attention back to me. "So, how is it going with that guy you're seeing?" he asked me.

"We...um...broke up, actually..."

"Oh, I'm sorry to hear that," Gabe said.

The strange thing was I genuinely believed him when he said those words. Even though I stopped seeing him to pursue Cash, there wasn't a hint of relief or malice in Gabe's voice.

"Here's that order for you," Madison said as she handed over the cookies that she divided into two oversized pink tote bags.

"Thank you," he said and started to take the bags off the counter.

I should have told him it was nice to see him and sent him on his way, but despite my revelations about Leon, a thought crossed my mind. Maybe this was a sign. What was the likelihood of running into Gabe in my sister's bakery, of all places? I didn't even know if I believed in signs but, whether I could admit I had feelings for Leon or not, I was terrified. Gabe's sweet face and almost limitless level of kindness seemed in direct opposition to the fear that still lingered over the possibility of ruining the most important relationship in my life.

"What are you doing right now?" I asked.

"Baby shower?" he said, holding up the bags to remind me.

"Right..." I said, trying to think of a reason to spend even a few more minutes with him. I had to know if this was just a coincidence or if his sudden appearance was more than that. "Can I walk with you? I need to get some air, and you look like you might need help with those," I said.

It was a poor excuse. I was sure that Gabe could handle two bags of cookies all on his own, but I was grasping at straws, and I had never really been good at thinking on my feet.

"Sure, it'll give us a chance to catch up," he said with a smile.

"Okay, I just need a minute. I'll meet you outside," I said to him. Gabe stepped out, and I immediately turned to both Nia and Elise with an apologetic look on my face.

"Who is that?" Nia asked me.

"The guy before Cash," I said.

"The nurse?"

"He's a caregiver, but yes."

"Jacey, do you really think this is a good idea?" Elise asked me, the worry returning to her voice.

"I don't know. We're just going for a walk," I assured her.

I expected a lecture, but Nia and Elise just looked at each other.

"Okay," my sister said before getting up and hugging me. "Let me know what happens?"

"I will."

Nia hugged me as well, and with that, I followed Gabe outside.

Forty-Two

The moment I left Gabriel Warren's apartment after I chose Cash, I began to wonder if I had made a mistake. Sure, Cash and I had passion, but Gabe and I had something else. We had a connection that I didn't know how to explain or even make sense of, but it was there. The moment I let it go, I began to miss it. I had never been religious, so I didn't believe in divine intervention, and while I liked the concept of fate, I didn't exactly subscribe to the idea that our lives were predestined.

But I had no other way to explain how Gabe walked through the door of my sister's bakery mere seconds after I'd decided to give a relationship with Leon a shot. If his sister had ordered cookies from another bakery, or I had come to talk to Elise an hour later, we would have missed each other entirely. Yet, at the exact moment I thought I made a decision, he appeared. *What did that mean?*

When I stepped outside the bakery, Gabe was waiting for me. I only needed one look at the smile that slowly formed on his face to remember just how quickly he could leave me speechless. Gabe was different in a way I could never quite put my finger on. There was something so honest and gentle about everything he did. It was hard for me to believe that there wasn't a catch and that Gabe was all he appeared to be.

"Shall we?" he asked me before we both started walking.

I wasn't sure where his sister's baby shower was or how much time I had with him, but I decided not to question it and let whatever stroke of fate put Gabe back in my life determine what happened next.

"Can I take one of those?" I asked, looking down at the bags from the bakery.

"No. You can't," Gabe said, though his tone was playful.

"Why?"

"I was raised by women. I guess you can call it childhood conditioning," he said with a shrug.

"You were conditioned not to let other people help you carry things?"

"It's more like I was conditioned to always choose the more chivalrous option," he explained.

"Okay, but what if I said I *wanted* to carry the bag."

Gabe stopped in his tracks and sighed heavily before handing one of the bags over to me.

"See, that wasn't so hard," I teased.

"Just don't tell my moms I let you do that."

I tilted my head to the side, unsure if I had heard him correctly. "Did you say moms? Like multiple?"

"Yeah, I guess we didn't get the chance to talk about our families much."

I realized just how much I didn't know about Gabe.

We spent hours talking to each other, yet there were still so many things about his life I knew nothing about. I told myself not to compare, but I kept thinking about how different my situation with Leon was. I knew everything there was to know about him. I could write the book on Leon, from how he took his coffee, to his favorite song, to the tiny town in Portugal where his mother lived. That was why the fact he hid his feelings for me for so long was hard for me to process.

I shook my head. I didn't want to think about Leon. At least, not right now.

"So you have two moms and a sister..." I said, putting together the pieces of what I knew so far.

"Three sisters," he corrected me.

"You weren't kidding about being raised by women!"

"Not at all," he said with a laugh.

"But the baby is a boy?" I said, remembering that the cookies Elise made were blue.

"I think I'm the only one who's not disappointed about that," he chuckled.

"I'm sure they'll get used to one more man in the family."

Talking to Gabe was always easy and comfortable for me. Being around him was like being wrapped in a warm blanket. He was so gentle. It was part of why I was drawn to him in the first place.

"So, how is Gail doing?" I asked, trying to keep the conversation light.

"She's good. She still asks about you all the time," Gabe said with a laugh.

"Me?"

"You don't get the effect you have on people, do you?"

I wasn't sure what he meant. I knew the whole reason

that Gabe and I started dating was that Gail demanded he get my phone number, but I hardly expected she would still be invested.

"I guess not," I said with a shrug.

I expected Gabe to drop the subject. Instead, he stopped and turned to me.

"You're kind of electric, Jacey. People don't just forget you."

"People, or you?" I asked.

"Both."

For the first time since I'd spotted Gabe at the bakery, I began regretting my decision. I could feel old feelings stirring in me. I knew nothing good was going to come out of this little stroll down memory lane and yet I kept smiling and walking along like there wasn't a war going on in my mind.

"So what exactly happened with that guy you were seeing? You seemed so sure about the whole thing."

It was a bold question, and one I certainly hadn't expected him to ask. I quietly wondered why he wanted to know. Was he still interested, or was this just a strange way to make small talk?

"Have you ever mistaken volatility for passion?"

It had only been twenty-four hours since my fight with Cash, but it was clear to me that I had been romanticizing him. He looked like the kind of man my mother would warn me about, he was a brilliant artist, and he had this uncanny way of getting under my skin. In my mind, that translated into some epic love story. I kept picturing this chaotic, passionate, wild love affair that would permanently alter me and the way I saw the world. Cash, however, wasn't capable of that. He was just possessive, quick to anger, and usually drunk. I didn't doubt that he was already looking for his next conquest by the time I'd reached my apartment last night.

"No, but I get it," he said.

Every time Gabe finished a sentence, I got the sense that he had more to say. He just seemed to be stopping himself from saying it. I wanted to know what was going on in his mind. Instead of wondering, I decided to face it head-on. "What's going on in your head?"

"A lot."

"Care to enlighten me?"

"It's not my place."

"But I'm asking."

He sighed. "I'm starting to wonder if this was a good idea because you are distractingly beautiful. I also want to ask if that means you're single now, but I don't want to come off like I'm angling for something because I'm not."

"You're not?"

"Alright, maybe I am, but mostly I just want you to know I meant it when I said I wanted to be a part of your life."

"You're pretty distracting yourself," I said honestly.

I paused for a moment before speaking again. I didn't know where I wanted this to go. Gabe was putting himself on a silver platter for me, but in the back of my mind, I kept seeing Leon's face. I didn't know how I had gone from being too afraid to date to catapulting between men, but I also knew I needed to tread lightly before I ended up hurting someone.

"The answer to that question is a bit complicated," I admitted.

"Complicated how?"

"I am single, but I'm also trying to figure some things out."

"That doesn't sound all that complicated."

"Someone I really care about just told me they have feelings for me," I explained.

I had no idea why I was being so honest. Telling someone I had once been involved with about the situation with Leon was a terrible idea.

"Do you have feelings for him?" Gabe asked me. I could hear a hint of nervousness behind his voice.

I was honestly a little stunned at how bold Gabe was being. He had always been so cautious and kind of shy up until now. Perhaps he felt there was nothing to lose. We had already stopped seeing one another, so it wasn't like something was going to change if he managed to upset me.

"Yes... I do, but he's also not the one I'm following around Manhattan, so there's that..."

Gabe smiled and looked away from me. As I watched him, I couldn't help but feel guilt slowly pooling in the pit of my stomach. Was I going to lead everyone on? Leon, Gabe, hell, maybe I'd call up Owen and see if he wanted his emotions toyed with. I knew that I wasn't doing any of this maliciously. I genuinely cared about both of them, but just because I wasn't trying to hurt someone didn't mean that I wouldn't.

We were both quiet for a while. It was a loaded silence. I felt like I had a hundred things to say, but didn't know where to start. I didn't even know what I was doing. I was supposed to be coming up with an answer for Leon. Instead, I ditched Nia and Elise and wandered around the city flirting with Gabe. The whole thing was starting to feel less like it was destined to happen and more like I was chasing my tail to avoid doing what I knew I had to.

"Do you believe in fate?" I asked.

"Not really. I think people just make choices and then do the best they can with the choices they make," he said.

"So you don't believe people are meant to be together?"

"Like soulmates?"

"Something like that."

"I know this probably isn't the most romantic answer, but no," he said. "Relationships are work, even the good ones. I think people that seem like they're perfect for each other are just people who found someone worth doing the work for."

I let that thought spin around in my head. If I had to choose, not just between Leon and Gabe, but if I had to choose anyone... Who was worth doing the work for?

We reached the outside of an apartment building, and Gabe slowed to a stop. "This is me," he said.

I handed him the bag I was carrying and then stood there, a little unsure of what to say.

"It was great to see you."

"You too."

I wasn't sure what I was expecting. Gabe's arms wrapped around me tightly? A declaration of how much he'd missed me? Some big dramatic sign from the universe that I was supposed to end up with Gabe? Instead, there was just an uncomfortable silence between us. He didn't know what to say any more than I did. Maybe there had never been a sign. Maybe Gabe was right, and it all just came down to a choice. Either way, I took it as my cue to go.

"Thanks for letting me walk with you. I'll see you around," I said, trying to sound upbeat before turning to leave.

I only took a few steps before I heard Gabe speak again.

"Hey, Jacey..." he called out.

I turned to look at him as he shifted nervously.

"I just wanted to say...the door is always open...."

Forty-Three

After my conversation with Gabe, I promised myself that I would take some time to think. I could talk to my friends or follow around guys I'd once had a fling with, but I knew that the only person who could decide what was best for me was me. I couldn't go home. I knew if I did, I would only be thinking about Leon and what he needed. Instead, I needed to think of myself. I walked for a while with no destination in mind. I just listened to the sounds of the city move past me as I spun circles of memories around in my head.

I thought of the night I met Leon and how he made me feel safe during the scariest moment of my life. I thought of the night I caught Brian in bed with Lexi and how he swooped in and rescued me. I thought of the way he made me laugh and how it took him less than five minutes to turn my entire day around. On the other hand, there was the way we fought and how

irresponsible he always seemed to be with women's emotions. I understood now that he had no emotional investment in them. However, that didn't make it fair. Plus, what would happen if he fell out of love with me once he had me? I was sure that I could handle a break-up; I'd done it before, but I couldn't bear losing my best friend.

My wandering led me to the subway, where I sat quietly in a crowded car. There was something strangely private about being among so many people. I took the train the entire length of its route and watched people get on and off at every stop. When it finally reached 28th, I got off and continued walking. This time, much closer to home. I was trying so hard to make sense of my thoughts, but no matter what I did, there seemed to be just as many reasons to be with Leon as there were reasons not to. I thought back to what Gabe said to me, that couples who seemed to be perfect for each other had only found someone worth doing the work for. I just wasn't sure it was that simple.

I glanced down at my cell phone. It was five-thirty. I asked Leon for the day and the day came and went. I slowly made my way back to our apartment. I hoped that along the way, something would click inside me again, and I would know what to do next.

When I reached the front door of our building, I could feel the return of knots in my stomach, and I dragged my feet as I ascended the stairs and followed the familiar hallways. When I got to the door that led to our apartment, I just stood there for a long time. I remembered how relieved I was the night before when Leon opened the door for me. Today I was terrified of what would happen on the other side of it. I knew I was stalling, and so I bravely put my key in the door and started towards whatever chapter of my life was about to come next.

"Leon?" I called out into the apartment as I pushed the door open.

A brief second of silence passed before he emerged from his bedroom. He was wearing this slate gray, two-button, single-breasted suit, and he looked painfully good. I didn't know how my brain had already settled into seeing him as more than a friend, but all I could think when I saw him standing there was how badly I wanted to get him out of those exquisite clothes. I was still conflicted, but clearly my eyes weren't because I couldn't take them off him.

"Um... hi..." I stammered out, sounding like an awkward school girl. *Why did he have to look so good?*

"Hey, go get ready. We have reservations at seven," Leon said.

"Reservations?"

"You wanted to have dinner, right?"

"Yeah, I just..."

"Then go get ready," he said with a smile.

I couldn't believe how calm he seemed to be. If the tables were turned, I would have been a wreck. Yet Leon didn't seem to be worried at all.

I didn't argue with him. I just turned around and headed straight up to my room. I was still unsure of myself or what I wanted. I reasoned that a few more minutes alone could only help.

Earlier in the day, I was relieved to be on my own in the comfort of my room. Once I saw Leon in that suit, however, I found myself rushing around to get ready as quickly as possible. I didn't realize it at first, but for the first time since I woke up that morning, I didn't want to be alone. I took my clothes off and narrowed down my outfit search to three options.

"Hey, can you come here?" I called down to Leon.

It was only a matter of seconds before I heard him coming up the stairs.

"Hey, is everything o-" he started, but stopped as soon as he saw me standing there in my underwear. "Um... hi...." he said, almost tripping on his words. He sounded an awful lot like I did when I walked into the apartment.

"I just need help picking a dress," I said as casually as I could despite my best friend's eyes nearly popping out of his head.

Leon took a step toward my bed, examining the options. He held up a dark red dress and handed it to me. "This one," he said.

It always amazed me how decisive men could be when they wanted to. Left to my own devices, I could have spent an hour trying to decide between the dresses on my bed, but it took Leon all of fourteen seconds.

"I'll be right back," I said before taking the dress from him and walking into my bathroom. I knew what I was doing. It probably wasn't wise, considering I hadn't quite figured out what I wanted, but I had to admit that I liked the way Leon reacted to me now that he wasn't trying to hide anything.

As soon as I had the dress covering most of my body, I opened the door to the bathroom. Leon was still standing there looking equal parts uncomfortable and anxious.

"Can you help me with this?" I asked, pointing to the open zipper on the back of my dress.

Leon stepped into the bathroom, moving behind me. I watched in the mirror as he slowly zipped up my dress. I could feel his hands shaking. When he looked up, our eyes met in the reflection. Suddenly, I couldn't breathe. I felt his hand graze my hip, and my whole body reacted as I felt his touch again. It was the one thing I never considered while trying so hard to figure this out. Physically speaking, we were on fire. There was no way I could go back to living in this apartment and acting as though nothing happened between us. He barely touched me, and I was already falling apart at the seams.

I looked at the two of us in the mirror. I wasn't sure how I'd never noticed how right we seemed together. Everyone else in my life saw it, but I couldn't. Not until that moment.

"If you don't stop looking at me like that, we're not going to make it to dinner," he said. His voice was low, and I bit down on my bottom lip, hard. I turned around to face him, my body inches from his.

"I'm okay with that," I said.

There was a hint of sadness that crossed his face. He reached up and stroked my cheek softly, and then stepped away from me.

"Not until I know what you want, Jace."

Maybe Leon wasn't as calm as I thought he was. He left my room without even glancing back in my direction. I took a deep breath, trying to steady myself, and then finished getting ready. I was still waiting for that "click" to happen. It happened once, in the bakery, but then I saw Gabe, and I wasn't so sure. I felt a long list of things for Leon; gratitude, love, adoration, and suddenly even lust, but I also felt doubt, and it was that doubt that scared me.

Leon wouldn't tell me where we were going. So I just sat with him in the back of a cab, watching his knee anxiously bouncing up and down. I couldn't bring myself to look him in the face. I didn't want to see how much my indecision was affecting him. Instead, I reached out and put my hand on his knee to stop him. He sat there motionless for a moment before he slid his hand into mine. Neither of us said a word; Leon and I just waited.

Privé was an ultra-exclusive restaurant in Tribeca with a bit of a reputation. Unlike traditional dining experiences, Privé had private booths where you couldn't be seen or heard by anyone but the waitstaff. The idea was to create an atmosphere where the diners could focus on the award-winning food instead of the people around them. At least, that was the concept, but there were more than a few stories about people hooking up instead of having dinner. It also wasn't uncommon for the wealthy older men of Manhattan to bring their dates to a place that made it so easy to avoid prying eyes.

"Am I your mistress now?" I teased as Leon opened the door of the cab for me.

"God, I hope so!" Leon said as he looked me up and down in an exaggerated way.

I couldn't help but smile. Somehow that one sentence lightened up a situation that until then had been much too heavy. I was still unprepared for the impending conversation, but it was a nice reminder that Leon was still my best friend.

Once inside, our hostess led us to a mahogany booth that reminded me of an oversized version of the 1960s phone rooms found in old hotels. We looked over our menus, and again, there was silence. We quietly stole glances at each other as if we were both waiting for the other to say something, but neither one of us was brave enough to breach the subject. By the time someone came to take our orders, I was starting to panic. I still wasn't sure what to say or do, and this whole thing began to feel like a bad first date.

"I think I'm going to go crazy if you don't say something," Leon finally said the moment our waitress left us.

"Okay... 'something'..." I joked. I tried to make light of the situation, but it was clear from the look on Leon's face that I was doing more harm than good.

"I'm serious, Jacey. Talk to me."

"I'm still scared," I admitted.

That was the truth of it. The reason I hadn't come to a decision wasn't that I needed to be sure. It was because I was afraid.

"Me too," he said honestly.

"What are you scared of?"

"Losing you, mostly."

I reached for his hand across the table. "You're not going to lose me."

"Are you sure about that? Because you seem like you're a million miles away right now."

"Leon, I love you. Maybe I'm not *in* love with you...yet, but I've loved you every day of the last ten years. That isn't going to change. I just don't want to make a mistake."

"How can this be a mistake, Jace?"

I started to respond, but before I could speak, Leon jumped back in.

"Am I on another planet here? Are you not feeling what I'm feeling?"

"What are you feeling?" I asked shakily.

"Jacey, I want you so bad I can barely breathe. I used to think that maybe the way I felt about you was all in my head, and no matter how great I thought we might be together, I was never going to find out. Then last night happened, and now I..."

My breathing slowed. "Now?"

"Now I'm even more in love with you than I was before, and I'm terrified. I am so fucking scared that this is all I'll ever have of you," he said in a rush.

Then it clicked.

I could date every man on the island of Manhattan, but none of them would ever feel the way about me that Leon did. I thought back through the five men who'd inadvertently brought me here. I thought about riding on the back of Owen's motorcycle and sparring with August's brilliant mind. I thought about running around in the ocean in the middle of winter with Alex and the way Gabe managed to take me on three of the best dates of my life all in one day. I even thought about Cash and how crazy he made me in all the best and worst ways. The truth, however, remained that none of them held a candle to Leon.

"Ask me," I said.

Leon just looked at me like a deer in headlights.

"I can't say yes to a question you don't ask," I explained.

The relief on Leon's face when he processed what I was saying could have easily been the most beautiful thing I had ever seen.

"Be with me, please?"

Wordlessly, I got up out of my seat and moved to the other side of the table, sitting down next to Leon. Instead of responding, I just kissed him. It was long and passionate and filled with so much emotion that I thought I might drown in it. I didn't know what came next. All I knew was I was sure.

Forty-Four

Love was never easy for me. Every relationship I'd ever been in was always complicated and painful. I remember my mother telling me that it was supposed to be simple, that the kind of love that lasted a lifetime wasn't a soap opera but a Sunday paper. I thought that's what I had with Brian, but it still turned into a soap opera in the end. I found myself wondering what was wrong with me. No matter how many times I tried, I was always wrong.

Until Leon.

When I found out about Leon's feelings for me, I could only think one thing: it would ruin us. For ten years, my relationship with Leon was the easiest thing in my life. I assumed that letting myself fall for him would twist things around and that I would no longer know how to navigate them but, I was wrong. I was beautifully and perfectly wrong.

It was almost unreal the way we fell into step with each other. All I had to do was say yes, and it was like everything just slid right into place. The more I thought about it, the more I realized that both Nia and Elise had been right. Leon and I were inevitable.

What followed was a month of takeout and horror movies and sex on every possible surface of our apartment. I felt like I was living in some tailor-made fairy tale. Despite all of my hesitation and fear, I somehow ended up with everything I'd always dreamed of.

Leon and I had opposite morning schedules. I was up at 5 a.m., and he didn't roll out of bed until at least nine. During the week, he would put up with my crack-of-dawn alarms, and on the weekend, we would stay in bed as long as humanly possible. It was one such Saturday morning that was slowly turning into Saturday afternoon. We both lay in bed wrapped around each other when, without warning, I started laughing.

"What are you laughing at?" Leon asked me.

"I just realized something..."

"What's that?"

"I lost the bet, and I still got my room back," I giggled.

Leon shook his head. "I mean, I could send you back upstairs if you'd like," he said sarcastically.

"You would miss me too much."

"Miss your snoring? I think I'd be okay."

"I do not snore!" I protested as I threw the comforter off my body and started to get up.

"Get back here." Leon grabbed my arm and playfully pulled me back down onto the bed with him.

"You'd be lost without me, admit it!"

"Completely," he said before leaning in and kissing me softly. He looked at me for a long moment before he spoke again. "I love you."

"I'm... almost there," I said, trying to sound playful, though I was sure that he was getting tired of hearing that.

By the time Leon and I decided to dive headfirst into a relationship, he already told me he was in love with me, so saying those three words was easy for him. For me, it was more complicated. The last two times I'd told someone I loved them had been a disaster. Loving Brian only brought me pain, and what I thought was loving Cash was nothing but a mistake. It wasn't that I didn't love Leon. I couldn't help but love Leon, but I told him I needed time, and he seemed to accept that. Most of the time.

"When are you going to admit you love me, Jacey Lange?"

"I don't know... probably sometime before I become Jacey Acosta," I said in a very matter-of-fact way. It was my way of telling him I loved him without having to say the words. It was clear that it worked because he immediately started smiling.

"Jacey Acosta..." he repeated, the smile never leaving his face. "What a weird name," he added.

"It doesn't really go together, but I'll make it work," I said with a shrug.

"Oh, will you?"

"*Sim meu querido.*"

"You're getting better."

By that, Leon meant that I was slowly starting to sound less like I had marbles in my mouth when I attempted to speak Portuguese.

"Maybe at speaking, but the reading and writing is still a mess," I complained.

"Okay, let's practice," he said before leaning over and

grabbing a leather-bound journal out of the drawer in his nightstand. He silently flipped through the pages until he found what he was looking for and then handed me the book. My eyes danced over sentence after sentence of handwritten Portuguese words. I could only pick out bits and pieces but not enough to know what Leon had just handed me.

"Start here," he said, pointing to a random paragraph.

"*É mais do que amar*," I read out loud.

"It's more than loving her," he translated back to me.

"*Sempre a amei.*"

"I've always loved her."

"*É o facto de não poder viver sem ela.*"

"It is the knowledge I cannot live without her."

"*Uma noite e eu estou para sempre alterado. Para sempre dela.*"

"One night, and I am forever altered. Forever hers."

"Holy shit..." I breathed. My words were hardly romantic, but they just came flying out of my mouth.

"What?" Leon asked.

"You really do love me."

He laughed and kissed me on the top of my head. "Did you think I was joking?"

"No, I just..."

I sat there staring at the words on the page. I assumed he wrote them after we slept together for the first time. I knew, on some level, how Leon felt after that night. There was just something different about reading it from his perspective. For as long as I could remember, I found myself hoping that someone would love me in this real, deep, earth-shattering sort of way, and now I realized that someone always had. I looked for him everywhere when he was simply in the next bedroom.

"Can I ask you something?" I said.

"Sure."

"Have you ever been in love?"

"Before you?"

"Yeah..."

"I mean... I was nineteen when we met, Jace."

"I know, but there were a ton of girls between then and now..."

Leon sighed, almost as if he knew this conversation was coming. "No, I haven't. Not unless you count the girl I dated in high school."

"Nerdy Leon had a girlfriend?" I asked teasingly.

"Shocking, I know," he responded.

"Not even Natalia?"

He signed again. It was clear I was pushing my luck. "No, not even Nat."

There was some part of me that didn't believe him. I knew Leon said that the reason he was such a wreck when he and Natalia stopped seeing each other was that I had just gotten engaged to Brian. But I had grown so used to seeing his tall, icy blonde, Slavic ex-girlfriend as the enemy that I couldn't wrap my head around the idea that he never actually loved her.

"What about you?" he asked me.

My eyes shifted back and forth. That was such a strange question. Leon knew everything about my love life. He was my best friend. I didn't even have a high school boyfriend or a fling in college he didn't know about.

"Um... yeah... I've definitely been in love before. I almost got married..." I said, wondering what planet he'd just floated off to.

"Yeah, but you told Cash you loved him."

I froze. I never told Leon that I thought I loved Cash. I *knew* I didn't tell him. I had been so embarrassed that I blurted out some half-assed declaration of love to an idiot like Cash that I did everything I possibly could to omit that particular detail. The truth was, I had never actually been in love with Cash. The fact that I had been so reckless with those words was part of why I couldn't bring myself to say them to Leon.

My mind started racing. How could Leon know that? I didn't keep a journal. I didn't talk in my sleep. Had I told Elise? Why would Elise tell him that? Was he guessing?

"Did I tell you about that?" I asked, trying to keep my voice even.

"Nia said something about it when she was dropping Nichelle off. I just assumed you told him," he responded.

I couldn't help but notice how quickly he rattled off his explanation. His response made sense, but there was something off about it.

"Does that bother you?" I asked.

"A little..." he admitted.

I rationalized that maybe what I was sensing was jealousy. I could only imagine how hard it must have been to hear Nia say something like that when he secretly had feelings for me.

"I didn't mean it. I just... got caught up..." I explained.

"It's just hard knowing you can say it to someone you dated for a couple of weeks, but you can't say it to me."

I took in a sharp breath. What Leon was saying was fair. If I were in his shoes, I would feel the same way, but that didn't make it any easier to hear. "It's not the feeling. It's the words..." I tried to explain.

"I don't understand."

Gently, I placed my hand on the side of his face.

"It's not that I don't...feel...that way, because I do. But both times I've said those words to someone, I wound up getting hurt, and when I said it to Cash, it was because I was trying desperately to hold onto something that was completely toxic. I'm not proud of that. When I say it to you, and it's a 'when', not an 'if', I want it to be something that neither you nor I ever have to question."

"Okay, that's fair," Leon admitted. He still seemed sad despite my explanation. I jumped right back in, hoping to save the situation.

"Can I just use different words?"

"What do you mean?"

"Until I'm ready? Can I say something else, so you'll know how I feel?"

"Like what?"

"I don't know, you pick," I said with a shrug.

"How about 'Leon, I didn't leave my clothes in the dryer,'" he said sarcastically.

"Only if yours is 'Jacey, I didn't put the toilet paper on the holder upside down,'" I responded.

"Or you could go with 'Leon, I've decided you're right. I'm not Amish. I don't need to wake with the sun.'"

I grabbed a pillow from behind me and hit him with it as hard as I could. "I hate you!" I said with a laugh.

He yanked the pillow away from me and tossed it on the floor before he grabbed me and pinned me to the bed. I tried to wiggle out of his grasp, but the truth was, I didn't want to get loose. There was no place on earth I wanted to be more than in that bed. Leon hovered over me, looking deep into my eyes.

"I hate you too," he said softly.

I had no question about what he meant. Leon kissed me, and I already knew that I wanted to hate that man for the rest of my life.

Forty-Five

There were still several months until Elise's wedding, but one thing that the ultra-wealthy loved to do was throw a party. Elise, and her fiancé, Nathan, were getting married in Bordeaux. Therefore, the Montgomerys decided to throw a huge New York high society engagement party for them so that anyone who wasn't flying to France could still be a part of the celebration. To me, the whole thing sounded like an excuse for the Montgomerys to show off how much money they had, but Elise was ecstatic about the idea. I was less than enthusiastic. However, as her maid of honor, there was no way that I was getting out of it.

I would have preferred to stay in with Leon. The only problem with living with someone while still in the honeymoon phase of a relationship was that the two of us were always staying in. For the last three months, we existed in this blissful little bubble that we both tried to

leave as seldom as possible. Going to an engagement party might not have been my idea of fun, but it was the first time my parents would get to see Leon and me together as a couple. Plus, I had an insanely hot boyfriend, and I wasn't exactly disappointed about the opportunity to show him off.

"Let's play how many things can I get done before Jacey finishes getting ready!" I heard Leon shout from the bottom of the stairs.

Leon and I now shared a bedroom, but we decided to keep my extensive wardrobe upstairs. Between the two of us, we owned far too many clothes to fit in one closet.

"You can't rush perfection!" I yelled back down at him.

"You know, I think I have my grandmother's Caldo Verde recipe around here somewhere. We don't have any kale, but I can probably grow some by the time you're done," he yelled again.

Unsurprisingly, the party was black tie, so I decided on a floor-length off-the-shoulder gown. I laughed as I checked myself in the mirror one last time and went downstairs. "I guess the kale will have to wait," I said.

The moment Leon laid eyes on me, all he could do was stare. I had to admit that I loved the way he looked at me. Plus, it made the two hours I'd spent getting ready seem worth it.

"This might be a bad idea," Leon said.

"Oh? Why is that?"

"Because I have no idea how I'm supposed to keep my hands off you all night when you look like that," he grinned as he reached for my waist and pulled me closer.

"Well, I have a surprise for you," I said with a coy smile.

"Please tell me we're not going."

I fluttered out of his grasp over to the clutch, sitting

on the small table near our front door. I pulled a key card out and then returned to Leon, handing it to him.

"What is this?"

"Just in case we need to ditch the party."

Elise's engagement party was at the Plaza Hotel. Ordinarily, there would be no way I would spend eight hundred dollars on one night in a hotel room. However, Nathan's parents already had a massive block of rooms reserved and the advantage of looking just like the bride was that no one at the hotel had a problem when I asked for one of them. I told Elise, of course, and according to her, half the rooms weren't in use, so I saw no harm in it.

"Have I told you how much I love you?" Leon asked me.

"Not in the last hour," I said playfully.

Leon took a step toward me before putting his hand on my hip and pulling me closer to him. "How the fuck did I get so lucky?"

"Well, you waited ten years. I'd say you earned it."

The cab ride to the Plaza was a short one. Unfortunately, it was just long enough that my nerves started to kick in. I didn't know why I was nervous. The party had nothing to do with me. I just needed to show up, drink free champagne, and support Elise, but for some reason, I just felt unsettled and I couldn't explain it.

When we pulled up outside the hotel, I took Leon's arm, and we found our way to the ballroom. Even though I knew how much money the Montgomerys had and how much they were spending, I was still shocked at how beautiful everything was. The party was so elaborate that it could have been the wedding itself. The room was already ornately beautiful all on its own, with intricate crown molding and a giant chandelier in the center of the room. The elegantly decorated banquet tables and the floral arrangements that were so large you could barely see over them made the place startlingly beautiful.

Leon and I immediately made a beeline for the bartender. We both knew that to put up with the pomp and circumstance of a party with a six-figure price tag, Leon and I were going to need alcohol and plenty of it. It was no surprise that when we got to the bar, I found my parents had the same idea.

"Can you believe this, Jeffrey? I knew Elise said they were spending a bunch of money, but Jesus Christ!" I heard my mother lean over and hiss to my father with a glass of red wine in hand.

"At least we didn't have to pay for it," my dad said with a chuckle.

I immediately started smiling. My dad's jokes were never actually funny. Most of the time, we weren't even sure if they were jokes. Yet somehow he always seemed to crack himself up. I realized as I watched the two of them just how much I'd missed them. Connecticut was only a two-hour train ride away, but there was so much going on in my life between work and my new relationship that I never had the time to come home.

"Don't worry, I don't plan on marrying a real estate heir, so you'll still get to pay for mine," I teased, interrupting their conversation.

"Hey, kiddo!" Dad beamed at me before pulling me in for a hug. "You hear that, Lisa! I'm still useful," he said to Mom.

My Mom rolled her brown eyes before turning her attention to Leon.

"Well, look at the two of you," she remarked as I pulled away from Dad and rejoined my boyfriend.

"Took you long enough!" Dad said with another laugh.

"Actually, Jeff, I wanted to chat with you about something if you have a minute," Leon said.

I looked up at him in utter confusion. What on earth would Leon need to talk to Dad about? My parents had known Leon for years, and they both loved him, but I had never once seen Leon go off and have a private conversation with my father. And yet, that's exactly what they did. I watched the two of them wander off, leaving me alone with my mother.

"He's going to ask your father for his blessing," my mother said bluntly.

I coughed loudly, choking on the cocktail in my hand. "We just started dating!"

I found myself wishing that I could read lips. Several feet away, Leon and Dad were talking like old buddies. I couldn't for the life of me think of a reason *why*.

"Jacey, don't be ridiculous. You might have just started calling it 'dating,' but you and that boy have been together since you were teenagers."

"Mom..."

"Honey, you live together, you cook for each other, you spend all your time together. You've been in a relationship for ten years. Leon's been in love with you all this time, and now he finally has you. I hardly think he's going to wait to propose," she explained.

I tilted my head to the side as I watched the two of them shake hands like they were conducting some business deal, but before I could try to rationalize what was happening, I saw my sister darting through the crowd toward me with a horrified look on her face.

"Jacey, I'm so sorry!" she exclaimed before wrapping her arms around my neck and hugging me. "I had no idea she would be here. I would have someone kick her out, but she's here with Nathan's cousin," she started rattling off.

I pulled back just enough to look at my sister.

"Who are you talking about?" I asked.

Then over Elise's shoulder, I saw exactly who she was talking about. Standing across the room on the arm of some man who looked like an investment banker was the last person I wanted to see.

Natalia Kasandrova was, in a word, breathtaking. She was the kind of woman who walked into a room, and every single person stopped what they were doing. It didn't matter that she smoked like a chimney or that she had an accent that sounded like throwing rocks in a blender, or even that she was as emotionally cold as the Russian tundra she came from. One glance at Natalia's long legs, platinum hair, and almond-shaped blue eyes, and people fell all over themselves.

I hated to admit that I had forgotten just how stunning Leon's ex-girlfriend was. I hoped I would never have the unfortunate experience of seeing her again, but there she was, at my sister's engagement party. I thought for a moment about the key card in my purse and about quietly trying to sneak upstairs with Leon before she saw that he was here. I was sure that Elise would understand, given the circumstances, but I quickly realized the ballroom only had one exit, and Natasha and her date were standing right next to it.

"It's okay," I said to Elise, trying to sound less uncomfortable than I felt. "It's your engagement party. Go, have fun! I'll be fine."

"You're sure?" she asked me.

"Go, Ellie. I'm fine," I assured her. I didn't feel fine,

but I wasn't about to let my sister spend her night worrying about me.

Leon and Dad returned, and while I desperately wanted to ask him what he and my father had just been discussing, I had a bigger problem on my hands.

"I think they're serving dinner soon. We're going to go find our seats," I said to my parents before grabbing Leon's arm and leading him away.

"Are you okay?" he asked me.

"We have a problem..." I said as quietly as I could.

He turned to look at me, and I nodded in the direction of Natalia.

"Shit," he exclaimed under his breath. I watched him look over at Natalia for several seconds before he turned to me again. "Do you want to leave?" he asked.

As much as I wanted to, I couldn't just leave my sister's engagement party before they'd even served dinner. Plus, whether Natalia saw us or not, she had to know whose engagement party this was, so she knew we were there.

"No," I said bravely. "We'll just avoid her," I added.

Leon nodded, and we found our way to our seats.

Luckily for us, the Mongomerys put my family on one side of the ballroom and Nathan's family on the other. That meant, while Leon, my parents, me, and even Elise's bridesmaids were all together, Natalia was situated clear across the ballroom with Nathan's cousin. Given the size of the floral arrangements and the massive room we were in, we couldn't even see her. As the night wore on, I started to forget that she was even there.

Natalia didn't forget me.

I had no idea if she had been waiting until I was alone or if she just happened to be in the right place at the right time, but as Leon and Nate caught up, I got bored and decided to take another trip to the bar. I ordered a Jack and Diet, and the moment I turned around, there she was.

"Jacey!" she exclaimed as if we were old friends.

I sighed heavily before forcing a smile onto my face.

"Natalia, it's been forever. How are you?" I asked.

I already hated this interaction. It was fake. We both knew it. I, however, wasn't about to make a scene, so I was forced to grin and bear it.

"I'm good, I'm good. How are you? Is Leon with you?" she asked in her heavy Russian accent as she scanned the room for him.

I stared in his direction, hoping that he would glance over and swoop in to save me, but he was too wrapped up in his conversation to notice.

"I'm well, thanks," I said tightly, ignoring the subject of Leon entirely.

"I heard you two are together now," she said. Her voice was completely saccharine but the way her nose started to curl up and the grimace that tugged at the corner of her lips told me everything I needed to know about her thoughts on the matter.

I doubted that she "heard" that information anywhere. I assumed she'd just been watching us all night and came to that conclusion on her own. I knew that Natalia had been sleeping with Leon while I was with Cash. I assumed that seeing him in another relationship so quickly was a blow to her overdeveloped ego.

"Where did you hear that?" I asked, calling her bluff.

"From Leon," she said with a shrug.

I blinked a few times. I wasn't sure if I heard her correctly. Of course, she could have been lying in an attempt to get under my skin, but Natalia wasn't a stranger to me, and while she was many things, a liar wasn't one of them. Plus, why would a woman who looked like that be threatened enough by anyone to lie to them?

"Oh, I didn't realize you two were still talking," I said calmly.

"Once in a while," she said.

The level-headed part of me knew that didn't mean anything. Natalia could have texted Leon wanting to see him, and he told her we were together. However, there was a very real part of me that wanted to march over to Leon and demand answers. I remained as detached as possible.

"Yeah, I'm sorry. I know you two were seeing each other for a while. I'm sure that was hard to find out." I said mirroring her obnoxiously sweet tone.

If she was going to play this game, I was going to play right along with her.

To my surprise, Natalia didn't snap back at me. She just looked confused, utterly, and completely confused.

"What do you mean?"

"A few months ago?" I asked, more than stated.

"What are you talking about? I haven't seen Leon in almost a year. We check in sometimes, but..." Natalia responded.

I just stared at her in disbelief. If Leon hadn't been seeing Natalia, then whose clothes were all over my living room? Where had he been disappearing to for months before we got together? Most importantly, why did he allow me to believe that Natalia was the cause for that behavior? I felt my voice catch in my throat. I didn't know what to say to her, but before I could even attempt to come up with something. I felt a hand on my arm.

"Hey Jace, Elise needs you," I heard Leon say.

I was in a daze. Without saying anything to Natalia at all, I let him lead me away from her.

"What happened?" he asked me once we were out of earshot of his ex.

"She... um..." I started, but I couldn't get my brain to catch up with my mouth. "When was the last time you two saw each other?" I finally asked.

"Why? What did she say?"

I glanced back over at the blonde, who appeared oddly satisfied with herself as she sipped on a glass of champagne. "That she hasn't seen you in a year... but you two were..." I said, unable to finish my thoughts.

"I wish it was that long," Leon said, rolling his eyes. "Natalia has an ego bigger than this room. She was probably just trying to save face."

I didn't believe him. I didn't know why I didn't believe him. I knew Leon far better than I knew Natalia, and so far as I knew, Leon didn't make a habit of lying to me. Yet something felt wrong. In that split second, I had to think; I decided not to make a big deal of it. I told myself that if Leon was lying to me, I was going to find out for myself.

"You're probably right," I said, and the two of us went back to the party as if nothing at all had changed.

Forty-Six

Nothing. I found absolutely nothing.

After my sister's engagement party, I convinced myself that Leon was hiding something from me. I didn't know what it was or why, but I was determined to get to the bottom of it. Yet, despite all my efforts, I came up empty-handed. I tried just about everything. I checked his phone, his calendar, and his laptop. Unbeknownst to my boyfriend, I spent the better part of a month covertly digging through his personal life. All I came to find was that his work friends made some incredibly stupid jokes and that he had an eye appointment on the 9th. I couldn't find the lie. I couldn't even find anything interesting. I became so desperate to get some answers that I marched into our bedroom while Leon was at work with a Portuguese-to-English dictionary in hand. I intended to figure out what he was writing in his journal, hoping that the answer would be there, but I never got

that far. Instead, I found a box.

It was small and burgundy, and I knew what it was long before I dared to open it. I no longer cared about Leon and Natalia. All that mattered was the three-carat marquise-cut diamond ring staring back at me. My mom was right. She was sure that, when Leon pulled my dad aside to talk to him at the party, he was asking for his blessing. I wasn't sure if that was true, but I did know that there was an engagement ring in my hand.

I immediately felt guilty about grabbing his phone every time he took a shower or second-guessing every word he said. I didn't want to be this person, and this certainly wasn't the girlfriend that Leon deserved. Here I was, doubting him, and he was planning the rest of his life with me. Leon hadn't done anything to give me a reason not to trust him. Why was I taking the word of a self-indulgent runway model with an ax to grind over a man I had known my entire adult life? Maybe he was right. Maybe Natalia was trying to save face. As beautiful as she was, I doubted any man had ever chosen another woman over her. I could imagine that fact bothering her enough to make her lie about the last time she and Leon were together. All the evidence I had told me to trust Leon.

There's a problem with knowing that someone is about to propose. You start to think the proposal is going to come at any minute. I wasn't even sure we were ready for that step. So far, I hadn't even been able to bring myself to tell Leon that I loved him, yet he'd already bought a ring. Plus, my last engagement hadn't exactly gone according to plan. I felt like I was bracing for Leon to pull the ring out at every turn, but before I knew it, months passed, and Leon and I were on a plane to Bordeaux for Elise's wedding.

This time, I was the one who was keeping secrets. Not only did I plan on finally telling Leon the three words he had been waiting months to hear, but Bordeaux wasn't the only place we were going. Keeping my plans a secret wasn't exactly easy, but somehow I managed to arrange an entire second trip without him being any the wiser.

When we landed, Leon and I more or less went our separate ways. The wedding was on a sprawling villa with a vineyard attached. Elise showed me the pictures while deciding between venues, but the photos didn't do the place justice. It was like something right out of a fairytale. Unfortunately, I didn't exactly have time to enjoy the beautiful views or the French wine. I was too busy chasing my sister around like a chicken with my head cut off. Elise was in full panic mode, and it took everything in me to keep her from losing her mind.

The first several days we were there, I barely saw Leon except when we slept. He seemed understanding, but I found myself missing him so much that I was relieved when the day of the wedding finally came. I counted the minutes until the ceremony was over and the reception began. As soon as Elise and Nathan kissed, I felt like I could finally breathe. My sister was now Elise Montgomery, she looked beautiful and indescribably happy, and beyond giving a speech, my duties as maid of honor were done.

Leon and I drank far too much wine, we danced to every song we possibly could, and overall, we were having the perfect night. That was, until the bouquet toss started and the nerves about telling Leon I loved him began to bubble up inside me. It wasn't a question of how I felt. I was madly in love with him. I'd come to accept that. It was just that every time I thought about telling him, I also thought about the last time I had loved someone and the way that crashed and burned. All I could do was reassure myself that it was just my insecurities.

I stood behind my sister in her giant white gown with a gaggle of other single women. I always found the tradition of hurling expensive flowers around rather ridiculous, but I promised Elise I would participate, and so I did. My sister faced away from the women in the crowd. I watched her give me a knowing look and then toss her pink and white bouquet behind her head. The women scattered as they tried to catch it but it was no use. The mass of flowers landed right at my feet, and I quickly bent down to grab it. The crowd clapped as I started back to my table with a crumpled bunch of peonies in my hand.

I could see Leon smiling from across the room, and when I got to him, I shoved the bouquet into his hands.

"Looks like you're getting married..." Leon said as he placed the flowers on the table in front of him.

"Oh, am I?" I asked with a laugh.

"You are if I have anything to say about it," he said.

I felt my pulse quicken. Once in a while, Leon and I would make jokes about getting married. His comment wasn't out of the ordinary, but now that I was aware of the piece of jewelry hiding in his nightstand, it was no longer a joke. I wasn't even sure I had worked out what I would say if he asked. On the one hand, I truly believed that Leon was it for me, but on the other, this relationship felt like it was going at lightning speed, and accepting a proposal so soon seemed irresponsible.

Leon looked at me expectantly, but I didn't know how to respond. Instead, I just leaned across the distance between our seats and kissed him softly. I felt him lace his fingers through the back of my hair. He held my face close to his as I pulled back from the kiss. It was the perfect moment to tell Leon that I loved him. The only problem was I found myself scared. I knew how ridiculous it was. I knew Leon loved me. "Can we go somewhere?"

Leon glanced around the room for a minute before his gaze settled. "Come on," he said as he stood up and held his hand out for me to take.

We walked hand in hand across the ballroom through a door leading onto the terrace. Luckily, we seemed to be alone. The other guests were too busy drinking and comparing the size of their bank accounts. My mind started racing, but I knew how long Leon had been waiting, and I promised myself I would tell him before we left Bordeaux.

"Okay, what's wrong?" Leon asked.

"Nothing's wrong... I just..."

"Jace!" he said, giving me a look that told me he knew better.

"I need to tell you something."

"Should I be worried?"

"No... just... can you ... just turn around?"

"You want me to turn around?"

"Yes!" I exclaimed in frustration.

Slowly, Leon did as I asked and turned to look out onto the property with his back facing me. I looked over at him as he stood there. The jet black hair, the exquisitely fitting emerald suit, the outline of the muscles in his back, the way he stood. He would always be the most beautiful man I had ever seen, and despite how confused I was about the ring, I was so in love with him.

I took a step forward and wrapped my arms around him from behind, holding onto him tightly.

"I love you," I said softly with my forehead pressed into his back.

I felt Leon tense.

"Can I turn around now?" he asked carefully. He sounded as if he were afraid he might startle me if he reacted too quickly.

"Yes," I whispered, though I didn't entirely feel ready.

Leon turned, and I took a step back. I fixed my gaze on the concrete below us. I couldn't look up at him, though I could feel his eyes on me. I just hoped he understood why this had been so hard for me and why I couldn't bring myself to tell him sooner.

He grabbed my chin, tilting my gaze toward his.

"Can we try that again?" he asked gently.

"Leon, I love you," I said, though my voice was still quiet.

It felt like tears were creeping in behind my eyes. It seemed so silly that three little words could affect me so much, but I couldn't help it. Loving someone meant they could hurt me, and I'd certainly been hurt before. I just needed to remind myself that this was the one man who had only ever loved me. I knew I couldn't guarantee that I would never be hurt again. I only knew that choosing my best friend meant I had a pretty good chance at it.

Leon leaned forward, resting his forehead against mine.

"Say it again," he murmured.

"I love you so much," I repeated. "I'm sorry it took me so long."

Leon shook his head. "I would have waited the rest

of my life to hear you say that," he said.

He leaned in and kissed me, and it was as if I could feel every ounce of emotion between us pouring into that one kiss. I had no more doubt. Leon was it for me. I couldn't imagine loving someone else as much as I loved him at that moment.

I looked up at him for a long moment as we pulled away from the kiss. "There's something else..."

Leon laughed. "What else could you possibly say after that?"

"I did something..."

"Okay, what did you do?"

I took out my phone, and after scrolling for a couple of seconds, I pulled up a travel itinerary. I handed Leon the phone and waited for his reaction.

"We're going to Faro?" he asked me with a confused look on his face.

"Well, we're flying from here to Faro and then taking a train to Tavira," I said.

"Why?" Leon asked apprehensively, his eyes rapidly moving from my face to the screen and back again.

That was not the reaction I was hoping for at all. The answer was obvious: Leon's mother lived in Tavira. In all the years I'd known him, I never met her or visited his hometown. Plus, I could barely remember the last time Leon went home to Portugal. Yet he seemed upset? I didn't understand.

"It's only a few hours away, and we're already in Europe. I just thought..."

"Without asking me?"

"Do I need to ask before I do something nice for my boyfriend?"

I had been planning this for weeks, and I was so

excited about Leon's reaction. I spent so much time figuring out how to get from Bordeaux to Tavira. I even learned how to say specific phrases so I could tell his Mom how much he meant to me, and *this* was his reaction?

Leon caught himself and immediately changed his tone. "You're right. I'm sorry. I'm just... surprised, that's all."

"We don't have to go if you—"

"No! No, I'm excited. I can't wait for you to meet my Mom. It's just unexpected," he rushed to explain.

"Okay..." I said, unsure of how to feel. I just stood there for a moment before I spoke up again. "Why do I feel like I did something wrong?"

"You didn't. I promise. You just caught me off guard."

"I guess I've done that twice now," I said, realizing I sprung two rather large things on him at once.

"Looks like I'm going to have to find some way to surprise you then," he said.

I thought again about the ring. He had already surprised me. He just didn't know he'd done it, and I didn't know what I was going to do when he finally decided to give it to me.

Forty-Seven

There were only a few things I knew about Constança Acosta. I knew she raised Leon on her own. I knew she and Leon moved to the United States for eight years while Leon was in school, though he never really explained why. I knew that she missed Portugal so much that she moved back to Tavira as soon as he graduated high school. I also knew that she spoke very little English. The rest was a mystery to me. I didn't even know what she looked like, although I imagined if Leon was her son, she had to be beautiful.

I was excited to meet her, but I was also more than a little nervous. Nerves were normal when someone met their significant other's family for the first time. Elise was terrified when she met Nathan's family. For me, there was the added pressure of a language barrier and a completely different culture to contend with.

Leon seemed to be determined to distract me. He

spent the entire plane ride to Faro telling me how much he loved me and how happy he was. Though he seemed hesitant when I first told him about the trip, he made up for it by telling me all the things he wanted to show me and how much his mother would love me. I wasn't sure what made him change his tune. Maybe he just had one too many drinks at the wedding, or maybe it simply took him a while to process what was going on.

Once we arrived in Faro, however, his disposition seemed to change again. His moods were switching so fast it was hard to keep up. The train ride was only forty minutes, but Leon kept uncharacteristically quiet and looked over his shoulder at every turn. I couldn't imagine what had him on edge, but I decided not to push the issue. Instead, I put in my earbuds, turned on some heavy metal, and watched out the window as we headed toward his hometown. Portugal was beautiful, and whether Leon was happy to be there or not, I was determined to enjoy myself.

The train slowly came to a stop. The platform itself was nothing remarkable, made of white concrete and surrounded by lush trees. Beyond a few photos online while booking the trip, I wasn't sure what to expect. Leon and I grabbed our bags and left the train station.

"We should probably get a cab," Leon said, still seeming a bit uncomfortable.

"How long is the walk?" I asked.

"Like, thirty minutes," he explained.

"Let's just walk. That way, you can show me around," I said cheerily as I slid my hand into his. I might not have known what was putting him on edge but I could at least try to put his mind at ease.

"Are you sure? You seem tired."

"I'm fine, plus I need to stop somewhere and get flowers for your mom."

Leon sighed heavily. I hoped that this emotional roller coaster of his wasn't going to last the entire trip. I was trying to be as understanding as I could, but he wasn't making it easy. Leon was cagey and uncomfortable. He held onto my hand a little too tightly and continued to look around as if someone might be following us. I knew there was a reason he left this place at such a young age. That had to be the explanation, he was too distressed for this to just be about my first time meeting his mother. I struggled to understand, but I was resolute to make the best of it.

"Come on, cheer up. You're home!" I said leaning into him playfully as we began our walk.

"You're my home," Leon corrected me.

At least he could be sweet even when he was acting like a weirdo.

I fell in love with Tavira immediately. It was like no place I had ever been. The stark white buildings, the terracotta roofs, and the Rio Gilão flowing through it were incredible. I couldn't imagine anyone ever wanting to leave. I felt like I was in a completely different world, especially compared to New York. Everything was so bright and warm. The people all appeared so happy and unbothered. Magical was really the only way that I could describe it.

Leon was quiet for a long time but he surprised me when he pointed to a bright yellow building in the distance. A flood of children in white and navy uniforms came running out of the wooden double doors. "I went to school there before we moved," he said.

His guard seemed to lower as we continued walking.

His body was less tense and he began to sound more and more at ease. He pointed out restaurants he loved, told me the history of the Roman footbridge as we crossed over it, and I found myself completely wrapped up in everything he had to say.

Eventually, we stopped at a tiny building sandwiched between a number of other shops. The aged sign out front translated to "tiny garden," and so I had to assume we'd found a florist. As we walked in the door we were greeted by a round cheerful looking old woman with long gray hair. "*Boa tarde*!"

I knew that the words meant good afternoon but I immediately looked to Leon, expecting him to translate for me. Instead, he laughed a little and shook his head. "You're not going to learn if I do all the work for you," he teased.

"*Boa tarde*," I responded. "*Tem...*" *Do you have...* I stared but quickly realized I didn't know the word for sunflowers which Leon told me were his mother's favorite. "*flores do sol*?" I finished hesitantly, hoping "flowers from the sun" was a good enough translation.

The woman just looked at me a little puzzled and Leon couldn't hold back his laughter. "*Girassóis*," he corrected.

"*Americana*?" the woman asked Leon, nodding in my direction.

"*Sim, ela está a tentar aprender português.*" Leon explained to the woman that I was trying to learn Portuguese.

She smiled brightly and took a few minutes grabbing a bouquet of sunflowers before handing it to me.

"You must love him very much to learn," she managed to say to me in English, though her accent was heavy.

"*Sim, mais que tudo.*" *Yes, more than anything*. I didn't

know if the sentiment made sense in translation, but when I looked up at Leon and the smile tugging at the corner of his mouth I could tell that at the very least *he* knew what I meant, and that was all that mattered.

"There's something you should probably know," Leon said after we left the shop.

"What?" I asked, hoping that he was finally going to explain his weird behavior.

"My mom... has some... alternative religious practices," he said hesitantly.

I laughed, mostly because I had no clue what that could mean. "Am I going to have to bathe in the blood of virgins?" I asked sarcastically.

"That, and maybe pledge your soul to the Dark Lord," Leon added.

"Oh cool, no problem."

"It's called *Feitiçaria*. I guess the closest thing I can compare it to is Wicca. They're not the same, but—"

"You're telling me your mom is a witch?"

"Yeah..."

"Great!" I said, unaffected by his statement. As a somewhat alternative teenager in the suburbs of Connecticut, I had my rebellious stage, and in it, I dabbled in Wicca as a way to upset my mother. It didn't stick, but my understanding of witchcraft was fairly practical. It was more a spiritual practice than some spooky supernatural phenomenon. I didn't know anything about Feitiçaria specifically, but I didn't find anything strange about what Leon said. I just expected there would probably be an altar set up somewhere or something like that. It wasn't like she would have bright green skin or fly around the house on a broomstick.

"That doesn't bother you?" he asked.

"Should it?"

"I don't know. I guess I just expected it to weird you out."

"Unless you're telling me that she's going to turn me into a frog, then why does it matter what she believes in?"

"You're amazing. Do you know that?"

"Because I'm not religiously intolerant?"

"Because you're fearless," he said.

I laughed. "I'm terrified, but I'm scared because I want your mom to like me, not because I think she's going to put a hex on me."

"She's going to love you," he assured me.

We walked for a while longer, and to my surprise, Leon seemed lighter. I couldn't imagine that his mom's alternative religious practices were the whole reason he was acting so strangely, but maybe that was the only issue. We got a few minutes outside of the center of town when Leon stopped at what appeared to be a hiking trail.

"We're here," he told me.

"Your mom lives in an invisible house, too?"

Leon shook his head and pointed above us. There, situated on the top of a hill, was a whimsical-looking, two-story blue house. Vines covered the entire building and reminded me of what a witch's house would look like if a witch took a sunny Mediterranean vacation. I loved her already. I just didn't love the idea of trekking up the hill.

I followed Leon up a winding foot trail. At this point, I was too curious to be nervous. I couldn't believe that I had known Leon all of this time, but I knew so little about the place he came from.

Instead of a front yard, there was a massive amount of trees and greenery covering everything. We navigated through it and under a garden awning before we reached the front of the house. Without knocking, Leon immediately opened the heavy, black front door. It opened into the kitchen, but I waited outside while Leon strolled right in.

"*Mãe? Onde estás?*" Leon called out into the house. At least that much I understood to be, *Mom? Where are you?*

All I heard in response was a literal scream of excitement and then the pattering of someone running toward the door.

"*Meu filho! O que é que estás aqui a fazer?*"

She wanted to know what he was doing there, but before Leon could even answer her question, his mother threw her tiny arms around his neck. She held onto him tightly before kissing both of his cheeks. I just stood there smiling as I watched the two of them reunite.

His mother wasn't at all what I expected. She was indeed beautiful, just different than I envisioned. She was tiny, roughly the same height I was, with waist-length black hair and wispy little bangs. Her face was small with a thin, slightly downturned mouth but a pair of giant doe eyes, the same color as Leon's. She reminded me of the actresses from old silent films.

"*A Jacey trouxe-me.*" *Jacey brought me*, he finally responded.

"Jacey?" Constança questioned as she turned her attention toward me. "*Entra, entra,*" she said excitedly, beckoning me into the house.

I came in and handed her the flowers. "*É tão bom finalmente conhecer-te!,*" I said, telling her it was nice to finally meet her in what was now becoming my signature broken Portuguese.

She kissed both of my cheeks just as she had with Leon. She said something to him, but this time I didn't understand. I waited for Leon to translate.

"She wants to know why I didn't tell her you were so beautiful," he explained, a slight blush spreading across his face.

"Good question, why didn't you?" I said playfully.

"Um... Can you give us a minute?" Leon asked me.

"Sure, where should I put these?" I asked, referring to our bags.

"The bedroom is upstairs," he said, nodding in the direction of the stairs.

It wasn't exactly like Leon to leave me to handle bags on my own and given that I didn't even speak the same language they did, I didn't know why Leon needed to talk to his mother in private, but he hadn't seen her in years, so I didn't call him out on it.

As I walked from the kitchen into the living room, I started to realize why Leon got ahead of telling me about his mother's practice. The whole place looked like a metaphysical store. I recognized some of the items, like dried smudge sticks and jars of herbs. However, there were other things I couldn't make heads or tails of. Thankfully, it wasn't hard to locate the winding blue staircase that led to Leon's childhood bedroom. There, things were far more normal.

I smiled to myself as I looked around. The bed was huge, but it had what sort of resembled a red and white circus tent over the headboard. There were still Mickey Mouse sheets on the bed and toys in a bin in the corner. I found it strange that the room had never changed. I also wondered who lived in this house while they were in the States. I reminded myself to ask Leon about it later. I set our bags down on the floor and followed a set of French doors onto a tiny balcony that overlooked the city. If I wasn't in love with Tavira already, I was now.

A few minutes later, I felt a pair of arms wrap around my waist.

"I'm sorry I've been acting so weird," Leon said as we both looked out over the view.

"Do you want to talk about it?" I asked.

"No, it's okay. I'm feeling better."

"Good," I said as I turned around. I reached my arms up around Leon's neck and kissed him. "Your mom is great," I added.

"She's really happy you're here."

"I am, too," I said.

"She's already started cooking."

"Crap!" I exclaimed as I shimmied loose of Leon's grip and started towards the staircase.

"What are you doing?" he called after me.

"Helping!" I called back at him from halfway down the stairs.

When I burst into the kitchen, Leon's mother just looked up at me, a bit startled.

"Posso ajudar?" I said, asking her if I could help.

"*Sim*!" she said with a smile and a nod.

I didn't exactly know how long it would be before we ran out of things we could say to each other, but so far we were doing alright. Constança placed a cutting board, a knife, and a bowl full of tomatoes in front of me. I could only assume I was supposed to start cutting them, and so I did. We were quiet for a while, and then I watched as she peered out into the living room as if she were checking to see if someone was there.

"Será que ele está a par desse bebé?"

I racked my brain for a moment. The only words from that sentence I understood were he, know, and baby. Maybe I was losing something in translation? Leon and I didn't have a baby, we didn't know anyone with a baby, and his mother certainly wasn't having a baby. Then it hit me. Maybe she was asking if I knew he didn't want babies?

I wasn't sure how to respond. I was well aware of how Leon felt about children. It was part of why I felt unsure about the ring. Not only had we not been together long enough for any reasonable person to think an engagement was a good idea, he also didn't want children. And unless he was serious about the adoption jokes we made while babysitting Nichelle, I wasn't sure that I was okay with the idea of never being a mother.

I decided to shrug my shoulders like I didn't understand. I was hardly prepared to have a conversation about children with my boyfriend's mother.

"*Não te preocupes, eu consigo guardar um segredo,*" she said.

Something about a secret? Understanding Portuguese that didn't come from a cartoon owl on an app was much harder than I thought. We continued cooking, mostly in silence.

The three of us sat around the dinner table for hours. His mother's food was delicious, and while Leon had to translate almost everything we said, there was still laughter and ease about being in her presence. I could see why Leon loved her so much.

For all of my nerves, I was happy I'd done this. There was something about seeing this part of Leon's life that made me feel closer to him.

Forty-Eight

After enough Portuguese wine, food, and words to make my head spin, Leon and I dragged ourselves up to his childhood bedroom. I didn't realize just how exhausted I was until I climbed into the outdated Disney sheets and rested my head on his broad chest. We were both quiet for a while, but being in Tavira, while incredible, brought up a million questions about Leon and his life here. It was almost like the only Leon I knew was the one who I met in that frat house, and he'd tried to forget everything that came before it. I didn't understand why.

"Who was living here when you were living in New Jersey?" I asked, as if the thought had just occurred to me.

"The house has been in our family for a long time. It just sat here. My mom couldn't bring herself to sell it," he responded.

"You know, I don't know much about your dad..."

"What would you like to know?"

"Is he alive?"

"No."

"Did you know him?"

"No."

"Did you ever want to?"

"No."

I sighed heavily and looked up at the ceiling. It wasn't that Leon's answers were wrong. He just seemed so closed off. I used to think I knew everything about the man lying next to me. Now, I was beginning to realize there was this huge part of him that was a stranger to me.

"Why didn't you want to come back here?"

"It's not that I didn't want to. It's just..."

I sat up in bed abruptly and looked down at him. I finally hit my breaking point. I had been trying so hard to be upbeat and supportive, but every time I would try to get him to open up, I hit a brick wall. If he were just some random guy I was dating, that would be one thing, but he wasn't. Leon was my best friend. Knowing full well there was a part of him that he wouldn't let me in on, I decided to play the only card I had.

"Do you want to spend the rest of your life with me?"

Leon laughed. "Are you proposing?"

"No, I'm asking a serious question. Is this what you want? Me and you? End game?"

Once he heard the tone in my voice, Leon sat up in bed with me.

"Jace, what is wrong?"

"Answer the question!"

"Yes!"

Leon took my face in both of his hands.

"I love you more than I've ever loved anything or

anyone. I want this," Leon said softly.

"Then let me in. I don't know what you're hiding or why, but I won't spend my life with someone I don't know."

"You know," Leon said as the realization of what I was saying hit him.

"About the ring? Yes."

Leon took in a ragged breath and looked away from me, letting his hands fall away from my face. "You're right," he said with his gaze still fixed on the French doors across the room.

He was silent for a long time before he spoke again. "I promise I will tell you everything, but they're things I've never told anyone, and some of them you're not going to like, so can you just give me some time?"

"Only if you stop shutting me out," I retorted.

"Okay," he agreed.

There was silence again, and it was deafening. We both just sat on the bed, avoiding eye contact with each other. I sat in the heaviness of that room for as long as I could. I waited until I couldn't stand it anymore and then spoke again. "I want you to know there's nothing you could say that would make me stop loving you. I get that you think that you love me more because you loved me first, but you're wrong."

"Am I? If I told you everything right now, I don't think you'd still be saying that."

"Then ask me."

"What?"

"Ask me to marry you! Right now!"

"Jacey..."

"I'm serious. Ask me!"

"This isn't the proposal you deserve," he said.

"Then propose again later, but if you want me to prove it to you, then ask."

Leon got up out of bed and paced the floor. I couldn't get a read on whether he was angry or just trying to figure out what to do until he stopped abruptly and turned to me.

"You really want me to do this?"

"Just ask, Leon!"

He shook his head in disbelief, and then right there in his childhood bedroom, wearing nothing but a pair of sweatpants, my boyfriend got down on one knee in front of me.

"I had a whole speech worked out, but I guess I'll save it since I'm going to have to do this again. I know that it hasn't been long enough, but for me, it feels like I've been waiting a lifetime, and I don't want to wait anymore. I can't wait anymore. You are my best friend. I love you. There has never been anyone for me but you, so... Jacey Lange, will you marry me?"

It was a fake proposal, or it was one that I pushed Leon to make in a misguided attempt to prove my love to him, but I felt it all the same. Tears started running down my cheeks before I could even bring myself to respond.

"Yes," I said, wiping the tears from my eyes as quickly as I could.

Leon got up and moved towards me, but I reached out and stopped him.

"I want you to hear me. I'm saying yes. I'm saying it before I know whatever you think will change things because I'm that sure of us. You can take whatever time you need, but when you're ready, I want you to remember I already said yes."

I could see tears pooling at the corners of Leon's eyes. In all the time I'd known Leon, I could only remember him crying once, and that was at the end of *Sons of Anarchy*.

"Now get over here," I said.

Leon immediately got up and crashed his lips into mine. I had been agonizing about that ring and that proposal for so long. Yet here I was, accepting it. I didn't forget about the fact Leon didn't want children or that we hadn't been in a romantic relationship all that long, but I also knew my best friend, and I knew he needed to know I loved him irrevocably, so I proved it to him in the only way I knew how. I just needed to believe we could work out the details somewhere along the way.

The following morning, I awoke to the sound of someone banging frantically at Constança's front door. Leon tended to sleep like the dead, and while the sound had me wide awake, he remained peacefully asleep next to me. I waited a while for the pounding to stop or for Constança to answer the door, but it continued, becoming more and more agitated. I threw the sheets off me and padded down the stairs. It wasn't until I stepped into the kitchen that I realized the person wasn't just repeatedly hitting the door, they were yelling at it, too.

"*Eu sei que ele está lá, Constança*!" a man's voice called out.

I was pretty sure that meant, *I know he's there*? Who? Leon? That, or Constança was having some secret affair and the man yelling at the crack of dawn was some angry jilted lover. I had no idea what was going on. All I knew was that this man wouldn't stop, and I didn't know what to do.

"*Estão todos a dormir*," I called out in a shaky voice,

telling the man that everyone was asleep.

The violent knocking stopped suddenly, and then there was no sound at all. I was more than a little creeped out, but when I didn't hear anything for a few seconds, I started to turn away slowly, intent on heading back up the stairs.

"*Desculpa, não te queria assustar,*" the voice said.

I wasn't entirely sure what that meant, but I understood the words "I'm sorry" and "scare", so I assumed he was apologizing for frightening me.

"*Volte mais tarde,*" I responded, telling him to come back later.

"*Eu sou o tio do Leondro,*" he responded through the door.

Leon's uncle? Leon never mentioned an uncle, but maybe I was mistaking anger for excitement? I didn't want to be rude, especially if this person was family, so I carefully started to open the door. I didn't intend to let him in. It wasn't my house, after all. I figured I'd attempt to explain more politely, and when the person saw that I was the only one up, they would go away.

I didn't get that far. As soon as the person on the other side of the door heard the lock click, they shoved the door at me so hard that it sent me flying backward onto the floor.

I hit the ground with a thud. I didn't know what this man wanted, but I was no longer interested in communicating with him. Instead, I just started screaming at the top of my lungs like some kind of banshee, hoping the sound would be enough to wake Leon.

The dark-haired man standing above me started yelling at me in Portuguese. He did look like Leon for whatever it was worth, but I no longer cared if they were related. I was terrified. I kept screaming. I was either going to wake up the whole house or blow out this man's eardrums, but I wasn't going to stop.

The next thing I knew, both Leon and Constança rushed into the room. The yelling between the three of them was so rapid and angry I had no hope of translating any of it. As his mother continued yelling at the intruder in her kitchen, Leon finally realized I was still on the floor and knelt to help me up.

"What the hell is going on?" My eyes darted between them full of both fear and confusion.

"We just need to get you out of here," he said.

Leon grabbed my arm and turned, intent on ushering me away, but before he could, I felt another hand reach out and grab me, yanking me backward with as much force as he could.

"Get the fuck off me!" I yelled as I struggled against the stranger, but it was no use. He was more than twice my size.

Leon shoved him back and then turned to his mother. *"Mãe, leva-a daqui para fora!"*

Get me out? Where was I supposed to go?

Constança grabbed me by my shoulders, shoving me out of the kitchen.

"No! Wait! What is going on?" I said, trying to push back against her.

"*Vais ficar bem*," she said before throwing open a door and shoving me inside. I watched the door slam. I heard it slam, and then.... waves?

At first, I thought maybe I got shoved outside, but the sound was too close for me to be outside the same house I had just been in. It was on a hill, not a beach. I turned away from the door slowly, only to find myself standing feet from cobalt-colored water.

Was I dreaming?

How did I get here?

I didn't start to panic until I turned back and saw the door was no longer there. Not only did I not know how I got here, but I didn't know how to get back. I didn't have a phone, and there were no people or buildings anywhere. There was just water and cliffs. I squinted, looking off into the distance, hoping I would see any sign of civilization, but there was nothing but a beach as far as I could see.

"Hello?" I called out, but there wasn't a sound.

Maybe this was a dream? I couldn't remember ever thinking that I was in a dream while actually in one, and yet I could hear all of my thoughts so clearly. Was I going crazy? I looked down at my arm where Leon's uncle, or whoever he was, grabbed me. I could see the bright red outline of fingers, and I could still feel a dull ache. I was also still wearing the clothes I'd slept in. I didn't know if I was more frightened for myself or Leon. I didn't know where he was or how to get back to him.

"I wanna wake up now!" I yelled again, but nothing happened.

There had to be a logical explanation for this. I told myself not to panic and tried to keep my breathing even. I had two options: I could sit and wait and see if something happened, or I could start walking and hope I found someone to help me. I decided that waiting was safer. I didn't know where I was, and even if I did find someone, I wasn't completely confident in my ability to communicate that I needed help.

Slowly, I sat down on the sand and pulled my legs into my chest. The sand below me felt real. The waves in front of me looked real, but unless I just waltzed into another dimension, there was no way this was possible.

Forty-Nine

I held no belief in things I could not see or quantify. I didn't believe in God, or ghosts, or other dimensions. There was nothing wrong with those ideas. I didn't judge anyone for believing in them, but they never resonated with me. So how did I find myself being thrown through a door in a house and transported to a beach?

My first thought was that I was dreaming; maybe it was the high altitude or the change in time zones that had given me one very realistic lucid dream. I thought I would wake up next to Leon any minute and tell him what a bizarre dream I had. How strange that I dreamt his mother tossed me through a door onto a beach in my pajamas. We would laugh about it soon and then eat breakfast and enjoy the rest of our time in Tavira.

That didn't happen. I sat and waited, and waited, and waited. I started forming tiny sandcastles and absently drawing shapes with my finger, anything to pass the time.

"It's just a dream," I repeated to myself.

I wasn't sure that I believed that, but it was the only sense of reality I had, and I was the only person there I could talk to. I had no way to know how much time had passed. It could have been minutes or hours. I didn't have a clock or a phone, so I was just stuck in this perpetual limbo, watching the tide roll in and back out again.

Just as I was starting to wonder if perhaps this was some puzzle I had to figure out, or if there was something proactive I could do to get myself to wake up, I heard a door open behind me. *When did the door reappear?* I stood up and turned around, only to find an exasperated and slightly disheveled Leon behind me.

"Are you dream Leon or real Leon?" I asked sarcastically, sounding more than a little annoyed. I was just so tired of being in this literal nightmare that I was starting to believe that I was never going to get out.

Leon hesitated. The pain on his face immediately scared me.

"Please tell me you're dream Leon," I said, slowly.

There was no way. No way in hell, this could be real. *Could it?*

"I thought it was better if we talk about this here," he said quietly.

"Talk about what, Leon? And where is here? What is going on?"

"You should sit," he said.

"Sit where?" I said, dramatically gesturing to the vast nothing all around me.

Leon gestured to a place in the sand, and immediately a red beach chair just appeared. My eyes went wide as I just kept looking from the chair to Leon and back again. I still wanted to believe that it was a dream. I didn't know how to process any other possibility. I swallowed hard and quietly sat down on the chair without saying anything. I didn't know what to say. First, I was tossed into some bizarre oceanside limbo, and now my boyfriend was making chairs appear out of thin air.

We were both silent, just awkwardly staring at each other. I wasn't even sure if I wanted to know what Leon had to say. If there was some possibility that I was actually conscious and truly experiencing this, I wasn't sure I wanted to know. However, I couldn't help but ask. "Is this real?"

"I guess it depends on how you define real," he said, shifting uncomfortably as he rubbed the back of his neck.

"Is this what you've been hiding?"

"Some of it," he replied.

I took a deep breath and remembered what I said last night. Whatever it was, I already said yes. "Okay, can you explain it to me?" I asked, trying as hard as I could to keep my voice even.

"There are two parts to this. There's what I am, and there's what I did..." he started.

"Okay," I said, though my voice shook.

Leon hesitated again, and I was sure I wasn't dreaming. His expressions were too real. Whatever this was caused him too much torment. I didn't know what was going on, but the space between us felt heavy. It was as if he was preparing to hurt me, and while I didn't know why, I did know that my brain wasn't capable of making this up.

"You know how I said my mom had alternative religious practices?"

"Yeah..."

"I might have understated that a little."

"She did this?"

"Yeah, she did."

"And you can also do... this?" I asked, motioning to the coastline around us.

Leon nodded.

"Okay, so...what *is* this?" I asked.

"A reality shift," he simply said.

"I don't know what that means."

"So your consciousness is here, but the physical you is in my mom's bedroom."

A chill ran through me. Despite how strange the concept seemed, some part of me knew Leon was telling the truth. That frightened me. Why couldn't I just be dreaming or, hell, even losing my mind?

"Why?"

Leon gave me a Look. "If I told you to stay put, would you have?"

I got his point immediately. I sometimes forgot just how well he knew me. I didn't know anything about the man in his mother's kitchen, but I wasn't just going to sit there and let something happen to Leon. It would have taken me all of four seconds to rush back in there.

"So, what was that in the kitchen?"

"That was my dad's brother," he said.

"I thought your dad was dead."

"He's very dead."

"Then why is his brother breaking into your mom's kitchen?"

"It's a long story," he sighed.

I rolled my eyes. "I have all day..." I said sarcastically.

"So my Mom has... abilities, as you can see, and so did my dad. His were just...different..."

"Different how?"

"My mom can change the perception of reality; my father could change the perception of... himself."

I wanted to slap Leon upside the head for being so intentionally vague when I was stuck here in some alternate reality without my consent, but I also knew that telling me this had to be hard for him. I tried to be understanding. I stood up from the chair I was sitting in and took both of his hands in mine.

"Hey, I know this is hard for you, but we're at the point where you just have to rip off the bandage. I already said yes, remember?"

Leon nodded. "This is going to sound crazy," he said.

"I've been sitting on a magical beach for an hour," I said with a shrug.

"My mom comes from a long line of women who have her abilities, but it's something you learn, not something you're born with. My father, however, was born with the ability to change forms."

I laughed. I didn't think what Leon was saying was funny but, I couldn't help it. It just came out of me. The whole thing was crazy. One minute I was leading a perfectly ordinary life free of magical creatures, and now my boyfriend was telling me that his mother was a witch and that his deceased father was some kind of shapeshifter? "So, what does that make you?"

"A little of both?"

"You can do both?"

"Yes."

"Which is why you never wanted to have children," I said as it finally dawned on me that these were the genes Leon didn't want to pass on.

"Yeah..."

"That still doesn't explain why there was a crazy man in your mother's kitchen."

"My mom didn't know what my father was when she fell in love with him. She said she knew he was different — darker than normal people, but she didn't know what that meant. He was in an accident and died before she found out that she was pregnant. When his family found out, they demanded that she give me to them because I might have the same abilities my father did. They thought they could do a better job raising me. Shifters don't usually develop any abilities until ten or so, so my mom managed to convince them to let her keep me until then."

"Which is when she took you to the U.S.," I said, now understanding why Constança abandoned her home and the country she'd spent her entire life in for no discernable reason. It was for Leon.

"Exactly."

"So why the theatrics?"

"The way I understand it is, my father had abilities that aren't common in shifters, which made him their leader, I guess. Because they suspect I can do the same things, they want me with them, to lead, and they've been trying to get me to come back for a long time. Someone saw us getting off the train from Faro, and that's why he showed up."

"Can you?"

"Can I what?"

"Do the same things?"

He nodded slowly before running a hand over his face.

"But you don't want anything to do with it?"

"Right. I just want a normal life...with you," he said.

I looked out at the scenic ocean in front of me. If I

had heard this without experiencing it, I would have thought it was mental, but there were just things in the world I clearly didn't understand. I had a lot to process, and if I was honest, what bothered me the most was that Leon had been hiding such a huge part of who he was from me for so long. I could see why he did it, but it hurt all the same.

"I have questions," I said, trying as hard as I could to sound neutral.

"Okay."

"Where is your uncle now?"

"He's gone," Leon said.

"So we can go home? We're not in danger?"

"He's not dangerous, just volatile. Ultimately, he can't force me to do anything."

"Seemed like he intended to try..."

"There are laws. He can't hurt his own kind," Leon explained.

The thought crossed my mind that just because he couldn't hurt Leon didn't mean that he couldn't hurt me, or Constança, but I didn't say anything.

"So you're telling me that you have these... supernatural abilities but that you don't want to use them? You just want to go home to New York and get married and be boring?"

"Desperately," Leon said with a laugh.

"Have you ever used them?"

"Yes."

"Have you ever used them on me?"

"I—"

"You know what, don't answer that."

"I can, if you—"

"No! I don't want to know."

Leon just looked at me, completely confused. I don't think I had ever confused him so much in all the years we'd known each other. There was a part of me that wanted to know the answer, but I knew that if he said no, I would always wonder if he was lying and if he said yes, I didn't know if I could look at him the same way, so I decided being ignorant was the best policy.

"I don't understand," Leon said.

"I already said yes," I repeated.

"Yeah, but—"

"I made you a promise. I said there was nothing you could tell me that would make me stop loving you. Granted, I wasn't expecting this, but I intend to keep that promise. There's no good answer to that question, so I don't want to know. I just want to know if you mean what you just said. I want to know that we're going to go home and be Leon the Art Director and Jacey the Designer and not Leon the Shifter-Witch and Jacey, the Confused Human."

I paused. I knew that what I was saying might not have been entirely fair but I didn't know what else to do. I woke up this morning completely unaware of any of this and now I was being asked to not only believe in the paranormal but simply accept that the most important person in my life was some sort of supernatural being. It was too much. "Wait, that's not what I mean. I just... this is a lot to process, and—"

"I mean it, Jace."

Leon took a step toward me, his thumb grazing my cheek. I thought maybe something would feel different now that I knew Leon and I weren't the same, but it didn't. He still felt like home.

"I love you so much," he murmured.

He leaned in and kissed me deeply, and by the time I pulled away from the kiss, I was back. I found myself lying on the floor of Constança's bedroom alone as if it had just been a dream. There was some part of me that wished it had.

Fifty

I never really aspired to be normal. From the time I was a little girl, I wanted to see my designs on runways in Paris and Milan. I wanted to make a name for myself. I romanticized the idea of the world knowing and loving my art. However, the moment I found out that my boyfriend was...less than normal, that was all I wanted. I didn't want to know anything more about witches or shapeshifters or any other mystical being I didn't know existed. I wanted the comfort of my apartment with its weird layout, I wanted to order Thai food, and throw blankets on the floor like a picnic, I wanted to start working on my next collection, and I wanted that ring sitting in the drawer of Leon's nightstand.

After the incident with Leon's uncle, we left Tavira immediately. Neither of us wanted to bring any more unwelcome guests into Constança's home. The flight back to New York was nearly fourteen hours, and while

I kept expecting the other shoe to drop and some other strange occurrence to happen, nothing did. It was a perfectly average flight with terrible movie choices and an even worse in-flight meal. When we got back to New York, our apartment was exactly the way we left it. That Monday morning, Leon went back to work, and I went back to the studio.

Weeks passed, and we didn't talk about Tavira or his family or any of the things I now knew. We just resumed the life we had before. I almost allowed myself to forget everything that happened. I suppose there was a part of me that wanted to forget. I didn't want to process the idea that there were forces in this world that had the power to change the things I thought were real, and I certainly didn't want to have to process the fact that the man I loved was one of them.

I knew that there was a possibility that I was in denial, but the denial was easy. At least, it was easy for me. I couldn't say the same for Leon.

At first, he seemed happy. He seemed just as determined to move forward as I did. However, as time wore on, Leon seemed to be carrying something around. Every time I would walk into a room or tell him something completely mundane, he would look at me like he was suffering. I wanted to understand. I wanted to be a good partner. I wanted to comfort him, but the truth was, I was afraid. Our whole relationship felt like it was hanging on by this thread of ignorance, and I knew if I looked too hard or too long, it could all fall apart.

It was a Sunday afternoon, and I was in the kitchen trying to decide what we needed from the grocery store. I opened the fridge, looking at various expiration dates and making mental notes, when I heard Leon's voice behind me.

"This isn't working," he said.

I froze for a second, unsure if I heard him correctly. I slowly turned around to find Leon sitting at the barstools that faced our kitchen. He couldn't look at me. He just stared down at the countertop.

"What isn't?" I asked, praying he was talking about something else.

He slowly lifted his gaze to meet mine. "I need to tell you the truth, Jacey."

"No, you don't," I said and turned back to the fridge.

"Jace—"

"I told you, Leon. I don't want to know."

"I can't do this anymore," he continued. He sounded so small.

"What does that mean?"

"You deserve to know the truth. If you still want this after that, then we can pretend it never happened, but—"

"Why can't we be happy now? Why does it matter?" I demanded.

"Because it's killing me," Leon said, his voice breaking at the end of his sentence.

I closed my eyes, swallowed hard, and then closed the fridge. I walked out of the kitchen, motioning for Leon to follow me as I made my way to the living room. Quietly, I sat down on the couch before I spoke again. "Okay, tell me."

"I don't know where to start," he hesitated.

"The beginning?"

"The guys you dated before me..."

"Leon— "

"It was... they were... they were me," he blurted out before I could manage to stop him.

My heart dropped into my stomach. I couldn't breathe. I grabbed the arm of the couch, physically bracing myself for the wave of pain that was making its way through me. I wasn't sure if I wanted to cry or scream. On some level, I knew there had to be more to all of this than I was willing to see, but it didn't hurt any less. It hurt more than anything I'd ever felt before.

"How? Why? I don't—"

I was struggling to form complete sentences. Leon tried to come toward me, but I held my hand out to stop him. His brows raised at my reaction and I could see the hurt on his face but the last thing I needed was him touching me.

"You know how I said my dad could do things other shifters couldn't..."

"You can turn into other people," I finished, putting the rest of the puzzle together.

"Well, all shifters can turn into other people, but I can— " he started to explain, avoiding my gaze.

I furiously wiped the tears that threatened to spill over out of my eyes. I looked up at him angrily, interrupting his explanation. "Why? What fucking reason could you possibly have for manipulating me like that?"

He immediately began defending himself. "I was so in love with you, Jace. I'm still *so* in love with you, but you never even looked in my fucking direction. I thought if I could just make myself into what you wanted, I— "

"Please stop," I said, feeling nausea rising inside me.

"I'm so sorry," he whispered.

"I still don't understand. They had friends and lives and apartments, and— " I stopped suddenly. I didn't even need to finish what I was saying. I knew the answer.

"You shifted my reality. It wasn't real."

"Only when I had to. Most of the time, I was just physically them, but there were times that I needed to change the reality so you wouldn't suspect what was going on," he explained, taking an unsteady step toward me.

"I can't—"

I started to speak, but the nausea wasn't just an emotional reaction, it was very real, and I couldn't hold it down anymore. I got up from the couch as quickly as I could, rushing into the kitchen and emptying the contents of my stomach down the kitchen sink. Thankfully, Leon didn't follow me. I turned on the water in an attempt to clean up the mess. I stood there staring at the running faucet for the longest time. Nothing I experienced in the last year had been real. The person I trusted most in the entire world betrayed me. My emotions kept switching from agonizing heartbreak to extreme anger.

I slammed the handle to the faucet down and stormed back into the living room.

"Show me!" I ordered.

Leon's mouth dropped open slightly. "What?"

"If what you're saying is true, then show me!"

"I don't—"

"If you want me to believe you, then you'll show me," I repeated.

Leon closed his eyes, and the room around me filled with a cloud of thick, dark smoke. It couldn't have been real smoke, however, because I could still breathe. I watched it curl up and consume Leon entirely until I could no longer see him standing there. After a moment, the smoke began to clear, and standing in front of me was Owen.

I covered my mouth with my hand to keep myself from screaming. It didn't matter how badly I wanted to deny the truth. It was right there, right in front of me, looking me in the face. I stood up slowly and walked around Owen. He was exactly as I'd remembered him. Tall, handsome, built like a house, he even smelled of those terrible cigarettes he smoked.

"Say something," I said, making further demands.

"What is the point of this, Jacey?"

My heart stopped at the sound of Owen's rough and weathered voice. I had been trying so hard not to completely lose it, but there was nothing left to deny. Leon was every man I'd opened my heart up to in the last year. He had been playing parts and telling me lies and changing the very fabric of my reality for no other reason than the fact he wanted to be with me.

"Please turn back," I begged through the tears that were now streaming down my face.

The same smoke filled the room again, and there Leon was, standing in the same position.

"I don't understand," I said as I continued to cry.

"I never should have done it. I know that now. I was just so fucking desperate, Jacey. I waited for over ten years, and I thought..."

"What if I fell in love with one of them? What if I wanted to settle down with August or Cash? What were you going to do then?" I demanded. I felt my fingernails digging into my palms as I clenched my fists.

"I was prepared to be whoever you chose for the rest of my life," Leon quietly said.

A sob escaped me as I covered my face with my hands. "Are you insane?" I said, though it was almost impossible to understand me through my tears. "You were going to take away my best friend? You were prepared to take away the most important person in my life and be someone else just so that I would be with you? That would have killed me! I would have spent the rest of my life trying to find you!"

"I don't know what I was thinking," he said, dropping his head.

"You weren't!"

I tried to pull myself together but the tears just kept falling.

"You know what's the most pathetic part about this, Leon? I still chose you. The real you. All you had to do was tell me how you felt, and I chose you."

"I know, that's why I had to tell you," he muttered.

I finally looked at Leon, really looked, and he was breaking. We were breaking. There was a part of me that desperately wanted to save us but I couldn't. I just couldn't.

"That's why Cash wanted me to choose between you..." I realized, remembering that awful fight.

"I had to know that you wanted him enough to lose me before I just... became him," Leon said, imploring me to understand.

"Harry Styles could have waltzed in our apartment and said he wanted to whisk me away forever, and I still would have chosen you, Leon!" I shouted.

I couldn't be in that apartment anymore. I needed to get away from Leon. It hurt too much to be near him. Even looking at him hurt. I abruptly got up out of my seat and stormed into our bedroom. I threw the door open to the closet and grabbed the first bag I could find. I started shoving the few items of my clothing that weren't upstairs inside it. Leon followed, watching from the doorway as I assaulted our bedroom.

I moved to the dresser looking for anything else I might have missed, but stopped abruptly when I came across my grandfather's watch.

"How did you get this?" I said, yanking it out of the drawer.

"I..."

"How?" I said angrily.

"Brian got mugged."

"What?"

"On 83rd, right after you broke up."

"You...?"

"As far as he knows, it was just some guy in a hoodie with a scar on his face."

If I wasn't so heartbroken, I might have laughed. "Did you hurt him?"

"No, I just scared him...a lot."

I stopped packing. I knew I couldn't stay but I couldn't help but feel an ache in my chest knowing that he had gone to so much effort to get back something I thought I'd lost. It would be so easy to hate him for what he'd done, but the same abilities he'd used to manipulate me, he'd also used to help me.

"Jacey, please don't do this," he said quietly.

"I can't be here right now, Leon."

"I made a mistake. We can work this out, please!"

"You didn't just make a mistake once. You did it five times! Five! Owen, August, Alex, Cash, Gabe—"

Leon jerked his head back. "Who the fuck is Gabe?" he interrupted.

My eyes went wide, and I stopped what I was doing, my hands still shaking from anger. "You weren't Gabe?"

"I don't even know who you're talking about."

I quickly remembered how angry Leon was when he found out that I'd spent the night at Gabe's apartment. Initially, I thought it was because I'd worried him, but it wasn't.

It was because Gabe was real.

I finished getting my things together and started for the door, but Leon blocked my path.

"Jacey, don't leave," he pleaded. Leon reached for me and for a split second I let him, for a split second I let myself forget the walls crumbling around me. His hand moved to my face, his thumb wiping away the tears remaining on my cheeks.

I wanted to stay but the reality of the situation kept hitting me in horrible waves and I knew I couldn't. I took in a sharp breath and I stepped away from him. "I need space. Please let me go."

"I can't!"

"You have to," I whispered, the anger finally falling away.

"I'm afraid if I let you go, I'll never see you again."

My eyes started to cloud. I was afraid of the same thing.

"I just need to think," I tried to assure him.

"Is this over?" he asked as he looked away from me.

"I don't know."

I pushed past him out the door. He let me go. I had no idea how I was standing upright, let alone what I was going to do. I didn't stop until I was outside the building, standing on the curb. My chest burned, but I tried to steady my breathing. I just needed to keep my head on straight long enough to figure out what to do next.

I couldn't go to Elise. I didn't want to ruin her newlywed bliss with my heartbreak. I couldn't go to

Nia. She had Michael and Nichelle. I didn't want to disturb her family. I could go home to Connecticut, but I wasn't sure I knew how to explain what was going on to my parents. I couldn't just show up and say, "Leon's a shapeshifter and he pretended to be every guy I've dated for the last year".

Well, all of them except one.

I pulled my phone from the pocket of my sweatpants and dialed before I could second guess myself.

"Hello?" the voice on the other end of the phone said.

I was trying to hold it together, but the moment I heard that voice, I fell into another fit of tears.

"Hello? Jacey?"

"Is the door still open?"

Roxanna Mason

is a debut paranormal romance author and formally trained actor from Los Angeles, California. It was her deep love of storytelling that led her to study theatre and that same love of storytelling that drove her to write her first novel. When not writing, Roxanna is binge watching horror films, creating vegan recipes, and dancing around her living room to Fleetwood Mac.

Jacey and Leon's adventure will continue in *Shattered*, coming in 2023.

Follow Roxanna on Instagram and TikTok @roxannamason or at www.roxannamason.com to stay up to date on the sequel.

Listen to the Official Companion Playlist for *Shifted* on Spotify.